Remembrance of Things to Come

OTHER BOOKS BY LAWRENCE WATT EVANS

Vika's Avenger
The Chromosomal Code
Touched by the Gods
The Rebirth of Wonder
The Nightmare People
One-Eyed Jack
Among the Powers
Shining Steel
(with Esther M. Friesner) *Split Heirs*
(with Carl Parlagreco) *The Spartacus File*

THE ADVENTURES OF TOM DERRINGER
Tom Derringer and the Aluminum Airship
Tom Derringer in the Tunnels of Terror
Tom Derringer and the Steam-Powered Saurians
Tom Derringer and the Electrical Empire

THE CASES OF CARLISLE HSING
Nightside City
Realms of Light

THE FALL OF THE SORCERERS
A Young Man Without Magic
Above His Proper Station

THE ANNALS OF THE CHOSEN
The Wizard Lord
The Ninth Talisman
The Summer Palace

THE OBSIDIAN CHRONICLES
Dragon Weather
The Dragon Society
Dragon Venom

THE LORDS OF DÛS
The Lure of the Basilisk
The Seven Altars of Dûsarra
The Sword of Bheleu
The Book of Silence

LEGENDS OF ETHSHAR
The Misenchanted Sword
With A Single Spell
The Unwilling Warlord
Taking Flight
The Blood of a Dragon
The Spell of the Black Dagger

Night of Madness
Ithanalin's Restoration
The Spriggan Mirror
The Vondish Ambassador
The Unwelcome Warlock
The Sorcerer's Widow
Relics of War
Stone Unturned
Charming Sharra

Remembrance of Things to Come

29 Science Fiction & Fantasy Stories
by
Lawrence Watt-Evans

Misenchanted Press

Bainbridge Island

These stories are works of fiction. None of the characters and events portrayed herein are intended to represent actual person living or dead.

Remembrance of Things to Come

"Remembrance of Things to Come" originally appeared in *Analog Science Fact/Science Fiction*, copyright by Davis Publications, 1999

"The Ghost Taker," "Natural Selection," "Harry's Toaster," and "The Night People" originally appeared in *Amazing Stories*, copyright 1991, 1992., 2018, 2019

"Short Lines" originally appeared in the Chattacon XVII program book, copyright 1992

"Foxy Lady" originally appeared in *Zoomorphica*, copyright 1992

"Dread Vengeance" and "He's Only Human" originally appeared in *Science Fiction Age*, copyright 1995, 1999

"Throwback" originally appeared in *Alien Abductions*, edited by John Helfers, copyright 1999

"Valedictory" originally appeared in *Release the Virgins*, edited by Michael A. Ventrella, copyright 2019

"The Last Bastion" originally appeared in *Far Frontiers*, edited by Martin H. Greenberg & Larry Segriff, copyright 2000

"That Doggone Vnorpt" originally appeared as by Nathan Archer in *Guardsmen of Tomorrow*, edited by Martin H. Greenberg & Larry Segriff, copyight 2000

"Advance Man" may have appeared in *Neverworlds*, copyright 2001

"Contraband" originally appeared as by Nathan Archer in *Low Port*, edited Sharon Lee & Steve Miller, copyright 2003

"Nif's World" originally appeared in *The 10th Science Fiction Megapack*, copyright 2015

"The Abduction of Ebenezer Scrooge" originally appeared as a holiday chapbook, copyright 2015
"An Evil Opportunity Employer" originally appeared in *Unidentified Funny Objects 6*, edited by Alex Shvartsman, copyright 2017

"Volunteers" originally appeared in *3SF*, copyright 2002

"Personal Space," "How I Found Harry's All-Night Hamburgers," and "When I See Rigel's Light Sleeting Through the Side of Heinlein Station" originally appeared in *Asimov's Science Fiction*, copyright 2019, 1989

"Sorcery of the Heart" originally appeared in *Lace and Blade 4*, edited by Deborah J. Ross, copyright 2018

"Paul is Dead" originally appeared in *Across the Universe: Tales of Alternative Beatles*, edited by Michael A. Ventrella and Randee Dawn, copyright 2019

"The House of the Spider" originally appeared in *Thrilling Adventure Yarns 2022*, edited by Robert Greenberger, copyright 2023

"The Jurors" originally appeared in *Three Time Travelers Walk Into...*, edited by Michael A. Ventrella, copyright 2022

"Distractions" appears here for the first time, copyright 2025

"The Prisoner of Shalott" originally appeared in *By the Light of Camelot*, edited by J.R. Campbell & Shannon Allen, copyright 2018

"An Interrupted Betrothal" originally appeared in *Lace and Blade 5*, edited by Deborah J. Ross, copyright 2019

"To See the New Jerusalem" originally appeared in *Grimoire: A Grim Oak Press Anthology for Seattle Worldcon 2025*, edited by Shawn Speakman, copyright 2025

Cover art by Luca Oleastri
Cover design by Lawrence Watt-Evans

Published by Misenchanted Press
www.misenchantedpress.com

Contents

Introduction

I sold my first short story in 1975. Since then I've had productive years and slow years, but the stories keep piling up. I had enough to fill a book in 1992, and that was *Crosstime Traffic.* I filled another, *Celestial Debris*, by 2002.

After that I did a bunch of theme collections – vampire stories, horror, fantasy, tall tales, and stories set in the world of Ethshar.

In 2023 I noticed that I had *almost* enough to fill another generic collection. In the summer of 2025, when "To See the New Jerusalem" appeared in *Grimoire* Vol. III, I tallied them up again and discovered that I'd missed a few in '23 – I have *more* than enough.

So here they are. The book's title comes from the first story in this volume, which originally appeared in **Analog** in 1999, and combines the first English version of Proust's *A la recherche du temps perdu* (*Remembrance of Things Past*, which is not an accurate translation) with H.G. Wells' *The Shape of Things to Come.* It was especially appropriate for the short story, but I think it suits the collection as a whole, too.

Some of these were originally published as by Nathan Archer; I haven't bothered to note which.

There's no particular theme, but they're all science fiction or fantasy. I didn't include any collaborations or licensed properties. I left out stories about librarian and monster expert George Pinkerton because I'm hoping to eventually have enough of those to fill a book of their own. A few stories I deemed unsuitable for other reasons.

But here are all the rest. I hope you like them.

Remembrance of Things to Come

An editor of my acquaintance mentioned receiving a bizarre cover letter for a story submitted to the magazine. It listed a bunch of disparate influences and ideas that were purportedly reflected in the story, everything from Marcel Proust to Marvel Comics.

While it was a silly cover letter I didn't think it was quite as ridiculous as the editor did, because really, writers work **everything** *into their stories.*

So I decided to write a publishable story using exactly the elements listed in that cover letter. I don't remember what they all were. I know Stan Lee was in there, and Proust, and Ursula K. Le Guin, and chaos theory, and literary criticism...

Anyway, I wrote a story using all of them, and entitled it "Remembrance of Things to Come," bastardizing Proust's Remembrance of Things Past *with H.G. Wells'* The Shape of Things To Come.

Here it is.

He stared at the student in shock.

"You think it's a *typo?*" he said.

"Well, yeah," the boy said, shifting his weight nervously from one foot to the other. "W is right above S on the keyboard; it'd be easy to type 'wet' instead of 'set.' And 'set' makes a lot more sense, doesn't it?"

"No," Williams said, his voice not entirely steady. "It changes all the imagery completely, don't you see that? 'He wet the blade on the floor' is the essential clue that he's killed her, that the floor's covered in her blood..."

"So maybe it isn't," the boy said. "Maybe she really *is* asleep, and he's decided to forgive her."

"But that's a completely different story!"

The boy shrugged. Williams stared at him in horror – didn't this smart-ass kid realize what he was trying to do? Williams had built his career on the careful analysis of Dorrie Ledbetter's short stories – hell, he'd written his doctoral dissertation on this very story, "A Sleeping Kiss," and had used it in class as a model for all his students to follow! His whole reputation had been founded on it. And now this...this *punk* dared to suggest that all the subtleties Williams had read into the story, based on that one final image of the protagonist wetting his knife in his wife's blood, were the result of a typographical error?

When the silence threatened to become awkward, Williams cleared his throat.

"It's an interesting theory," he said, "but for now, we'll just have to deal with the story as it was originally published, all right?"

The kid shrugged again. "Okay," he said. "I just thought I'd ask. 'Set' seemed to make so much more sense."

"Well, things don't always make obvious sense," Williams said. "Now, run along, I need to lock up."

The boy turned, gathered his books, and trotted up the aisle, out of the classroom. Williams stared after him.

Then he pulled out his own battered copy of *Seven Endings* and thumbed it open to "A Sleeping Kiss" and began reading.

At supper that evening he poured out the whole thing to Dr. Garrand, his regular dinner companion. She was in the physics department, but pleasant company all the same.

"One word!" he said. "One *letter*, and it's an entirely different story!"

"That's fascinating," Garrand said. "A classic example of a sensitive dependence upon initial conditions. I'd never thought that would have applications in *your* field – though I suppose I should have; chaos theory certainly does seem to turn up everywhere once you start looking..."

Williams blinked. "Chaos theory?"

"Of course."

"Isn't that a mathematical thing? What's it got to do with literature?"

"It's mathematical in nature, yes. Chaos theory is a way of looking at systems too complex to predict by ordinary means..."

"What?"

Garrand sighed. "It's like this," she said. "In physics, or any other science, we look for models that will predict what will happen under certain conditions. Then we create those conditions and see what happens, and see whether our prediction is correct. If it is, that's good; if it isn't, we throw out our model and start over. But sometimes, there are things that are so complicated we can't say what will happen, even if our models are right. There might be a situation where the tiniest little fluctuation can completely change the outcome – the classic example is the flap of a butterfly's wing stirring the air at just the right time, in just the right place, to start a cascade. That one tiny movement means that a breeze is ever so slightly stronger, so a branch falls that wouldn't have, and that changes something else, and it builds up and builds up until you have a hurricane that wouldn't have happened if that butterfly hadn't been there."

"For want of a nail, the kingdom was lost."

"Something like that, yes," Garrand agreed. "Ordinarily, the flap of a butterfly's wing would be lost in the noise, canceled out by other events; but if everything's just right, it can tip the balance and change everything. That's a sensitive dependence on initial conditions – your starting set-up determines what effect that butterfly has."

"And that one letter is the butterfly."

"Yes!" Garrand nodded. "If the letter is W you have the story you always thought was there, about a grief-stricken murderer; if it's S, then you have a story of forgiveness and redemption."

"But how do I know which is right?"

"Well, if this were quantum mechanics I'd say you *can't* know, that the Heisenberg principle is in effect – but it isn't physics, it's literature. You can open Schroedinger's box and see if the cat's alive or dead by contacting the author and *asking* her whether she meant to say 'set' or 'wet.'"

Williams had no idea who Heisenberg or Schroedinger were, or what cats had to do with anything – Ledbetter hadn't been one of the

Beat writers, she was after that. He did, however, understand Garrand's basic suggestion.

"Dorrie Ledbetter's dead," he said. "She died before the story was published, in fact. Heart failure, at age forty-seven."

"Oh," Garrand said. Her face fell. "Maybe her editor? Or her heirs?"

"I can ask, I guess," Williams said thoughtfully.

Two weeks later he and Garrand dined together once again after a longer hiatus than customary, and Garrand had to struggle to hide her dismay at Williams' appearance. He hadn't shaved for at least three days, and his hair, normally fussily neat, was uncombed. There were circles under his wild eyes.

"You want to know something awful?" he said. "*Nobody* knows. I'm not sure *Ledbetter herself* really knew!"

"Well, of course she did," Garrand said soothingly. "She must have known what story she was writing."

Williams smiled crookedly. "You'd think so, wouldn't you? But I'm not sure. I tracked down the original manuscript, you see, and got a photocopy."

"So which is it in the manuscript?"

Wordlessly, Williams pulled a paper from his pocket and unfolded it.

Garrand leaned forward and looked at it.

"Oh, my," she said.

The manuscript was typed, not computer-printed – and the key word was spelled with *both* an S and a W, one typed over the other.

"And even the experts can't tell which one was first," Williams said wearily. "She used a non-correcting electric typewriter, and each letter was a single stroke, no white-out, no repeat. Maybe if someone did a microscopic fiber analysis of the paper, to see which fibers were stretched how by the impact – but Ledbetter's niece won't allow it."

"So you aren't the first person to wonder about this?"

Williams snorted. "No," he said. "But it's been kept quiet; the publisher doesn't like to admit they might have made a vital mistake in one of their reliable sellers."

"So nobody but Ledbetter herself ever knew which was the correct version?" Garrand asked, as she stared at the photocopy. "Huh. Or maybe *she* didn't know, either – maybe she planned it *both* ways. Maybe she wrote the story as a wavicle, a quantum indeterminacy..."

"What?" Williams stared at her.

"I'm sorry, I'm just babbling," Garrand said, as she slid back down into her chair.

"But you think she might have done it *on purpose*?"

Garrand shrugged. "Who knows? Maybe. Don't writers do things like that sometimes? Maybe she couldn't decide which version she liked better, and wanted to let it be determined by chance, like Marcel Duchamp and his standard curves."

"Or she wanted to let it be determined by the typesetter," Williams said morosely. "Making him an unacknowledged collaborator."

"She trusted the universe to make the correct decision," Garrand said. "Everything for the best, and all that."

"Ha!"

"Oh, come on; what's the problem? Everything will work out fine..."

"No, it won't!" Williams burst out. "Don't you see that? *I'll never know!*"

Garrand hesitated. "Ledbetter didn't leave a diary or anything?" she asked. "No correspondence with her editor?"

Williams shook his head. "Nothing," he said. "She was sort of secretive; she liked to wait until everyone had had a chance to read her stories before she said *anything* about them. Except she died before anyone read 'A Sleeping Kiss.'" He sighed. "If only there were some way to go back and *tell* her to leave a note, that she wouldn't live to see this one in print..."

Garrand bit her lip. "You know," she began, then stopped.

"What?" Williams asked.

Garrand hesitated, started to speak, stopped again. At last she said, "There *might* be a way to tell her."

"How?" Williams demanded. "She's been dead for thirty years – are you planning to hold a seance or something?"

Garrand shook her head quickly. "No," she said, "not a seance. But we've been working on something in quantum physics lately..."

Williams stared at her. "A time machine?"

Garrand grimaced. "Well, not in the traditional sense," she said. "We can't send matter through time – that's not allowed under our current working model of spacetime."

"Energy, then?"

"Energy and matter are the same thing," Garrand said.

Williams frowned. "What else *is* there, besides matter and energy?"

"Information."

Williams sat back in his chair and stared silently at her for a moment.

"Okay," he said, "I give up. How do you send information without sending matter or energy?"

"We're back to Schroedinger's cat," Garrand said. "Let us suppose you have a particle that decays into two other particles, one with a positive spin and the other negative..."

"Never mind," Williams said, interrupting her. "I don't want to hear about any cats or quantum stuff. I just want to know what *form* this information would take. It can't be a piece of paper, or even a radio signal, right? So what would it be?"

"Memory," Garrand said. "We think we have a way to record the quantum state of a present-day brain onto a brain somewhere in the past in such a way that the patterns in the receiving brain will duplicate those in the source brain, and that as a result the receiving brain will acquire the memories of the source brain. And since memories and brain patterns are all we are, it'll be as if the personality of the present-day person were transported into the brain of the person in the past."

"What, you mean they'd swap bodies?"

Garrand sighed. "No," she said. "Not at all. The present-day person wouldn't change at all; the information is being *copied*, not moved. And the recipient ought to acquire the sender's memories and personality, but there's no reason the recipient's *own* mind would be affected. There's plenty of room in a human brain for two personalities and two lifetimes of memories."

"So it'd be like a split personality? Could they talk to each other?"

"I don't see why not," Garrand said.

"So you could send a copy of my memories back to her, to warn her?"

"That's the theory. The fact is, though, we've been looking for some way to test it, but we ran into a lot of ethical issues..."

"But we want to *warn* her that she's going to die! Surely that can't be unethical!"

"Well, that would depend..."

"No, it *can't* be." Williams leaned forward across the table. "Don't you see? You've got to do it!"

Four days later, as Williams lay motionless on the slab and the MRI scanner slid over him, one of the other researchers leaned over and whispered to Garrand, "Warn some poet that she's going to have a heart attack? Why don't we do something *worthwhile*, like warn the crew of the Titanic that there's ice ahead?"

Garrand didn't bother to correct the misstatement of Ledbetter's chosen form; instead she shrugged. "This is safer," she said. "We don't know how much history might change if we did anything big. Even *this* wouldn't get past the ethics committee if we'd bothered to ask them."

"We didn't ask...?"

Garrand smiled. "With great power comes great responsibility," she said, "but I don't think anyone's responsible enough to resist testing this thing at least a little, no matter what the rules say."

An hour later Williams sat up and reached for his shirt.

"Now what?" he said.

"That's it," Garrand told him. "Either Dorrie Ledbetter got a copy of your memories, or she didn't. Now we just need to find some evidence of which it was."

"What sort of evidence?"

"Whatever she remembers would get to you."

* * *

She woke up suddenly and stared at the ceiling, momentarily confused. She remembered lying on a platform in some sort of machinery – was that a dream? She was here, safe in her own bed...

But it wasn't her bed, was it? The ceiling was the stained and flaking ceiling of her boarding-house room, but she lived in a pleasant little apartment just off campus.

She blinked. Campus? Apartment?

She lived in a furnished room in a crumbling Edwardian disaster of a boarding house, with her cat and her typewriter, and here she was.

But she *also* remembered a sunny room on the fourth floor of an apartment house, a little kitchen on one side, a tidy little bedroom on the other, and that didn't come before the boarding house, before this she'd been in the basement apartment that always smelled of mildew, and before that she'd lived with her parents in the nasty little ranch house in Poughkeepsie – where did a fourth-floor apartment fit in?

She tried to remember. She'd taken the apartment when she first came to Queensbury College (she'd barely *heard* of Queensbury, had never been there!) right after the turn of the century, in March of 2001...

She blinked again and sat up.

It was 1978. She knew that.

But it was 2010, and she *also* knew *that.*

She looked around the room, at the digital clock and the faded curtains and the battered IBM Selectric. This was *definitely* 1978; there wasn't a computer screen anywhere in sight, and a typewriter like that would be a museum piece by 2010.

So why did she remember lying down in 2010, on a sort of hospital table surrounded by machinery? And how did she *know* typewriters would be obsolete, replaced by computers, by the turn of the century?

A dream was the only explanation, but it was one *hell* of a dream, to have this kind of effect on her! Usually the hard part was remembering dreams, keeping them from fading away, but this one seemed to be getting stronger with every second she was awake, trying to crowd out *real* memories.

She got up and pulled on her robe, then headed down the hall to the bathroom. She used the toilet, then stood and turned to the mirror. Her hand reached automatically for her razor.

She stopped dead. Razor?

Well, of course, she had to shave, didn't she?

Shave *what*? She'd stopped shaving her legs back in college, when she finally gave up any idea that she might someday play the ugly duckling and turn out a swan instead of the fat pig she was.

What the hell was wrong with her? Why did she remember another face, a man's face, that ought to be in the mirror? Had she suddenly developed a split personality, like Sybil?

But Sybil's personalities hadn't confused memories like this. She *remembered* being male – and a very strange, uncomfortable memory it was. She reached up and touched her shoulders, her arms crossing across her breasts, then looked down at herself.

She was unquestionably female. Dorrie Ledbetter, age forty-seven, weight a mortifying two hundred and fifteen pounds, critically acclaimed but dirt-poor writer, teacher of creative writing at the adult education center six blocks east, where she was paid two dollars per student per hour to tell little old ladies that their inept moral tales of heroic pets and naughty children showed real promise but still needed work.

But she remembered so *very* clearly being Richard Williams, assistant professor of English at Queensbury College, several inches taller and only slightly overweight, with a potbelly that he knew he could eliminate any time he was willing to work at it a little.

This couldn't be a premonition; she didn't believe in them, for one thing, but for another, how could she foresee being someone else? And a member of the opposite sex, at that – she wasn't one of Le Guin's Gethenians, able to choose her role; she was a woman, and would always be a woman.

Was this some bizarre hallucination? A flashback to her one experiment with LSD, back in '69, perhaps? It didn't *seem* anything like that experience of crawling colors and time distortion; the sink looked completely normal, white porcelain with greenish stains around the drain, and time seemed to be ticking past at the usual rate.

She was Dorrie Ledbetter – she had Dorrie Ledbetter's body and was in Dorrie Ledbetter's room – so why did she remember being Richard Williams?

What exactly did she remember? She leaned heavily on the sink and tried to think.

She had eaten alone the night before, sat up late reading, and gone to bed. But what had Richard Williams been doing last night?

She remembered lying on a table in a laboratory, and this huge machine like something out of "2001" moving across her. An MRI scanner, Garrand had called it...

And that was absolutely her last memory of Richard Williams; that was what had woken her up this morning, the memory of lying there while her/his memory was copied.

She'd been sent a copy of memories from the future.

Her mouth fell open, then snapped shut.

That was crazy; that was science fiction.

She stared at herself in the mirror.

Richard Williams had wanted to know what she'd meant in one of her stories, so he'd sent a copy of his memories back in time, into her sleeping mind, so she would leave him a message.

And why did she need to leave him a message? Because she was about to die! She wouldn't live to see "A Sleeping Kiss" published.

She turned and stared out the bathroom door at the table against the wall, the little table where a manila envelope stood propped up, waiting to be mailed – an envelope containing the manuscript of "A Sleeping Kiss."

"Oh, fuck," she said.

Then it sank in, and she shouted it. "Oh, *fuck!*"

She was going to *die*, and this callous bastard Williams had told her about it *just so he could find out what she'd meant in one of her stupid little stories?*

She gripped the edge of the sink and steadied herself.

Wait a minute, she told herself. Just wait. Think about this. Memories from the future? And she *believed* that?

Well, she *had* to. The other possibility, that she was imagining the whole thing and was therefore going insane, wasn't any better.

And what kind of an imagination could it possibly be that would spring this on her all at once? Why would these memories all appear full-blown like this? She could remember what it felt like to be a man – and a nasty, uncomfortable memory it was, too. She could remember the Gulf War, and the huge celebrations at the turn of the millennium, and the fall of the Berlin Wall, and the Challenger explosion...how could she have made all that up overnight?

Something she – no, Williams – had said came back to her. "So it'd be like a split personality? Could they talk to each other?"

"Hello?" she said. "Anyone there?"

No one answered; no little voice spoke up in her head. It appeared Garrand had been wrong. If she were a split personality, suddenly manifesting this new, invented identity for the first time – which didn't *at all* fit her understanding of how MPD worked, in any case – then why would *she* have all of Williams' memories?

No, Garrand had been wrong. The memories were *not* the personality. Her brain was still entirely hers; she just had a lot more jammed into it now.

And it must be real. No other explanation made sense.

After all, why *shouldn't* someone invent something like this, someday? Apollo 11 must have seemed just as unlikely to her parents.

So Williams' memories were true. And she knew the future – or thirty-two years of it, anyway.

But she wouldn't live to see it.

"Well, screw *that*," she said, looking in the mirror again. "And screw *you*, assistant professor Richard Williams! You selfish, self-centered, egotistical, petty *bastard*! Why the hell should I care whether *you* know what my story's about?" She stamped out of the bathroom, crossed the room, and snatched up the envelope, tearing it open.

She had to see whether she really had typoed that word; she hadn't caught it.

And if she hadn't, then she'd need to retype the last page; she couldn't expect to get the S and the W lined up properly if she just put the existing one back in the typewriter. She'd make *sure* that son of a bitch didn't know which she'd intended, not unless she was still alive to tell him!

She found the right page and scanned it. No typo. She'd had it right.

She began tearing the page into little pieces, which she would burn at the first opportunity; she could copy the carbon, and then she'd destroy *that*, too.

For a moment she considered destroying the entire manuscript – but she needed the money, especially now that she *knew* it would sell the first place she tried it, and besides, she wanted Williams to experience that horrible moment, years from now, when that smartass kid would point out the typo.

She sat down at her desk, sandwiched carbon paper between two fresh sheets of mimeo bond, and rolled them into the typewriter.

"Forewarned is forearmed," she muttered to herself as she typed "Ledbetter/Kiss" and the page number at the top. "A heart attack, huh? Because I'm too goddamn fat? Okay, you son of a bitch, then I'll stop being fat! You think I can't? You think just because I'm a woman I'm too passive and stupid to do something about it? I'll *live*, you bastard, and what's more I'm going to be rich, because *now*, you moron, I know what's coming! I'll bet on Reagan in 1980, I'll bet against the '86 Red Sox – thank you, Bill Buckner! I'll invest in Intel and Microsoft. You wait and see, Williams – one day I'll show up on your doorstep and spit in your face!" She snorted derisively as she rapidly typed through the next sentence. "You went and wasted this on my stupid *story*? You didn't warn someone about Adolf Hitler, or Pearl Harbor, or Vietnam? Someone gave you a time machine, and all you want to do is *fix a typo?* Jesus, that's like, I don't know – destroying the planet to send a message, or something. You don't want to interfere, my ass – God, you *deserve* to suffer!"

She slowed, and carefully typed "set," then backspaced and typed a W over the S.

"There," she said. She spaced forward and continued typing.

Water and celery, she told herself silently. She would live on water and celery until she'd lost fifty or sixty pounds. She'd been meaning to lose weight for years, she'd known she ought to lose ninety, maybe even a hundred pounds, but she could never force herself to diet and exercise – it wasn't as if she'd had all that much to live for, after all.

But now – now she knew she'd be at least moderately famous. Now she knew she could be rich. With *that* for motivation a few weeks of starvation would be nothing.

She laughed to herself as she typed "The End" at the foot of the page.

"I'll show *you*, Dickie Williams!" she said. She ripped the page from the typewriter, and rummaged in the drawer for a new manila envelope.

Ten minutes later she dropped the envelope in the corner mailbox and jogged, panting, toward the park.

* * *

The medical examiner shook his head. "Damned stupid fad diets," he said, tossing the folder on his desk.

The police lieutenant glanced at him.

"This Ledbetter woman," the ME explained. "She hadn't eaten a decent meal in weeks! She was living on carrot sticks and water. Lost forty pounds, sure – but the strain on her heart was too much." He leaned back in his chair. "She couldn't afford a doctor – I guess no one warned her just how risky a crash diet like that can be!"

"She was still pretty hefty," the lieutenant remarked. "She must've been really something, if she'd lost forty pounds."

"Yeah," the ME agreed. "She might've had the heart attack anyway." He shrugged.

"I guess we'll never know," he said.

"I can live with that," the lieutenant replied.

The Ghost Taker

This story started with a question I asked myself. What, I wondered, if some people have souls that can survive after death, and other people don't? Suppose it's a mutation that's arisen in some population...

He knew the dust of the road from a thousand previous journeys, from a million weary steps taken in the past. This was the same road he had always followed, and his teachers, his ancestors before him. He knew everything about it, yet still he studied it, trying to see it anew, as if he were a young child walking it for the first time.

The dust changed, of course. Everything changed, for that was the way of the world. The grass on the verge was thicker here, taller there; one tree had died, another grown. The dust had swirled and shifted and lay now in a low central mound between two shallow ruts where once it had been almost even, but lowest in the center. Even the roads had changed with the arrival of the Strangers, even the dust; was it any wonder that men and women had, too?

Ah, but had they changed in any fundamental way? A man was still a spirit bound up in flesh, seeking the good things of the world. That could never change.

Ahead he could see the village that had once been home to Franzaver Shaman, whose soul he had captured three years ago. He had never known a name for the place; he had needed no name but Franzaver's for it. The Strangers put great faith in names, trusted more in names than in essences – as was only to be expected of creatures that did not acknowledge their own souls – so the village would certainly have a name now. The dust of the road, in its gentle mound, told him as much.

He walked on, looking ahead now, and saw that the village had changed. He remembered it as Franzaver had known it, a score of great houses arranged about an oval market, not as a collection of forty or fifty mismatched structures. The great houses were still there, but so were several sheds of the sort the Strangers used to store their machines, and several small shops. A gatehouse stood at the roadside.

He paused, looking at the gatehouse. He could circle around it readily enough, if he chose. He knew that he would probably not be made welcome here; the village had plainly taken up the Strangers' ways wholeheartedly. Still, he was an honest man pursuing an ancient and honorable duty; he would not sneak in as would a thief. He walked on down the center of the road.

The gatekeeper emerged, and the traveler stopped, shocked. The man was a Stranger.

Franzaver had known the village gatekeeper, a huge man with black hair and a bristling beard, Simagis by name. Huge and dark, yes, but Simagis had been no Stranger. Franzaver had known him, and so the traveler knew him, and this man was not Simagis.

Behind the Stranger a second figure appeared, a familiar face. Ignoring the alien intruder, the traveler called a polite greeting.

Simagis, the village gatekeeper, studied him over the Stranger's shoulder, while the Stranger stood, silently glowering, between the two. "Do I know you?" Simagis asked at last.

"I bear the soul of Franzaver Shaman," the traveler replied.

"A priest?"

The traveler nodded.

"We need no priests here," Simagis stated with firm finality. The Stranger nodded agreement, and a hand fell to the butt of an instrument on his belt, an instrument the traveler knew for a weapon.

"Yet I was drawn here," the traveler replied, ignoring the hostility.

"We need no priests here," the gatekeeper repeated, glancing at the Stranger as if seeking approval.

"You heard him," the Stranger said, speaking in a harsh, deep voice, "Get lost."

The priest tilted his head, feeling the world around him, and answered, "Someone in your village is dying, Simagis, and I have come here to collect his soul." He paused, then added, "Or hers," as an afterthought, "I can't tell who it is."

"Nobody sent for you," Simagis insisted.

"Oh, there was no need to summon me; I have taken enough ghosts to know without being told when and where I will be needed."

"Witch doctor, you aren't wanted here," the Stranger said. "Go away."

"Wanted or not, I am needed. Would you have this person's spirit wandering about the village, alone and blind and frightened?"

"The spirits of the dead do not linger," Simagis replied. "That is myth, it is superstition. The Terrans have told us this."

The Stranger, the Terran, nodded confirmation.

"What do the Strangers know of it?" the priest demanded.

"The Terrans know far more than any of our people ever have!" Simagis gestured at the man standing before him. "Look at their machines, their clothes, their medicines, their size and strength; the Terrans are wisdom made manifest."

"But what do they know of *us*? They may know that their own souls do not roam, lost and crippled, after death, but what do they know of ours?"

The Terran replied, "We're all human, little priest. We had your kind on Earth long ago, but we learned better eventually."

"You see?" Simagis said, "They say we are the same, that our ancestors were Terrans like themselves who were stranded on our world."

The priest studied the two men. He wondered, not for the first time, what the homeplace of the Terrans must be like. If they were in truth the same as his own kind, yet did not allow the taking of souls, what could their world be like, with all those ghosts roaming free, blind and frightened, striking out in terror at the mind of anyone they touched? A world of madness, surely.

"I have heard that we are the same," he said. "I do not say it is false, for I do not know; no one remembers so very long ago. However, we are a part of this world now, wherever our forefathers might have come from, and we are no longer Terrans. In our world, ghosts walk, screaming in terror, if no priest is there to catch the last breaths of the dying and take their souls into himself."

The Terran snorted in derision.

"You priests lie," Simagis insisted. "It's all tricks to deceive us and make us dependent upon you, so that you have no need to earn your keep as honest men do. We need no deceivers in Galoran. Go away, priest."

"I am no deceiver! I bear the souls of two hundred and forty-one people, in addition to my own – souls I have captured myself, and the souls brought to me by those priests whose dying breaths I caught. I *know* them, Simagis; I know these souls, know that they are real, know that I saved them from blind wandering throughout eternity."

"The Terrans say you lie."

"And *I* say that the Strangers are wrong! They have lost the truth, and now seek to destroy it here. Will you believe them, and not one of your own?"

"Yes, priest, I will! Go away!"

"You heard him," the Stranger said, "Go away!"

The priest fought himself calm, fought down all of his various feelings. "I have come to provide a necessary service for someone who will die here, very soon. If you do not wish to pay me the traditional tithe from the belongings of that person, so be it, I will forego my fee. I will ask nothing of you or your village or anyone in it, save that you let me catch the dying breath and take the ghost with it."

"It's superstition, and we want none of it! No one here is dying! Go away!"

The priest looked up at the implacable face of the Terran, into the empty brown eyes, then stepped back in sudden shock and turned away.

– What are you doing?, asked Franzaver's ghost frantically.– One of my people is dying!

– Something troubles you, another soul said.

– They will not have us, he replied.– Would you have me force my way in, like a thief, and steal the soul?

– No!, clamored several spirits, – We are not thieves!

– A vote, suggested a thin and ancient soul, one that had almost faded into the mass, surely not one he had taken himself, or even one Franzaver or the other priest, Avaunas, had taken, but one that had been passed on through many priests.– Put it to a vote.

He agreed, and tallied the results on his fingers in binary notation, but did not really need to. He knew what they would be from the urgings he felt pulling at him. When the ghosts were stirred up he had little will of his own left.

There would be no intervention. He would walk on, carrying out his duty where the people permitted it, and hoping that the rest would come to their senses before too many souls were scattered and lost. Surely, when the initial glamor had faded from the Terran strangers, his people would see their self-assurance for the arrogance it was.

Or perhaps the Terran scientists would realize their mistake, see what he now knew beyond any possible doubt, that his people were *not* the same as Terrans any longer – he did not have the words to tell them, to convince them. His language held no word for mutation that he could make the Strangers understand, but he knew that some sort of change had taken place if his people were, in truth, descended from Terrans.

He knew, because he had seen into the mind behind the Terran's eyes, and had seen that there was no soul there, nothing that could escape the body at death and be caught by another.

No wonder, then, that the Strangers thought the priests mere tricksters and parasites! Among Terrans they would be no more than that.

Surely, though, some day, his people would realize the truth and would again accept the priests, and would test their children for the holy talent and allow them to be trained as new priests.

Surely, some day, that would happen – for if it did not, he and the two hundred and forty-one souls he carried would die, with no priest to save them, and he had no wish to die as the soulless Strangers did, the moment his body ceased to work, so very, very long before his time.

He turned away, unwanted, from Galoran, suffering with the knowledge that a soul would soon be wandering the night there with no brain to hold it, no eyes to see through, screaming in terror until it faded away to nothing – as his soul might someday wander and fade, if no more priests were trained, as the souls of all his people would wander and die. Tears stung his eyes, and to hide them he looked down at the road, looked at the dust beneath his feet with two eyes that led to more than two hundred souls.

Natural Selection

This story is just me taking a slightly different angle on an often-seen science fiction situation: If only a few will survive the end of the world, how do you choose who they will be?

EYES ONLY

EXTREME ULTRA

Unauthorized Reading or Reproduction of This Document is a felony punishable by not less than five years imprisonment

Report of the Committee on Personnel
for Extraterrestrial Survival
May 3rd, 1996

Review:

This Committee was formed by executive order to advise and consult on the offer made July 23, 1995, by an extraterrestrial intelligence, through coded transmissions received at Andrews Air Force Base. This offer was to transport six hundred and seventy-six (676) human beings to a habitable planet orbiting the star Lambda Aurigae, so that the species would not be wiped out by the approaching supernova of our sun.

The Committee on Astrophysics has independently confirmed the statement by the extraterrestrial intelligence (hereinafter referred to as the ETI) that the sun will indeed go supernova within the next two to five years.

The Committee on Security reports that to date, the general public remains unaware of the existence of the ETI, or of any impending threat to our planet or civilization.

The previous report of the Committee on Personnel covered arguments for and against several methods for choosing the six hundred seventy-six persons who would be transported to the Lambda Aurigae system, but reached no firm conclusion as to the best to use.

This previous report apparently became irrelevant a few hours before its completion, however, when the ETI, for reasons it has refused or been unable to explain, informed its contacts at Andrews that final selection was to be made by a single individual, who would be chosen at random by the ETI itself.

Additional Background:

Since our last report, the ETI has made its selection. The individual chosen was one Jeremy Cathcart Rollins, 19, of Ararat, Ohio; male Caucasian, 5'10", 175 pounds, brown hair, hazel eyes; graduated 1994 from Ararat Public High School; no college. Last known employment, day laborer with Tollerman Construction, laid off Jan. 4, 1996. Unmarried, no known children. Lives with his parents, Arthur and Dawn Rollins, at 114 Apple Street, Ararat. An older sister is married and residing in Cleveland with her husband and infant son.

Jerry Rollins was taken into protective custody by the FBI on March 27th, 1996, and brought to Washington, D.C. for briefing and consultation.

Mr. Rollins was understandably concerned, but appears to accept and understand his position. He has been allowed to communicate with his family under strict security.

Further discussion with the ETI in hopes of convincing it to alter its insistence on Mr. Rollins as the sole selection authority has been unavailing. The ETI is adamant that the transportees must be freely selected by Mr. Rollins and no one else.

Report on Conversations with Mr. Rollins:

Members of the Committee on Personnel have met repeatedly with Mr. Rollins between his incarceration on March 27th and yesterday, May 2nd. Every effort has been made to provide him with information that could help him in his selections, and suggestions for methods of selection, including the complete text of our previous report, have been provided as well.

We hoped to influence his choices, and increase the chances that the new community would survive and flourish, but we met considerable resistance to our suggestions.

Naturally, the possibility of allowing selections to be made by others for his approval was brought up. A transcript of his response follows:

"You said this alien left it up to me, right?"

"That's right, Jerry. But you're free to take advice..."

"Hey, if I want your advice I'll ask for it! If I let you guys do the picking, I'll wind up with a bunch of hot-shot politicians and generals, right? What the hell kind of world would *that* be?"

Further argument proved unavailing.

The suggestion that selection be made on the basis of proven intelligence or value to society was also dismissed:

"Nah. I've known too many high-I.Q. geeks. If I'm gonna spend the rest of my life on some other planet, I don't want to be surrounded by geeks."

The assumption that Mr. Rollins would himself be included among the transportees was noticed and commented on, and a reply given:

"What, you think I'm stupid? Of course I'm going. I don't want to fry, and if I get to choose, I'm goin'."

The possibility of a single planned community was then brought up.

"You mean, like take an entire town? 'Cept with less than a thousand guys it'd have to be a pretty small one; even Ararat's bigger'n that."

"Well, yes, the idea was that in a small town, the distribution of labor and the interpersonal relationships would already be well-established, which would smooth the transition."

"Who gives a shit about the transition? That's only gonna last a couple of years, tops. And I don't want to spend the rest of my life surrounded by a bunch of small-town rednecks, even if it is on some other planet. 'Sides, the only town I ever lived in is Ararat, and I sure don't want to take half of that stupid little burg, and if I picked anywhere else I'd be kinda odd man out, wouldn't I?"

The possibility of trying for a particular ethnic or geographic mix was greeted with the following:

"Why?"

"Why what, Jerry?"

"Why you want to go and make trouble? You pick people that way, you'll wind up with all the same crap we got here. If I take a Jew and an Arab, and a mick and a limey, and like that, we'll probably be fighting wars before the alien even leaves."

In desperation, a lottery was suggested. Mr. Rollins was offended.

"Christ, you think I can't do a better job pickin' 'em than a damn slot machine? What if you get a cripple or a bunch of old ladies or somethin'?"

Finally, on April 13th, members of the Committee conceded defeat. Mr. Rollins was determined to make his own selections, using his own criteria, and he flatly refused to discuss those criteria with us in advance. We therefore provided him with a committee member to act as his stenographer, and asked him to make his choices.

We had assumed that he would select his own family and friends, which would provide a dangerously-limited gene pool and cultural background. Our member was startled by the following exchange:

"I suppose we should start with your parents, Jerry?"

"Nah. I mean, I love Mom and Dad, but they're old, they're all settled – what would they do on another planet? Besides, they aren't about to have any more kids, and the idea is to keep the human race going, right? So they can stay. I'll miss 'em, though."

"Ah... you mean you'll knowingly leave them to die?"

"Yeah, I think so. We all gotta go sometime, and there's gonna be five billion other people dying – my folks are special, but y'know, they aren't *that* special."

After that awkward beginning, Mr. Rollins went ahead with his list, which is appended to this report.

The Selection Process:

The actual choosing took some time, of course. Several interruptions were necessary while Mr. Rollins did research, after his fashion. We were called upon to provide several current magazines, as well as accompanying him on trips to the area's college campuses.

At first, we were shocked by his methods of selecting who should survive, out of all the five billion inhabitants of Earth, but we really should not have been. After all, this is clearly simply a case of natural selection.

His choices include twenty-three old girlfriends and former classmates, one hundred and seven actresses, seventeen fashion models, three hundred thirty-two women who posed for men's magazines, one hundred ninety-one female college students chosen from nearby universities, two women encountered walking on the streets of Washington, and two secretaries he saw working at the Pentagon.

He did accept one suggestion, and included an obstetrician as his final selection.

They are all, needless to say, and including the obstetrician, female.

Conclusion:

Although there is some concern about the inbreeding that must occur in the coming generations, Mr. Rollins' selection certainly does provide for rapid population increase, and all the subjects chosen are obviously young and healthy. Since we have no say in who is to live, all we can do is hope for the best, and to acknowledge that Mr. Rollins could certainly have done far worse.

For example, had he in fact chosen on the basis of past accomplishments in public affairs or the sciences, it is an unfortunate fact that the resulting group would have been comprised mostly of males and largely older than optimum.

And in closing, at least one member of this Committee feels it necessary to point out that if the person doing the choosing was going to do it on the basis of sex appeal, it's a damn good thing that the ETI chose a heterosexual male.

Good luck, Jerry Rollins.

You'll need it.

Short Lines

Once again, I wanted to do a new take on a standard element of classic SF – why do you need a spaceship to access hyperspace?

Those damn fool science fiction writers always talked about subspace like as it wouldn't be any use anywhere except outer space, zipping around between stars like bees hopping from the honeysuckle to the hibiscus. Shows what they know, don't it? Same as they had their space navigators using slide-rules, and their computers using cams or filling up whole buildings or all that shit. I'll tell you, those boys could maybe spin a good yarn, but they weren't any better at guessing the future than my cat.

Well, I don't suppose they could've known. Wasn't till the fall of '98 that anybody ever figured out even that subspace was real, let alone that it was so easy to get into.

And it wasn't a durn thing like those old books.

I know, that ain't what you asked. You asked me why we do this the way we do. You already knowed the stories was wrong.

Well, hell, it's simple, really. It's all in how subspace works.

You need gravity to open into subspace. I guess that was something none of those folks ever thought of - in fact, I recollect a few who guessed 'twould work just the opposite. But it don't; you need a good strong gravity well to punch through. And when you've got that opening, you need to anchor it, or it's gonna drift all over hell and back, and you can't use just something sticky like asphalt, because it'll stretch and crack and break apart, but steel, steel works just fine. Steel will hold it right in place, solid as you like, and you won't find yourself coming back out the ass end of nowhere because the portal slipped a bit when you weren't looking.

So they knew right away they'd want rails.

And the distances are shorter in subspace, all right, but they ain't that much shorter. It's no four or five light years to Alpha Centauri, but it's still a few billion miles, and aiming's a royal bitch, because the match-ups ain't what you'd call exact, and there's that damn drift, and that's just about random as far as they've figured it yet. So nobody's going to cruise to Mars for the weekend just by taking a shortcut through subspace.

So they knew they weren't building no starships.

But the real corker - well, they found it quick enough, but it took a good long while before they figured out what they'd found. What it was - electricity don't flow through metal in subspace, and don't ask me to explain that, because I can't and neither can anyone else on God's green earth. You can just thank whoever you pray to at night that electricity still works up here, in the old noggin, and in your muscles, because otherwise anyone who set foot through a portal'd be dead as yesterday's lunch.

Anyway, that all put a few limits on what could be done, sure enough. Weren't any starships gonna go cruising out there without their computers and fancy equipment. Weren't any cars or airplanes going anywhere without sparks in the cylinders.

But they found land and air in subspace, and steel rails would hold just fine, and it wasn't but a mile from the Atlanta portal that Turner set up to the Chattanooga opening, and two miles from New York to Philly, five from New York to Boston. A man's muscles can swing a hammer here, and a spike will hold a rail to a tie, and steam will drive a piston just as hard as it ever did anywhere. Alcohol lamps'll burn just fine - can't use whale oil any more, o'course, not like they did on the old trains.

And it's what you'd call a tested technology, tried and true; wasn't any question but that it'd work up to expectations. Which it did.

Did you know that a good steamer can top a hundred miles an hour hauling a full load? They make the Boston to Washington run in about fifteen minutes. Not a jet built that could compete with that; hell, it used to take that long just to get everyone on the plane and taxi out to the runway.

Listen, there's the whistle; break's over. Now, you just take that sledge and start driving those spikes, boy; it's a good five miles to L.A. yet. I think I've answered your question about why we brought back the steam trains instead of building starships. No, don't try another one – I don't know who thought it up. First subspace train came out of a museum somewhere, so we make the tracks to fit it, but they're building them new now.

And think of it this way - if subspace wa'n't what it is, you wouldn't have this here job, would you? You'd be rotting in a drunk tank somewheres, most likely. Or if you did have a job you'd probably be cookin' up a good case of skin cancer out in the sun, instead of bein' here in the nice cool dark. There's a sun in here, too, or we'd freeze, but it's all in the infrared, you can't burn if you try.

Out there in normal space there isn't much work for a man with more muscles than brains, but in here we do just fine. I figure we'll do fine right up until we've covered this whole damn mudball in here with rails.

Those damn writers with their scientists zippin' around subspace didn't know what the hell they were talking about.

Don't you sass me, boy.

Hey, listen, hear that? That whistle, that's the San Diego mail train – she takes the western line, about two miles over. Not another sound in the two worlds like that.

Lonely, ain't it?

The folks I feel sorry for are the ones that lived out their lives without ever hearing that.

Now, swing that sledge!

Foxy Lady

An editor asked whether I'd ever written any fiction about "furries." I said no, but I'd be willing to give it a shot. Here's the result.

Al stared at the board, trying to concentrate, trying not to sweat.

"This one's for the grand prize, folks!" the MC announced, in those infuriatingly jovial tones he did so well. He gestured in the general direction of the display. "Are you ready, Al?"

"Ready as I'll ever be," Al replied, trying to sound as if he were having fun, rather than struggling to hold down his lunch.

Watching at home, he thought, you never saw how nervous the contestants were, or how small the studio was, or how that stupid board was knocked together out of plywood and cheap laminate.

"Then you have thirty seconds. Go!"

The central two screens lit up.

People. They were faces, two men.

"Presidents," he said, recognizing Ronald Reagan and John Kennedy. Kennedy disappeared, replaced by Marilyn Monroe. "Movie stars." Reagan vanished, replaced by Madonna. "Blondes."

"Try again," the MC called.

"Sex symbols, actresses..."

Monroe disappeared, and a new face he couldn't identify replaced her, a vaguely familiar male face with long hair and wire-rimmed glasses.

"Singers," he guessed.

Madonna was replaced by Kennedy. If he could figure this one out he'd be all the way around the circle and would win, but he couldn't figure out who the guy in the glasses was. A singer? Connected with Kennedy?

"Ten seconds," the MC said.

He'd seen the face, he knew he had. The hairstyle gave him a clue.

"The sixties," he guessed.

"Try again."

He tried to think. What was Kennedy noted for? "Uh...assassination victims?"

A bell rang and the studio audience burst into cheers.

"Congratulations, Al Roebuck!" the MC announced, coming forward to clap him on the back. "You've won the grand prize! Bill, tell Al what he's won!"

John Lennon, Al realized, that's who it was. He turned, a bit dazed.

"From the New Gene Corporation," the announcer said, as the pale blue curtains parted, "She's friendly, intelligent, and beautiful, and she's all yours! She's their top-of-the-line model, carefully cloned and hand-raised from a kit, every gene selected and tailored to make her the perfect household companion and servant. She's the New Gene Corporation's Mark Five Vixen, Salome!"

Al stared.

"Yes, made from the germ plasm of the common fox, the Mark Five Vixen is fluent in both English and Spanish, and trained to perform a wide variety of common household chores, from mopping floors to massaging backs. With a life expectancy of seventy-five years, she should last you a lifetime. She has a retail value of six hundred and fifty thousand dollars, but, Al Roebuck, she's *all yours*, for playing Missing Links!"

"Wow," Al said, still staring.

She was beautiful.

She was standing on a melon-colored rotating pedestal, one knee forward, one hand on her hip and the other hanging by her thigh; her pointed muzzle was raised proudly, her tail swishing gently behind her, the only part of her not held motionless. She wore only a simple red tunic that covered her from shoulder to mid-thigh, accentuating, rather than hiding, the swelling curves of bust and hip, and a black leather collar around her neck. Fine orange fur covered her legs, arms, and upper face; her hands, feet, and muzzle were white, toes and fingertips black. A white ruff and black forelock resembled a human woman's head hair.

Al hadn't expected anything like this. He'd figured they'd give away a car, or some furniture, or something, but not a gene-tailored companion!

"Isn't she something?" the MC asked, his arm around Al's shoulders. "And she's all yours!"

"Wow," Al said again. "She's beautiful."

The MC gave a phony chuckle, then turned to the studio audience and said, "Bill, what about our other players?"

"Richard, all contestants on Missing Links receive the home version of our game, and today we also have the pocket edition of the Encyclopedia Britannica, compatible with any standard reader..."

Al wasn't listening; he was still staring at the fox-woman on the pedestal.

Then the red lights on the camera went out, and a gofer came to lead Al away. Still dazed, he signed half a dozen assorted releases and tax forms, and twenty minutes later found himself standing at the studio door, lost and confused.

A stagehand walked up, holding a leash; the other end of the leash was clipped to the fox-woman's collar. He held out a clipboard.

"Sign here," he said.

"What is it?" Al asked, accepted the clipboard and a pen.

"Acknowledging receipt of your prize," the stagehand explained. "If you don't want it, sign on Line 3, and we'll pay you a percentage of its cash trade-in value, instead. It'll be mailed out in about ten days."

Al looked over the form. "Where do I sign if I *do* want her?"

"Line 1," the man replied. He pointed.

Al signed on Line 1. The stagehand took back the clipboard, pulled out two copies of the form (one pink and one yellow), and handed them to Al.

"If you change your mind, you have ten days to call the number here and arrange for pick-up," the stagehand explained, pointing. "They'll deduct a charge for the pick-up – see Paragraph Four? And your check will go out in about two weeks."

Al nodded, not looking.

The stagehand looked at him, glanced at the Mark Five Vixen, then shrugged and handed Al the leash. "She's all yours," he said.

She was shorter than she'd looked up on the pedestal, Al realized – scarcely over five feet tall. That made sense, though – foxes weren't very big animals. He looked down into her huge dark eyes.

"They said you probably wouldn't want to keep me," she said, in a throaty alto.

"They were wrong," he said. He looked down at the leash. "Uh...you sound intelligent. Do you need this thing?"

She cocked her head to one side. "I don't know," she replied. "They always said we had to have them any time we went out in public, but I don't know why, really."

"It's so you won't run away, or get into trouble," Al said.

"Why would I want to run away?" she asked.

Al had no answer for that. "Maybe we'd better leave it for now, just in case," he said.

Holding the leash loosely, he led her out onto the sidewalk. She flinched slightly at the noise of the traffic, her pointed ears folding back somewhat, her tail wrapping about one leg. "Come on," Al said, leading her toward the corner.

The first two taxis passed them by, but the third pulled up in response to Al's frantic waving, and they got in. The fox-woman looked over the worn upholstery and faded gum wrappers with fascination as Al gave the name of his hotel.

The driver said nothing on the way, but after seeing the size of his tip he growled, and pulled away with horn blaring and tires squealing.

A few people stared as Al led the fox-woman through the lobby to the elevators. Anthropomorphs were still new and rare, toys of the very rich, and this hotel, while respectable, was hardly a haunt of billionaires.

Giving one away on Missing Links was probably an attempt to broaden their appeal, to sell them to the merely wealthy – prices were reportedly coming down, after all. A year ago there reportedly hadn't been more than a hundred sold; now the number was said to be over a thousand.

They had the elevator to themselves, and Al asked, "They call you Salome?"

"That's my model name," she said. "There were twenty of us in my creche. I was Number Eight."

"You didn't have a name?" Al asked, shocked.

The fox-woman cocked her head in what Al was beginning to realize was her equivalent of a shrug. "They couldn't tell us apart, half the time," she said. "After all, we were all clone-sisters."

"Can I name you, then?"

"You can do anything you like, I guess – I'm yours, aren't I?"

"I guess so," Al agreed, "I'm having trouble believing it, that's all. I never won anything more than a Big Mac before."

"Really?"

"Really. I mean, I was on vacation here, and signing up for a game show was just a whim, you know?"

She blinked at him, batting eyelashes longer and lusher than any mere human had ever possessed.

"I'm going to call you Sally, I guess," Al said. "For Salomé."

"All right. And should I call you Master? That was what they taught us to do."

He hesitated. All his childhood training, to respect others and treat everyone as equals, came back to him – but this person, this thing, was *not* his equal, she was property. Legally, she was a *pet*, not a person.

"That's right," he said.

* * *

He had argued when the airline had insisted he buy Sally a ticket, claiming that she was cargo, and not a passenger.

They had responded by showing him their pet regulations – pets had to be in approved carriers, and if they didn't fly in the cargo compartment and didn't fit in the overhead luggage compartment, then they needed tickets, just like passengers.

They were willing to accept the collar and leash as a carrier, but if he was going to *argue*...

He bought her a seat.

At least the hotel hadn't tried to charge for her. They hadn't allowed her in the restaurant – no pets except guide dogs, the sign was right there – but they hadn't charged anything extra beyond the higher room service prices.

He was beginning to see that keeping an anthropomorph could be an expensive proposition. She ate just as much as a human, needed a seat on airplanes – that could add up.

Clothing was no problem, though. He had discovered as soon as they reached his hotel room that she was wearing nothing underneath the tunic, because as soon as he closed the door behind them she reached up, unclipped the leash from her collar, and pulled the tunic off over her head.

He had been rather startled by that.

She had been puzzled by his surprise.

"But I've got *fur*," she had said. "Why would I need clothes? I know I'm supposed to wear them out in public, since I look so much like a woman and we don't want to embarrass anyone, but why should I in private?"

He had had no answer; he simply stared. The short white fur on her belly, and the fluffy white on her breastbone that stood out a good three inches, had fascinated him. The fur was longer again between her legs, providing a discreet cover – she really *didn't* need clothes.

Except, perhaps, to cover her nipples, which were exposed and hairless.

She had tidied up the hotel room while he lay on the bed, resting and watching her. Since the maid had been in that morning, there hadn't been much tidying to be done, but she had done her best, hanging up her tunic, straightening the shirts in Al's suitcase, and so on.

She really was shaped almost exactly like a woman, Al had seen. Except for the fur, and the long bushy tail, and her head, she could have been human.

They'd done an amazing job, starting with a fox and producing her!

When she was satisfied with the room's condition she had come and sat beside him.

"What should I do now, Master?" she had asked.

He had reached up and done what he had not had the nerve to do up until then, and had stroked the fur on her arm. It was soft and sleek.

She had taken this as a cue, and had responded by stroking him back, and then unbuttoning his shirt.

He'd made a vague attempt at expressing his doubts and reservations about the propriety of this, since they were different species. He had said something about voiding the warranty, about physical compatibility, but she had swept that aside.

"Oh, they knew it would happen," she had said as she crouched over him, tail waving. "It was one of the things they designed us for, right from the start, and they trained us for it, too. They can't *advertise* it, of course, but I think everybody knows."

Her fingers were amazing, and he was delighted by how little her tail got in the way. The fur added a whole new element. Even so, she made love like a woman, rather than a fox, which was just as well. Al did not care for any nipping, and was pleased to have her on top and facing him.

Of course, those pointed little teeth and the shape of her mouth did limit things somewhat, and he would want to keep her claws filed down, but all in all, it was quite an experience.

He remembered that on the flight home, and decided that she was definitely worth the extra airfare.

* * *

She settled in quickly. His apartment achieved and maintained a degree of cleanliness he hadn't believed possible; she answered the phone when he was out, and took messages flawlessly.

He was rather surprised, as he had been so often by her, when he realized she could read and write.

"It's useful," she said, "So they taught us."

The woman he had been dating, one Mandy Charpentier, dumped him because of Sally – she didn't make a big scene, but she did call him a pervert.

"Hey, I didn't go out and buy her, I *won* her, on TV!" he protested.

"And you *kept* her, didn't you?" Mandy shot back. "Are you trying to tell me you couldn't have traded her in, or sold her somewhere?"

Al was basically a truthful person; he let Mandy go.

He worried about it, briefly – *was* he a pervert? The new term that was being used by the inevitable campaigners against the immoral use of anthropomorphs was "furvert." Was he a furvert?

He eventually decided it really didn't matter whether he was or not. He dated other women, took some of them to bed – and when they weren't there, Sally was.

His friends met Sally, marveled at her. A few were offended; a few were intrigued. For reasons he couldn't explain, he never let anyone else touch her – except once, after a particularly wild date, when he brought the woman home and the three of them wound up in bed together. The human woman had seemed almost obsessed with Sally's fur; Sally, for her part, had been fascinated by the woman's smooth hairlessness.

That particular woman wanted nothing to do with Al after that night.

His food bills more or less doubled, which left him with less disposable income than he was used to, but he got by. He went to fewer shows, bought cheaper clothes.

He taught Sally his favorite recipes; she already knew how to cook, but her repertoire was sadly limited at first.

His electric bills went up; Sally preferred sleeping a few hours each day, and staying up most of the night reading or watching TV. He could have ordered her not to, but that seemed needlessly cruel, and the bills weren't unmanageable.

A small price to pay for having a household companion.

For having, he admitted, a slave.

There were ads on TV for anthropomorphs – more and more of them, it seemed. There were a few dozen varieties of cat-person, there were seal-people and dog-people and pig-people. There were vixen-ladies up to Mark Six now, and fox-men to Mark Four. Bear-men, lion-men, swan-women.

Al marveled at how human the New Gene Corporation could make all those different species. He wondered why other companies didn't seem to be able to, even though NGC didn't claim to have any patents on their processes. Their nearest competition came from Polyform Biologicals, and PB's Poly-Pets were small and stupid, limited to perhaps a hundred words of vocabulary and a few simple tasks.

Sally seemed as bright as he was – maybe, he admitted to himself, brighter. He wondered if the genetic engineers might not have overdone it.

"You know, Master," Sally said one night, as he got ready to crawl into bed after a late date, "I know I shouldn't, but sometimes I feel jealous of those women you go out with."

Al turned and looked at her.

"I know, I know," she said, "I'm just an animal, and you're a human, but I *do*. I won't do anything about it, of course, but I wanted to let you know – just so, you know, if I get angry or say anything nasty, you'll understand why."

He hadn't answered; he didn't know how.

Instead, he had canceled his dinner date for next Saturday, and stayed home with Sally.

He had had her almost a year when it happened.

He came home from work and let himself in; she was not waiting there to greet him. That wasn't particularly unusual; sometimes she was asleep. He hung up his jacket and turned.

She wasn't asleep. She was sitting in the living room, staring at the TV. Her eyes were fixed on the screen with an intensity he had never seen before.

"What is it?" he asked, crossing to her.

"Shh!" she hissed, without turning.

Puzzled, surprised that she had dared to shush him, he sat down beside her on the rather battered sofa and looked at the TV. A toothpaste commercial was just ending, to be replaced by a news desk.

"Welcome to the second half of Channel 8's Eyewitness News," the anchorman said. "Recapping tonight's top story, FBI agents have arrested most of the management of the New Gene Corporation on a variety of charges, including fraud, slave-trading, and murder. Four NGC executives are reported to have attempted suicide, two of them successfully, while others are still at large. Authorities say that genetic testing has demonstrated that the so-called anthropomorphic pets marketed by NGC are, in fact, human-derived, rather than animal-derived as the company claimed, and that under present law, all such anthropomorphs are human beings, free citizens, entitled to the full protection of the law..."

It was Al's turn to stare in shock at the TV, while Sally slowly turned to stare at him.

When the news switched to something about central Africa, Al looked at Sally.

"I didn't know," he said. "I swear I didn't know!"

"Neither did I," she replied. She hesitated. "So if I'm human – do all humans feel like this? Confused and unsure all the time, and trying to hide it by working at little things, to distract themselves from the big ones?"

"Probably," Al said. "*I* do."

They stared at each other for a long moment.

"I can't keep you," Al said. "I mean, I'd be glad if you stayed, but I can't make you, I can't tell you what to do. They said something about a settlement..."

Sally nodded. "We're all going to collect damages – they're liquidating NGC and parceling it all out. If there's enough, they might pay back some of what the owners paid. You could..."

"There won't be enough. There can't possibly be enough to cover what they must owe all of you!"

Sally blinked.

"Besides, I didn't pay anything, I won you," Al pointed out.

Sally got up from the couch and headed for the door.

"You'll need your tunic," Al called. "And it's chilly; take my tan coat."

"But..." Sally turned. "But I won't be..."

"Don't worry about returning it," Al said, "It's the least I can do."

She put on the tunic, and took the coat.

Al sat alone on the couch until very late that night, not really thinking, but simply missing her.

* * *

At the end of the first week his apartment was a mess, worse than ever – he had become accustomed to leaving things around for her to put away, and it took awhile to break the habit.

By the end of the second week the place was spotless again; he had gotten fed up with his own slovenliness and, as a sort of tribute to her, had thoroughly cleaned the entire apartment.

He was wavering about whether to keep it that way – specifically, whether to carry his used coffee mug back to the kitchen or just let it sit – when the doorbell rang.

If he was going to have to get up anyway, he might as well take the mug, he decided. He picked it up as he rose, and carried it with him to the door.

He almost dropped it.

She was wearing a black suede jacket, a pleated black skirt, and a broad-brimmed black hat with an ostrich plume on one side — the effect was startling.

She cocked her head to one side. "We don't exactly blend in, regardless of how we dress," she said, "So why not have fun?" She held out an arm; his tan coat was draped across it. "I brought your jacket."

"Come in!" he said, gathering his wits, "Come in!"

She did.

She draped his coat on the back of the sofa and looked around, and he thought he saw a trace of disappointment flash across her face.

"I'm glad you came," he said. "I've wanted to know how you've been doing. I've been watching the news reports, of course, but they don't get very specific."

She nodded. "You've kept the place neat, I see," she said.

"I try," he said, suddenly reminded of the coffee mug in his hand. "Listen, can I get you something to drink?" He headed for the kitchen. "There's all the usual stuff."

"A glass of milk would be nice," she said.

He put the mug in the sink and got her milk.

When he returned to the living room she had doffed her hat, which now adorned an end table, and unbuttoned her jacket, revealing the familiar red tunic beneath. She took the milk with the odd half-grin that was the closest her fox-like mouth could come to a smile.

"So what's been happening?" he asked, settling on the couch beside her.

"It's been pretty awful," she said. "They've been talking about plastic surgery and hormone treatments and things, to make us all look more normal, and they don't seem to listen when most of us say we don't *want* to look normal, we *like* the way we look. They say it's just the conditioning we got from NGC, but even if that's true, so what? It doesn't make it any less real."

"Hormone treatments?"

"For the fur," she explained. "To make it fall out."

"Oh, that would...what a waste!"

She nodded. "And they want to cut off our tails. But I'm keeping mine – they can't *make* us."

"Of course not!"

"They talk about us as if it's our fault, sometimes – I heard someone say that at least the problem's not permanent, since we're all sterile we'll all die off in a generation. I don't see why we have to be a *problem* like that."

"You don't," Al began, but she interrupted him.

"And there are the stories the others tell about their old owners – torture, and beatings, and abuse – I knew I liked you, and everything, but I didn't realize how lucky I was that you'd won me, instead of my being sold to some rich, sadistic furvert."

"People can be thoughtless," he said feebly.

She shook her head. "They weren't thoughtless," she said. "They did it on purpose."

He didn't argue.

She looked around the room again and asked, "So, have you been seeing someone?"

"No," he said.

"Oh. I thought you might have been lonely, with me...I mean, living alone again."

"I am," he said. "But it's okay."

"I've been living in a hotel," she said. "With three other anthropomorphs. They put us all up there until we could find places of our own. And we're all entitled to welfare, as well as a share of the NGC settlement – that could be about sixty thousand dollars apiece, they think."

He nodded. "So what are you planning to do?"

"I don't know," she said. She looked around the room again, a little desperately. "I was sort of hoping I could...could maybe work cleaning people's homes."

"You're good at it," he said. "But it's not a very good job."

"I know," she admitted. "I always hated it."

"You *did*?" That was the first thing she had said that had really surprised him. He sat up straight and stared at her.

"Of *course* I did!"

"Then why did you *do* it?"

She stared at him as if he was obviously insane. "Because I *had* to, of course! It's what a household companion is *for*!"

"Well, if you'd ever *told* me you didn't like it, maybe I would have done some of the cleaning myself, but I thought you *liked* it! I thought it had been programmed into you, or it was something foxes did, or something."

"No! I was trained for it, but I never *liked* it!"

"Well, did I *ask* you to keep the place so spotless?"

"No, but I thought you liked it!"

"I *did* like it, but if you didn't like *doing* it, it wasn't important."

"Why didn't you *tell* me that?"

"You never asked!"

She stared at him.

He stared back, and in a much calmer, quieter voice he added, "There were a lot of things I never told you."

"Like what?"

"That I love you."

* * *

An hour later they lay together on the floor, naked; he stroked her furry back, and she brushed her tail along his thigh.

"Only an idiot would want to make your fur fall out," he said. "Or cut off your tail."

She nipped gently at his nose. "I love you, Mas... I mean, Al."

"You can call me anything you like, in private," he said.

"And I can stay?"

"As long as you like."

"That might be a long, long time – I'm really not sure."

"Whatever."

"I'm glad to be back. Except..."

"Except what?" He stopped stroking.

"Well, there's one thing that'll have to change, or I just *can't* stay."

"What?"

"Oh, don't look so worried!"

"I *am* worried! What is it?"

"From now on," she said, laughing, "*you* wash the pans that don't go in the dishwasher! I hate what the detergent does to my fur!"

Dread Vengeance

A story about propaganda, inspired in part by something the Roman emperor known as Caligula reportedly said: "Oderint dum metuant." Which means, "Let them hate me, so long as they fear me."

The Earthman in the holographic image was small and scruffy, a scraggly growth of beard scraping at the air filter that covered his mouth and nose, greasy fingerprints on his dark goggles; he staggered slightly as if intoxicated – or already wounded.

He was hurrying, fleeing across an alien courtyard, and the image moved with him, the camera following his flight.

Behind the Earthman came a dozen or more creatures even smaller than himself, moving on four legs apiece, each holding something in its prehensile snout; sunlight whiter and sharper than anything that had ever shone on Earth glittered from mica-bearing paving stones and blades edged with volcanic glass.

The Earthman glanced back, his expression hidden by his protective gear, and quickened his pace, but that only served to trap him in the narrow end of the cul-de-sac courtyard that much sooner. He turned, a beast at bay, casting about for something he could use as a weapon in his defense.

A flung stone struck his shoulder; he started back, the filter-mask moving as he shouted, and stooped to retrieve it. Another stone caught him on the side of his head as he did so, throwing him off-balance and knocking his goggles out of line.

He caught himself against the wall to keep from falling, and reached up with his free hand to straighten the crooked eyepiece.

Another stone caught him on the hand; blood gleamed a vivid red as he dove for a stone.

The next missile bounced squarely off one lens, but he ignored it as he regained his feet, a shard of rock in his fist.

The creatures were closing in, and when they saw the weapon they ceased their slow torment; a hail of stone battered at him. The goggles flew off, and he flung an arm across sun-blinded eyes; his scream loosened the filter-mask. Blood streaked his hair and trickled down his jumpsuit. He fell.

The arrival of the military airsled two minutes later, its flashing multicolored lights only dimly visible in the glare of the white sun, was an anti-climax; the attackers were already fleeing, and the Earthman was obviously quite dead. His crumpled body sprawled awkwardly against the wall. Blood trickled from nose, mouth, and eyes, from a hundred wounds, and pooled on the cobbles.

As the airsled's human crew emerged and began efficiently cleaning up the mess and gathering the corpse aboard, a deep voice spoke.

"This incident was recorded by one of the automatic cameras that were studying the city at the time; unfortunately, the equipment had not yet been programmed to automatically summon help at the sight of a bleeding human, and only the failure of the victim's heart, reported by the required internal monitor carried by all off-Earth personnel, alerted the emergency crew. The victim was beyond hope of revival by the time help reached him."

The scene cut abruptly to a shot of the same Earthman, alive, sitting at ease and speaking to a woman behind a desk.

"The victim was Alan McCrae, an unskilled volunteer attached to the mission. He had been dismissed from his position and was awaiting transportation back to Earth at the time of the incident. Later investigation revealed that he had used the free time resulting from his unemployment to swindle several of the local inhabitants, selling them 'medicine' which proved to be whiskey cut with sugar-water. The metabolism of the *Sh'chinei* reacts badly to alcohol, and a young female died of McCrae's medicine, precipitating the attack. None of the *Sh'chinei* reported McCrae's actions prior to the attack; had they done so, McCrae would have been bound over for trial and in all likelihood turned over to the *Sh'chinei* for punishment."

Another cut, to eight men and women seated about a table.

"Despite the circumstances, the Council refused to alter the official policy. A human life had been lost, and policy requires that the killing of any human by any non-human sentient must be promptly avenged, in the interests of preventing recurrences. Accordingly, the *Sh'chinei* city was destroyed."

The scene changed again, and the audience watched in horror as the strange town vanished in a fireball even brighter than the light of that world's white-dwarf sun. The burning cloud rose ominously upward on a tower of flame, then spread horizontally in what any Earthman would recognize as a mushroom cloud.

"The results were satisfactory," the narrator said calmly, as a camera panned across glowing, molten ruins beneath darkened skies and a rain of black ash. "The surviving *Sh'chinei* were warned that a second incident would result in the destruction of their entire civilization."

"By every power," one of the watchers hissed in its native tongue. "How can this be so?"

"For a single murderer they did this!" another replied.

"Suppose," said a third, "that we had not seen this, and an Earthperson had slain one of our own young. Would we not have slain him in turn, and perhaps all died as a result? Let us thank the powers that allowed us to see this record in time!"

"Dare we continue to deal with the Earthpeople?" the second asked.

"I think that we can," the third replied. "Did not our friend Anna Twombley bring us to see this record, though she was told not to? Some among the Earthpeople wish us well, and surely the benefits to be derived from trade with them are obvious. But oh, we must be cautious!"

"We must spread the news among all our people," said the first. "No Earthperson may be harmed, under any circumstances."

"Agreed," said the second.

"Agreed," said the third.

"We must leave, before the Earthpeople find us here," the second said; the others clapped their consent, and together they left the little viewing room that Anna Twombley had elaborately smuggled them into.

From another viewing room, Twombley watched the results of her handiwork. "Not bad," she said, leaning on the back of her younger companion's chair.

"I couldn't follow it," the young man replied. "To me that language of theirs just sounds like white noise."

"I can play it back and translate, if you like, Bill."

The young man looked at the third human, an older man in a military uniform. The soldier shook his head.

"Don't bother," the younger man said. "We'll take your word for it."

Twombley leaned forward to hit the stop-and-rewind tab. "I don't think we'll have any problems at all with these people from now on," she said. "They're good and scared."

"That's the whole idea," the older man said. He leaned back in his chair, satisfied.

Bill frowned. "You know, Colonel, Anna, it occurs to me that someday we're going to hit a culture that has a movie industry of its own and knows special effects as well as we do, and when that happens this little stunt isn't going to work."

Anna shrugged. "It might work anyway. How could they be *sure* it was a simulation? Would they dare call our bluff?"

"They might," the young man said. He hesitated. "You know, it occurs to me, Anna – is it really a bluff? *Would* we retaliate like that?"

"We don't *have* to – no one's going to call us, not after they see the recordings."

"How do we know? These are aliens we're dealing with."

"They still have an instinct for self-preservation – that's universal."

"Is it? Well, I suppose so." He shrugged. "Still, seems to me there are plenty of times in human history when bluffs have been called. Sometimes they were bluffs, sometimes they weren't." He studied the player with interest. Then his expression changed as an idea struck him. He glanced at the colonel, then asked uneasily, "Do we even know for sure that this holo is faked?"

Anna stared at him, then she, too, threw a quick glance at the colonel, who was sitting silently, listening, with an odd half-smile on his face.

"Of course it is!" Anna said. "Of course it's a bluff! We wouldn't nuke millions of intelligent beings over one human! It's unthinkable!"

"Hey, relax," Bill said. "I'm just throwing ideas around, thinking out loud."

"Well, stop it. It's...it's...." She turned away, unable to find the right word, and picked up her beltpack; her eyes wandered back to the holographic cartridge in the player.

"Unthinkable?" the younger man asked, following her gaze.

"Of course it is!" she repeated, "We'd never do it. The public would never stand for it."

"Not if they knew," the young man said, with another glance at the colonel.

"You're saying we'd lie to our own people?"

"Why not? We lie to *them*," Bill said, gesturing at the player.

"We'd never do it!" Anna insisted. She strode to the door. Then she paused, and turned back to look at the two men, her eyes worried.

"Would we?" she asked.

he two men glanced at one another. The colonel crossed his arms over his chest. Anna felt as if a weight had just settled on her own chest.

"*Have* we?" she asked.

Bill shrugged.

"You don't want to know," the colonel said.

He's Only Human

Long ago, a fellow named Dan Goodman posted a few story ideas he wanted to see used somewhere. I liked this one, and with his permission I wrote this and sold it.

The Speaker of the House stared at the President Pro Tem of the Senate. "You can't be serious," he said.

"Oh, yes, I can," she replied. "I'm *very* serious."

"But he's the President of the United States! I know he's not our party, but he can't... I mean, you're *sure*?"

She nodded.

"What about the vice president? The Cabinet? Are any of *them* aliens?"

The senator glanced at the office door, making certain it was securely closed – it would not do to have anyone overhear. "Human, all of them," she replied. "Not a single extraterrestrial in the lot."

"But how could this *happen?*" the Speaker protested. "How could we have completely lost control of the executive branch? Isn't there something we can do?"

She shrugged. "Do you have any suggestions, Mr. Speaker?"

He looked helplessly around the office. "Is it too late to make a substitution? Can't we infiltrate somewhere? I mean, leaving the country in the hands of *humans* – it's not safe! How could the Commission ever have let it happen?"

"Someone got careless, I suppose."

"Carelessness on *that* level is the exact reason we came here in the first place! Are we getting as sloppy as the humans, now? Did someone get overconfident just because their Cold War has been over for a couple of decades?"

The senator shrugged, a human gesture she had become rather fond of.

"We have no way to infiltrate the White House and replace him?"

"Oh, we can certainly get in there," the senator said. "We have the equipment – but we have no one accredited to take the job, and no costume ready. It would take weeks to grow a disguise good enough to pass muster."

"Well, something must be done, and immediately!" the Speaker said, getting to his feet. "We'll just have to *remove* the president and vice president. I'm next in line, and I can get some of our people into the Cabinet and line things up for the next election."

The senator was silent for a moment, then said, "That's a bit drastic, isn't it?"

"It's a drastic situation. We can't trust humans with spaceships and nuclear weapons!"

"Should we contact the Commission first, to let them know our plans?"

"There isn't time; the next relay ship isn't due for almost a month. They've always trusted field agents to act responsibly, and I think it would be totally irresponsible to leave a human president in the White House."

"It's your decision, sir – you're the senior agent – but I admit I'm a little reluctant to interfere so directly. Removing *both* the president and vice president..."

"It's necessary, clearly," the Speaker told her. "We'll go tonight."

* * *

They had removed their disguises, of course – if by some horrible mischance they were spotted, it would hardly do for the Speaker and the President Pro Tem to be seen sneaking into the president's bedroom. The senator had suggested substituting some other human guise, but the Speaker had refused, for two sound reasons: *Nobody* had any business sneaking into the president's bedroom, and besides, it would take too long to grow them.

If anyone saw them, that person would probably assume he was dreaming, and certainly wouldn't be believed if he talked about it later. Two three-foot-tall aliens creeping through the White House corridors, using mysterious machinery to open locks and evade security devices, would surely seem more like a Secret Service agent's nightmare than a real possibility.

They moved silently down the corridor, thanks more to a dampening field than any natural stealth, and used light distorters to make themselves effectively invisible in the shadows whenever they had to pass near a human being – though the distorters had the rather severe drawback of impairing the users' own vision as well, limiting their usefulness.

The door to the presidential bedroom popped open at the touch of a handheld device, and they stepped cautiously into the darkened room...

And the lights came on suddenly, leaving them blinking foolishly at the sight of four Secret Service agents pointing weapons at them.

And the weapons weren't the standard-issue human-made 9mm automatics, but Krung neural suppressors.

"Well, I'll be damned," someone said, and they looked past the black-suited guards to see the president standing beside his bed, wearing a bathrobe and slippers. "They told me they'd spotted some extraterrestrial shenanigans goin' on, but I didn't think they'd actually catch two of you sneakin' in here!"

"Urk," the Speaker said.

"Now, just who are you, and what did you boys want with me?"

"Uh..." the President Pro Tem said.

"This one's not a boy, sir," one of the Secret Service agents said, gesturing at the senator. "It's a female."

"Oh? How can you... no, don't tell me."

The Speaker and the senator looked at one another. No human would have recognized the senator's sex – which meant that though the president was human, at least one of his guards was not. And judging by the Krung weapons and all the rest, the president knew it.

That changed everything. She asked, "What's going on? Why weren't we told?"

The president laughed. "Seems to me that it's *you* who have some explaining to do, little lady! Who are you two, anyway?"

"I am Heo designate Fu-jerin, from the fourth planet of Epsilon Eridani," the Speaker said.

"The Speaker of the House of Representatives, sir," a Secret Service agent explained.

The Speaker and the senator looked at one another again.

"It's a set-up," the senator said. "An ordinary agent wouldn't know your name."

"Probably a test of some kind," the Speaker agreed. "I suspect we just flunked."

"I'm afraid so," the Secret Service agent said. "The Commission was considering you for a new post, now that we're turning Earth over to the natives, and set up this situation to see how you'd handle it. I think if you go back through the e-mail you've let pile up over the last few weeks you'll find some interesting reading."

"I don't have time to read my own e-mail!" the Speaker protested. "I've been busy running the country! We didn't want this one to fall apart the way the Soviet Union did..."

"Running the country is *my* job, Mr. Speaker," the president said mildly.

The Speaker glared at him with immense green eyes. "It shouldn't be!" he retorted. "You humans would've blown each other up fifty years ago if we hadn't intervened!"

"That was then," the Secret Service agent replied. "This is now. You really should have kept up on the reports, Fu-jerin. We've been discussing a gradual reversion of control for the past two years."

"I saw some of the discussions, but I didn't know it was being *implemented...*"

The Secret Service agents didn't reply; they just stared at him over their Krung suppressors.

"Someone should have told me," the Speaker protested weakly.

"Tell that to the Commission," a Secret Service agent said.

"What's going to happen to us?" the senator asked.

"You're going to leave peacefully and go back to your normal activities," the Secret Service agent said. "I wouldn't recommend running for re-election, though."

"You aren't going to do anything to us?"

"What would we do? You think we want headlines about aliens trying to kidnap the president?"

"I suppose not." She looked forlornly at the president. "Our apologies, sir," she said. "We meant no harm."

"No harm done," he said, waving a hand in dismissal. "If it's any comfort, these boys do keep an eye on me, just in case I do somethin' stupid." He gestured at the Secret Service agents. "We're taking it one step at a time."

"Yes, sir."

"And while you're here, I'd just like to say somethin'" the president continued. "Maybe it's just me bein' a little too proud, but I like to think we would have managed to not blow ourselves up even if you fellows hadn't interfered. You comin' in and secretly takin' over the governments of half a dozen countries the way you did was a lowdown sneaky thing to do, and you didn't have any right to do it. It came as one hell of a shock to me when I found out just what all you'd done, and I was madder 'n hell at first."

"But..." the Speaker began.

The president stopped him with a raised hand.

"That said," he said, "I gotta say, you kept up your end of the bargain. You could've stomped us all flat, or let us blow ourselves up, and you didn't, and now that your High Commission's decided we can be trusted, you're pullin' out, little by little. It's plain you meant well. So while I can't quite bring myself to say thanks for takin' over the world, I *will* say that I appreciate the thought. Now, get out of here and let me get some sleep; I've got a lot of work to do in the morning."

And with that, he turned away, while the Secret Service agents escorted the two intruders out of the room.

As the two aliens made their way through the secret network of tunnels under the Washington streets, back toward the workshop where they had left their human disguises, the Speaker said bitterly, "It's all very well having infiltrated the Secret Service, and telling the president the truth, and that was a pretty speech he made, but I still don't like it. When you come right down to it he's still only human."

The senator glanced at her companion, and would have shrugged if she were wearing shoulders.

"They could do worse," she said.

Throwback

The thing about alien abduction reports is that they never give an explanation for what the aliens want with their victims, or how they choose them. What are they looking for? After the first half-dozen, what more is there to learn from anal probes?

Maybe they're really looking for something else entirely.

The highway was empty as far as he could see – and since it was dead straight right to the horizon in both directions, that was quite a distance. The speed limit was nominally 65, but he couldn't see any reason to abide by that on a night like this, and was roaring down that empty asphalt at close to ninety.

Not, he reminded himself, that he was in any great hurry to get anywhere. The job he had waiting in Chicago didn't start until Monday, and it probably wasn't exactly going to launch a brilliant career in any case. It was just another stupid dead-end position he'd keep for a year or two before he got bored and quit.

But that was all he ever found.

Not that he'd looked all that hard; he'd rather spend his time fishing than poring over want ads or sitting there sweating through interviews.

He blinked, then rubbed his eyes – first the right, then the left, never both at once, not at this speed. He always kept one hand on the wheel and one eye open.

And when he looked out at the highway again there was a bright light coming from somewhere overhead.

"Oh, crap," he said. A police helicopter, presumably – but what was it doing out here in the middle of nowhere, in the middle of the night? And why hadn't he heard it coming?

For that matter, he *still* didn't hear it...

And then his car's motor died, for no reason he could see, and he struggled with the wheel as the vehicle started to slew to the right. He was able to keep it on the road and coasted to a stop.

The light was brighter now, and changing colors, and he still didn't hear any aircraft – in fact, with his own engine off, he didn't hear anything but his own breathing.

He turned the key to off, then cranked down the window and stuck his head out, trying to see where the light was coming from...

And then he was inside the alien craft, with no memory of how he got there; he was strapped to a table and three of the aliens – short, big-eyed, gray-skinned – were leaning over him, studying him.

Something closed around the top of his head for a moment, then vanished. Long grey fingers pulled open his shirt and prodded his chest; he tried to shout a protest, but he couldn't make any sound emerge. Something seemed to be blocking his throat, though he could still breathe freely.

He remembered the stories he'd read describing alien abductions, stories about mysterious surgery and sexual abuse and weird mistreatment, and he tried to scream, but still couldn't make a sound.

The aliens spoke amongst themselves, fluting and chittering at one another, but of course he couldn't understand any of it. He struggled against his restraints, but could not move.

Then an alien hand clasped his neck for a moment – not squeezing at all, just placed around his throat, held there for a few seconds, then removed – and he let out a moan of terror.

It was a sound, though. His voice was back. "Who are you?" he asked – which was, he realized, a stupid question – they were *aliens*, for Chrissake! Who else could they be, the Boy Scouts? "What do you want with me?"

One of the aliens looked down at him and waved a metal thing that looked vaguely like a curling iron his sister had once had.

"I'm Michael Bostic," he said. "I'm just a clerk. I grew up in Illinois. I have one sister – why am I telling you this?" He looked at the curling-iron thing. The alien tilted its head; it wasn't a nod, but Bostic understood the gesture to mean the same thing as a nod.

"You made me talk," he said. "With that thing."

The alien's head tilted again. Then it looked at its companion and made chittering noises.

One of the other aliens stepped forward and spoke. Bostic wasn't certain whether it was actually speaking English, or whether he was somehow understanding another language.

"Are you of sufficient interest?" it asked. "Our evaluation is inconclusive."

"I don't understand," Bostic said.

"We operate under limitations," the alien said. "We are permitted to keep a set maximum of your kind – we cannot keep all we take. We choose carefully. Most we decide easily. Amelia Earhart was of great interest and we kept her. Ambrose Bierce we kept. Sidney Messerly we kept. Others we returned. You we have not evaluated clearly."

Bostic wondered who the hell Sidney Messerly was, but he saw an opportunity here.

"I'm no one," he said. "I'm boring. I'm dull."

"You do not wish to be taken from your home," the alien said.

"Damn right."

"That is a point we will consider."

"You do that," he said. "I promise, I'm boring."

The alien turned away.

Bostic stared at the back of the alien's head, but the alien did not turn to look at him again. Bostic tried looking elsewhere, but the other aliens had withdrawn as well, and he could not focus clearly on the ceiling, nor could he see the walls at all.

"I'm boring," he repeated.

And, he realized with an unpleasant shock, he really was, too. He wasn't lying to save himself. He *was* boring. He tried to worry about telling the aliens too much, making himself sound interesting, and was horrified to discover he couldn't do it. He couldn't think of anything interesting about himself.

Except, of course, that he had been kidnaped by aliens. That was certainly something out of the ordinary.

But it was the *only* thing he could think of.

"I *am* boring," he said, wonderingly.

He had never thought about it before. The subject had never come up. Friends had drifted away over the years, but no one had ever come up and told him, "Michael, you're unbelievably dull." They'd just stopped calling or writing. Now that he thought about it, though, he hadn't been able to hold their interest, had he?

"We will return you," the alien said, and then everything went gray, until he woke up in his car.

He sat up with a start and stared out at the empty highway. The sky in the east was turning from black to blue. Had he dozed off at the wheel? He'd had this weird dream, about being snatched by a UFO...

If it *was* a dream.

He looked down at his hands; they were sunburned. He touched his face gently, and winced; that was sunburned as well. But it was *night*, and he hadn't been sunburned when he fell asleep, so far as he knew...

Maybe it hadn't been a dream at all.

But that meant he really had been abducted by aliens – and then they'd released him.

Or really, they'd thrown him back, like an undersized fish – because he was boring. He stared out at the empty highway, letting that idea run through his mind.

He was so boring the aliens wouldn't keep him. He was dull, ordinary, uninteresting. There was no question about it. He thought that over, and came to a conclusion.

He didn't *want* to be boring.

Of course, now he had been abducted by aliens, however briefly. Wouldn't that make him interesting? Not to the aliens, perhaps, but to other people?

He remembered his own usual reaction to abductees on talk shows – changing the channel. No, endlessly rehashing an abduction was boring, too. If he wanted to transform himself into someone fascinating he'd have to find another way.

He peered at the road ahead and told himself that by God, he *wouldn't* be boring. He'd go to Chicago and take that job, but he wasn't going to *stay* there...

* * *

The talk show host tried not to stare at Bostic's hair, but couldn't help giving it a glance or two, and the first thing he asked once they were both seated was, "Is the hair new?"

"Same hair I've been growing since I was a baby," Bostic said, grinning. "But the style's new, yeah."

In fact, he'd spent the morning working on it – the "skunk" he'd been wearing for the past few weeks had been getting old. Now the right side of his head was shaved from the center of his scalp to just above his ear, and the left side sported a great swoop of gelled chartreuse wave. It stood a good six inches high.

"It's different," the host said.

Bostic shrugged. "It's nothing," he said. "Just a little experiment."

"Think it'll catch on?"

Bostic smiled. "You know, Dave," he said, "I really don't care whether it does or not. I'm not trying to start fashions – I know I *have* started 'em, but I'm not trying to. I just don't want to be boring."

He did sudden double-take, as if he had just seen something somewhere off-camera, but of course there was nothing there. The studio audience laughed.

"Seems to me," said the host, "that you've dedicated your *life* to not being boring."

Bostic's smiled broadened. "That's exactly right, Dave. That's just what I've done. The stunts, the books, the music, the clothes, the hair – it's all to keep from being the really dull, ordinary person I am underneath."

Some of the audience laughed uncertainly.

"No, really," Bostic said. "Six years ago I was the most boring person you'd ever care to meet."

"Uh huh," Dave said doubtfully. "So what made you decide to change?"

"Well, six years ago I was abducted by aliens."

"Oh, really?" Dave sat back in his chair. "I hadn't heard this one."

"I've never mentioned it before," Bostic said. "Mostly because I didn't think anyone would believe me. They'd think I was a nut."

"Of course. Bright green hair, parachuting off the Sears Tower, books about the secret erotic life of furniture, that's all sane."

"Oh, hey, that's why I'm telling you now," Bostic said. "Now everyone *knows* I'm a nut, so what harm can it do?"

"You tell me."

"None that I can see. So yeah, six years ago I was snatched out of my car by the crew of a UFO. They threw me back because I was boring, though, so I promised myself I'd never be boring again."

"Is *that* what happened?"

"Exactly what happened. Here, hold this." He pulled something from an inside pocket and handed it over.

The host accepted the soft plastic lump and asked, “What is it?”

“A silicone breast implant,” Bostic explained. “Ever wondered what they look like before they’re installed? Well, there you are.”

“Aha,” the host said, staring at the thing in his hand. “Don’t they usually come in pairs?”

* * *

After the show Bostic was wiping off his makeup – both the regular pancake and his own fluorescent designs – when he noticed a production assistant standing nearby, watching him. He straightened up and turned around.

“Did you want something?” he asked.

“Well, I had a question, but if you’re busy it’s not important,” she said, clutching her clipboard to her chest. He noticed she was wearing a blouse based on his half-leather style of the year before.

“I’m not busy,” he said. “Busy is boring. What’s your question?”

“Were you *really* kidnapped by aliens?”

He smiled at her. “I think so,” he said. “Either that, or I fell asleep at the wheel one night and had one hell of a dream.”

“And that’s really why you...why you started doing all the things you do?”

“I got my ears pierced that same day,” he said. “Starting small, you know. I added the warpaint the day after, and started thinking about what to do next.”

“And it’s because the aliens sent you back?”

“That’s right.”

“So...so you wanted them to keep you? Are you hoping they’ll take you again, and keep you?”

The question startled him; amazingly, he had never really thought about it. He had been too busy finding ways to make himself interesting to consider why. “No,” he said. “I just didn’t like the idea that even space aliens could see how dull I was.”

“Well, you aren’t dull now – so what if they *did* recapture you? I mean, in the stories, don’t they sometimes pick up the same people over and over?”

He stared at her thoughtfully.

“I suppose,” he said slowly, “that they’d keep me. If they did pick me up again, I mean, and in six years I’ve never seen any sign of them so I don't think it's likely. But hey, if I disappear mysteriously, figure that's where I've gone."

"Okay," she said. "Thanks, Mr. Bostic."

She turned and was gone, and Bostic stared after her for a long moment.

Would the aliens pick him up again? And if so, would they really keep him?

And if they did, would that be good or bad? Being taken to their planet, meeting the other people they'd taken...

Well, at least it would certainly be *interesting.*

* * *

The aliens watched the broadcast from Earth in silence, but when it was over they spoke quietly among themselves, in their own language.

"That one turned out well," one of them said. "It will be very amusing. It has kept their culture fragrant."

"All superficial," another replied. "I would prefer to smell a stronger perfume. Bodily adornments, arrangements of words – this is all just a whiff to be blown away by the first breeze."

"It has cultivated the unexpected," the first insisted. "That keeps everyone's nostrils open, and encourages others to spread their own scents."

"Are you suggesting we should leave it in place, to create these rich new odors?"

"No, certainly not. We have waited long enough. It has done its part and become entertaining. We will pick it up in a few hours and begin the journey home."

"It will in all probability abandon its bizarre behavior shortly after being put on display," a third crew member warned. "Its actions have been primarily socially driven, rather than internally driven. Without the presence of its own species it will quickly abandon these behaviors."

"We have recordings," the first replied. "Its memory will be available for experience."

"Will there not be other members of its species?" the second asked. "Several still survived when I last viewed the menageries."

"I am unsure," the third admitted. "But even if others survive, their numbers may not be sufficient to maintain complex social responses."

"We are not concerned with its long-term value," the first said, dismissing the issue. "We are charged with finding provocative new exhibits. This creature now qualifies. Let us prepare for his acquisition."

Everyone chittered agreement to that.

* * *

When Michael Bostic failed to appear for his next several appointments, and his car was found abandoned on the shoulder of I-80, everyone took it for granted that he was simply planning another stunt. It was three weeks before even his friends grew seriously concerned.

The rumors that he had indeed been abducted by aliens did not begin until much later.

Valedictory

I was invited to contribute a story to an anthology entitled ***Release the Virgins.*** *The one requirement was that each story must contain the phrase "release the virgins." I'm a fantasy writer; you say "virgins," and I think "unicorns." Start giving commands like "release the virgins," and I assume an organized unicorn hunt, and here's the result.*

Lisbet looked up at the huntmaster's eyrie, towering above the wall of the reserve. She knew her father was up there, but she couldn't catch so much as a glimpse from this angle. She hoped she wasn't going to embarrass him – or herself. The unicorns couldn't *really* tell, could they? Not when it was just the one time. *Surely* they couldn't. That was merely a legend.

She knew a lot of girls wouldn't have risked showing up for the hunt afterwards, but wonderful as her night with Kraddig had been, she was not about to give up her annual opportunity to see and touch a unicorn, to hear its musical whinny and look into its eyes as it laid its head in her lap, just because of that one little slip.

Of course, she would only have the unicorn to herself for a moment; then the netsmen would swoop in and bind the unicorn up, holding it securely so that the surgeon could safely remove its horn, while Lisbet was pulled clear on her swing and hoisted clear of the animal's wild struggles.

Lisbet remembered how that felt, soaring safely up out of the enclosure as the netsmen secured their quarry – it was thrilling, but sad, too, knowing she would not see or touch a unicorn for another year.

The first time Lisbet had almost cried, feeling as if she had betrayed the beautiful animal, but her father had comforted her, assuring her that the unicorn would be released unharmed as soon as its horn had been removed, and that it would not hold the ruse against her – and sure enough, she was almost certain that it had been the same unicorn that followed her into the trap two years later, its horn regrown, her treachery forgiven.

Many people argued that the mere fact that the unicorns allowed themselves to be captured repeatedly, year after year, meant that they did not really mind. Some people thought that the beasts must consider it an elaborate game; others thought that perhaps they *wanted* to be rid of their horns, before they grew too inconveniently long. The scholars, though, said that the unicorns simply didn't remember, that as part of their magical purity they were incapable of recalling anything unpleasant. If that was true, then the unicorns would forget the whole thing the instant they were freed, so any suffering or sense of betrayal would be short-lived.

The girls' feelings were not so transient, but Lisbet had long since learned to live with hers. Seeing the miracles of healing made possible by the powdered horns easily outweighed any guilt over tricking the unicorns, and she had happily signed up year after year, eager to once again see one of the beautiful creatures up close, to feel the impossibly soft fur of its muzzle, to smell its sweet breath and look into the sparkling depths of its eyes...

She looked around at the other girls. Most of them were younger than she was. Oh, Tassa was still there this year – Lisbet thought Tassa intended to die still eligible, though the hunting committee did not allow any of the lures to participate after their thirtieth birthdays – but Lisbet was one of the half-dozen oldest. Most of the friends she had made in her six previous years in the hunt were gone now.

Sharan had said she would be here, but then she had met Orin and withdrawn her name. Lisbet couldn't blame her; Orin was an attractive man. Not as nice as Kraddig, but still charming.

Almost half of the girls were complete strangers, most of them here for the first time. The repeaters were eager, looking forward to seeing unicorns again, but many of the new ones looked nervous, or even scared. A few seemed downright terrified.

Lisbet had always considered herself a natural leader here because of her father's position, but now she had seniority, as well; she could only see three or four who had done this more often than she had. Lisbet could not resist giving a few words of encouragement.

"Don't worry," she said to them, speaking loudly. "No one wants you to get hurt – not the hunters, and not the unicorns. They're all trying to *protect* us. We haven't had an injured lure since I was a baby, when a silly twit named Filiana tripped over a root and broke her wrist." She smiled, and saw a few of the younger girls smile timidly back. "And the unicorns are so wonderful!" she continued. "You'll see. They're more beautiful than you can imagine, and you won't just *see* them, you'll touch them. You'll look into their eyes, and feel their..."

She had intended to say more, but before she could continue her father's voice boomed out from the speakers, interrupting her. "*Are the locksmen ready?*"

Lisbet could not see the response, but she imagined it – she remembered watching from the eyrie when she was little, seeing the blue flags waving from the entrance of each trap.

"*Netsmen?*"

Those flags were orange, and there were half a dozen for each trap.

There wasn't time for any more encouraging speeches. "You all know your numbers?" Lisbet called. "You know where to lead your unicorn?"

Most of the girls nodded; she didn't worry about the ones who didn't. Most of them would manage just fine once they were out in the reserve, and any who didn't – well, most years saw a few traps remain empty, for one reason or another. In peacetime forty or fifty horns should be enough to supply every healer in Berunia; they didn't need the full sixty-four the reserve could handle.

"*Release the virgins!*" her father cried.

Then the big doors swung open, and sunlight poured into the waiting area.

"All right, girls," Lisbet called. "Let's go lure!"

She had rather hoped for a cheer – most years at least *some* of the girls cheered – but this was a relatively somber bunch, and they surged out of the enclosure with only a little chatter and a nervous giggle or two. Eager to prove herself still able, Lisbet ran ahead of the others, scanning the forest for any signs of their quarry.

She didn't see any. Usually she spotted a flash of white or a silver sparkle almost immediately, but this time she saw nothing but trees and grass.

She had been assigned Trap #51, well around to the right; the entrance the girls used to enter the reserve was between #32 and #33, and those two traps always went to the youngest, least experienced girls, but the others were supposedly assigned at random. Lisbet glanced back to see the other girls spreading out along the wall, alternately watching for their own places and peering into the woods, looking for the unicorns.

Lisbet heard a rustle, and turned to see whether one of the unicorns was approaching her – while they could move through the forest silently if they chose, they didn't like to startle the virgins, and would usually allow a glimpse or make some small sound before drawing near.

She didn't see anything, but off to her left she heard someone exclaim, "Oh!"

Then another girl murmured, "So beautiful!" and a whole chorus of surprise and delight sounded around her as the unicorns emerged from the forest, driven by their inexplicable urge to place their heads upon virgins' laps.

But Lisbet didn't see any. She hurried into the trees, away from the wall. She imagined her father up in his eyrie, staring down, watching her failure, and she wanted to get out of his sight, under the canopy of leaves.

She could hear the other girls running on the grass, leading their prey toward the numbered traps. The cries of wonder had mostly died away, but there were still distant giggles and coos.

Then she heard the rumble and slam as the first trap closed, and the cheers of the locksmen at a successful capture. One unicorn had been boxed in, so that even its magical stealth could not save it from the ropes of the netsmen.

She looked back at the wall and saw Trap #51, the big door open and waiting for her. She saw a sunny little patch of grass beyond, with the swing for her to sit on, all surrounded by a ring of bushes where the netsmen were hiding.

A dozen yards away she saw a flash of color as a girl in a flowing sky-blue gown dashed by, and then the gate of #50 rolled into place, the locksmen quickly securing it. Another virgin had done her job, and would be hoisted out while the netsmen and surgeon did theirs.

More gates slammed; more men cheered.

And she had yet to see or hear anything of the unicorns themselves. She felt her face flush red. She had never before resorted to such a thing, but she called quietly, "Unicorn? I'm here!"

There was no response.

The horrified realization sank in that the unicorns really *could* tell, even if it was only once. She hadn't wanted to believe it, but there was no other explanation. And when she, the huntmaster's own daughter and an experienced lure who had never before, in her six years in the hunt, failed to attract and capture a unicorn, and returned to the wall without having so much as glimpsed one of the elusive beasts, everyone else would know what she had done, as well. She had been a fool, signing up as a lure again this year.

But how *could* the unicorns tell? She wasn't any different, not really.

Magic, she supposed. Magic could do the impossible. That was rather the *point.*

#52 closed. The pace of traps being sprung slowed, though she could still hear the shouting of the netsmen struggling to corner their prey without harming it or being gored, and the excited squeals of girls being lifted from their traps.

And the gate of #51 still stood mockingly open, the little carefully-cultivated glade beyond still empty, the locksmen and netsmen no doubt waiting impatiently. They were probably speculating on what was taking so long.

She looked up to see little Vivin from Green River being hoisted away on her swing, her face flushed with excitement and her pink skirts billowing. Lisbet thought she saw tears in her eyes, though, as she was carried away from the unicorn she had just been fondling.

Lisbet finally realized, as Vivin vanished over the outer wall, and as the shouts of the netsmen faded away as the last animal was bound, as she looked around at the woods and did not see any trace of hoof or hide or horn, that she was never going to see a unicorn up close again. She was too small to be a netsman or a locksman; those were always big men, not petite women.

And she had disqualified herself as a lure.

Tears started in her own eyes, tears of frustration and loss and embarrassment. For a moment she wanted to blame Kraddig and say it was all his fault, that he had seduced her, but she knew that wasn't true. She had wanted it as much as he did. Blaming him wouldn't be fair.

But then she heard a rustle. She turned, peering deep into the woods of the reserve.

And there it was – a unicorn, a *big* one, watching her, but not approaching. Sunlight sparkled from its silver horn and dappled its pure white hide as it looked directly at her.

"Unicorn?" she whispered, her tears drying. She took a step toward it.

It backed away a step and shook its head, its mane fluttering like a cloud.

She understood. She was not going to capture it. She was not allowed to touch it. But it was giving her one last look, a chance to say goodbye.

"Thank you," she said. In a moment of inspiration, she blew it a kiss.

It nodded its head, and then in a blur of white and silver it was gone, vanished among the trees.

She stared after it for a few seconds, then let her shoulders slump. That was it, then; it was over. She would never touch another unicorn, never smell one's sweet breath again. She turned, and began walking toward Trap #51.

As she approached the door she waved to the locksman. "It's not coming," she said. "It's just me." Her eyes were welling up again, and her voice shook, but she knew she had to own up to the truth. The men might tease her, might make bawdy jokes, but it would surely be worse if she tried to pretend.

No one said anything as she walked to the swing and sat down. She beckoned to the netsmen. "We're done here," she said. "Send me up." Her throat tightened, and she was barely able to add, "I'm sorry I wasted your time."

No one answered; there were none of the crude remarks she had expected. She closed her eyes as the netsmen emerged and began coiling their ropes; she held on as the swing began to ascend.

And then, as she cleared the top of the wall, she opened her eyes and saw two men waiting for her on the platform – her father and Kraddig. She swallowed, barely able to keep from bawling.

When she stepped off the swing onto the platform she could barely stand, and for a moment she thought she might fall at her father's feet, but Kraddig rushed forward to catch her. She was startled to find herself wrapped in his strong arms, his cheek warm against hers, as he murmured words of comfort.

Looking over his shoulder she found herself meeting her father's gaze.

"Kraddig told me what happened," he said. Even in her state of abject misery, she was dimly aware that he did not sound angry, which puzzled her.

"I'm sorry, Daddy," she said, her voice muffled against Kraddig's tunic. "I didn't believe they could really tell."

"Oh, of course they can tell! You've known that since you were a baby! How could you not believe it?"

"I don't know, I thought...I don't know," she sobbed.

"You didn't *want* to believe it," Kraddig suggested.

"I didn't," she admitted. She snuffled, and tried to stop crying. Rather to her surprise, she mostly managed it.

"Well, now you know," her father said. "You can have the unicorns once a year, or you can have Kraddig, but you can't have both."

"Well, it's too late now," Lisbet said. "I don't have a choice anymore."

"No," her father agreed, his voice gentler. "You don't."

Kraddig said, "I may not be as wonderful as a unicorn, but at least I'm here a lot more than once a year."

She managed a weak smile at that, and pressed herself more tightly against him. He *was* there all the time, and while he might not be as beautiful as a unicorn, he had uses they did not. He didn't just want to rest his head in her lap.

"He's a good man," her father said. "When he realized you were really going through with it, he came to warn me. He talked his way past the guards, and told me he would take all the responsibility and I shouldn't blame you."

"Oh, that's not right!" Lisbet said, pulling out of Kraddig's embrace. "It's very generous, but it isn't true. I'm sorry to disappoint you, Daddy, but it was as much my doing as his."

"I'm not disappointed. I thought it might be," her father said. "You've always gotten your own way."

"I didn't today. The unicorns wouldn't have me."

"But *I* will," Kraddig said, pulling her close again. She raised her lips to his, and kissed him.

That kiss lingered until at last her father cleared his throat.

"So," he said, "with that settled, is it too soon to talk about grandchildren?"

The Last Bastion

Another anthology story. This time the requirement was a story set far away in time and space.

Two human beings stood alone in the observation chamber, looking at projected images of the Milky Way Galaxy. On the central diagram a harsh, hostile orange tint stained most of the gigantic whirlpool of stars, leaving only a tiny sliver of friendly green, covering no more than a hundred stars, at one edge.

"There's nowhere else to go," Wang said, gesturing at the screen. "We stand or fall here."

"But there are millions of other galaxies out there!" Lee protested.

"Oh, of course there are," Wang agreed. "But we can't *get* to any of them. They're simply too far away to reach in a single lifetime. The best minds we have have been studying the problem for centuries, and there's no way to exceed the fivespace constant."

"That's what they said about fourspace," Lee said, "but even if there isn't, or if we can't find it in time, why do we need to do it in a single lifetime?"

"You want to spend a thousand years in stasis, at the mercy of a bunch of self-maintaining machines? You have more faith in our technology than I do."

"I was thinking more along the lines of a multi-generational journey – boost an oneill or even a small planet into fivespace. It's just a matter of engineering..."

Wang shook his head. "We don't have the resources on hand," he said. "If our ancestors had given the matter some real thought, and started preparing, then yes, it could be done, but now it's too late. We don't have the energy sources we'd need to ramp an entire planet into fivespace, we don't have the resources to keep an astellar ecology stable for a journey that long – remember how dark and empty it is in intergalactic space! Not enough light to power anything important, not enough matter to collect for anything."

"You've run the numbers?"

"Of course. To see our descendants safely to M31 would require everything we have, and would have a safety margin so small the odds of completing the journey are fifteen to one against." He sighed. "And just in case, I checked my conclusions with the top theoreticians among the other groups. They all confirm my figures."

Lee grimaced at the mention of the other surviving individual-human factions; her own clan was Purist, and had always opposed any cooperation with cyborgs and genengineers. Events had forced the alliance when she was still a child, despite its unpopularity, but she had never entirely reconciled herself to it. The others weren't really *human* any more, by her standards.

But they were still close. They were still individuals, still had human concerns. And they had joined the naturals in fleeing here, to the edge of the galaxy.

The cooperation was so complete now that the galactic map didn't even show the three factions as separate territories; all their systems were shared.

They had all fought so long and so hard to maintain their individuality – and now Wang, the coordinator for their defense, said the fight was over.

"There must be *some* way," she said.

"I've told you my proposed solution."

"I'd rather try that thousand-year stasis. The odds sound better."

Wang sighed. "We don't know the odds on negotiating; nobody's tried it in millennia. The Link may have changed. It's got the rest of the galaxy; why should it insist on taking our pitiful handful of systems?"

"Because that's what it *does*, Wang!" Lee said. "It's *hungry*. It wants data and energy and matter, as much as it can get. It's pursued humanity everywhere we've gone, trying to absorb us."

"The old stories say that it thinks it's doing people a favor by assimilating them," Wang said. "It thinks it's doing it for our own good."

"That's what it *says*. I don't believe it."

"Oh, I think it's sincere, even if I don't want to be assimilated any more than you do."

Lee looked very doubtful indeed, but didn't argue further. Instead she asked, "Have you spoken to the others?"

Wang nodded. "I left your clan until last – I knew you'd be the hardest to convince."

"They've all agreed?"

"Yes. Some of them imposed conditions, but they've agreed."

"They're all ready to surrender?"

"It's not a *surrender*," Wang insisted. "It's a negotiation."

"It's offering to stay on the reservation," Lee said. "It's offering to become its pets, a bunch of animals in a zoo, a museum exhibit. *I* call that a surrender."

"A surrender would be letting the Link assimilate us," Wang said. "I won't do that."

"You may not have a choice."

With that, Lee turned and stalked away, toward the lift.

Wang watched her go. He understood her feelings, but he also understood reality.

He looked up at the galactic map. That sliver of green was so tiny, the orange smear so vast...

* * *

"I still can't believe they agreed to talk this way," Lee said as she watched the ship descend smoothly, sliding gracefully down through the cloudless blue sky. "I thought the Link never let any of its units detach for even an instant!"

"I told you they would be reasonable," Shmit said.

Lee grimaced at the unnaturally musical sound of the cyborg's electronically-enhanced voice and fought back a bitter remark. The Link had been *created* by cyborgs, thousands of years ago – of course Shmit would be more tolerant of the Link than it deserved.

And Lee didn't want to listen to any machine man telling her "I told you so."

The ship settled gently onto the pavement, and Wang and the others started forward. Before they had covered half the distance an opening appeared in the ship's side, and a figure emerged.

It *looked* human enough, but Lee knew better. She reluctantly began walking closer, but she didn't hurry; let the others get the preliminaries out of the way, she thought. The less time she spent close to the Link representative, the better, so far as she was concerned.

The representative wore a smooth, form-fitting red garment that made it plain the creature was neither male nor female; its skin was a lovely golden brown, its black hair trimmed short. It was inhumanly sleek and beautiful – but it moved awkwardly, unevenly, as it stumbled down the ramp the ship had extruded.

"Welcome to Refuge," Wang began when his party and the Link representative were a couple of meters apart.

The representative held up a hand signaling for him to wait, staggered, then straightened up. It took a deep breath, let it out, and then spoke.

"I'm sorry," it said. Its voice, as lovely as Shmit's, was unsteady. It cleared its throat, and added, "This is *hard* for us – for me. Give me a moment."

"We appreciate your willingness to meet with us under these conditions," Wang said.

"It's important," the representative said. "We know that, so we'll try to cooperate. But you've all had years of practice being unlinked; it's new for us. For me."

"I understand," Wang said, though Lee doubted that he actually did. The cyborgs, with their implants and gadgets, might have some idea what it would be like for a single unit of the Link to be detached and forced to operate independently, but a natural human like Wang – or Lee – could have only the vaguest understanding of the experience.

The representative took another deep breath, then stood up straight and recited, "You understand that as a single individual, I cannot make a final decision for the entire Link if you present me with an option we had not previously considered?"

"Of course," Wang said. "We wish to make our proposals, discuss options, then send you back so that the Link can think the situation over."

"Good. That's what we want, too. What *I* want."

Lee had now joined the group, and got a good look at the representative. Up close it looked considerably less human – wiring was visible along its fingers and neck, there were slits that Lee thought might be gills, and some of the black fibers on its head, clearly not human hairs, moved independently. Its eyes had tiny insets that Lee guessed were added sensory equipment, and the gleaming blue biting surfaces in its mouth were definitely not teeth.

Some of its distant ancestors had been human, but it was not.

"Shall we go inside, where we can sit down?" Wang suggested.

"That would be good."

A few moments later the entire party was gathered around a conference table. Wang had offered to wait until the representative had rested and adjusted to the local climate, but the representative had declined the offer.

"The sooner I get this done and can rejoin myself, the better," it explained. "You have no idea how uncomfortable this is for me – it's like being blind and alone."

"You aren't alone," Wang said. "We're here."

The representative didn't answer, but simply stared at him in astonished disgust.

"It's not the same, I'm sure," Lee said. "Now, can we get down to business? I'm not that much more comfortable than our guest is." She gestured at the others gathered around the table.

They were all individuals, not part of any hivemind Link, and they were all of human ancestry, but Lee was the only Purist. Wang, Mez, and Kita were fellow naturals, their flesh unpolluted with machinery, their genes perhaps cleaned a little but still entirely human.

But Shmit, Maet, and Das were cyborgs, with metal and plastic built into them. Llur, Saffa, Berene, and Tiril were genens, their genes modified at their ancestors' whims, and each had visible features – skin, eyes, hair – that had never evolved on Earth.

And Ashi and Ho were both genetically engineered *and* cyborged.

A hundred years ago, this gathering could never have happened – the human factions had kept themselves separate. Pressure from the Link had driven them to this mixing, which Lee could only see as pollution.

Wang stood up. "We all know the situation," he said. "The Link wants the entire galaxy, and we prefer to remain as we are, independent individuals not part of a network, free to arrange our societies as we choose. Up until now the Link has pretty much expanded as it pleased, driving us into a smaller and smaller volume of the galaxy, and we've reached a point where we can retreat no farther. Rather than simply give in, though, we've asked you to come here to give us a chance to convince the Link *not* to assimilate our paltry handful of worlds. We asked you to come here as an individual, not part of the Link, partly because of our distrust of you and our fear that if the Link were permitted the tiniest access to Refuge that the entire planet would be absorbed into the system before we could do anything to prevent it, but also – and this part you may not have realized – because we wanted to remind you what it's like to be an individual human being. We think it's a very special experience, one that the Link tends to forget or underrate, and we don't want to see it eliminated from the galaxy. Surely, the Link can see some value in maintaining the few of us here, as a possible resource, a source of diversity?"

The representative stared silently at Wang for a moment, then said, "There's so *much* you don't understand."

"I'm sure you're right, that we don't appreciate how much better and happier we would be as part of the Link, but nonetheless, we want..."

"No, no, *no*," the representative interrupted. "That's not what we... what I mean at all."

Wang blinked.

"What *do* you mean, then?" Llur sang.

"We need these systems," the Link representative said. "We need them urgently. We don't want to harm you, though – we understand you better than you might think. What we propose to do is to pay you for them."

"What good is *payment* if you're going to absorb our entire world?" Kita demanded, before Lee could say anything.

"It depends what form the payment takes, doesn't it?" the representative asked, lisping slightly. "We propose to pay you with the resources of several star systems, including technology we don't believe you have, that will permit you to launch two or three planets into fivespace, bound for whatever destination you choose."

"You want us out of your galaxy entirely, is that it?" Lee demanded, rising angrily to her feet. "Damn it, you monster, it's *our* galaxy, too!"

"Not any more," the Link representative said. "Individual consciousness has been driven into this tiny fringe; wouldn't you rather have an entire new galaxy?"

Several voices spoke at once, growing louder as they tried to assert themselves, and in a moment everyone was shouting. Wang held up his hands for order, and eventually silence returned.

"You said you *need* our systems," he said. "For more space? What will you do then, when you've filled it? Follow us to M31?"

"There are millions of galaxies," the representative said, which Lee found an eerie echo of her own words of just a few days before. "You take one, we'll take another."

"Will just one more be enough?" Kita asked sarcastically. "If *this* one isn't big enough for you..."

"We won't have this one much longer," the representative said.

A stunned silence fell.

"Why *not*?" Lee asked at last.

The representative struggled to find the words it needed. At last it said, "There was an experiment. An accident. A few centuries ago. The Link was attempting an upgrade, and the test portion became something else. We call it the Oneness." It pulled a display chit from its pocket and tapped a command; a galactic map appeared in the air above the conference table.

"Here are your stars," the representative said, and a familiar sliver turned yellow. "Here are ours," and a broad expanse of blue covered perhaps a third of the galaxy – but only a third, a huge crescent around one side of the galactic disk, the yellow sliver a patch on its outer edge.

"This is the Oneness," the representative continued, and a great broad ring of red appeared, nested against the blue crescent and centered on the old Sagittarian sector. "And this last portion," it said, as the white patch in the middle of the ring turned orange, "we call the Transcendence."

"The *what*?"

"The Transcendence." The representative sighed, and explained, "the Oneness experimented, as well. The Transcendence came into existence about a century ago."

"What do these names *mean*?" Shmit demanded. "Aren't they just Links that for some reason separated from yours?"

The representative shook its head. "No," it said. "The Link is a group mind – each of its constituent parts is linked to the whole, but we are still separate minds, even if we aren't individuals by your standards. We share data and sensation and memory, and a given consciousness may not be attached to a specific body, but there are still multiple consciousnesses in the Link, even if the boundaries between them are weak and variable. A fivespace datalink is fast, but it's not instantaneous – we can't maintain a true single consciousness across interstellar distances.

"But the Oneness *can.* We don't know how; we don't understand it. It's as alien to us as we are to you. I was able to detach myself from the Link and come here to talk to you; I don't think a constituent body of the Oneness could do that, any more than you could take off one of your fingers and send it to do an errand. And the portions of the Link that have tried to communicate with it have been absorbed into it."

Lee looked around the table at the faces of the others, and could see that they were all thinking the same thing she was – that the Link was getting a demo of its own programming.

"And the Transcendence?" Wang asked.

"The step beyond the Oneness," the representative explained. "We *really* don't understand that one. It seems to be something that combines space, time, and consciousness into a single entity and it's the only thing that scares the Oneness, which means it *terrifies* us."

"Wheels within wheels," Lee said, looking at the galactic map.

"So this Oneness is taking the galaxy away from you?" Shmit asked.

"Gradually, yes. And the Transcendence is then taking territory from the Oneness. Waves of expansion, spreading outward – a very, very old story."

"So you intend to push us out of the galaxy entirely to buy yourselves a little more breathing space," Kita said.

"More than that, we hope," the representative said. "It's not your *space* we need it's your *worlds.* It's mass, in big convenient chunks."

"You have half a galaxy!" Wang protested. "What do you need with a few hundred rocks?"

"You haven't been listening," the representative said. "We *don't* have half a galaxy, not for long. We need to get out of here while we still can."

"I don't understand," Lee said.

The representative looked about as if seeking inspiration, then said, "It's a long way between galaxies. You couldn't make the jump without us because you don't have enough energy, enough technology, to ramp entire planets into fivespace before we overrun your territory, and nothing less than a planet can safely sustain your civilization for so long a journey. Well, we have the same problem many times over. We are the Link – we are all joined into our single community by fivespace datalinks, and without that connection we're nothing – or at least, we aren't what we want to preserve. And a fivespace datalink can't function over intergalactic distances."

"So you'll send a community to another galaxy, and build a new Link there..." Kita began.

"*No!*" the representative protested. "No! We don't want another Link; we want *our* Link, our life. It's the difference between sending your children to safety and saving yourself we'll settle for creating a new Link if it's the best we can do, but we want to *live*, not die. We want to stay Linked."

"Well, how can you..." Shmit began.

"A bridge," the representative said. "A bridge of planets, spaced at distances that allow proper Linkage, stretching out from this galaxy to another. And when it's complete, we'll transfer whatever is left in this galaxy to the other. It'll take thousands of years, of course, but we can handle that."

The sheer audacity of the concept left the humans stunned.

At last, Lee spoke up.

"You have millions of planets already," she said. "You don't need to buy ours."

"It's a long, long way to the next galaxy," the representative said. "And we're steadily losing planets to the Oneness. Even a few hundred could make the difference between success and failure."

"It's more than that," Lee said.

"Of course it is," the representative said. "Believe it or not, we *like* you. You're family."

"The idiot cousin," Kita suggested.

The representative flushed. "Well, yes," it admitted. "Or maybe the dotty old uncle would be a closer comparison. We'd like to see you have a chance at survival, and we really don't want to fight you on one side and the Oneness on the other if things turn nasty."

"And we're your test pilots, aren't we?" Lee asked. "To see if there are any unforeseen problems in ramping planets into fivespace and sending them out between galaxies."

"That, too," the representative admitted. "We don't want to risk detaching an entire inhabited planet from the Link."

Lee nodded thoughtfully. "I like it," she said. "On behalf of the Purists, I vote to accept the Link's offer."

Several of the others stared at her in astonishment. Clearly, they had expected the Purists to put up unreasoning resistance to anything so radical.

"A bridge between galaxies," Lee said, musing aloud. "That's quite a proposal. I wish you luck with it, so long as it's not *our* galaxy you aim it at."

"Thank you," the representative said.

Lee smiled. "There's one thing that puzzles me," she said.

"Oh?"

"I wonder what method the Oneness will use to reach a new galaxy, when it flees from the Transcendence?"

That Doggone Vnorpt

Back around the turn of the century I planned to write a series about Amelia Hand, owner/operator of a small starship. A story entitled "A Breath of Fresh Air" appeared in the comic book series **Dark Horse Presents**, *I planned two novels that I still haven't finished (***Earthright*** and* **Technoplague***), and this story wound up in an anthology called* **Guardsmen of Tomorrow**, *despite not really fitting the guidelines.*

Amelia Hand didn't notice the first obvious sign that something was wrong at the Busted Fin. The fact that the huge service doors were standing open somehow didn't register; she was too concerned with getting inside, out of the blinding white Daedalus sunlight, and getting herself some decent beer and a look at the local talent. Seven weeks alone aboard her ship with nothing to drink but water and condensed fruit juice had left her desperate.

Once she set foot inside, though, she immediately knew there was a problem.

"What's that smell?" she demanded, before her eyes adjusted to the gloom of the interior. The usual odors of spilled beer and hot oil were overwhelmed by a stench she didn't recognize.

Then she saw the vnorpt, and stopped dead in her tracks, her hand dangling near the butt of the blaster on her thigh.

It was standing at the bar – or rather, towering over the bar, its crest stooped slightly to avoid scraping the ceiling – talking to Al, the bartender. Hand had never seen a vnorpt in the flesh before, but there was no mistaking it; no other sentient stood five meters tall and three meters wide.

And no other sentient smelled quite so awful, either.

"He was a *pet!*" Al was shouting. "A companion!"

"Oops," the vnorpt said, in a bone-shaking rumble. It belched. "Sorry."

Hand looked around the room. Half a dozen humans cowered in the booths along one wall; the stools at the bar, and the other tables, were all deserted. A waitress stood cringing in one corner, staring at the vnorpt. She and Al were the only employees in sight, and the six in the booths, the vnorpt, and Hand herself the only customers.

There were at least six assorted freighters in port, a Patrol cruiser, and the starliner *Dreamship III*, as well as Hand's own *Tristan Jones*; the Busted Fin should have been jammed with people, some of them as eager for human companionship as Hand was.

"What's going on?" Hand demanded, her fingers lightly tapping the blaster.

Al looked past the vnorpt and said, "He ate Barnstable!"

Barnstable was Al's dog; Hand had never liked him much. She'd never had much patience with pets, and Barnstable, half bulldog, half basset hound, and half-witted, had been even less lovable than most.

"Was an accident," the vnorpt rumbled. "Thought it was snack. Pay for damages, yes." It dropped a credit chit on the bar with one of its feeding claws.

"You can't just..." Al began.

"*Said* was sorry," the vnorpt interrupted. "Now, beer, yes?"

"You ate my dog! You get out of here!" He pointed toward the service door.

"Uh uh," the vnorpt said, lifting one of its hands off the floor and waving the stubby talons in Al's face warningly. "No racial incidents, yes? Treaty says vnorpt travel freely in public areas of human settlements, no refusal just for being vnorpt."

"I don't care if you're a vnorpt or a l'antar or a goddamn treefrog! You ate my dog!"

"Was *accident*," the vnorpt insisted. "*Very* sorry. Pay insurance value three times, yes? Now, beer."

"You ate my dog and chased away all my customers!"

"Not responsible for unfortunate prejudice of clientele. Beer, third time asked." This final sentence sounded very much like a warning.

Hand decided that it was time to intervene – and not by pulling a blaster. "Give him his beer, Al," she called, as she strode up to the relatively small section of bar not blocked by the vnorpt. "And file a protest about Barnstable later. You don't want to make this fellow angry."

Nobody *ever* wanted to be around an angry vnorpt.

Al glowered unhappily at her, but picked up the credit chit with one hand and a pitcher with the other, and opened a tap.

The vnorpt looked down at Hand. "Thanks," it said. It took in her size and general appearance, and said, "You little guy, yes? Kinda cute."

"Thanks," Hand said, not meaning it. She looked up at the vnorpt.

It was roughly egg-shaped, covered with bony brown armor; four long, multiply-elbowed arms hung from its middle, and four feeding claws were arrayed below its gigantic maw, ready to shove in whatever got within reach. Four eyes on stubby stalks bracketed the immense mouth, all of them currently tilted toward her, and a greenish-yellow crest topped it off. Something yellowish was seeping between plates of bone on one side of its head – if it *had* a head – and Hand suspected that was the source of the worst of the foul smell. Nothing corresponding to ears, nose, or other human features was visible.

A typical vnorpt, in other words, completely nondescript to anyone but another vnorpt. The only thing that made this one unusual was its location, in a human-run bar in Daedalus Port rather than out in vnorpt territory.

This character, Hand told herself, was clearly a problem that had to be dealt with. The Busted Fin was the only worthwhile bar in the entire port, as far as Hand was concerned; the others were all over-priced tourist traps that would be full of the passengers off the *Dreamship III*. Hand was eager to find a little action – a nice big freighter crewman would be very welcome – but she was not about to waste her time on a bunch of overdressed twits who thought tooling around on a starliner made them spacers.

And they probably wouldn't want to waste time on her, either, if the truth be told. She was no exotic offworld beauty, just a stubby middle-aged woman with a blobby nose that she kept meaning to get fixed but never had yet.

Freighter crews weren't so picky about details like that. But freighter crews weren't going to set foot in the Busted Fin so long as this mountain of alien meat was stinking up the place; vnorpt were known to occasionally smash skulls or break human legs "accidentally," just as this one had "accidentally" eaten Al's dog. They generally didn't actually eat humans any more, not since the treaty, but even that wasn't impossible if a vnorpt got drunk enough. It would mean apologies and reparations and warnings from the Patrol, but that wouldn't do the vnorpt's dinner any good.

"What brings you to this part of town?" Hand asked. She had hopes of convincing it to move on to a different bar – the Stardust Lounge, maybe, where the tourists would probably be just *thrilled* to meet a real, live alien.

"Beer," the vnorpt replied. "Good beer here. Not like the others."

Al finished filling the pitcher and handed it to the vnorpt, which transferred it to a feeding claw, then tossed it down in a single gulp, like a human drinking a shot of whiskey.

"Can't argue with that," Hand said. "So you've tried the others? The Stardust?"

The empty pitcher dangled from the tip of the claw, swinging back and forth as the vnorpt said, "Tried Stardust. Beer there tastes like dirty water. Here is *real* beer." It reached up and dislodged the pitcher; Al dove forward in time to catch it as it fell. "More beer," it said.

"I'll have one, too," Hand said, as Al reached for the tap. "Just a half-liter, though, and make it a stout."

Al grumbled something and began refilling the pitcher.

"I didn't know that vnorpt like beer," Hand said, as she waited for her drink.

"Yes," the vnorpt said. "Tried some because humans talked about it so much. Good stuff. Got more respect for humans now; anyone who invent beer is okay."

"Then you don't make your own? There's no vnorpt beer?"

"No vnorpt beer, because no vnorpt hops, no vnorpt yeast. Dumb question, little guy." A vnorpt hand lashed out in what was probably intended as a comradely gesture akin to a slap on the shoulder; the impact slammed Hand off her feet.

She reacted completely automatically. By the time she hit the floor she had her blaster out of the sheath on her thigh and pointed at the vnorpt's head.

"Oops," the vnorpt said, but Hand wasn't looking at that – she was looking at Al, behind the bar, who had put down the pitcher and was now nodding vigorously, drawing a finger across his throat.

"Self-defense," Al said. "I'm a witness."

Hand hesitated.

The vnorpt hadn't intended to hurt her, she was fairly certain. Al was mad about his dog and what the vnorpt was doing to his business, but the vnorpt was still a sentient being and probably hadn't really meant any harm. Shooting it wasn't called for unless it actually attacked someone.

Besides, she was only carrying a standard-issue urban blaster, where penetration was deliberately kept low so that random shots wouldn't punch through entire blocks and take out innocent bystanders; she wasn't sure what it would do to vnorpt armor.

She lowered the weapon, but didn't return it to its holster.

"Sorry, sorry," the vnorpt said, and before Hand could get back on her feet one of those long arms had reached out and grasped her shoulder. It picked her up, and two of the vnorpt's other arms began brushing her off. "Very sorry," it said. "Low gravity tricky, yes?"

"I'm fine," Hand said. "Put me down." The gravity in Daedalus Port was 1.08 gees – not low by human standards at all, though Hand usually boosted her ship at higher acceleration than that, in the interest of saving flight time.

Vnorpt had apparently evolved under much higher gravity. Nobody really knew much about their origins, but that much was widely believed.

"Just checking for broken bones, things like that," the vnorpt said, as it stuck a hand in her crotch.

She really hadn't *intended* to fire, but that was too much. The blaster bolt spattered glowing plasma across the brown armored face.

The vnorpt dropped her, and she landed sitting on the bar. The stench of vnorpt was now worse than ever – whatever that yellow stuff was, it smelled even ghastlier when it burned.

"*Ouch!*" the vnorpt said, dabbing at a singed eye.

"Oops," Hand said, smiling broadly. "Sorry, sorry."

The other three eyes swung around to glare at her. It made a noise she had never heard before, and never wanted to hear again; she wasn't sure whether it was a laugh or a growl or what. "Beer," it said to Al. "And wet cloth."

Al was staring up at the vnorpt in astonishment, his mouth hanging open.

"*Beer,*" it said again. "And wet cloth."

Al remembered himself, and handed up the refilled pitcher and a bar rag. When the vnorpt took them, he leaned over and said to Hand, "You *shot* it!"

She stared at him silently as she slid off the counter and landed standing at the bar.

"You shot it in the face at point-blank range, and it isn't even *hurt*!"

"I think it stung a little," Hand said.

"But you shot it in the face!"

Hand sighed. "Al," she said, "I have some buddies who fought the vnorpt in the Eridani campaign. They told me that the way they used to work was they would systematically cut the vnorpt ships to pieces, and then would go in and potshot the individual vnorpt as they drifted in vacuum. The vnorpt would shell up, to hold in their air as long as possible, and they could live a couple of hours like that, long enough for another vnorpt ship to rescue them, so our side didn't just let them alone, they went in and picked them off. It usually took a couple of shots to punch through the armor and let the air out, and that was with a ship's heavy plasma cannon, not some dinky urban sidearm. Sometimes even the cannon wouldn't do the job, and they'd knock 'em down into the nearest star, instead." She shook her head. "I used to wonder sometimes whether those guys were exaggerating, or whether the vnorpt crews wore extra armor, besides what nature provided. I guess not."

Al drew her a half-liter of stout while she made this speech; he passed it over and stared up at the vnorpt.

"Better," the vnorpt said, dropping the rag, which was now coated with yellow slime, onto the bar. "Yes, vnorpt pretty tough, compared to humans. Good side to that and bad side, yes?"

"Yes," Hand agreed. "No hard feelings?"

"No anger. Pet eaten, eye shot, bumps, thumps, pokes, no big deal. Tolerance required. Accidents and inappropriate things always happen when people from different cultures interact, yes?"

"Yes," Hand said again. In a way, she was almost beginning to like the vnorpt, clumsy and obnoxious though it might be.

But she didn't want it in the Busted Fin. There were too many of those inappropriate things happening. "Al," she said, "I bet our friend here would like to meet Mickey Finn – think he'll be in tonight?"

Al looked at her, then at the vnorpt. "He might be, at that," he said. He looked up at the vnorpt. "Want another beer?"

"Yes," the vnorpt said, handing down the pitcher.

Al started filling it, and glanced sideways at Hand. He needed her to distract the vnorpt so he could add something to the drink, of course.

"So," she said, "did you fight in the Eridani campaign?"

"Didn't fight," the vnorpt said. "Not a fighter."

"So you never saw a blaster before?" Hand asked, raising her weapon again.

"Saw lots of blasters, here and there. Never shot before, though." The vnorpt's eyes were all focused on the blaster. Hand couldn't read its expression, but thought it was wary, worried that she'd shoot it again.

"Really? What'd it feel like?"

"Hot," the vnorpt said. "Stings. Like poke in eye with sharp stick. *Very* sharp stick. Very hard poke."

"Does it still hurt?" Al had a vial of something out, and was pouring the entire contents into the pitcher of beer.

"Some."

"So does my butt," Hand said.

The four stalked eyes all seemed to stretch toward her, and she could hear the creature's surprise. "Just from fall on floor? In this gravity?"

Hand nodded. "We aren't built anywhere *near* as tough as you." Al's vial was out of sight again. She put the blaster back in its holster.

"Sorry," the vnorpt said. "Was accident. Truly."

"Here's your beer," Al said.

He and Hand watched as the vnorpt downed the entire five or six liters of lager in a single gulp. Then Hand asked Al, "So when do you think Mickey will show up?"

Al shrugged. "Could be any minute now, Captain Hand. Ought to be here in ten minutes, fifteen at the outside."

"Then I'll wait," Hand said. She looked the vnorpt up and down and sipped her own beer. "Say, would you be interested in renting a cargo lifter, later tonight?"

"I might be, at that." He glanced up at the vnorpt.

The vnorpt dropped the pitcher on the bar, and smacked its lips. "Better and better!" it said.

Hand blinked, and asked the vnorpt, "So what brings you to Daedalus?"

She and the vnorpt made small talk for the next twenty minutes, while Al grew steadily more upset, glancing constantly at the clock on the wall. The sun set as they chatted, and the glaring white of a Daedalus day gave way to the multi-colored glare of the port's neon-enhanced night.

The other human customers had all managed to slip out by the end of that time, and the waitress vanished into the back room and stayed there. Various potential customers and curiosity-seekers looked in, but once they saw the vnorpt they hesitated, then withdrew – no one but Al, Hand, and the vnorpt set foot in the bar.

At last Hand said to Al, "Mickey's late. Got any way to give him another call, maybe?"

Al looked up at the vnorpt and shrugged hopelessly. "I used all I had last time," he said.

"Got something you can substitute?" She looked up at the vnorpt. "Maybe something appropriate for a toast in Barnstable's memory? After all, accidents happen. Even fatal ones."

Al looked at her. "You think so?"

"I think that vnorpt are big and tough enough that yeah, they do." She looked Al straight in the eye.

He knew what she was saying – she was advising him to go ahead and poison a paying customer, on the theory that it probably wouldn't kill something as monstrous as a vnorpt.

Of course, if she was wrong, they might be guilty of conspiracy to commit murder and treaty violations, but at this point Hand no longer cared. She wanted the vnorpt out of the bar. She wanted to be able to smell something again; her nose had long ago shut down in protest at the vnorpt's stench. She wanted other customers to come in here, so she could find some decent company to drink with and maybe take back to her ship.

"Let me see what's in the back room," Al said.

Hand kept the vnorpt occupied for the next several minutes; at last Al reemerged with a box. The vnorpt didn't notice.

"Want another beer?" Al asked.

"Yes!" the vnorpt said.

A moment later it gulped down another pitcher. Then it hesitated, and said, "Um."

"Is something wrong?" Hand asked.

"Didn't taste right that time."

"Maybe you've had enough, then," Hand suggested. "You wouldn't want to get really drunk, would you?"

"Wouldn't," the vnorpt agreed. It pulled in its eyestalks and folded its feeding claws, while dropping the pitcher to the bar. "Feel bad all of a sudden."

"You've just had too much to drink," Hand said. "It hits all of a sudden like that, sometimes. Get some fresh air, walk it off, and in an hour you'll be fine."

"Beer does this?"

"If you drink too much, yeah."

It started to say something, then belched instead. "Um," it said. "Oops."

"Fresh air helps a lot," Hand said cheerfully.

It dropped its four hands to the floor, then lifted itself up. "Fresh air," it rumbled. It picked its credit chit off the bar, then turned and staggered toward the big service door.

Hand watched it go, then turned and hissed at Al, "What did you give it?"

"The first mickey was chloral hydrate," he said. "A *lot* of chloral hydrate."

"Yeah, but it just shook that right off," Hand said. "What did you give it the *second* time?"

"Rat poison," Al said, holding up the empty box. "A full kilogram."

"A *kilo* of arsenic?"

"Hey, it worked, didn't it?"

"Al, that much might even kill a vnorpt!"

"Wouldn't bother me if it did," Al replied defensively. "It ate Barnstable, and chased away my entire clientele and most of my staff! It stank up the place – I'll have to put the recirculators on emergency overload to get the smell out. It was self-defense!"

Just then they heard a sound unlike anything either of them had ever heard before, coming from just outside the service door – a deep tearing gurgle, followed by splashing.

It seemed to go on forever, but Hand knew it wasn't really more than a minute or two.

After it ceased there were several seconds of silence; then the vnorpt called in, "Feel much better now. Go home, sleep it off."

Neither Al nor Hand replied; they were both overcome by the incredible new reek that had managed to penetrate even their overwhelmed noses. They stood, gagging, as the vnorpt staggered away down the street.

At last Hand managed to gasp, "Better get those recirculators pumping."

Al nodded, still unable to speak. A moment later the hum of the vent-fans climbed into audibility, and the air stirred.

Unfortunately, it stirred in the wrong direction, sucking air in through the service door, which meant it carried that unbelievable new stench.

"I didn't know anything *could* smell worse than vnorpt," Hand muttered. "But it figures that if anything could, it would be vnorpt vomit."

"I'm ruined," Al gasped. "The bar'll stink for weeks! They'll probably ticket me for a public health hazard..."

"Drastic measures are called for," Hand said, pulling out her blaster.

"What are you..."

She ignored Al as she marched across the barroom floor and looked out the service door.

Sure enough, an immense puddle filled several square meters of the street there; only the raised threshold had kept the dozens of liters of yellowish fluid from spilling into the Busted Fin.

"I hope this works," Hand said, as she fired her blaster into the center of the pool.

And with that, Hand discovered an even worse smell, one that made her senses swim and the world fade away as she tottered on the verge of fainting – the scent of *burning* vnorpt vomit.

Hand didn't falter; she kept firing, waving the blaster back and forth.

And at last the smell faded, and she found herself firing an almost-discharged blaster at empty, entirely-harmless plastic pavement.

Slowly, as the fresh evening air began to clear her mind, she slipped the blaster back into its holster and looked around thoughtfully.

The quantity just a single vnorpt had consumed was truly astonishing. An entire planet of vnorpt would be a huge market.

"You know," she said to no one in particular, "I see an opportunity here for an enterprising trader. Like me."

Then she turned and went back inside, headed for a barstool.

Selling a few shiploads of beer to the vnorpt might make her rich, but it could wait. Right now, she wanted a drink. Whiskey, maybe, or gin.

But not beer.

Advance Man

I came up with the premise of "Advance Man" a long, long time ago – I don't remember how far back. It was inspired, more or less, by an old DC Comics science fiction story from the 1960s. My story wasn't remotely the same, but the DC story was the first place I'd encountered the concept of an advance man, and that was where I got the idea. It's about what aliens might want from us – clearly not money or power or technology...

When that first real alien ship arrived it didn't act much like all those "flying saucers" that people had reported over the past fifty years. It showed up on radar just fine. It didn't appear out of nowhere, or dodge around like crazy. It was spotted for the first time halfway between the Earth and the Moon, and it came in in a perfectly sensible approach curve. It made a smooth entry into the Earth's atmosphere somewhere over the Pacific, passed over California at about 40,000 feet, and cruised its way across much of the American west in broad daylight, descending slowly.

And we certainly didn't try to hush it up, the way all the saucer nuts always said the government would. NASA and the Air Force held a joint press conference, and the FAA issued an advisory bulletin to all aircraft.

The press conference and the bulletin didn't say much, of course – nobody *knew* much yet. Mostly, they announced that yes, what appeared to be a genuine spaceship had arrived, and we didn't know where it came from or what was aboard or what they wanted, and any pilot flying near it did so at his or her own risk.

Pilots went near it anyway, of course – reporters, mostly, but also some curiosity seekers. By the time it crossed the Mississippi ordinary planes could keep up with it, and half a dozen did – along with a fighter escort, courtesy of the Air Force.

There was much speculation about what these strangers might want, and very few answers. The craft certainly didn't look hostile, with this open approach, and those nightmare scenarios about invasion from space had never made very much sense to begin with, since anyone with a technology advanced enough for interstellar travel ought to be able to make anything they need, rather than taking it from lesser civilizations.

But on the other hand, even if they were friendly, what could people with such a technology want from *us*? Were they explorers? Missionaries? Traders?

Would they want to deal with us at all, or were they just scientists here to collect a few samples and leave?

We didn't know, so we watched the ship closely. When it finally landed on a cow pasture in Indiana it was surrounded by police cars, traffic helicopters, and federal agents in a matter of minutes.

I didn't get there until hours later, though.

I was President Digby's science advisor; the president himself hadn't gone because it was considered too risky, but the White House needed to send someone, and I was the logical choice. I was on a plane to Indianapolis twenty minutes after the ship landed, and by mid-afternoon I was in the back seat of a black Lincoln, bumping my way down a dirt road to the Stoddard family's farm, being brought up to speed over my cell phone.

We passed half a dozen police checkpoints – each one had a big sign reading "Proceed At Your Own Risk," but they let us pass.

Ms. Stoddard didn't, though, until we'd paid ten dollars apiece for me, my aide, and our driver. She and her kids had the farm gate closed and had cleaned up the "Posted - No Trespassing" sign on the fencepost next to it, and the oldest boy had his father's shotgun cradled in his arms. Reporters, cops, military brass, White House staff, the Stoddards didn't care – everybody paid. When a gold mine falls out of the sky into your back yard, you don't give free samples.

It wasn't worth arguing. We paid. She took our money with a smile, then pointed. "Around that side," she said, "and don't you *dare* drive over any of my garden. Don't worry about the barking, the dogs are chained up. My husband will show you where to park."

So we drove around back to the pasture, and there was the ship.

You know, you'd expect a spaceship to look really out of place on a farm, but it almost didn't. It wasn't gray or silver like in the movies; it was bright yellow, just a shade lighter than a backhoe, with big red and purple symbols on it – circles and lines and things like crooked asterisks. And it didn't look so much like a flying saucer as like an overweight starfish.

I got out of the car and left the driver to follow Mr. Stoddard to the next field – this one was full, with cars and helicopters everywhere. I hurried up to the crowd of people, and pushed my way to the front.

I almost tripped over the alien pilot.

It was short and fat, with oily maroon skin, and looked like an upside-down octopus on an uprooted stump. It pointed a tentacle at me and said, "New guy. You who?" The voice came from a black box that was slung on what might be considered its shoulder, rather than from anything like a mouth.

I introduced myself. They'd told me on the plane that it was learning English at a fantastic rate, that the black box was some sort of translating computer and a reporter's pocket dictionary had been scanned in, but I was still startled to hear it. For one thing, it had an Indiana accent.

"President is reddest local authority, confirm?"

"Reddest?" I asked.

"Highest, it means," a reporter told me.

"What's it mean by local?"

The reporter shrugged.

"The president is the most powerful official on Earth," I said.

"You represent the president?"

"Yes."

"Good! Now we start."

"Yes," I agreed. "Now we start." I had already been told that the alien had refused to say why it was here until it had the highest possible authority present – and that was me, as the president's representative.

It had, however, assured everyone that it was not here to conquer Earth, or steal anything. "We want water, take ice from comets. We want metal, take metal from asteroids. We want food, grow our own. You think we want your women, you need to take another look at us."

I couldn't argue with any of that.

"You come inside. We talk privately." It turned toward the ship, and a panel rolled open.

I hesitated for half a second, then followed it.

We talked for more than an hour, just the two of us – we wanted to be absolutely sure there were no misunderstandings. I explained that the president didn't speak for the entire planet, but reassured it that he *did* speak for all the territory it had flown over since reaching land, and together we went over several concepts, to be as certain as we could there was no confusion. We reviewed permits, and licenses, and liability, and taxes, and entertainment. Its people had recorded some of our radio and television broadcasts, and made some observations, and it wanted to be sure nothing important had been misinterpreted. It wanted to know about governments and corporations and property rights and advertising, and I did my best to explain.

And then it did its best to explain to *me* what it had come for.

I had trouble believing it at first, and went over everything all over again, but at last I knew I was right. I knew what they wanted from us.

Together we emerged from the ship, to find a dozen cameras and a hundred microphones were pointed at us. I pulled my cell phone out and got my direct line to the president, and then I made my speech.

"Mr. President," I said. "Ladies and gentlemen. Our friend here, who has no name we can pronounce but who has asked us to call it George, has come to Earth not as an ambassador of some alien government, nor as a representative of its world or species, but only on behalf of a group of individuals – a group we might call a company, or a family, or by some other term entirely. It has come here not to trade with us or threaten us, but only to make an announcement on behalf of that group. It withheld that announcement until it was certain that it would not violate any regulations or taboos, that it would not offend our sensibilities, and that it would be using terms we would understand correctly."

That whole crowd was staring at me, and I realized that millions of people were probably seeing this on TV and hearing every word I said. I couldn't resist hogging the spotlight a little – especially after what George had told me.

"George's people are very different from our own, as anyone can see, but we share some of the same urges. Most of those are easily satisfied at home – George's people have no need of any material goods we can provide, nor any knowledge we possess. However, we can give them one thing they want very much – a new audience. The urge to show off, to be admired for one's unique talents, is apparently universal.

"Advertising may also be universal, and that's what George does. It's here to advertise on behalf of its group, to get them the biggest audience possible when they arrive next week."

I took a deep breath, and then I said it, as loudly and clearly as I could.

"Ladies and gentlemen, children of all ages! George came here to tell us that the greatest show in the galaxy is on its way to Earth – the circus is coming to town!"

Contraband

This one was written for an anthology dedicated to the less glamorous side of starport life.

The ship's afterjets were still smoking as Jeffers trotted out onto the blast apron, the display panel in his hand showing the manifest the crew had transmitted from orbit. He'd snagged this one the minute he saw the read-out, before Ota or Singh got a look at it, and all because of one word: Pets.

As far as Jeffers was concerned, pets were a struggling customs officer's wet dream. He could claim they were diseased or dangerous, he could demand endless documentation, genetic scans, certifications from half a dozen governments or organizations – basically, he could delay the shipment indefinitely.

And pets needed care and feeding, which would eat into someone's profits for every day the cargo was delayed, and the animals would be getting older and less valuable, and might get sick or die, which would make them worthless; their owner would want them delivered as quickly as possible.

Which meant that Jeffers could expect a very healthy fee to "expedite" the process. With luck, he could wind up with half the captain's profits going onto his own card.

And it was all far safer than "overlooking" drugs or weapons; exotic alien pets were legal, after all, and the people who transported them were therefore far less likely to shoot an overly-greedy customs inspector. He wouldn't be threatening anyone with arrest, deportation, or reprogramming – just with bureaucratic delays. Nobody liked red tape, but only a lunatic would shoot anyone over it, while drug dealers and gun-runners shot each other with depressing frequency.

Of course, the *Lord Lucan* might be smuggling contraband, as well as its official cargo, which could make the haul even richer, albeit riskier. Jeffers smiled happily as he tapped the phone keys on his display.

"Musashi Port Customs, requesting permission to come aboard," he said.

"Just a minute, Customs," a woman's voice replied, though no image appeared. "I'm checking on the cargo restraints. Wouldn't want anything to hit you on the head."

"Whenever you're ready, Captain," Jeffers said. He stood on the apron, waiting patiently, as the sound of heavy objects thumping on metal surfaces came over the display speakers.

At last the woman spoke again.

"Opening the lock, Customs; stand clear."

Jeffers booted up the atmospheric sensors on the display, then tucked the panel under one arm and watched as the outer door of the airlock swung open and extended itself downward to become a boarding ladder. Before the bottom rung had entirely stopped moving he grabbed the rails and began climbing.

At the top he waited while the airlock cycled – apparently the captain wasn't in any hurry to expose herself to Musashi's air. At last, though, the inner door opened and he found himself facing the *Lord Lucan*'s captain. She was a sturdily-built woman with coffee-colored skin, wearing a standard shipsuit that was drab blue at the moment.

"Madis Tyler," she said, holding out a hand. "Is Maintenance coming?"

Jeffers shook the offered hand. "Karl Jeffers," he said. "I haven't heard anything from Maintenance; that's between you and them."

"They said they'd send someone right out."

"Shouldn't be more than an hour or so, then. They're a bit backlogged." His curiosity got the better of him. "What needs maintenance?"

"The main drive. That's why I put down; I wasn't planning to land at all. If this place had a decent orbital station instead of just that stupid navigation post, I wouldn't be here, wasting time and fuel, I'd have made the repairs in orbit."

"Then your cargo isn't bound for Musashi?"

"Oh, hell, no; I've got buyers waiting on Telemachus III. I'm just here because I was using the Musashi beacon for transition, and the drive went unstable and dumped me out of hyper about fifteen light-minutes off the point. I didn't want to risk jumping again until I found out why."

This took the edge off Jeffers' enthusiasm; if the ship was going to be delayed for expensive repairs anyway, and the impatient buyer wasn't here on Musashi, his bargaining position wasn't quite as good as he had thought. He couldn't demand payment before allowing the pets to leave the ship, because they weren't *going* to leave the ship here. He could probably still manage something, but this wouldn't be as lucrative as he thought; if he got too greedy the *Lord Lucan* would probably just launch without clearance and run for it, and there wouldn't be much anyone in the Musashi system could do about it. Musashi did not have many patrol ships, and the Confederacy Guard was unlikely to waste one pursuing someone whose only crime was not bribing the port officials adequately.

"I'll still need to take a look," Jeffers said apologetically. "Port rules, you know."

"I figured you would," Tyler said with a sigh. "Every port in the galaxy has rules and bureaucrats. I suppose there'll be paperwork?"

"Oh, I think we can keep it to a minimum, since you aren't offloading anything," he said. "In fact, a small service charge might expedite the process..."

"How much?"

"Well, that depends on the exact nature of your cargo."

"They're pets. Sixty of them. Furballs indigenous to Fomalhaut IV. Do you need the species name? It should be in the manifest."

Jeffers took the display board from under his arm and looked at it. The atmosphere indicators showed a bunch of non-standard trace organics – that would presumably be from the cargo's breath or waste. There were no traces of anything that looked like illicit drugs or outgassing from explosives, unfortunately, which meant Tyler probably wasn't smuggling anything and Jeffers couldn't extort even more.

The manifest did give a species name – *Ardemanus ardemani fomalhauti* – that was amazingly uninformative, and tapping the query button elicited "No data on file."

He hesitated. He knew he should just name a fee, but he wanted to see what these things looked like. There might be some excuse to charge more if they looked especially valuable.

And a thought struck him. "You only have sixty? On a ship this size?"

"They're *big* furballs, not just hamsters or something, and I've got to haul the food and water for them."

Big animals? That meant he might be able to make an accusation of inhumane treatment, or transporting dangerous livestock; that could raise the price. "I'll need to take a look," he said.

"Yeah, fine. This way." Tyler led the way to the central core, where they ascended a ladder to the main hold.

The smell reached Jeffers before the door slid open, and he almost gagged; there was no question that the *Lord Lucan* was transporting animals. A glance at the display showed four red indicators on the atmosphere readings – but steady red meant "unidentified," not toxic.

Then he looked at the cargo, and saw why Captain Tyler had called them "furballs."

There were about a dozen of the creatures in this compartment. Each stood about five feet tall and about three feet wide, thick legs supporting almost-spherical bodies covered in luxurious fur in a variety of colors. It took Jeffers a moment to puzzle out exactly what he was seeing, beyond walking balls of fur, but at last he understood.

They were tripodal – a leg on either side and one at the back, the back one jointed differently, which Jeffers suspected meant it had evolved from something like a tail. Plastic restraints encircled every leg, each creature tethered to a cargo ring on the bulkhead.

Between the front and back leg on either side of each furball was what could only be considered an arm, though the resemblance to human arms was slight; each was equipped with four things somewhere between fingers and pincers at the end, and also with something clawlike at the lower elbow. There were no actual hands.

And between each pair of front legs hung a long neck ending in a flat, pan-shaped head, equipped with four eyes and a mouth, and other openings that might or might not be ears and nostrils.

Most of those many eyes were staring back at him.

"Whoa," he said. "Who'd want *those* for pets?"

"Rich people," Tyler said. "On Telemachus III."

Jeffers shrugged. "I suppose some people will buy anything." He looked at his display. "I'll want to take some readings."

Tyler didn't reply; she just frowned. Then her com twittered. "Maintenance, waiting to come aboard," it said. "What's the nature of the problem?"

"I'll be right there," she said. Then she turned her attention back to Jeffers. "Don't touch anything," she said. "They're docile, and they're tethered, but that doesn't mean they can't step on your foot or butt you accidentally if you get too close." Then she spun on her heel and marched back out to the ladder.

Jeffers watched her go, then turned back to the furballs.

He didn't really care what they were, or what the readings said; he just wanted to figure out how he could maximize his income from this.

They were odd-looking creatures, and the way they were all watching him made him nervous. The smell didn't help.

"You guys stink, you know that?" he said.

"Sorry," the nearest replied, in slightly-accented Commerce.

Jeffers almost dropped his display. "You can talk?" he demanded, once he was sufficiently recovered to speak.

The furballs exchanged glances; one said, "The captain lady said we mustn't talk to you." Two of the others turned to glare at it.

Jeffers glanced around for cameras, and spotted three – but he knew how to deal with that; anyone who conspired with smugglers had to be able to alter records. He hurried to the compartment's com port and punched up a link between the ship's systems and his display board, then selected one of the display's files and quickly entered a few parameters.

That would generate synthetic images of utterly innocuous behavior in the cargo hold, starting from the moment Captain Tyler descended the ladder.

"She can't hear us now," he said, turning back to the furballs. "Now, what were you saying?"

"We're sorry we stink," a reddish-brown one said. "We haven't had a decent bath since we came aboard, and the food doesn't agree with us."

"Or the air," a bluish one interjected.

Visions of a charge of inhumane treatment, and the bribe it would take to have it dismissed, arose in Jeffers' thoughts, only to be immediately dismissed by a far more basic issue.

These things weren't pets.

Oh, there were talking pets – parrots and mynah birds and Sirian mimic hounds – but those couldn't hold real conversations. A mere pet would not apologize for its smell and complain about a lack of bathing facilities, would it? Those flat heads didn't look big enough to hold much brain, but not every species kept its brain in its head.

"What *are* you?" Jeffers asked.

The furballs exchanged glances.

"Well, our own word for our kind is..." It made a gurgling noise.

"It just means 'people,' really," another explained.

"The captain lady calls us her cargo," said the reddish one.

"Or furballs."

"Or slaves."

Jeffers stared at them. "Slaves," he said.

"That was the word she used, yes."

There was clearly more going on here than a little smuggling. "Not pets?"

The furballs exchanged glances.

"No."

"I don't think so."

"What are pets?"

Jeffers ignored the question and asked, "Do you know what slaves are?"

"Workers," the reddish one answered promptly. "We're to cultivate crops, and run machines, and do whatever we're told. If we don't, our families will be killed."

Oh, this was just getting better and better, Jeffers thought. Kidnapping, slavery, and maybe even murder if Tyler had demonstrated that her threats were serious. Not to mention that she was probably suppressing knowledge of an intelligent species, in violation of the contact laws.

This was not something he wanted to be part of.

Jeffers knew he was not a law-abiding citizen. For the right price he could look the other way when spacers decided to bring in drugs or weapons, because after all, their customers chose to buy the stuff. Drugs might ruin lives, but the owners of those lives had taken the drugs in the first place of their own free will, despite all the warnings in their schooling and entertainment. Weapons might kill people, but people could improvise weapons readily enough, or kill each other without them – human beings had demonstrated great ingenuity in their long history of violence. He could tolerate drug-smuggling and gun-running, and still consider himself a fairly decent human being; he had no trouble facing himself in the mirror most mornings. He lived with that sort of crime easily.

But slavery? That was an entirely different level of wrong.

And what was the point? Why weren't the farmers of Telemachus III using robots for their labor?

Slaves were probably cheaper, especially if these things would breed in captivity. If Telemachus was a metal-poor system, or if it had an environment that corroded metal or circuitry, robots might be expensive there.

Slaves might be more versatile; the furballs seemed pretty bright.

Or maybe there wasn't any sound economic reason. Maybe the Telemachans just liked the idea of slaves. Jeffers shuddered at the thought, but he knew it was possible.

It wasn't really any of his business, he told himself. He shouldn't get involved...

But slavery?

Still, what could he do about it? Reporting it to the cops here wouldn't do any good; Tyler would just bribe them, or maybe launch before she could be arrested. Jeffers knew very well just how corrupt the local law enforcement was. He also knew what would happen to his own reputation among both cops and smugglers once the word got out.

And if by some fluke he found an honest cop, and Tyler got hauled off to jail, and did *not* manage to flee, then what? He'd be called to testify, and if Tyler managed to find even a halfway competent lawyer the jury would then be treated to all the lurid details of Jeffers' own past. Juries were notoriously unlikely to believe crooked officials.

And the other smugglers, the people who made it possible to live decently on his salary, would all hear about it. Losing half his income was the *best* he could hope for; turning up dead in an alley was far more likely.

No, the sensible thing to do here was to take a moderate bribe and keep his mouth shut, slaves or no slaves.

But he looked at the furballs, at the dozens of eyes staring at him, and wished there were another way.

He blinked, closed his eyes, and tried to clear his thoughts. This wasn't really so different, he told himself. He'd let gun-runners through, after all, and he knew those weapons weren't just for target practice. And he'd seen what happened to people who got too fond of the drugs he'd let in.

It wasn't any of his business. Drugs and guns and slaves were going to be smuggled in no matter what he did; he might as well take his money and keep quiet. He had long ago decided that – well, he had long ago decided that about drugs and guns, anyway; slaves had never come into it before.

He wished they hadn't come into it now, either.

He opened his eyes and found the furballs were looking past him; he quickly tapped the abort on his display and turned to find Captain Tyler climbing back up the ladder.

"They're looking at the drive," she said. "Can we get this paperwork out of the way so I can go keep an eye on them, and make sure they don't break anything they can add to my bill?"

"Of course," Jeffers said. He looked at the display and began entering commands. "So tell me about Telemachus III," he said. "I've never been there – hell, I've never been off Musashi. I love to hear the stories, though."

"I don't know what to tell you," Tyler said with a shrug. "It's just another damn colony. The Confederacy runs the port, but mostly people there just mind their own business."

"They're rich enough to buy your cargo, though; how'd that happen?"

"Oh, the local fauna's good for scents and flavors; real complex stuff, easier to grow it than synthesize it. They've got whole plantations of weird plants they export."

"Sounds interesting," Jeffers said, with a glance at the furballs. That explained what these things would be doing.

"Yeah, and it gets lonely out there in the backwater plantations, so they'll buy fancy pets. Now, do you have the papers ready? Got the fees figured out?"

"Just about..."

Tyler's com twittered.

"Yes?"

"Maintenance, Captain. Looks like you've got a blown balancer."

Tyler grimaced. "Which one?"

"Portside, number three."

"That son of a bitch. I'll be right down."

"I could just transmit..."

"No, I want to see it." She turned to Jeffers. "Show me where to thumb, and tell me what it's going to cost to get out of here as soon as Maintenance has my drive working."

Jeffers decided that he didn't want to drag this out. He held out the display and pointed. "Right there. And I think that, say, sixty kay will cover everything and get you cleared."

"Sixty kay? Try twenty."

"Well, I was allowing for extras, you know how it is. Say fifty."

"Thirty-five. The Telemachans aren't *that* rich."

"I can't be sure to get it all done for less than forty."

"Forty's good enough. Give me your card."

Jeffers held out the card, and accepted the funds transfer. Then he took back the display and tapped more keys.

Tyler glared at him. "I thought you said that would cover it."

"It will," he said, not sure himself why he was delaying. "I still need to do the data entry, that's all. It'll just be a minute; I'll be out of here long before they have a new balancer aligned."

"Fine. You know the way out. Don't bother the furballs, okay?"

"Sure."

She wasn't even nervous; he marveled at that. She hadn't asked whether the furballs had done anything, wasn't worried about what he might see or do. She had weighed him in her mind and found him harmless.

Jeffers stood and watched as Tyler once again descended out of sight; the minute she was gone he reactivated the camera jammer and turned back to the furballs.

"Listen," he said, only then realizing what he was going to do, and what he would say, "this is *your* ship, you understand? You bought it, and hired Captain Tyler to fly it for you, and then she chained you up and you don't know why. Got it?"

The furballs exchanged glances.

"No," one of them said. "It isn't true."

"No, it's not true, but it *should* be, and you *tell* anyone who asks you on Telemachus that that's what's happened, and they'll make sure that you can go home and that your families will be safe."

"I don't understand," the reddish one said.

"Just *do* it!" Jeffers said. "If anyone asks. If no one asks, forget I said anything."

"But..."

"I don't have time to argue," he said. He turned and headed for the ladder.

He glanced over his shoulder as he descended, and saw the furballs looking at one another in confusion. He hoped they could manage their role – but it shouldn't be too demanding. All they had to do was act like wronged innocents – and that's what they were.

He started working up the new manifest while waiting for the airlock to cycle, but didn't finish it until back in his own office. It was a bit tricky; he had to make it look as if his substitute was the original, and the freight list a fake pasted over it. He also had to make sure that the Confederacy officials at the port on Telemachus wouldn't miss the revised version.

It was a safe bet that Captain Tyler would never check it, but he didn't dare just leave the modified version out in the open; the Confederacy would never believe that...

At last he was satisfied, and transmitted the files, along with a customs clearance for the *Lord Lucan* – a deliberately faulty customs clearance, so that the Confederacy would double-check it.

If it worked – and he thought it would – when Tyler landed at the port on Telemachus and had her documents checked, it would look as if she had been hired to fly sixty passengers to the Contact Authority on Sirius II, and had instead kidnaped them to Telemachus III to be sold as slaves, with altered records calling them pets.

He hoped that the Confederacy officials on Telemachus III were less corrupt than his co-workers on Musashi. They *should* be; the Confederacy had a reputation for clean, if ruthless, administration.

Tyler must have had some way to get past the customs officials there, though. Would the "pets" designation have been enough? Perhaps she knew who to bribe. But the risk in letting a manifest *this* damaged through...

Well, Jeffers had done his best. He could only hope it was enough. The more he thought about it, the more he wanted those furballs safely returned home. He wished there were a way to find out what would happen to them on Telemachus III, but he doubted the news would ever reach Musashi.

An hour later he watched the launch, wondering whether he had done enough – and why he had done anything.

He hadn't known he had any real scruples left, but obviously he did.

As he watched the glowing dot vanish into the heavens he wondered whether it might be time to find another line of work, perhaps even time to get off Musashi once and for all; Musashi Port was clearly not a good place for a man with scruples.

He had tried for years to do without them, but he had discovered today that there were some he was not willing to lose, and the discovery was strangely comforting.

If he settled somewhere new, he would try to do better than he had here, to be a better person. He wondered how honest he could be if he worked at it.

To his own surprise, he thought he would enjoy finding out.

Nif's World

Many years ago I was on a convention panel with an unusual gimmick: several writers were shown a painting – "The Planet Growers," by Steven Vincent – and asked what we would do if we were basing a story on it. We all took very different approaches – which was sort of the point, to show that writers all work differently. One panelist wrote a poetic opening, another a set of notes, and I wrote the first draft of what you see here.

Nif watched, enraptured, as the colors poured out through the worldstalk, blue and green and white. Her fingers tightened around her companions' hands in a final squeeze before they separated into their individual environment bubbles and soared apart, each bound for her own sprouting worldlet.

Nif did not take the first worldlet she saw, nor the second; she knew what she wanted, and in time she spotted it. Ahead, a little to one side, a worldlet was blooming outward, already a full sphere and approaching its final dimensions, with all the green-coated land on one side, the shining blue of the ocean on the other. That was what she needed, a world with only a single continent.

She flapped a wing and steered for it. Her wings were non-functional in the vacuum of space, of course, but the environment bubble registered the motion and fed the information to her propulsion unit.

She exulted at the sight of her chosen miniplanet. She had been planning this for pentads, dreaming and scheming for the day when she would at last sail into the pocket universe, the shaping power placed ready in her mind. She knew that her teachers doubted her talents, and she was determined to prove what she could do.

The purple mists of ylem were clearing as she swooped down toward the globe she had selected and prepared to nip it free of its nurturing tendrils.

Once she cut it free of the stalk there was no going back; that would commit her to shape this worldlet and no other. She did not hesitate, but sheared the stalk quickly and let the planet spin free.

It was all hers. She was on her own now. In her classroom assignments she had never been alone, not really; she had had her textmemories to refer to, and more importantly, she had had Qui and Skir to help out.

Now, though, her two best friends were off to their own worldlets, and she had nothing she could draw on but her own skills and talent and desire.

The desire was there, certainly. She wanted to be an artist, a world-shaper, more than anything else she could imagine. She had always wanted that. The talent, she was certain, was inside her somewhere, lurking within, buried still beneath the awkwardness of her youth, waiting an opportunity to blossom forth.

The skills, however, were lacking. She knew that. She simply was not very proficient with the shaping power. Her conceptions were not clear enough, not detailed enough, for the enabling mechanisms to follow them through quickly and easily. She had to go over every little thought and image over and over, correcting flaws, filling in gaps, and even reshaping concepts. Often, unfortunately, her concepts didn't work.

It was an unfathomable wonder to her that Qui could bring forth her ornate creations in a single sweeping work, whole invented realities purring and ticking like fine machinery – though of course, until now, Qui had never had to fill an entire *world*. In her earlier projects, though, Qui had never been troubled by details, and Nif had no doubt that world-shaping would go as well for her. Qui's creations always worked, and worked right the first time, without tinkering.

Skir was almost as good, creating her works not all at once, as Qui did, but in a smooth progression, like a flower opening.

Nif's were more like a child's card-houses, rickety and uneven and likely to collapse under close inspection.

All the same, skills lacking or not, she had made it this far. She had reached the Competition. She had skirted the very edges of cheating to do it, of course, getting the most help that she could possibly be allowed from Qui and Skir and the household AIs. She had spent pentads plotting and planning, thinking what she could do that would impress the judges with her undeveloped raw talent, that would show she had the audacity to be a fine world-shaper even if she lacked the polish of her competitors.

She had known that any wholly original concept would not work. Under the intense pressure of the Competition, with the terrifyingly short time limit, she knew that she could only botch one of her own muddled ideas. She wouldn't have the time to go back and patch it together after the initial shaping.

She had searched for something she could adapt, instead, a concept she could take, ready-made, to shape a world. She had dug back through history and myth for something clear and simple, so that she could handle it, but so stunningly appropriate and powerful that the judges would have no choice but to recognize its value.

And, at last, she had found what she wanted.

She approached her chosen worldlet and studied it.

Yes, it was just as it should be. Ready to drop from the stalk, it was roughly three kilometers in diameter – in the warped reality of the Competition's artificially-opened pocket universe, that would support a fully-realized miniature Earthlike environment.

It had a molten metal core, a thick stone mantle, a fragile crust of tectonically-active plates that she could manipulate if she chose, and enough water to cover almost four-fifths of the surface with oceans, all in perfect miniature. The land surfaces, both dry and suboceanic, were coated with a thin layer of easily-modified, high-speed genetic material, ready for her to shape.

She reached out, in communion with the shaping power, and began to bring forth her dream. The gene-stuff grew and blossomed at her command, burgeoning wildly, until it had entirely covered her world's single continent with a tame, peaceful, luxuriant garden. She needed no deserts, no mountains, no badlands for her creation, simply a single continent-sized garden.

When that was done she reached out again – thinking, as she did, that Qui was probably done already, with some magnificent, intricate work – and raised up fauna from the newly-formed, still-unstable flora. Beasts that crawled and walked and flew, that swam or burrowed, she brought forth as many as she could devise, all herbivorous, all calm, placid, peaceful. Her world was to be a paradise, not a battlefield.

When the beasts were finished, adequately if not well, she concentrated on the small open plain at the center of the single continent. There she put a single great tree, a tree bearing biocybernetic fruit. Each fruit carried a semi-sentient pseudo-organism, self-contained, which, if ingested by a humanoid, would become a symbiote bonded to the human nervous system, feeding information and the accumulated moral knowledge of the human race into the eater's mind.

She had worked on that aspect, all by itself, for more than a pentad, in planning her project. She had mentioned something to Qui about her preparations, and Qui had laughed.

"You can't plan everything, Nif," she had said. "You need to see what fits on the world you choose. The judges want to see us make the best use of the material we're given, not just impose our own order upon it."

That was all very well for Qui, Nif thought, but not everyone was as skillful as she.

She was ready for the centerpiece of her work now. She reached out to a pair of near-apes, one male and one female, that she had kept handy, and placed them beneath her biocybernetic tree. There she reshaped them, shifting and sorting their genes until they were virtually indistinguishable from true humans, save for their size, the speed at which they lived, and the peculiar nature of the other-universal matter that made up their bodies.

She herself, of course, was not exactly a true human, since her ancestors had been modifying their genes to suit their whims, or the whims of fashion, for millennia. Her wings were the most obvious manifestation of that. She was not interested in creating beings in her own image, however, and stuck closely to the natural genetic blueprint for humanity, as it had originally evolved.

Adam and Eve, she called them when she was done, and the worldlet, of course, was Eden. She registered this name with the Competition's administrators mere moments before the three judges sailed into view, their environment bubbles gleaming golden in the warm light of the artificial sun.

Nif saw them approaching and waited expectantly. As she had been instructed she ascended, watching but well away from her work, so as to allow the judges their first look without interference. When they were ready she would swoop down and explain it all, tell them of the ancient myths, explain how her Tree of the Knowledge of Good and Evil worked, and then, modestly, she would await their assessment.

She was certain that she had created her masterpiece. Qui would probably outdo her, and Zik, and maybe Skir, but there were a dozen openings to be had this time around, and she would surely rate one of them.

The judges were taking their first good look at her world, and she found herself unable to resist. She had a trace of the shaping power left, and she used it, almost without meaning to, to tap into their private communications as they judged her Eden.

The first judge spoke almost immediately after reaching the planet, before she could possibly have seen more than the most obvious features, and her words froze Nif's heart.

"Oh, Creation!" she said. "Not Adam and Eve again!"

"That's the third Garden of Eden this time around," the second judge remarked, bemused.

"You'd think the kids would learn," the third said, "but every time it's the same old things, Eden or dinosaurs. Don't they realize we've seen that a hundred times before?" He registered a rejection for Nif's world; neither of his fellows countered it. Without speaking to Nif at all, they prepared to move on to the next worldlet.

The Abduction of Ebenezer Scrooge

My wife and I create our own holiday cards most years. Sometimes I write a story, and we use that. Here's one such story, based on wondering whether Scrooge's reactions to his ghostly visitations actually made any sense.

The junior scientist waved a tentacle politely. "We have returned the subject to his residence and observed his actions for the following four days," it said.

"Report," the mission director said. "What have you learned?"

"We...are unsure." The scientist s antennae slumped. "Our results do not match our expectations."

"Explain."

"Our intent was to assess the creature's reaction to extreme emotional stress, beginning with experiences when his sensory input did not match his understanding of reality. Would he adapt to this new data, or reject it? Would he alter his behavior to suit these new perceptions? Would he display curiosity, or fear, or anger? You are familiar with such experiments, of course."

"Of course. Go on."

"We also wanted to evaluate how traumatic experiences would affect his subsequent behavior. Previous studies had suggested we could expect to see hypervigilance, depression, anger, and a breakdown in social function. Because of these anticipated negative consequences, we chose a subject with no immediate family and few social contacts, to minimize the damage. We also selected an individual of fixed habits, one whose movements normally remained within a constrained area, so that any disruption of his normal surroundings would be immediately obvious to him. We also chose a subject of firmly fixed ideation, one given to expressing strong opinions, so that changes in his beliefs would be readily detectible."

"I understand. Continue."

"Our subject is a financial operator named Ebenezer Scrooge. If his name has any meaning or significance, we were unable to determine it."

"We have observed that human names often have no meaning beyond a simple designation of a specific individual. Continue."

"Yes. We had observed this Mr. Scrooge intermittently for several years, so as to have a firm basis for our experiments. On the night of our experiment we waited until he returned to his domicile upon completion of his daily labor, and then projected a simple holographic image of a dead former co-worker upon the door of his residence."

"And?"

"We had anticipated an exclamation, or some other demonstration of surprise or fear, but saw no reaction whatsoever."

"None?"

"None."

"Are you sure he saw it?"

"Yes."

"Go on."

"He did display some concern once he was inside his home, checking each room for irregularities. This was not part of his customary routine. We assume it was prompted by the hologram of his co-worker s face. Encouraged, we decided to see whether an auditory phenomenon might provoke an interesting reaction, and used a focused ultrasound to cause every bell in the structure to ring. While that drew his attention, he still failed to demonstrate an emotional response, and we proceeded to the next level of our experiment. We projected a full-sized image of that same dead co-worker, and held a lengthy conversation in which we warned Mr. Scrooge of a dire fate awaiting him in the afterlife – you do understand this culture's curious belief in an existence after death?"

"Of course. Go on."

"Yes. Mr. Scrooge professed to believe that he was hallucinating, but he continued to converse with our projection, and while he gave few outward signs of fear or terror, his brain-waves did indicate agitation."

"Our specter told him to expect three further supernatural visitations, and warned him that his failure to react appropriately to what these manifestations showed him would condemn him to an eternity of suffering. He should have been overcome with dread, according to our theories, but he continued to conceal his emotions, and we withdrew our image.

"He then retired to his bed, where we sedated him, and brought him aboard our ship, where we could attach him to the neuro-inducer for the next stage.

"With the inducer providing direct access to his memories, we then presented him with a series of images from his past, reminding him of past tragedies, missed opportunities, and irrevocable mistakes. We had assumed this would produce a state of despair and frustration with his inability to alter any of these past events.

"This was followed by images of his acquaintances enjoying their holiday celebrations without him, intended to alienate him from his social setting and add loneliness to the pre-existing matrix of despair and frustration.

"And finally, we caused him to imagine his own death, to add futility to the mix. We expected this to leave him a broken man, his confidence destroyed.

"That done, we returned him to his residence.

"We hoped that we had not driven him to suicide, but we expected him to be in a state of emotional collapse when he awoke."

"I see. And was this what you observed?"

"No." The junior scientist's antennae twitched. "Instead he displayed every sign of delight at his experiences and situation. His behavior showed a drastic alteration, but he did not become paranoiac or depressed; instead he seemed...well, giddy. He proceeded to perform several acts of generosity that were completely incongruous with his previous behavior, and generally displayed great joy."

"Interesting. And what do you conclude from this?"

"Director, my only conclusion is that I don't understand these people *at all.*"

The director waved a tentacle. "Well," it said, "that's a start."

Volunteers

This is a story about how people's actions often don't match their words.

It had been about six weeks since the alien fleet settled into orbit and the ambassadors landed at Dulles, and most people were over the initial shock and getting back to normal, when the announcement came. There were hints and warnings, of course – everyone knew something big was coming as soon as the White House and the UN called their press conferences, and the nets were instantly awash in rumors.

But then, the nets had been awash in rumors ever since the first radar contact with the approaching ships. The nets are *always* awash in rumors about *something*. The intensity did ramp up a little once we got a look at their ships, and at their lumpy purple bodies and eyeless upside-down faces, and then jumped again when word of the press conferences came, but there were limits to how much speculation and gossip anyone could handle.

I'd been ignoring the rumors since about the second week. I figured we'd find out soon enough what the story was, and I was more or less right. It was pretty clear we weren't being invaded, since the aliens didn't all land, didn't blow anything up or make any obvious threats, and beyond that – well, we'd find out in time.

My brother Jason read every tidbit or theory, though, no matter how trivial or loony. It drove his fiancée nuts. Emily kept trying to talk to Jason about ordinary things – wedding plans, whether they wanted kids, where to eat dinner, that sort of thing – and Jason would sit there looking attentive, and then say, "Do you think maybe they're an advance party, here to negotiate a surrender?" Or, "Someone said the radar signature of the ships looked like that old Soviet space station, Mir – maybe they modeled their ships on that, to look less threatening?"

So Jason knew something was up hours before I heard about the news conferences, and he was already locked into his chair, with CNN on one screen and a webfeed on another, when I came in from the garage and started to ask if he'd heard.

I should have known.

Anyway, he shushed me before I got the question out, and I looked at the screens and concluded nothing was happening yet, so I went out to the kitchen to nuke up some popcorn.

Emily arrived just as the popping began to subside, which meant she'd left work early – she obviously thought this was an important event she should share with her intended. We said our hellos, and I asked if she'd like some popcorn and whether there was anything I could get her to drink, and she came in to help me fetch and carry, which meant that five minutes later, instead of me walking back into the family room with a bag of popcorn and a couple of beers, I walked back carrying a tray that held three bowls of popcorn, a shaker of salt, a dish of melted butter, a dozen chocolate chip cookies, a bowl of pretzel sticks, a glass dish of carrots and celery sticks, a glass of onion dip, and a stack of paper napkins.

"Emily's coming with the drinks in a minute," I said as I put the tray on the coffee table.

"Shh!" Jason said, staring at the screen.

I sat down and grabbed a handful of popcorn, and watched as the CNN anchor tried to fill airtime telling us the obvious – that the reporters were all in their seats waiting for the officials, and the press conference called for 4:00 Eastern should start at any moment.

Since it was 4:06 by the inset clock, I could have guessed that part.

Then some guy in a suit stepped up to the podium and began speaking.

I missed the first few words because Emily was trying to arrange the drinks on the table and Jason was desperately shushing her, but it was all just ritual noises; it took a few minutes to get to the meat of the matter, and by then all three of us were settled on the couch, listening intently.

"As you know," the spokesman said, "our extraterrestrial visitors have been learning English, and our linguists have been learning their methods of communication. As yet, neither side has approached fluency, but we are able to make ourselves understood through a computer-assisted pidgin."

"They *think* they're understood," Jason said with a grimace. "God only knows what misconceptions are going to come around and bite us on the ass later."

Emily threw him a glance, but didn't say anything; I was still focused on the screen.

"Naturally, the first thing we wanted to know, once communication had been established, was why they had come to our planet."

"Duh," I said. Jason threw me a dirty look.

"Our guests answered that question weeks ago, and our people have been working day and night since then to get a clearer and more detailed explanation of that answer. We have not been able to do so, and the aliens are growing impatient. They have made a request of us, one they know we can easily fulfill without knowing *why* they made it, and they consider our reluctance to act until we know their reasons to be uncooperative. They think we're stalling, and they're growing more hostile with every day we postpone taking action. Therefore, we have reluctantly agreed to do as they ask, and make the announcement they have requested."

"Get *on* with it," Jason growled.

"On behalf of our visitors from the fourth planet of Lambda Aurigae, we are issuing a call for volunteers."

He paused, and a puzzled silence hung in the air, both at the press conference and in our rented house.

"Volunteers for *what?*" someone finally called from the floor of the press conference.

"Well, that's just it," the spokesman said, smiling a politician's smile. "We don't know, and the aliens either can't or won't tell us. We've been trying to get an explanation for almost a month, and are making no headway at all. They don't seem to understand the question – or perhaps they just can't believe we're asking it. It's been very frustrating for all of us, as I'm sure you can imagine."

"It's a cookbook," I muttered.

"Shut up," Jason said, punching my arm.

"Here's what we do know," the spokesman said. "The fleet in orbit is here to transport up to twelve million volunteers, though they don't really expect that many. The volunteers will be transported out of our solar system at speeds faster than light. Most of them, perhaps all of them, are not expected to return to Earth, though we don't know why, or when *any* return would take place. We are not able to get a definite answer on whether the volunteers would be going to the aliens' home system of Lambda Aurigae, or somewhere else entirely. And when we get to the question of what the volunteers will *do* out there, communication breaks down completely. We don't *think* our visitors intend to eat them, or kill them outright, but we can't even be sure of that. All we really know is that these beings want to load lots of human volunteers onto their starships and fly them away.

"Now, I'll take questions."

Jason stared at the screen in disbelief. "That's *all*? That's all they know?"

"It's all they're telling us, anyway," I replied.

"So what's really happening, then?" Emily asked.

"*I* don't know," Jason snapped.

"What's the word on the nets?" I asked. "What do all the geeks think?"

"Shut up," Jason said, pointing at the screen.

I realized a reporter had asked a question, and the spokesman was repeating it, and I'd missed half of it.

"No, we do not have any assurances that the volunteers will not be harmed," he said. "We do not have assurances of *anything*. That's why we put off making this announcement until now."

"Are the aliens *threatening* us, then? If you had not announced today, would they have taken action against us?"

"Like everything else, that's not really clear. We had the distinct impression that if we continued to delay that yes, they would have taken action independently – but the nature of that action is unclear, and saying it would be 'against us,' or that this was a threat, isn't really justified. The prevailing theory among our experts, and it is, I reiterate, *only* a theory, is that our visitors would have found other channels of communication and made the public announcement themselves."

"But they might have done more?"

"That possibility cannot be ruled out," the spokesman admitted.

"They're getting off the subject," I said, irritated. "I want to know what they want the volunteers for."

Jason was looking at the other screen, and said, "Biljo thinks they're trying to weaken us by stealing our best and brightest, to make it easier to conquer us."

"Biljo is an idiot," I said. "Our best and brightest are bright enough not to buy into this sight unseen. The volunteers are going to be losers and misfits. And twelve million of them, out of seven billion, won't matter anyway."

"What, losers?" Jason glared at me. "Man, this is a chance to go to the *stars!* They'll get the dreamers, the guys who always wanted to be astronauts."

"Yeah, the losers and misfits."

"Oh, fu..." He remembered Emily, I guess, and cut himself off. "Screw you, Jeff," he finished.

"Both of you shut up," Emily said. "I want to hear this."

"...said how the actual mechanics will be handled. As we understand it, the volunteers are to be shuttled up to the orbital fleet as quickly as they arrive at Dulles. They're leaving the details of getting them to Dulles up to us. Yes, you in the back."

"Can Dulles Airport handle twelve million passengers? I wouldn't have thought it had the capacity."

"It doesn't. We're still working out the details, and we don't really expect the full twelve million. Yes, in the third row."

"You say you don't expect the full twelve million – how will you know when you're done, then? Is there a deadline?"

"We don't know. Our visitors are, as on many subjects, very vague on this point. It's our impression that at some point they'll just decide they're done, using their own criteria, and that will be it."

"Are we getting anything in exchange for these volunteers?"

"Ah, now we arrive at the *good* news – yes, we are. Our guests will be turning over significant equipment for our scientists and engineers to study. Exactly *what* equipment remains to be determined, and before anyone asks, we do not yet know whether it will include any weapons, or their stardrive. The nature of the equipment appears to be linked in some fashion to the number and quality of the volunteers, and how quickly they arrive – and no, we do not know what they mean by 'quality' in this context."

"Probably how well-marbled they are," I muttered.

"Will you shut up with that?" Jason said, punching me lightly.

"Okay, fine," I said. "They aren't going to eat them, they're just going to pull out their brains and use them to run machines, factories and farm machinery and the like. Or send them to zoos all over the galaxy. Or experiment on them to see what it takes to turn human beings into starship fuel."

"Or use them as shock troops in an interstellar war," Emily said. "The enemy won't have seen humans before, won't know how they think or how they fight."

Jason had been preparing to hit me again, but now he turned and looked at Emily.

"That might be it," he said.

"If creatures that advanced need infantry at all," Emily replied.

"Maybe they're just weeding out losers to improve our gene pool," I suggested.

"Or to pacify us by taking all the guys willing to take chances, the guys out to prove something," Emily said.

"Culling the herd," I said, and Jason punched me again, harder this time.

"Twelve million won't make much of a difference to the gene pool," he said, as I rubbed my arm.

"Do we really know that?" Emily asked. "Maybe there's a gene for a certain sort of risk-taking, or volunteering, and it's a lot rarer than we realize." She looked at the video screen. "Are they going to say anything else important?"

"Probably not," I said.

Jason didn't answer; he was leaning over the other way, reading the webfeed.

"So what's the flash crowd saying?" I asked.

Jason snorted. "They're asking each other who's going," he said.

"Is that loudmouth Biljo going? If he thinks they want the best and the brightest, I know *he* thinks he qualifies."

"No," Jason said. "Now he's talking about first wave versus second wave on the frontier, and how the first wave mostly all dies, but that clears the way for the second wave. He says he'll go in the *second* wave."

"What makes him think there will *be* a second wave?" I asked.

"What makes him think that it'll happen in his lifetime, if there is?" Emily asked. "I mean, we're talking about interstellar distances here, right? The aliens were saying most of the volunteers won't come back – maybe that's just because the trip's going to take so long that most of them will die of old age."

"But they have a stardrive," I said. "They must have, if they got here in the first place!"

"Well, what's that mean?" Emily asked. "What sort of a stardrive?"

"She's got a point," Jason said. "I mean, sure, they must travel faster than light, if they got here at all, but that doesn't mean they can go bopping around the galaxy like Captain Kirk. Maybe all they've got is Warp Two, or whatever."

"Maybe they don't even have that," Emily said. "Maybe they live for centuries, so spending fifty years on a starship is no big deal."

"Ask someone," I said, pointing at the keyboard with one hand while I grabbed popcorn with the other. "Has anyone mentioned that?"

Jason didn't bother to answer; he was already typing.

And that pretty much killed the conversation; after that Jason was caught up in the online argument, and too busy to talk to us peons in the material world. I finished the popcorn, and Emily cleared away the tray, and the press conference went on for another hour and a half without saying anything useful.

I'd thought Jason had been bad before, when there were just rumors, but now he was worse than ever, because now there were *theories* instead of guesses. We knew what the aliens wanted, but we didn't know why.

And now there was other news, as well. The first volunteers started arriving at Dulles less than an hour after the news conference, and by the time they did overseas volunteers had begun clamoring for help reaching America.

It took three days for the U.S. to agree to use military transports to bring the volunteers to Dulles – or rather, to Andrews, where they were loaded on buses and driven over to Dulles. Collection points were set up in a hundred countries, all over the world.

By then the aliens had collected the first load, a crowd of four hundred people; apparently they all fit onto the ship, but it was tight. Some had brought hundreds of pounds of baggage, others hadn't even brought a toothbrush; the aliens didn't seem to care. Landlords and homeowners all over Dulles and Reston and Chantilly were leasing out crash space, taking cars or clothes or computers in payment for a few nights on a couch or daybed.

I found myself wondering how the aliens intended to *feed* twelve million volunteers. Were those orbiting behemoths *that* big?

If so, no wonder our boys never considered refusing the aliens' demands.

The news media were going crazy, of course. Everyone had a theory about what the volunteers were for, but nobody knew anything; reporters were interviewing volunteers, their families, their friends, the officials handling the exodus, people who started to volunteer and then backed out...

What they *really* wanted, of course, was an interview with one of the aliens, but none of them ever managed that.

A few facts did trickle out – maybe. The trip to Lambda Aurigae would reportedly take between three and four years, one way, and that was assuming that the aliens really did mean *our* years – the scientists had done their best to get that settled, using models and diagrams, but no one was really convinced there hadn't been a misunderstanding somewhere in the process.

And the question of feeding the volunteers was brought up, but the aliens just said it wouldn't be a problem.

Two weeks after the announcement some eight thousand volunteers had been shuttled up to orbit, and none had come back down, nor had any reports from any of them. Some people on Earth were starting to scream that the volunteers had all been murdered, and demanding that the government do something about it, and so far the government was just shrugging its collective shoulders and saying, "What do you want us to do? They volunteered."

And Emily was demanding that Jason get the hell offline and do some serious wedding planning. She had finally given him an ultimatum; I didn't know the details, but he had agreed to eat dinner with her at a restaurant with no net access, without bringing his laptop or pocket box, and with his phone turned off. I thought it was probably a good thing, and not really any of my business – until I got asked to play chauffeur, chaperone, and referee.

"Why do you want *me* there?" I asked. "I thought this would be a good chance for just the two of you to talk, you know, without a fifth wheel in the way."

"Because there may be yelling, someone could storm out, I expect to do some drinking and may need a designated driver..."

"Why?" I was honestly puzzled. "What's the big deal? You're planning a wedding, not negotiating a divorce – you're supposed to be in *love*, for heaven's sake! I mean, if you're having second thoughts about it, Jase, you should have said something before this."

"It's not..." He stopped, frowned, and started over. "It's not Emily. I do love her and I want to marry her, and I don't think she's going to go nuts over getting every detail right or anything, but I just... this isn't the *time*, with the aliens up there. I can't concentrate on anything else. You remember, when we were kids, I wanted to be an astronaut, or make millions of dollars so I could pay to go into space, and here's my chance, I could not just go into orbit, I could visit another *star*, but..."

"But it's crazy, and you don't know what you'd be letting yourself in for."

"Well, that, but mostly there's Emily. I mean, do you think *she* would ever want to volunteer? You know what she's like. And I'm afraid that when I tell her I'm thinking about it she's going to get, um..."

"Royally pissed off?"

"You got it."

"Um."

"So I want you along, Jeff, to keep things calm. I mean, if we can just keep it together until the aliens leave, and I don't have that option open any more, then I'll be able to focus on Emily again. So I don't want a big scene now, I don't want a break-up, I don't want anything we'd have to undo – or that we *couldn't* undo. So can you come along and just *be* there for us? A calming influence?"

I shrugged. "I guess I can try," I said.

So I tried. I dressed up a bit, filled my pockets with everything I thought might be useful, from my address book to aspirin, and drove Jason there in my old Saturn.

Emily had come straight from her office. She met us in the parking lot, and our table was waiting.

"If you ever want me out of the way, I won't be offended," I said, as we sat down. "I can always just go drink at the bar."

"You're driving," Jason said.

"So I'll drink ginger ale."

Emily tucked her skirt under her, pulled in her chair, checked to make sure her purse was somewhere no one would trip on it, shook her hair away from her eyes, then looked at me and said, "So why'd Jason bring you?"

That was quicker and more direct than I'd expected.

"Ask him," I said.

She looked at him, but didn't say a word.

"Moral support," Jason said.

"Why do you *need* moral support? What are you going to say that I'm not going to like? Believe me, I'm not going to make a scene over the shape of the cake or how many entrees to offer."

"I know, I know. It's the aliens."

She stared at him in a way I would not want to ever see from a woman I intended to marry. "What *about* the damned aliens?"

"Well, I..." Jason looked helplessly at me, but I just shook my head slightly; I had no guidance to offer. He hesitated, then plunged ahead.

"I've been thinking about volunteering," he said.

She stared some more, but her expression had changed; it was far more thoughtful and less hostile. This was obviously not the reaction Jason had expected; he stared back for a moment, then glanced at me, then looked back at Emily.

"So are you going to?" she asked at last.

"Well, no, because I don't want to leave you," Jason said.

"What makes you think I wouldn't come with you?"

Up until then the silences could have been called "awkward," or "puzzled," or most particularly "confused," but the one that followed had worked all the way up to "stunned."

"But you never...I mean, you didn't seem interested. I never heard you talk about going into space or anything."

"Did you *ask* me?"

"No, but... but I thought I knew you well enough that I didn't have to."

"It never hurts to ask, Jason. If you were seriously thinking about volunteering to spend the rest of your life on an alien spaceship, don't you think that's something you should discuss with your future wife?"

At that point I noticed the waiter hovering quietly. I picked up my menu and said, "I'll have a ginger ale."

"Rum and Coke," Emily said, without shifting her gaze from Jason's face.

Jason, on the other hand, was glad of an excuse to break eye contact; he looked up and asked, "What beers do you have?"

And after that we just talked about the wedding plans and the food.

Emily's heart didn't really seem to be in it, though, and Jason was clearly far more concerned about not offending Emily further than anything else. The wedding date was still six months away, so of course there was plenty of time for changes if they later regretted anything.

My presence was pretty thoroughly superfluous, I thought, but at least the food was good, and Jason was paying.

And then it turned out to not be quite totally superfluous, after all, when Emily announced that she would be going to her mother's place instead of coming home with Jason; that meant I got to drive Jason home.

We were walking out to the cars when Jason caught Emily's arm and said, "Listen, we need to talk about this volunteering thing. I wasn't going to volunteer without talking to you. I was still thinking about it, that's why I hadn't asked you; I didn't know yet what *I* wanted to do, so it didn't seem right to ask *you* yet."

"Do you know what you want now?" she asked.

"No," he said. "I mean, if we knew what they want the volunteers for..."

"Jason, they want *volunteers.* If they were going to do something terrible to them, wouldn't they just take people without asking?"

"Who knows? They're *alien*, they don't think the way we do."

Emily didn't answer that; instead she just said, "Good night, Jason," and got in her car.

We watched her drive away before we got in my car.

And in the morning I got her e-mail; I suppose she sent it to me instead of Jason because she thought he'd be up all night, and she didn't want him to get the news until morning.

The wedding plans were off. The wedding itself was not necessarily off, though – if Jason got aboard the same transport she did, they could be married on the way. There was bound to be a clergyman or a ship's captain or someone who could perform the ceremony.

And if they didn't get the same ship, well, then it wasn't meant to be.

"Tell Jason there are those that want," she said, "and there are those that do. Which is he?"

I printed the e-mail out and took it up to Jason's room – which had been Emily's, too, until then. I handed it to him as he came out of the bathroom. I didn't say anything, I just gave him the paper and waited.

He sat on the bed and read it; then he handed it back to me and said, "Crazy bitch."

"So are you going?" I asked.

He looked up at me. "No," he said – the first time he'd ever given a definite answer. "I thought about it, and it's crazy. I decided last night. I'll wait until the second wave, or until we have our own goddamned stardrive, or until I have a few million dollars to buy a shuttle seat and a week at the lunar Hilton. Volunteering to go off with a bunch of alien monsters – it's nuts."

"Emily went," I said.

"Maybe she did, maybe she didn't," he said. "Maybe she just dumped me and doesn't want to admit it; she's just hiding somewhere until the aliens are gone, and then she'll come out and pick up where she left off. And if I was dumb enough to actually buy her story and fly off to Lambda Aurigae, then ha ha, she's well rid of me. She probably thinks I'll do that, thinks I'm a crazy dreamer who'd fall for anything to get into space."

"And if you don't go?"

"Then when she comes out of hiding we can start fresh. We'll know neither of us was stupid enough to volunteer."

I looked down at the print-out in my hand, then at Jason. "You really think she didn't go?"

"I don't know, and I don't care. Go to hell." He fell back on the bed, staring at the ceiling.

I didn't go to hell, but I did go back downstairs. I made a few calls.

Emily really had gone to her mother's place, and had told her she was volunteering, and had packed some of the clothes and things she still kept there, and done a lot of loose-end tying and farewell-saying before driving off in the direction of Dulles in the middle of the night; Ms. Halloran was pretty upset about it. Emily had e-mailed a resignation to her office, and called or sent notes to several friends, before she left.

If she was faking, she was being pretty thorough about it.

When Jason finally came downstairs I said, "You might still be able to catch her at Dulles and talk her out of it."

"Screw it," he said. "She's gone."

"What are you going to do with her clothes and stuff?"

"Send them to her mother, I guess. Eventually."

"So she's not affecting your decision now," I said. "You aren't going to volunteer?"

"I told you I wasn't. Why, you want the whole house to yourself?"

I gave it another month, just in case Jason changed his mind. When the government started hinting that the aliens were getting ready to leave, though, I signed over my half of the house and a bunch of other assets, packed a bag, and left.

I don't think Emily's on this ship, but they say we'll be able to transfer between them later, if we want, and we can start sending messages as soon as we leave orbit. Until then it might interfere with the project – they don't want anyone back on Earth to have any real confirmation that we're okay until the selection process is complete.

It'd be good to see her again.

Yes, they've told us what we've volunteered for, at least part of it, and I think I understand why they didn't announce it on Earth. It's not easy to explain, especially not in an improvised pidgin. We'll be building a community to link their culture with ours – sort of – and they'll be studying how we do it, so they can understand our species. We'll be a colony and an embassy and a blending, all at once. The process works better if the participants don't know in advance what's planned, they say.

But once we're all aboard, they'll re-open communications, and we can send back messages. This will be mine. I wanted a record left behind.

Maybe Emily really was just hiding somewhere, and she and Jason will get married next year and laugh at poor dumb Jeff who flew off to the stars. Maybe whoever reads this will decide I only volunteered to show my brother what a jerk he was. I don't much care. I'm here, and it's what I wanted.

Some people want, Emily said, and some people do – but I don't think that's right.

Some people don't know what they want, I'd say.

And some of us do.

An Evil Opportunity Employer

I found myself wondering about the difference between a minion and a henchman, and just what the rules are for each, and why would anyone sign on as either one...

Read the contract. I tell everyone that – *everyone.* You know how many people actually do it?

Okay, I don't know either, but it isn't enough of them, I can tell you that. I swear half my business and 90% of my losses come from people who didn't do it. I don't suppose I should complain, since that's also at least half my income, but I get so fed up with clients who have no idea what they've signed that I just want to punch someone, even if I have to do it in my civilian identity.

Yeah, I admit it, I'm one of those dual-identity vigilantes – I hesitate to say "superheroes," because quite aside from any trademark issues, it sounds so boastful. It's not for me to say whether I'm a hero, let alone "super." I'm not going to tell you my *nom d'aventure*, but you'd probably recognize it; I'm not one of the really big names, not one of the Kryptonians or Asgardians or anything, but I have certain special abilities and I've earned a few headlines.

What I *haven't* earned from crime-fighting is a living, so I have a day job as a contracts attorney.

And I know what you're thinking – contracts? Not criminal law? Yes, contracts, because unlike *some* attorneys I could name, I understand the concept of conflict of interest. I also understand how difficult it is to keep from being recognized in court by someone with whom you've just had an epic two-hour brawl. Masks can slip and tear, and people *do* recognize voices and body language.

Most thieves and thugs don't sign any contracts before robbing a bank or taking a busload of commuters hostage, though, so I can put my law degree to use without worrying about constantly confronting people from my other work.

But there are exceptions, and I'm here to tell you about one of them.

This big guy with a battered old briefcase walked in wanting advice on whether he should sue his employer. Nothing out of the ordinary there. I was nodding and getting some papers ready and only half-listening at first because I get these all the time. He'd been asked to do stuff he thought was outside his job description and pretty clearly illegal, and he had agreed because his boss has a mean streak, but now he was having second thoughts, and he wanted to know what I thought he should do.

But then I asked who he worked for, and he answered, and I sat up straight and stared at him.

"Say that again," I told him.

"I work for Dr. Catastrophe," he repeated.

"Dr. *Alice* Catastrophe?" I asked, just to be sure, because yes, Catastrophe is an unusual name, but you never know.

"Yeah. The Doctor of Disaster. Her."

I sucked in my lips and considered this. I don't really like to call people "super-villains" any more than I like to call myself a superhero, but I have to admit the term fits Dr. Catastrophe better than any other description I can think of. I'd never gone up against her myself, at least not directly, but several people I knew had, and they all spoke of her with respect. I had the impression that if they weren't all professionally fearless, they'd speak of her with abject terror.

The guy – I'll call him John Doe – had my full attention now. The possibility of getting a lead on Dr. Catastrophe's current whereabouts definitely caught my interest, not so much as a lawyer as for my other line of work. "Tell me more," I said. "What exactly is it you do for Dr. Catastrophe?"

"I'm a henchman."

"What kind?"

"Non-specific."

"So you're not a lawyer or engineer or scientist or lab assistant or experimental subject?"

"No. I'm just a henchman. I run errands, operate equipment, do some security work, some light construction and maintenance, occasionally chauffeur the boss or her friends around."

"And you think she's asking you to do something outside your duties?"

He nodded.

I drummed my fingers on my desk. I knew something about the hireling business, albeit only from the outside, so I had a pretty good idea what henchmen and minions and serfs and underlings and the other categories did, but the exact lines were often vague. "Mr. Doe," I said, "I don't quite see how that's possible; are your duties *defined* anywhere?"

"Yes, they are," he said, lifting his briefcase onto my desk. "I'll show you."

I had a moment of alarm there, thinking that maybe this was all a set-up of some kind and he had one of Dr. Catastrophe's diabolical devices in there, that someone had found out about my other identity and decided to take me out, but then he flopped a sheaf of ordinary paper from the case onto my desk. He shoved it toward me.

"That's my employment contract," he said.

I just stared at it for a moment, then pulled it over and began reading.

It was indeed an employment contract, but not quite like any I had ever seen before. Parts of it were standard modern boilerplate, but other parts were strangely archaic, even more so than ordinary legalese, such as a clause giving the party of the first part – that is, Dr. Catastrophe – "full power under such circumstances to do with the party of the second part at her pleasure, be it either body, flesh, blood, or goods."

It also defined half a dozen different jobs, including henchman, but when I got to the signature page I noticed something odd.

"So all of Dr. Catastrophe's people sign this?" I asked.

"That's right. Apparently she's had some problems in the past with her employees double-crossing her, so she had this drawn up."

I knew something about *that* – Dr. Catastrophe spent eight years in prison after some of my crime-fighting compatriots convinced several of her flunkies to turn on her. Two full pages of this contract had been written specifically to prevent a recurrence, providing elaborate but carefully legal-sounding penalties for disobedience or betrayal. I had doubts about whether these provisions would hold up in court, given the various whistle-blower laws – in fact, since her entire operation was probably a criminal enterprise the whole contract should be unenforceable – but they certainly *looked* good enough to deter most hirelings.

But that wasn't what I had been looking at. I turned the contract back around to show him the signature page. "This is you?" I said. "You signed this?"

"Yeah, that's me. I'm not claiming I didn't sign, but paragraph 36..."

I interrupted him, still holding it open to the signature page. "Paragraph 36 doesn't apply," I said. "Look here." I pointed to a list at the top of the page where one box was checked, and only one.

"What did...I don't..."

"You aren't a henchman," I said. "You're a minion. It says so right there."

He leaned back, shocked. "But I applied to be a henchman!"

"Doesn't matter. What matters is what you signed, and it says right there that your employment category is entirely at the discretion of your employer, and cannot be changed once the contract is signed. You're a minion."

"The doctor *said* I was her henchman!"

I shook my head again. Hirelings are always surprised when they find out their bosses have lied to them. *I* used to be surprised when they were; what do they *expect* from criminal masterminds? But I'd gotten used to it. "Doesn't matter," I said again. I flipped pages. "Paragraph 83 – the party of the first part shall have full authority to lie to the party of the second part, to mislead, deceive, or defraud in service of her goals and purposes. She can call you anything she wants, but the *contract* says you're a minion."

He glared at the contract, his face going red. After a moment he said, "So how does that change things?"

"Well, the rules are different for minions; I'm sure you know that. Minions swear total obedience – to fetch and carry, to serve without question. See Paragraph 38? You're required to obey any order she gives you, no matter how stupid, if it doesn't directly endanger your life – or if you're in her presence, even if it *does* directly endanger your life. Henchmen get more latitude on what orders to obey, and how much they can argue. But there's a trade-off there – see Paragraph 44, reasons for termination and methods of termination? She can't just shoot you if she's angry, the way she can a henchman. Henchmen are responsible for their screw-ups, and minions aren't, because henchmen are assumed to be using their judgment and minions are supposed to be mindlessly obedient."

"So she thinks I'm a moron."

I managed to resist pointing out that he *had* signed the contract without noticing the big black check-mark in the "Minion" box at the top of the page, which did not speak well of his intelligence. Instead I tried to be conciliatory. "She may not have had any henchman openings left. It's hard to find good minions."

"So does this affect my case?"

"I'm afraid it pretty much *destroys* your case," I said. "Paragraph 38. *Nothing* she tells you to do is outside your job description. As for it being illegal, come on, Mr. Doe – you're working for Dr. Catastrophe! *Everything* she does is illegal, pretty much."

"So I really need to go steal all those kittens?"

I did a double-take. "Kittens?"

"Yeah. She wants...well, never mind." He picked up the contract and dropped it back in his briefcase.

"Kittens?" I said again.

I admit it, I have a soft spot for kittens. My two cats at home, Bruiser and Caliban, are both grown and both fixed, but...kittens. I love kittens.

If Dr. Catastrophe was going to do something horrible to kittens, I had to stop her.

"Hang on," I said, getting out of my chair and crossing to my reference shelves. "I'm pretty sure there's a precedent on this. Uh... do you know what Dr. Catastrophe *wants* with the kittens?"

"No."

"How many kittens are we talking about?"

"She said she needed at least forty, and fifty would give her a margin, just in case. She assigned three of us to fetch them."

"I think there's a precedent about minions and cute furry things. I'll need to look that up." I began scanning the shelves for the volume I wanted. "By the way," I said, as casually as I could, "did you notice that henchmen who try to leave can be hunted down and killed – it says 'terminated,' but we both know what that means – for their disloyalty? But minions who desert are ignored. The contract assumes they don't know enough to be dangerous."

He looked puzzled for a second, then realized what I was saying. "Wait – so I could just walk away?"

I nodded. "You'd be out of work, of course."

"But I wouldn't need to steal any kittens."

"That's right."

I could see he was thinking that over as I found the book I wanted and carried it to the desk.

"I think I'll do that," he said. "Thanks for the advice."

I waved it away. "It's nothing," I said.

"No, I appreciate it. Thanks. I guess you won't be representing me, but I've taken up your time, so what do I owe you for the consult?"

"Nothing. Really. I haven't accepted you as a client, and I'm not going to. I won't accept a cent from you."

"What? Why not?" He frowned. "Because I'm just a minion?"

"No," I said, as I flipped pages without looking at him. "Because if you're my client, this whole conversation would be privileged communication, and I couldn't tell anyone about it without your permission. If you're *not* my client, then we're just a couple of guys chatting, and if I mention any of this to anyone I'm not breaching confidentiality, which would be an ethics violation, I'm just making conversation."

"I don't see...oh." He lost a little color. "Maybe I do."

"Mr. Doe, have a good day – and I really think you're making the right decision not going back."

Then he picked up his briefcase and hurried out, and I put the book back on the shelf. I never did find that precedent. Maybe cute furry animals don't actually have any special legal protections.

But I took the rest of the afternoon off, and made a few calls, and that night a coalition of costumed vigilantes used their superhuman abilities to track the sound of mewing kittens to Dr. Catastrophe's lair, and to put her back behind bars.

Personal Space

This one actually started out as a story treatment for "Twilight Zone," back in the 1980s; some elements were specifically chosen to keep the budget manageable. I got paid, but the episode never got made, and eventually the rights reverted to me. Some time later – much later, really – I wrote this version of the story. It had to be updated, since the world's geopolitics had changed drastically in the intervening decades, but the basic concept still worked fine.

He clicked "Print" and sat back in his chair, then glanced at the clock on the office wall. Startled by what he saw, he checked the time on the computer screen. It matched.

He pulled out his phone, and that, too, gave the time as 6:20. He flipped to his list of contacts and tapped "Anna," then held the phone to his ear and listened to it buzz while he watched the Madison agreements print out.

The buzz stopped. "Hi, Gary," Anna's voice said. "What's up?"

"Hey, Annie," he said. "Look, I'm running late – I came into the office to catch up on some stuff, so I could start the day Monday with a clean desk, but it took longer than I expected. I'm still here."

"At the office?"

"Yeah."

"So are we still on for dinner?"

"Of course! But could you meet me here? Seems silly to come all the way out to your place and then back into town when I'm two blocks from the restaurant, and we're going to be late for our reservations as it is."

The printer stopped, but the screen said "Load Paper," rather than reverting to "Ready." He grimaced.

"Oh, sure," Anna said. "I'll be right there. Meet you out front of the office?"

"Sounds good. See you soon!" He tapped the red button, dropped the phone back in his pocket, then got up and headed for the supply closet. He had time; Anna's apartment was twenty minutes away.

He found a ream of paper and loaded it into the printer, then waited while the contracts finished printing. He put them in a folder, slid them into his desk drawer, then headed out. He turned off the lights, closed the door of the office and made sure it was locked and that his keys were in his pocket, then turned around.

And there was Anna, standing in the corridor halfway to the elevators.

"Hey!" he said, startled. "How'd you get here so fast?"

She jerked, obviously as startled by his presence as he was by hers, and stared at him.

"Weren't you at home when I called?"

"Yes, I was," she said. "But I made good time."

"You couldn't have! Not *that* good! And why are you up here? I thought we were meeting out front. And how did you even get in?"

"I...I don't..."

He realized he had almost been shouting, and quickly forced himself to calm down. Anna was prone to nerves – not surprising, with her background. "I'm sorry," he said. "I didn't mean to yell. But you *startled* me!"

"Then we're even," she said. "I thought you'd be out front waiting by now."

"The printer ran out of paper," he explained. "And I knew you wouldn't be here for another ten minutes at least, so I didn't see any need to rush, and...here we are."

"The reservations are for 6:30, aren't they?"

"Yes, they are, and we aren't going to make it, but we can still keep it close. I'll call the restaurant to say we're on our way."

He did just that as they hurried to the elevators and started down the fourteen stories to the lobby. That done, he put the phone away, and the two of them rode the last few floors in silence. They crossed the lobby, let themselves out through the security door, and made their way along the sidewalk, his arm around her waist.

Gary still couldn't figure out how Anna could possibly have been in that corridor if she had been at home when he called. Had she actually been in one of the other offices, catching up on some of her own work? But if that was it, why hadn't she just said so? Why would she have said she was at home?

They got to the restaurant, and their reservation had been held; they were seated, water was poured, menus delivered. Their waiter recited the list of specials and recommended the tilapia, then left them to it.

"They push the tilapia because they get it cheap," Gary remarked a moment later. "I'm going for the scallops."

"I think I want the grilled chicken," Anna replied.

That settled, Gary put down his menu and waited a few polite seconds, then asked, "Seriously, Annie, what were you doing outside my office?"

She silently shook her head, and kept her eyes on the menu.

"Were you working overtime, too?"

"No," she said.

"Then why were you there, instead of home at your apartment? I mean, I said I'd pick you up at six, and I know I was late, but..." He let the sentence trail off.

"I *was* in my apartment when you called!" she said, setting the menu down. "I said I was home, and I was! I was right there waiting for you, all dressed up and ready!"

"But you couldn't have been! I mean, it couldn't have been ten minutes between when I called and when I found you."

"So?"

"So you couldn't possibly have gotten your car out of the garage and driven eleven miles and parked somewhere and walked to the building and gotten the doorman to let you in and come up to the fourteenth floor in ten minutes!"

"I didn't take my car," she said. "Or talk to the doorman or use the elevator."

"But then how did you get there? Magic?"

She hesitated, and he thought he saw a...blush? A reddening of her cheeks?

"I don't know what it is," she said. "I mean, I know what it is, but I don't have a name for it. I don't know if it's magic or what."

"What?"

"The waiter's coming."

She was right. They placed their orders, handed over the menus, and then stared across the table at each other.

He broke the interlocked gaze first. He took a sip of water and said, "I've got to say, this dinner isn't going the way I expected."

"I'm not enjoying it as much as I expected, either," she replied. She straightened up. "Look, Gary, I do have a secret. I admit it. I haven't told anyone about it since I was a little girl, because when I *did* tell people, they never believed me. They thought it was just my imagination. They never gave me a chance to prove it."

"Prove what?" he asked, confused.

"I'll show you after dinner, all right? For now let's just have a nice meal and talk about other things, okay?"

He struggled to do as she suggested, but his thoughts kept circling back to finding her there in the corridor when she should have miles away. It didn't make any *sense*. He barely tasted his scallops as he ate them.

Anna did not seem to have any such problem. She ate her chicken with enthusiasm, and talked at length about her neighbor's adorable new cat. Gary was aware that he was not holding up his end of the conversation, but he simply could not focus on the meal.

Anna did not seem to mind; in fact, she seemed happier than usual as she rambled on and on about that stupid cat.

Finally, though, the waiter cleared away their plates and asked whether they would like to see the dessert menu. Ordinarily Gary would at least have taken a look at it, but tonight he was too eager for the promised demonstration, and started to wave it away. At the last second he caught himself, and said, "Unless you...?"

Anna shook her head. "No, that's fine."

He knew it was probably not fine; she loved sweets. She was deferring to him. Normally he would have encouraged her to stand up for herself, but not tonight. "Just the check," he said.

They did not make the usual small talk as he led the way back to the building where they both worked and showed his badge to the doorman. They rode up to the fourteenth floor in uncomfortable silence, and emerged into the reception area. There Anna took the lead, heading down the corridor.

She did not go to his office, though, nor to the workroom where she and three other administrative assistants looked after the everyday details that kept the firm running smoothly. Instead she led him to the ladies' room.

Or more precisely, to a blank stretch of corridor wall next to the door to the ladies' room.

She stopped. "Here," she said.

"Here, what?" he said, looking around.

She hesitated. "I haven't tried this here before, bringing someone else along, but it should work."

"*What* should work? Anna, you aren't making any sense."

"Gary, I'm about to show you my biggest, most personal secret, something I haven't shown anyone since I was a little girl. I haven't even *told* anyone about it since I was twelve, and no one ever believed me, so for you I'm going to *prove* it. Give me your hand."

"Anna, I don't – "

She did not wait for him to finish his sentence; instead she grabbed him by the arm with both her hands and stepped forward, pulling him with her.

He reared his head back as he was dragged toward the wall, expecting to bang his nose against the beige wallboard, but there was no impact; instead he passed *through* the wall, into a place he had never seen before.

It wasn't the tiled interior of the ladies' room, nor any of the familiar offices; it was not a room that belonged in an office building at all. In fact, he wasn't sure it was actually a *room*. It was a *space*, with black, featureless walls and floor.

And ceiling, on which he bumped his head. Instinctively, he ducked and looked up.

The ceiling was completely, utterly black, and mere inches away, even now that he was stooping. He turned, though, and saw that Anna was standing upright without any difficulty; that blank, dark ceiling was a few inches above her head.

"I hadn't thought of that," she said, looking up at him and seeing how he was crouched. "I'll want to raise that if you're going to come in here much."

"Come in *where*?" he asked. "Where *are* we? Is this a secret room of some sort?"

"Sort of," she said, taking his hand and leading him forward.

The black room was not empty, he saw. There was a big overstuffed chair, worn and battered, next to a small table piled with paperbacks. A battery-powered camp lantern was perched on a cheap set of shelves, the sort of étagère you could buy at Target or Wal-Mart and assemble at home. The shelves also held a few cardboard boxes and framed photos, as well as more books. A large, ragged old teddy bear sat on a kitchen stool beside the shelves. The entire place had something of the feel of a college dorm room, furnished as cheaply as possible, with no concern for esthetics, but still comfortable.

These were all in an area maybe a dozen feet on a side, but he had the feeling the place was considerably larger than that. The completely featureless black walls were effectively invisible, so it was impossible to judge the size accurately. The little bunch of gently-lit furniture seemed to be floating in an empty, infinite void.

"Have a seat," Anna said, gesturing at the chair. For herself, she picked up the teddy bear and settled on the stool.

Gary settled onto the upholstery and looked around, baffled. At least when he was seated he didn't need to worry about hitting his head.

"What *is* this place?"

"This is my *secret* place, Gary," Anna replied. "It's where I go when I want to be alone, or to get away from something. Or someone." She gazed at him expectantly.

He still did not grasp the situation. "Here in our office?" he asked.

The look she gave him was not flattering. "No. We aren't in the office building. We aren't *anywhere*. It's my own special place."

"I don't understand. And what does this have to do with you showing up early?"

She sighed. "We came in over there," she said, pointing. "There's an opening there that comes out next to the fourteenth-floor ladies' room." Then she turned and pointed in another direction. "And over *there* is an opening that comes out in my apartment, in the corridor that connects my bedroom and the living room. So I can get from one place to the other in about two minutes, and I never need to go out in the rain or snow to get to work. It saves on gas or bus fare, too."

"But...how? How is this possible?"

She shrugged. "I don't know. It's just something I can do. I found it when I was five, when I was a little girl in Pyongyang. My father had done something suspicious, and the police took him in for questioning, and my mother thought they might come for us, too, so she hid me in a closet. She kept me hidden there for about two days – just me, alone in the dark, with nothing to do and scared half to death that those men might come and take me away, so I tried *very, very hard* to be somewhere else, where they could never, ever find me.

"And then I *was.* I was in a little place that wasn't much bigger than I was, but it felt warm and safe, so I just stayed in there – in *here*. But then I got worried about my mother, so I came back out and peeked out to make sure she was still there. I found out I could go in and out any time I wanted – I could just crawl through the back of the closet as if it wasn't even there, just the way we came through the wall, and could come back out the same way. I could make the opening bigger, and it would *stay* bigger, and I could push back the walls and ceiling in here and make *it* bigger. I could bring things in and out."

"You found all this out in two days?"

"No, I don't...well, I don't remember for sure. It was a long time ago. But we lived in that same apartment for almost another year, and I came here lots of times when I wanted to feel safe, or when my mother told me to hide. But then they took my father away again, and this time we knew he wouldn't be coming back, so my mother and I left, and we got to the border and escaped into China, and honestly I don't really know most of what we did or where we went, because I was only six and most of the time the people around us weren't speaking Korean and I hadn't learned any Chinese or English yet." She picked up the teddy bear and held it out. "There was one place where some people took care of us, and let us sleep in a real bed, and a nice lady who had the lightest hair I had ever seen up to then gave me this bear, and I've kept it ever since, everywhere I went. It's my comfort bear. Her name is Gom." She looked at Gary expectantly.

"But we didn't get here from a closet in North Korea."

"No, of course not!" She set the bear back on her lap with an expression of mild disappointment. "I was getting to that. That first night in China I was scared again, and I found out that I could still get into my secret place – I could make *another* door, just like in the closet, and there I was. I could go back out into the closet in Pyongyang, or come out in the house in China; then my secret place had *two* doors." She waved a hand. "Now it has at least a dozen. I can make a new one any time I want, though it takes a few minutes. I brought in the furniture, and the lantern – it's much nicer now. And bigger; I've pushed the walls back a lot. I smoothed out the floor, too." She smiled. "If I'm going to bring in people as tall as you, though, I guess I need to push the ceiling up."

He looked around, amazed. "So can you just step out *anywhere*?"

"No, I can only make new doors coming *in*. I can go out any door I've already made, but I can't make new ones from inside."

"Who else knows about it? Are there *other* people who can do this?"

"I don't know of anyone else, but how would I? I told my mother about it, and some of the people who helped us get from China to America, and some of my friends when I was little, but no one ever believed me. I even brought one of my friends in here when I was about ten, but she thought it was a trick and *still* didn't believe it was real. I didn't have any furniture in here back then, I used a flashlight so we could see, but of course there wasn't anything *to* see. So she thought I was playing a joke on her and she got mad at me and we stopped playing together after that. She tried to get in without me pulling her, and she couldn't do it, and that got her even angrier. I think she was mostly mad that she couldn't figure out how I did it."

"It probably scared her," Gary said. "It scares *me*, a little."

"Maybe. But why be scared? It's my *safe* place!"

"But it's not *my* safe place. This is all a lot to take in!"

"But you're here with *me*. I trusted you enough to tell you the truth and bring you here, Gary. I've never done that before, not since Emily when I was ten."

"Well, you had to explain, after you appeared like that." He looked around again. "So you just came through here?"

"Yes. I thought you'd already be out on the sidewalk waiting for me, so I could come this way and sneak out behind you and go around the block to meet you. But you were running late because of the printer, and you caught me." She grimaced. "I could have made up a story, but I...well, you're special. So here we are."

"Are you sure we can get out again?"

She laughed. "I've been coming here since I was five, and I've never had any trouble getting out."

"But can you get *me* out?

"Sure! I got Emily out. I bring stuff in and out all the time; why would you be any different?"

"I don't know, this is all..." He let his voice trail off.

She looked down at Gom, then set the bear on a nearby shelf. "Well, now you've seen it, shall we go? I assume you have your car in the underground garage, so we'll go back out through the office."

"Wait – where else could we come out?"

"Well, my apartment, but I don't...I'm not ready for that. I have a door near some of my favorite shops downtown, and one at my mother's house, and some others. I suppose I could even go to the farmhouse in Liaoning, or the closet in Pyongyang, if they're still there, but I haven't been back to either of those since I was little." She shuddered. "Why would I *want* to?"

Gary found himself starting to imagine reasons she might want to, but he put that aside. "What about that shopping one? Could you show me that, just so I can see how it works?"

"I guess." She slid off the stool. "Take my hand and follow me."

He rose from the chair and took her hand, keeping his head down to not bump the black ceiling, and let her lead him across the black floor to a black wall that looked just like all the others. She stretched out a hand, and tugged at his arm so that he stumbled....

And they were on a street, midway between streetlights, and he recognized it as Michigan Avenue, halfway across the city from the office.

"Oh," he said, straightening up as she released her hold. "Wow." He tried to take it all in. He put a hand on the wall behind them and felt only stone.

After a few seconds Anna asked, "Should we go back for your car now?"

He took a few steps away from her, staring at the stores and the lights and the cars. "Wow," he said again.

"Gary, I didn't come here to go shopping," she said, wrapping her coat more tightly around herself.

"I know, but...it worked!" He looked up at the touch of a raindrop; the skies had clouded over, and it was beginning to sprinkle. "We're here, across town!"

"That's right. Can we go back now? I want to get home."

He turned to look at her, and realized she looked unhappy, though he did not quite grasp why. "Sure, of course," he said. "How does it work?"

"I showed you," she said. "Come here." She held out a hand.

He took it, and let her pull him up to the blank limestone wall – and *through* it, back to the black space.

He stumbled as he hit his head on the ceiling, then ducked. She let go of his hand. He looked at the chair and the stool and the shelves, then turned and reached out.

His hand hit the wall. It was absolutely solid and unyielding, but he could not *feel* anything; there was no texture at all, no temperature. It wasn't warm, or cool, or smooth, or rough, it was just solid – the only way he could tell it was there was that his hand stopped and would not go through it.

"This place is amazing," he said. He looked up, trying to see where the wall joined the ceiling. There was no visible distinction; it was all just blackness.

"It is, isn't it?" He thought she smiled again, though it was hard to see her face; her back was to the lantern that provided the only light.

"So it isn't really anywhere at all?" he said. "You'd be safe in here no matter what was happening outside, wouldn't you?"

"That's right."

"So if there was an earthquake, or a hurricane, or even a nuclear war, you could just come in here until it was over."

She tilted her head; he could no longer read her expression at all in the limited illumination. "I guess so," she said.

"You could bring friends in here to keep them safe."

"I...I suppose," she said. "But it's a *private* place. I don't want other people to know about it."

"Oh, but think about it! You could bring people through to get them out of a disaster area – bring them in from wherever they are, then take them back out somewhere safe." He looked around at the sparse furnishing. "You could go on vacation somewhere, then make an opening there, and be back home in five minute – no more airfare! You could spend every weekend at the beach!"

She did not reply.

He wandered back to the area around the chair, and looked at the lantern. "Could you run electricity in here? What happens if the battery dies?"

"If the battery dies, it gets dark. It's happened. I can find my way out without it. I tried running an extension cord in once, as an experiment, but current wouldn't flow through it, and when I let go of it, it got cut in half – half in here, and half in my apartment, cut apart as if I'd snipped it with a pair of scissors. Nothing can go through any of the doors unless I'm holding it."

"But anything you can carry can go in and out?"

"Well, yeah."

He gestured wildly. "Then...could you make an opening inside a store, or a bank? You could step through in the middle of the night and just take whatever you want!"

"I'm not a thief," Anna said, her tone flat.

"No, no, of course you aren't," he replied hurriedly. "But there are so many possibilities! You could carry things for people, run a courier service."

"I'd need to open a lot more doors to do that," she said. "And I'd need to carry every package myself."

"That's true, or...maybe you could open these doors in cities all over the world, so you'd be able to carry things from China or London without spending fourteen hours on a plane. Or, or you could volunteer as one of Elon Musk's Martian colonists, and after you land on Mars you could open a door *there*, and instead of two years in a cramped spaceship you could come back home in two *minutes*!"

"Gary," she said, "this is my private place. *My* place. It's not for Elon Musk or bank robbers or refugees."

"But it's got so many possibilities!"

She took his arm. "Let's get you back to your car," she said. "It's getting late."

He let her drag him away from the chair, and a moment later they were in the fourteenth-floor corridor, next to the ladies' room. He turned to stare at the blank wall. "You can't *see* anything," he said.

"No, you can't," she agreed, releasing her grip. "Thank you for dinner, Gary. It was a lovely meal." Then she took a step back, and was gone. He was alone in the corridor.

He studied the wall, running his hands over the wallpaper, but he could not detect any sign of an opening. There were no edges he could see or feel, no softness or give.

He spent ten minutes at his investigations, then finally stepped back, took a final look, and headed for the elevator.

He did not hear from Anna again that night; she did not call or text. He did not hear anything Sunday, either. Several times he debated calling her, but he always decided against it. He didn't know what he could say about the astonishing experiences they had had together – though they had not astonished Anna; she was used to her abilities.

Sometimes he wondered if perhaps he had dreamed the whole thing, but he remembered it so clearly that he knew he hadn't.

Monday he arrived at work early, and waited by the elevator for twenty minutes for her to come in – and then realized that was stupid. He turned and headed up the corridor.

She was already in the workroom, talking to Janice the social media guru. She glanced up when he entered, then continued her conversation with Janice. He waited.

Before he had a chance to say anything to Anna, though, his boss appeared in the doorway. "Have you seen...oh, there you are! Do you have those contracts?"

Reluctantly, Gary allowed himself to be led away to his own office to do his job.

It was almost 11:00 by the time he finally got an opportunity to talk to her, catching her in the corridor.

"Anna!" he called.

She ignored him.

"*Anna!*" he called, more loudly.

She stopped, and waited for him to come around to face her.

"Hi," he said. "I'm sorry I didn't call yesterday."

"It's all right," she said.

"I didn't know what to say. What you showed me Saturday was just so *amazing*! There's so much potential!"

"I don't know what you're talking about," she said, and started to walk away.

"No, wait!" He followed and grabbed her arm.

She stopped, looked down at his hand, and said quietly, "Let go of me."

He released his hold, a little hurt by her coldness. "I'm sorry," he said. "I was just...your secret place is..."

She looked him in the eye. "What secret place?"

He was momentarily speechless, but when she started to turn away again he said, "The one you showed me after dinner on Saturday!"

"I don't know what you're talking about."

"Anna, wait!" The possibility that he had dreamed the entire thing occurred to him again, and again he dismissed it. He didn't have dreams like that. He ran after her and said, "We had a dinner date Saturday, right?"

"Of course we did. It was a lovely meal."

"And afterward you showed me...we..."

"Afterward I went *home*, Gary, and I assume you did, too."

"But you showed me something, this place..." He pointed down the corridor toward the ladies' room.

"I don't know what you're talking about," she repeated.

"Look, I didn't *imagine* it!" he said, his voice rising. "You showed me this incredible thing you can do."

She flushed. "If you're implying I know some secret Asian sex technique you never saw before, Gary Brannon, then you're *definitely* imagining it. I just went home after dinner. You didn't even drive me there." She spoke at a normal volume.

"No, I don't mean anything like that!" he said. "You *showed* me...!"

"I didn't show you *anything*, Mr. Brannon. Now, if you don't mind, I have work to do." She marched back to the workroom, leaving him in the passageway.

He realized that half a dozen other people were staring at him; he hesitated, realized anything he might say would only make it worse, and then retreated to his office.

He tried to work, but could not concentrate. Finally he stopped pretending he could think about anything else and wrote her an e-mail, being very, very careful to send it only to her account.

"Anna," he wrote, "I'm sorry if I offended you. I'm not sure what I did, but whatever it was, I apologize."

He was not sure that was the best way to start, but he didn't want to take time to revise it. He continued, "That place you showed me is a miracle, and it could be worth a fortune. I don't think you understand how important it could be, for you and really, for all of us. If scientists studied it and learned to duplicate it, it could change the world! You could be rich and famous. Or even if it can't be duplicated, there are so many ways it could be used! It could be so much more than just your hiding place and personal shortcut. Please, let me discuss some of my ideas with you."

He signed it "Gary" and clicked SEND.

He waited, but there was no response. Finally he sighed and went back to his own duties, promising himself he would catch her at lunch or after work.

He watched for her in the corridor around lunchtime, but did not see her; eventually he gave up and went for his own meal.

At the end of the day he went out to the corridor and waited. He worried that she might have left early, but he did not see a viable alternative. He positioned himself near the wall where her "door" was, hoping she hadn't decided to take the bus to avoid him.

He was about to give up when the door to the ladies' room opened, and Anna stepped out.

"Anna!" he called, positioning himself in front of where he thought the door was, and hoping he had remembered the location correctly.

She glared at him, then started past him, headed for the elevator lobby.

"Come on, Anna," he said, grabbing her arm as she tried to pass. "Stop playing games. I know what I saw on Saturday, and we need to talk about it."

She tried to pull her arm free, but he held on. "No, we do *not* need to talk about it. Let me go."

"Please, Anna! This ability of yours is important! All the things you could do with it – did you read my e-mail?"

"I read it," she said. She stopped struggling, and faced him, clearly trying to stay calm. "It's not important to *me* what *you* want to do with it. Gary, do you think I haven't thought of all those things? I've been able to do this since I was *five.* Do you really think I didn't experiment when I was a teenager? Do you think I haven't read up on everything that might help explain it? Do you really think I'm that *stupid*?"

"Uh..." His grip loosened, but then he tightened it again.

"Yes, I have a door on a beach in the Bahamas. Yes, I have a door in New York, and a door in Boston, and a door in New Orleans I use to go to Mardi Gras every year. I have a door in Disneyland, and one in Vail, and a couple in California. I am the *queen* of the one-way ticket, Gary – but you never even *asked*, you just assumed that because I'm a little Korean girl five years younger than you and a couple of levels lower on the corporate ladder that I hadn't thought of any of that.

"Maybe I just didn't want to *tell* you, did *you* ever think of *that*?"

He stammered something, but before he could put together a coherent response she continued.

"As for letting some damned doctors study me and poke around in my brain, does that sound like fun to you? Like something *you'd* want to do, for the greater good of society? Because it doesn't sound like anything *I* want to do."

"I don't..."

"I tried to share a very important and private part of my life with you, Gary," she told him, "and all you could talk about was finding ways to exploit it – to exploit *me*. I told you about hiding in a closet for two days, and my father being taken away, and you never tried to comfort me or ask what happened to him – not that we ever found out, but you should have *asked*. I showed you Gom and told you where she came from, and you didn't say a word about her. My dearest, oldest possession, and you never so much as looked at her. You never said a word about *me* at all – all you would talk about was my private place, and it was all about what we could *do* with it. You never looked at the pictures I'd put there, never asked what any of it meant to me. You never said anything about Emily when I told you about bringing her in. You never paid any attention to *me*; you only wanted to know more about the place. You just wanted to *use* it. Well, forget it, Gary! It's *mine*! You tell anyone you like, and they'll just think you're crazy. I know you're not crazy, but you *are* stupid and inconsiderate. Good night and good-bye!" She pulled her arm free and stepped toward the wall.

But he was not about to let her get away that easily. He grabbed her again, ducked his head, and let himself be pulled through the wall into that cozy black void.

"Let go of me!" she said, trying to twist free.

"No," he said, tightening his hold. "Not yet, not in here – you could leave me stuck in here."

She stopped struggling. "And give it up myself? Why would I do *that*?"

"It wouldn't be forever; you could just wait until I died of thirst."

"You think I'd *do* that?"

"I don't *know* what you'd do!" he exclaimed. "That's why I want to talk about this place, and what you do with it!"

"If you're trying to convince me to cooperate with you about *anything*, you aren't going about it very well."

"You won't let me do it any other way! I *tried* to talk to you nicely, and you wouldn't listen!"

"Maybe you should have taken the hint!"

"Maybe you should have talked to me! I'm only trying to help you."

"I don't *want* your help, and I don't need it. None of the things I can do, none of the places I can go, are any of your business, Gary. This thing I have is mine, and you don't get to tell me what to do with it."

"But you don't have any right to keep it to yourself!"

"Why *not*? It's part of me!"

"Look, can we go somewhere else to talk about this stuff, about you keeping it private? Somewhere back in the real world?"

She studied his face for a moment, then said, "All right. We can go to my apartment."

"Fine. Lead the way."

She did, guiding him across the space and around behind the chair. He frowned.

"This isn't where you pointed when we were in here before," he said.

"No, it isn't," she agreed, stepping into the blackness.

And then they were somewhere else, and she led him forward out of a closet into a drab, empty apartment lit only by faint twilight.

Startled, he looked around. The floor was bare concrete, the walls roughly finished. "This is your apartment?" he said.

"Let go of my arm," she said.

"It doesn't look right."

"*Let go of my arm*!" She began tugging again.

Puzzled, he released his hold. "Where *are* we?"

"My apartment," Anna replied. "The one I lived in when I was five."

Stunned, he whirled to face the nearest window. "In *Korea*?"

"See for yourself," she said.

He pulled aside the ragged remains of a yellow curtain and looked out on an unfamiliar city-scape lit by the first glow of dawn, the skyline dominated by a strange triangular building that he thought must be a hundred stories high. "We're in Korea?" he exclaimed.

"*North* Korea," she said. "The People's Democratic Republic of Korea. I don't suppose you speak any Korean, or have your passport with you?"

In a sudden panic he turned and tried to grab her again, but she dove into the closet, closing the door behind her before he could catch her.

He tugged at the doorknob, but she held the door closed.

"Gary," she said from the closet, "this is your last chance to apologize and back down. I won't leave you to die in my own private place, but if you won't give up your obsession with *using* me, I can leave you *here*."

"Apologize? Obsession? But don't you see, Anna, what your... your place means? It only took us five seconds to get here, not a fourteen-hour flight!"

He thought he might have heard a sigh. "That's still all you have to say?"

"*We could be rich*!"

"We?" There was a brief pause, and he thought perhaps she was coming to her senses, but then she said, "Goodbye, Gary."

Suddenly the knob turned freely in his hand. He opened the door, but she was gone. He stared, unable to believe she would really desert him, could really leave him here. He waited a few seconds for her to reappear, to laugh at the joke, but the closet stood dark and empty, and his nerve broke.

"Anna!" he screamed, as he pounded on the unyielding back wall of the closet. "*Anna!*"

In the street below the window, two policemen looked up at the sound.

Sorcery of the Heart

Some years back I created a fantasy setting called the Bound Lands specifically designed for romance and swashbuckling adventure. I plotted out more than a dozen stories set there, including two novels that made it into print – ***A Young Man Without Magic*** *and* ***Above His Proper Station.*** *A couple of shorter stories were written for the "Lace and Blade" anthology series, including this one.*

Merilsa Albier studied her surroundings as she stepped into Lord Ashur's dining hall, from the gilded crown moldings to the polished marble floor tiles, from the crystal chandeliers to the velvet curtains that hid the far end of the room. For a town as small as Posieron, the burgrave's manor house was quite impressive.

The gathering being held there was rather less so. There were only about a score of guests. Lord Ashur was handsome and fit enough for a man well into middle age, and dressed himself as well as he did his home, but his wife, Lady Kieras, wore a surprisingly plain gown and clearly enjoyed the pleasures of the table rather more than she should. The rest of the company tended toward clothes several years out of fashion, and none of them seemed particularly interesting...

Or rather, almost none. One young man whose well-tailored coat was merely in last year's style, rather than a fashion from Merilsa's childhood, caught her eye; he was tall and broad-shouldered, his eyes large and dark. He also seemed to be looking directly at her.

"This is my daughter Merilsa, my lord," her mother said, pulling Merilsa forward and startling her from her thoughts. Merilsa recovered quickly, and curtseyed to the burgrave.

"I believe we have met before, years ago, when last you visited," Lord Ashur said, nodding. "She was a delightful little girl, and I see she has only gained in charm now that she is a lovely young woman. Merilsa Albier, allow me to introduce my nephew, Lord Dieryn Cabriet, who is newly arrived in our humble town."

Lord Dieryn proved to be the very man Merilsa had been watching; as he stepped forward he smiled broadly, a warm and welcoming smile. He took her hand and held her fingers to his lips, his eyes still locked on her own. "A pleasure, to be sure, Mistress Albier."

A small thrill ran through her at his touch, and she found herself staring into those deep, dark eyes. She felt her mouth start to fall open, and she caught herself.

"The pleasure is mine, my lord," she said, looking down.

Just then a footman whispered in the burgrave's ear, and he nodded. The footman hurried away, and Lord Ashur raised his hands.

"My dear friends!" he called to the little crowd. "I am so glad you could all attend, and I hope you will enjoy your evening with us. I am informed that our musicians are ready to begin, so those who choose to do so are invited to dance a few rounds before we dine. You will see we have cleared a space."

Indeed, as the burgrave spoke curtains that Merilsa had taken as the far end of the room were being drawn back, revealing not the wall she had assumed to be there, but a dance floor, and a stage where a quartet was beginning a gentle tune. To her surprise she recognized the cittern player as a young man she had encountered before, a traveling musician by the name of Volber Taraz; they had met last year in a village called Clemin, where she and her mother had gone to purchase a particularly interesting relic of the Old Empire that a farmer's plow had turned up. He had seemed interested in her, but she had ignored him. She had never expected to see him again, and had not found him particularly appealing. He looked up from his instrument and seemed to be staring right at her – perhaps he was *still* interested.

The other musicians were strangers. The melody they were playing was familiar, though – one of those gloomy ballads that mountain people seemed so very fond of.

Then Lord Dieryn was beside her again, saying, "I understand that their next tune will be a little more lively. Would you consider joining me in a dance?"

She looked up at him, past the lace collar of last year's jacket to those delicious eyes, and smiled. "I would be honored, my lord." She gave him her hand once more, and allowed him to lead her past the dinner table to the dance floor, where it was less than a minute before the musicians concluded their mournful melody and burst into a much more lively tune. Lord Dieryn whirled Merilsa out onto the floor, her skirts flying.

He was, she discovered, an excellent dancer. As four or five other couples joined them Merilsa found herself enjoying herself more than she had ever expected. Her mother had dragged her to this dinner party because Lord Ashur, who claimed to have some interesting artifacts he wanted to sell, had invited them both, and one could not offend someone with whom one hoped to do business, but Merilsa had anticipated a dreary evening of eating overcooked, under-seasoned food while listening to strangers gossip about people she had never heard of. To find herself instead dancing in the strong arms of a handsome young nobleman was a marvelous surprise. She looked up at his face as they made the next turn and saw him smiling gently, his eyes fixed on her own.

The song ended, and Lord Dieryn asked, "Another?"

Merilsa nodded, not trusting herself to speak. Her heart was racing, and she did not think it was merely from the exertions of the dance.

But for the third number they were separated; a woman a few years older than Merilsa insisted on Lord Dieryn's attention, and Merilsa found herself in the arms of an eager young fellow who managed to not step on her feet, but for whose dancing ability little more good could be said.

The fourth dance found them with new partners once again, but before the fifth tune the burgrave announced, "Our last dance, good people, for my cooks tell me dinner is almost ready to be served!"

At that, Lord Dieryn crossed the dance floor with a speed and determination that verged on rudeness and claimed Merilsa once more. He swept her around the room with a grace and vigor that exhilarated her, and she spent the entire time gazing into his eyes. She knew that nothing good could come of any mutual interest between a lord and a commoner, but she told herself she could still enjoy the moment, even if it would not lead anywhere.

When the music ended Dieryn kissed her hand and slipped wordlessly away while the others were still applauding the musicians; his sudden departure startled Merilsa. Had she done something to offend him? She turned to see him speaking to Lord Ashur, who was nodding and smiling. She wondered what that was about. Servants were bustling about the dinner table, making final preparations, and Dieryn was saying something to one of these attendants.

But then a bell chimed, and the burgrave announced, "Please find your places, dear friends, and let us eat!"

A moment later the guests were sorting themselves out according to place-cards on the table, and Merilsa was startled to find herself well up toward the head, while her mother was seated down near the foot. She had assumed they would be near one another.

Then Lord Dieryn was holding her chair for her; she sat down, and saw that his name was on the card to her left.

"You rearranged the place-cards!" she said, as he settled into his own place.

"Of course," he said. "Or rather, I asked one of the footmen to see to it. With my uncle's blessing, I hasten to add. I could not pass up an opportunity to see if you are as delightful a dinner companion as you are a dance partner."

She blushed. Before she could compose herself sufficiently to reply, the first course arrived.

Through the entire meal Lord Dieryn seemed only interested in speaking with her; he ignored his aunt, who was seated to his left. Lady Kieras did not seem very upset about this.

The man to Merilsa's right seemed content to focus his attention on the food; she did not even get his name.

On the other hand, she heard a great deal about Lord Dieryn's background – how he was the fourth son of the burgrave of Balvoran, and as a fourth son entirely unneeded in his home town. Consequently he had done a good deal of traveling, and when he had returned home last season, expecting to remain there for a time, his mother had instead sent him to stay with her brother in Posieron, out of the way of his father and older brothers, until he decided what he wanted to do with his life. He suspected that she had thought he would find Posieron, small and backward as it was, so boring that he would quickly decide on a career of some sort simply to escape the dreary little town.

Merilsa also explained her own history – how the family had been trading in art and antiquities in Kallai, selling to Walasian and Quandish alike, for generations, and how her father had been crippled when a runaway coach had crushed his leg so badly that even the margrave's sorcery could not heal it. That had forced her mother to take over the traveling necessary to their business, and Merilsa was being dragged along to teach her the details she would need to know when she, as the only child, inherited their gallery.

She did not mention her mother's ulterior purpose. Merilsa knew that her parents wanted her to find a suitable husband somewhere who could take over the business and provide them with grandchildren to carry on the line. She had already rejected virtually every possible suitor in their native Kallai, but the empire was full of eligible young men.

Up until now, while she had no particular objection to marriage and children in theory, she had never found anyone who made the prospect appealing. The idea of settling down somewhere with Lord Dieryn, though, definitely had its charms.

But she knew that was ridiculous. He was a noble of the Walasian Empire, which is to say a sorcerer, while she was a commoner who could no more work a spell than she could stop the sun in the sky.

She knew her mother had brought her to the burgrave's dinner party in hopes of finding a potential husband, and while there were very few candidates to begin with, she felt a little guilty that she was spending her time here with a man who she knew would never marry her. Sorcerers married sorceresses, to keep the magic in their blood concentrated from one generation to the next. Oh, a nobleman might keep a commoner as a mistress, but *marriage* was forbidden, by custom if not law, and as the sole heir to her parents' considerable wealth she was not in a position to settle for being a sorcerer's plaything.

But then she looked into Lord Dieryn's eyes, listened to his voice, and she did not really care about any missed marital opportunities. Whatever the future might hold right now she did not want to be anywhere other than at his side, sharing his past and her own, enjoying the sight and smell of him, strong and masculine. Whenever he smiled – which he did often – she felt a warmth in her belly that had nothing to do with the food they were eating.

When the final course was served the musicians began playing quietly again. Lord Dieryn glanced at them.

"They play well, but I hope they will not make conversation difficult," he remarked. "I would rather hear your voice than the finest musician."

"Oh, I think they can control themselves," Merilsa replied. "I know the cittern player, and I'm sure he'll be considerate."

"You know him?" Dieryn asked, startled.

"Why, yes," she said. "Or at any rate, we have met. His name is Volber Taraz. He travels, as do I, and this is not the first time our paths have crossed."

"Really?" Dieryn glanced at the little stage. "Do you know the other three musicians, as well?"

"I do not recognize them."

Lord Dieryn considered this, staring intently at the quartet for a moment – particularly at the cittern player. He frowned. Then he said, "When we finish our meal, let us go speak to them, and see whether they remember you – though how anyone could forget *you* I cannot imagine."

That seemed rather pointless to Merilsa, but she said, "If you like."

A quarter hour later, as the musicians were packing up and most of the guests were moving into the drawing room, Merilsa followed Lord Dieryn over to the stage. The cittern player looked up from the leather case that now held his instrument. "My lord," he said. "Mistress Albier. Can I help you?"

"Master... Tazar, is it?" Dieryn began.

"Taraz," Merilsa corrected him.

"Taraz, my lord," the musician confirmed. "Volber Taraz."

"Ah, my apologies. I understand you know Mistress Albier?"

The musician glanced at her, and Merilsa did not like the look in his eye – she thought he was still interested in her, and it appeared a more predatory interest than a companionable one. "We have met, my lord."

"And the rest of you?"

"I think I saw her in Clemin," the rebec player said. "We did not speak."

The others said nothing.

"Ah," Dieryn said, his eyes fixed on the cittern player. "And is it merely a coincidence, Master Taraz, that you and she meet once again, here in my uncle's house?"

The other three musicians looked baffled. "What else might it be, my lord?" Volber asked.

"You did not come here to see her?"

"Until you led her out onto the dance floor, my lord, I had no idea she was in Posieron."

"You look familiar; have *we* met before?"

"I do not recall any previous encounters, my lord."

Lord Dieryn nodded, relaxing. "Then I am sorry to have troubled you. Thank you for an evening of fine music!" With that he passed Volber a guilder, then turned away, leaving the musicians to finish packing.

Still confused, Merilsa accompanied him, but before they reached the drawing room door she asked, "My lord, why did you do that?"

"Hm? Oh, I was concerned for your safety, my dear. I feared that man might be following you, for reasons best not dwelt upon. And he *does* look oddly familiar, though I can't imagine where I might have seen him before."

"Well, if he *were* such a scoundrel as you fear, which I do not believe him to be, would he answer you truthfully?"

"In fact, he would," Dieryn replied, as he stepped aside to let Merilsa precede him into the drawing room. "You forget, I am a sorcerer – not a great or notable one, but good enough to cast a simple binding upon an unprepared and unsuspecting commoner, *compelling* him to answer my questions truthfully."

"You did that?" she asked, startled.

"I did, though it was harder than I expected. I hope you don't mind; I had only your own safety in mind."

"Of course. I'm flattered."

In truth, though, she was somewhat disturbed by the incident. Not only did it serve as a reminder that she and Dieryn came from very different parts of Walasian society, but it seemed presumptuous, or at least rude, to cast a spell upon someone so casually without any warning or permission.

But then, Dieryn was a nobleman, and Volber merely a wandering musician. It was certainly within the rights of Dieryn's class to use magic in such a fashion.

Then they were in the drawing room, where she was immediately swept up in conversation – Lord Ashur inquired how she had enjoyed their supper, and her mother made a jest about she had obviously enjoyed the company. Merilsa blushed as Lord Dieryn spoke up in her defense.

The remainder of the evening passed pleasantly enough; Dieryn remained close at hand, but did not dominate her attention as completely as he had at the table. It was almost midnight when at last the two women departed; a servant brought them their shawls, and another carried a lantern to light them safely back to their inn.

Lord Dieryn had kissed her hand yet again when saying good night, but had taken no other liberties nor made any suggestions, improper or otherwise.

Back at the inn, after they had undressed, Merilsa lay on her narrow bed in her shift, reviewing the evening. Lord Dieryn was so very charming! But she could have no future with him; he was a sorcerer, and she was a commoner. She wondered why he had bothered to spend the entire time with her. True, there had hardly been a surplus of presentable young women, but his attentions had perhaps still been a bit much. Did he think she would succumb to his unquestionable charms and wind up in his bed, despite the impossibility of marriage? The idea was not without its appeal, she could not deny that, but she dared not yield to such temptation. The risks were too great.

Though, she reminded herself, she had heard that sorcery could eliminate some of those risks. It was said that no sorceress ever bore a child unwillingly; their magic granted them control over conception. Indeed, it was quite unusual that Dieryn was a fourth son; peasants might burden themselves with a dozen children, but Merilsa had never before heard of a noble family with more than three. Most sorceresses did not care to undertake the risks and burdens of pregnancy more often than that, and it seemed unlikely that sorcerers were any less prone to lust than commoners. In fact, the more salacious stories she had heard implied that quite the opposite was true – there were rumors that sorcerers held secret orgies as part of their magical rites.

If Dieryn could ensure that a brief liaison would not result in either disease or pregnancy...

Well, that made it even more tempting, but she would still resist.

For one thing, that incident with the musicians helped to discourage any romantic fantasies; a man who could so casually bind another's will was not entirely to be trusted.

If, indeed, he really *had* enchanted Volber. She had only his word for it.

Thinking about Dieryn made it hard to sleep, and she lay awake for at least an hour before finally managing to put him out of her mind and doze off.

She did not sleep as late as she had expected, so her mood was not the best when she and came down to the inn's common room for breakfast. Her mother had left a note saying that she had gone to the burgrave's manor to discuss business, leaving Merilsa to her own devices.

Merilsa hoped that warm food and a cup of tea would help her disposition. She was seated at a table and just starting on a buckwheat cake when someone called her name. She looked up to find Volber standing nearby.

"Might I join you, Mistress Albier?" he asked.

She looked at him and seriously considered saying "no," but there was no reason to be rude. "If you wish," she said. She added, "Though I doubt I will be pleasant company just now."

"Thank you," Volber said, taking the chair directly across from her.

She ate another bite of buckwheat cake, took a sip of tea, then asked, "Did you wish to speak to me?"

"I did," the musician said. "First, I must ask you – do you plan to see Lord Dieryn again?"

"I fail to see how that is any concern of yours."

"Then I will assume that the answer is yes. I fear, Mistress Albier, that he has ensorcelled you."

She blinked, and put down her mug. "What are you talking about?"

"I believe that he has placed a spell upon you, binding you to him."

"And on what do you base this bizarre theory?"

"On three things, Mistress. On his behavior last night, most particularly on that peculiar moment when he came to speak to me, to determine whether I had any claim upon you; on your own behavior, when you devoted every instant of your attention to him, ignoring your host, your own mother, and everyone else at the party; and most importantly, I thought I sensed magic when he spoke to me."

"*Sensed* it? How?"

Volber shrugged. "They say that music is akin to magic in some respects; perhaps that explains my sensitivity to it. I can sometimes feel when magic is present."

"I think you misjudge the situation," Merilsa said. "That I should take an interest in a handsome young man, and he take an interest in me, can surely be explained without resorting to sorcery. As for detecting magic in use, yes, I believe you did sense it, though I had never before heard that musicians were any more sensitive to it than the rest of us. Lord Dieryn told me later that he had enchanted *you*, so that you could not lie to him. He claims he thought you might be pursuing me from town to town with some ill intent."

"Did he?" The musician frowned, and seemed to hesitate. "Perhaps his concern was genuine, and I have troubled you needlessly. I assure you, Mistress, that we traveling musicians are nowhere near such scoundrels as we are often portrayed, and I had no designs on you; I thought it a pleasant coincidence to see you last night, and nothing more."

"I never doubted it, Master Taraz."

For a moment the musician said nothing, but at last he responded, "Then I will leave you to your own interests, but I do ask, Mistress, that should you find yourself involved any further with Lord Dieryn, you consider the possibility of sorcerous influence."

"I appreciate your concern."

With that, Volber rose, tipped his hat, and departed.

Merilsa, bemused by the encounter, watched him go. To have two young men taking such an uninvited interest in protecting her from one another was quite unexpected, and unlike anything she had previously experienced. She did not know what to make of it.

She remembered, though, how thoroughly she had focused her attentions on Lord Dieryn the night before. Yes, he was a very personable young man, and there had been no others remotely as appealing at the party, but perhaps there *was* something more than natural attraction at work.

But even if that were true, she could not see that any harm was done. After all, here she was, unscathed by the experience, with no expectation of seeing Lord Dieryn again, nor any intention of inflicting herself upon him further, despite what the musician had thought. She felt some mild disappointment at that – or really, now that she gave it some consideration, perhaps not all that mild – but she had enough common sense to know that there was no future in any relationship with him. That hardly seemed like any sort of meaningful enchantment. What was she to do, go knock on the burgrave's door and demand to see his nephew? Perhaps if she were truly under a spell she would do exactly that, but she was not, in fact, so out of touch with common decorum.

She finished her breakfast, brushed any lingering crumbs from her dress, then rose, with the intention of making her way back to her room to await her mother's return. She had just set her foot upon the first stair when the door of the inn burst open and Lord Dieryn appeared. She turned to stare at him.

"Mistress Albier!" he called. "I am delighted to have found you!"

"My lord?" she said, taken aback. She still had one foot on the bottom stair, the other on the floor.

"My uncle and your mother have just completed their negotiations, so I knew you would be leaving soon, and I realized that I could not bear to let you go."

"Lord Dieryn, what are you talking about?"

"Mistress Albier, I think I have fallen in love with you. All night I could think of nothing else; when I did sleep, I dreamed of you."

She felt her cheeks redden. "My lord, are you mocking me?"

"No! By the Father and the Mother, I mean every word!"

This was mad, Merilsa thought. "May I remind you, my lord, that I am a commoner, but a woman of good family and a proper upbringing? No relationship between us more intimate than casual friendship is possible."

"But that's not true, my dear Merilsa! It would be true if we were confined to the Walasian Empire, but we are not! I sat awake half the night thinking about this, and I have seen how we can be together without sullying your honor. We can be married in Quand. The Quandish make no link between magic and nobility, and intermarriage between sorcerers and ordinary folk is common there. I would give up my title by abandoning the empire, of course, but that's of no consequence; as the fourth of my father's sons I would never have had any role in the empire's governance in any case. My departure would be no loss to the empire or myself. Your home is in Kallai, on the Quandish border; if we made our residence just beyond you could return as often as you chose to visit your parents or see to the family business. I could earn a living as a sorcerer for hire – I have heard that such things are common in Quand."

Merilsa stared at him in astonishment. If either of them was ensorcelled, it would appear to be *him*, rather than herself, to spout such nonsense. Yes, his scheme was *possible*, but it was ridiculous. They had known each other less than a single day!

"Do you really think you would be happy living as an ordinary citizen of Quand?" she asked. "Do you even speak Quandish?"

"Only a few words," Dieryn admitted. "But I could learn!"

She continued to stare, her thoughts in a tumult. *She* knew Quandish – she could not claim any great fluency, but she had indeed grown up in a city where trade between the two nations flowed freely, a town where Quandish traders and travelers were an everyday presence, and she had naturally picked up the basics.

But this was absurd.

"My lord," she said, "just what are you proposing?"

"I am saying, my dear Merilsa, that I love you, and I want you to emigrate with me to Quand, so that we can be wed." He took a step closer and knelt, there in the hallway of the inn, then took her hand and asked, "Will you marry me?"

She felt her heart leap, and her belly grew warm again, but she refused to let her body overcome her common sense. "This is madness, my lord," she said. "We barely know one another!"

"Then let us know one another better!"

That had the sound of an indecent suggestion, and Merilsa snatched her hand away. "No, my lord. Excuse me, but I must retire." She took a step up the stairs.

"Please, my Merilsa," Dieryn said, still on one knee. "Surely you do not find me so very distasteful?"

"Not distasteful so much as preposterous, my lord. I would..."

She stopped in mid-sentence as another figure appeared in the doorway behind her suitor – Volber had returned. Before she could react he reached for something, and she thought that this was a very odd time to play music, but it was not his cittern that appeared in his hand. It was a drawn sword.

"Get away from her, Lord Dieryn," he said.

"What?" Dieryn rose, turning to face this new arrival.

"Step aside and let her pass. I am taking her to her mother, and you will not interfere."

"You're...the musician? What are you doing here?"

"Step aside, I said!" He raised the sword.

"Volber, this isn't necessary," Merilsa cried.

"I am afraid that I cannot trust your judgment, Mistress Albier. I still believe he has enchanted you."

"If he had, I would have agreed to his insane proposal a moment ago."

"Then perhaps he had not cast the spell *yet*, but had I not arrived he would have." The sword was pointed at Dieryn's chest. "Step aside, my lord."

"I agree with Mistress Albier that this is unnecessary," Lord Dieryn said, "but I will oblige you." He moved sideways, into the inn's common room.

"Now, if you please, Mistress Albier, come with me to your mother, where you will be safe from this sorcerer."

Confused, Merilsa cast a glance at Dieryn, then looked up the stairs and down the corridor toward the kitchen in hopes of seeing the innkeeper or someone else who might intervene. She saw no one.

And perhaps, she thought, Volber was right. Certainly, Lord Dieryn's behavior had not been rational. She hurried down the steps and past Volber, out the door into the village street. There she stopped and looked back.

Volber turned away from the inn door, sword still in his right hand, and with his left he took her by the arm, rather more forcefully than necessary, and began leading her away. She let him guide her, but she looked back as Lord Dieryn stood in the doorway looking baffled and angry.

This was all so very bizarre! She did not understand any of it. She had certainly had men interested in her before, but nothing like Lord Dieryn's obsession. And to have Volber come to her rescue – well, it had probably been unnecessary, but it was still somewhat comforting. What if Dieryn had followed her up the stairs?

She looked at Volber, and then at the street, and something registered.

"Wait a moment," she said. "This is the wrong way. My mother is at the burgrave's mansion."

"No, she isn't," Volber said, his voice a trifle unsteady. "I warned her what the burgrave's nephew was up to, and she left. We'll be joining her at our camp outside the village."

"No, I..." Merilsa began, but then Volber's grip tightened and he tugged harder on her arm. She tried to free herself, and his grip tightened still further. She realized that something was *very* wrong. The musician was not *rescuing* her; he was *abducting* her.

She debated what to do – struggle? Protest? Scream? But he would claim she was enchanted, and he was saving her from the villain responsible. He had his sword ready. If she screamed, someone could be hurt or killed.

What in the world did he think he was doing? What did he want with her?

For now she would play along, let him think she believed him, and wait for an opportunity. She did have a dagger under her skirts; any sensible woman who traveled the empire without male protection, as she and her mother did, would always to be armed. Perhaps Volber didn't realize that, or thought she would have left her weapon in her room at the inn.

What *did* he want with her, anyway? There was, of course, the same thing any man would want with a healthy young woman, but surely a handsome musician had no need to resort to such methods.

She allowed him to lead her out of the village and into a grove of maples; there he stopped. The ground here had been well-trampled, but there were no tents nor cook-fires, nor anything else that could reasonably be called a camp.

"Where is your camp, and your companions?" she asked, looking around. "Where is my mother?"

"We had already broken camp," he said. "Your mother should be here any minute. Have a seat, and we'll wait for her."

"I prefer to stand, thank you." Sitting would make her more vulnerable, less able to flee. She pulled her arm free, and this time he released his hold.

"It may be some time," he said. "You might as well make yourself comfortable."

"I am quite comfortable on my feet. I thought you said she would be here any minute."

"I said she *should* be, but something might delay her."

"Then perhaps we should endeavor to meet her halfway, to be sure she is not in danger."

At that his facade finally cracked. "Sit *down*, Mistress Albier!"

"No, Master Taraz, I will not."

He raised the sword. "I tell you, you have been enchanted, and I have come to free you from the sorcerer's thrall! Now, do as I say!"

She ignored the blade in his hand; he would not dare use it. She was worth nothing dead, and her murderer would be hunted down by the burgrave and his men. "I do not believe for an instant that Lord Dieryn has enchanted me! Now, let us return to town and find my mother!"

He grabbed her arm again and stared into her eyes, and suddenly she found herself sitting on the root of a great tree with no memory of how she got there. "I did not want to do this, but if it is the only way to overcome your stubbornness, then I will do what I must," Volber said.

"What have you done?" Merilsa cried.

"*I* have enchanted you!" His voice rose. "Not that worthless fop, but me, the outcast, the sorcerer's bastard! I have placed a binding on you and you cannot leave this grove until I allow it."

She stared at him, astonished. "Sorcerer's bastard" – that explained a great deal. "You did something to Lord Dieryn, then?"

Volber grinned. "Indeed I did. The fool never suspected...Well, no, I cannot say that. I believe he *might* have suspected. I think that was why he came to speak to me after the dance; he knew something wasn't right. I had been watching the two of you, and working my will on you, ever since Lord Ashur drew back the curtains. *You* were never enchanted, my dear, until now, but *he* was; I was able to slip through his defenses while you held his attention. I may not have the raw magical power he does, but I have had to learn subtlety. I was able to usurp his natural and genuine interest in you and force it into a loop, building upon itself, so that he would be driven to possess you. And when he suspected something and came to speak to me I was able to turn away his feeble truth spell, which he kept ridiculously weak to avoid detection."

"Why? Why are you doing *any* of this?"

"So that he would pay anything to ransom you, of course! Or perhaps your mother will pay, or the burgrave; it doesn't matter to me."

"If you wanted to kidnap me, why bother with all this? Why not just waylay me and take me by force, or bind me on the spot?"

"I had *hoped*, my dear, that I could convince you I was actually rescuing you, so that you would come willingly and cooperate with me in negotiating the terms of your release. I would have said the ransom was merely a fee for my services."

"I don't see why you would want to resort to kidnaping me in the first place. If you are a sorcerer, surely there are better ways to obtain money! Cannot you claim your birthright among the empire's nobility?"

"No, I *cannot*," he said bitterly. "My father forbade it. He would not allow me to stand the trials, lest his infidelity be exposed. He swore he would kill me rather than permit me to stir up gossip. Indeed, as I grew older and came to look ever more like him, he banished me from his lands entirely, lest anyone see the resemblance and guess the truth."

"But after you left..."

"I have no sponsor, no training! I cannot gain admission to the trials, and without training, could I pass them? They do not permit a second attempt, should a candidate fail. And my father has sworn that he will make sure I am never recognized as his son or his equal. I do not know how far his power extends, and I do not wish to find out."

"Who *is* your father?"

"He has placed a binding upon me; I cannot speak his name or full title, but I can tell you he is a landgrave, ruler of a province to the south of here, and a very powerful man."

"He sounds very cruel!"

"He is a hard man, but he has been generous with my mother, and he made certain that I had skills that could earn me a living. It was at his insistence that I was tutored in both cittern and sword – but the binding that forbids me his name also forbids me earning my living by magic, so I cannot even act as a witch, selling my magic to commoners. Yes, if you call him cruel, I will not deny it."

That rendered moot any question of why Volber had not done as Dieryn suggested he himself might, and gone to Quand or the Cousins to practice his sorcery.

"So you have devised this scheme instead? Have you fared so poorly as a traveling musician?"

"I have done well enough, but when I saw how Lord Dieryn looked at you I could not resist the opportunity to make a nobleman look foolish, and bring myself a few guilders in the process."

"And you must drag *me* into your crusade against the sorcerers?"

His self-assurance faltered, and his eyes fell. "I...When I saw you in Clemin, I...But you would barely look at me. You thought yourself far above a mere traveling musician. But when a *sorcerer* sought to dance with you, you were willing and eager, even though you know he cannot marry you. Had you known *I* was a magician, would you have dismissed me so casually?"

Merilsa stared at him for a moment, and decided there was no answer she could give that would improve her situation. The truth was that had she known he was a sorcerer's bastard she would have actively avoided him, as a danger and an unknown, while as a musician she found him moderately interesting – but no more than that. No thought of romance had crossed her mind, and his rank, or lack thereof, had nothing to do with it; he simply did not appeal to her.

And now, it seemed, she was paying for her lack of interest.

"I...I know I am behaving foolishly," he said. "I know this scheme is ill-advised. But I could take no more, watching the two of you."

"But you made him *more* interested in me! Would it not have been more sensible to turn him *away* from me, and then enchant me to love you?"

"I don't...I am untrained, as I told you." The sword drooped. "I cannot always...I did not know how. I can strengthen what is already there, but not reverse it."

"But then you must know I don't want you."

"Of course I do! But at least I can make him pay for you."

She was groping for something to say when a voice called, "Volber Taraz!"

He turned quickly, his sword ready again; Merilsa leaned over to look past his legs, and saw Lord Dieryn approaching through the trees. He, too, carried a bare blade.

"Ah, my lord!" Volber replied, saluting with his own weapon.

"What are you doing with Mistress Albier?" Dieryn demanded.

"Luring you here, my lord." He took two long steps toward his foe and brought his blade up to guard position.

Merilsa quickly reached under her skirts, unconcerned with modesty, and found her knife.

"Drop your sword, musician," the sorcerer said, advancing into the grove.

Volber smiled; his sword did not move.

Merilsa thought Dieryn looked puzzled for a moment, but then his face cleared and he raised his own weapon. "I see," he said. "You have magic of your own. Later, if we both survive, you must explain your situation."

She did not see who made the first move, but suddenly there was a clash of steel and the two men were fighting, swords flashing as they thrust and parried at one another. In addition to the natural movements, though, Merilsa saw other things, as well – swords that bent in strange ways, hands and heads that twitched oddly for no visible reason – and she realized that the two were fighting with sorcery as well as steel.

To her surprise, the two were evenly matched. She had assumed that Volber, who had boasted of his training, would be the better swordsman – and perhaps he was, but Lord Dieryn was the more powerful and better trained sorcerer, and was able to use his magic to compensate. Merilsa had seen a sorcerer take down an armed bandit once, and that had been over in seconds; the bandit's sword had dropped from a numbed hand, and had bent itself into uselessness as it lay on the ground. Here, though, the combatants both had sorcery at their command, and the difference in power and training was not enough for Dieryn to immediately overcome his opponent.

The duel continued, metal flashing in the sun, blades clashing against each other, for what seemed to her to be hours, though she knew it could not really have been more than a few minutes. The two men dodged from side to side, occasionally using the trees as cover, as they fought.

And then Volber gained ground, forcing Dieryn back a step; the sorcerer seemed to be tiring.

That would not do. Merilsa stood, her dagger in her hand.

She could not leave the grove, she knew that, but Volber's binding did not otherwise restrain her, and both swordsmen were under the trees. She ran forward, ducking behind the trunk of a towering maple; Volber's head twitched just then, whether because he heard her or because he was resisting another of Dieryn's spells she did not know. Whatever the reason, he could not turn to look for her; Dieryn was pressing him too hard.

And then she came around the tree and plunged her dagger into the musician's leg.

He jerked sideways, and the wounded leg buckled beneath him; he tumbled to the ground, the sword falling from his hand, and then Lord Dieryn was standing over him, the tip of his blade at Volber's throat.

"Yield, sir," he said.

Merilsa lifted her dagger, ready for another blow should it prove necessary. She did not want to kill Volber, or even cripple him, but she could not allow him to continue fighting.

Volber struggled for a moment, then fell back, his hands opening. "I yield," he said.

Without taking his eyes from his fallen foe Dieryn asked, "Are you unhurt, Mistress Albier?"

"I am, my lord," she replied.

"Then could I ask you to please fetch my uncle as quickly as you can? I dare not leave this person unguarded, and sorcery is required to restrain him."

"I understand. I will be as quick as I can." With that, Merilsa started toward the road – and stopped. Her feet refused to carry her out of the shade of the trees.

"I cannot leave the grove," she called. "He placed a spell upon me."

"Release her," Dieryn said, pressing his sword's point into the flesh of Volber's neck – not enough to break the skin, but enough to indent it slightly.

And then it was as if a weight she had never noticed was gone, and Merilsa was able to first walk, then trot, and finally run out of the maples and toward the village and the burgrave's mansion.

Villagers stared as she passed, but no one interfered as she ran up to the carved oaken doors and pounded upon one of the panels. A footman answered, and a moment later she was gasping an incoherent appeal to Lord Ashur – and her mother, who had still been in the burgrave's parlor. One more thing Volber had lied about.

She did not try to explain; she simply said, between breaths, "Your nephew needs you at the maple grove. Sorcery."

The burgrave made admirable haste, and moments later he, Merilsa, and her mother arrived at the grove to find Dieryn still standing over the fallen musician, sword in hand.

Both men appeared somewhat more relaxed, though, and an improvised bandage had been wrapped around Volber's wounded leg.

"Uncle Ashur!" Dieryn called, as he saw the burgrave's approach. "Welcome!"

"What's going on here?" Lord Ashur demanded. "Who is this man?"

"He calls himself Volber Taraz," Dieryn replied. "He played the cittern at last night's festivities."

"The musician? But what..."

"It would seem, Uncle, that he is a sorcerer's bastard, and had the misfortune to inherit both his father's talent and face, making him an outcast, and understandably bitter."

"Face?" Lord Ashur looked down at Volber.

"I thought he looked familiar at the dance," Dieryn said, "but I could not place him. When he told me his sad story, though, I knew why. The face I know is at least twenty years older. Have you ever met Lord Olbrigan, landgrave of Vaun?"

"Lord Olbrigan? I know the name, but no, we have not met. You say this man is his son?"

"If not, then the resemblance is quite an astonishing coincidence. I met the landgrave in Lume when I attended the emperor's court two years ago, and this man's face is remarkably similar."

At that point Volber spoke up. "My lord, why am I here, with your nephew's blade at my throat?"

"I don't yet know," the burgrave replied. "Dieryn, why *are* we here?"

With that, Dieryn explained how he had seen Merilsa led from the inn, and that Volber had said she would be taken to her mother, but then guided her in the wrong direction. Concerned, Dieryn had used his sorcery to track Merilsa to this grove, where he found her at Volber's mercy. They had fought, and he had sent Merilsa to fetch aid.

"He kidnaped her," he concluded, "and must face your justice."

"I did nothing of the sort!" Volber protested. "I rescued her from your nephew's unwanted advances!"

Lord Ashur turned to Merilsa. "Well, Mistress," he said, "which is it?"

Volber looked up at her hopefully. "He abducted me," Merilsa said.

Volber's face fell.

"My lord, he has done more than that," she continued. "He placed a binding upon me, and claimed to have done the same to Lord Dieryn, yet he is no nobleman. That makes him a witch, does it not?"

Lord Ashur's expression turned grim. "It does," he said.

Merilsa held up a hand. "But he says that he did not undergo the trials to be admitted to the aristocracy as a sorcerer because his father enchanted him so that he could not do so. Would that be a mitigating circumstance?"

The burgrave paused, considering this.

"This is beyond me," he said at last. "I think perhaps we should all go back to my house, dispel *all* magic involved here and remove any bindings placed upon any of you three, and *then* see where we stand."

No one objected.

While most of the spells were easily broken, removing Lord Obrigan's binding upon his illegitimate son required the combined efforts of both legitimate sorcerers as well as the spell's target; there could be no doubt that the landgrave was a very powerful magician indeed. In the end, though, every enchantment was broken, whereupon the burgrave cast a new one upon all present, requiring them to speak the truth, and the details of the morning's misadventures were determined.

In the end it was decided that Lord Dieryn and two of the burgrave's men at arms would escort Volber to Lume, to let the emperor's magistrates sort out what should be done with him – and with his father. Lord Ashur agreed to act as his sponsor should he be allowed to undertake the trials to become a registered sorcerer, and preemptively pardoned him for any crime of witchcraft he might be determined to have committed in Posieron.

But not, he was careful to explain, for the crime of abducting a woman, nor that of casting a compulsion upon a nobleman.

"While I understand your father's desire to maintain his reputation and spare his wife embarrassment, I believe that preventing anyone from taking the trials is a crime under imperial law," Lord Ashur explained. "He exceeded his authority, at the very least. But I cannot say that the fact that you were wronged, Master Taraz, excuses your offenses against others."

Lord Dieryn's party left for Lume the following morning; as they prepared to go the sorcerer found time to take Merilsa aside. The two settled on adjoining chairs in an alcove.

"Mistress Albier," he said, leaning toward her, "I regret any embarrassment I may have caused you by my obsessive attentions. I will say, though, that even with the spell broken I do not regret them, for it was a delightful evening."

"The evening was lovely," Merilsa agreed. "It was the morning after that left something to be desired. Your behavior at the inn was quite ridiculous."

He straightened up. "Oh, surely not so ridiculous as that! Running away to Quand may seem like romantic nonsense at first glance, but I rather think I might like to try it."

"Well, give it a season or two," she jested, as she rose to go, "and if you still think it tempting, come find me in Kallai and we can discuss it further."

He smiled. "I may do that."

And then he kissed her hand in farewell and departed.

Merilsa and her mother left for Kallai that same afternoon, having purchased a few trinkets from Lord Ashur that Siltheria thought might bring a decent price at the gallery.

Half a season later a messenger stopped by the gallery to give her a letter from Lord Dieryn, and she learned that Volber – now *Lord* Volber – had passed the trials and been accepted as a sorcerer, but was serving a half-year sentence in the palace dungeons in lieu of a fine that would have taken him several years to pay off. He had been allowed to keep his cittern, and reportedly entertained the guards and other prisoners in exchange for small luxuries.

The political situation was such that Lord Obrigan received only a mild letter of censure, and that was an end to the matter. The letter ended with florid compliments that she took as meaningless politesse.

But a season after that Merilsa answered the gallery bell to find Lord Dieryn standing there. She gaped at him, too astonished to say a word.

He doffed his hat and bowed. "Mistress Albier," he said. "There is a matter you suggested we might discuss further. Would you perhaps consider joining me on a visit to Quand, where we can consider every aspect of it at length?" He gestured toward the street. "My carriage awaits."

She barely hesitated. She knew that the idea was ridiculous, but she found she did not really care. She smiled up at those dark eyes and said, "Let me fetch my coat."

The Night People

As a young man I led a fairly nocturnal life, regularly staying up until the wee hours of the morning and then sleeping until midday. I wasn't the only person doing this, and I spent some time observing the other night people. I wondered where they were during the day. Then it occurred to me that maybe they weren't **anywhere** *during the day.*

It was around 3:00 a.m. when he finally gave up trying to sleep; the pain in his tooth was just not going away, and the dentist couldn't see him before 8:00. He'd already taken all the aspirin he'd had left, but it hadn't done much, and it had worn off around midnight.

He considered finding an all-night pharmacy or 24-hour market to get more aspirin, or maybe some other pain reliever, but he wasn't sure it would be safe to take any more; he'd already taken a lot. Still, he got out of bed and put his clothes back on because anything was better than lying there feeling his jaw throb.

He took the elevator down to street level, left the building, and began walking east, then turned south onto Third Avenue.

The drugstore on the corner was closed; the card on the door said they closed at midnight, which was reasonable enough, if not very helpful. He reached into his pocket for his phone, to check what might be open, and didn't find it; annoyed, he realized he had left it in his apartment.

It wasn't worth going back for, he decided; he would walk until he found somewhere, and at the very least the fresh air felt good. It was a warm night, just pleasant, not hot, with a gentle breeze blowing, and the air was clean – the streets weren't *empty*, but there were only a few widely-scattered vehicles instead of the usual motorized flood, so the customary cloud of exhaust had dissipated. The city's usual racket was reduced to a faint background hum; he could hear a subway train somewhere, passing below a distant grate, and a siren that might be coming all the way from Brooklyn. The sounds were just enough to remind him the city never really slept, and to distract him from the pain in his jaw.

But then, as he walked further down the block, he heard the unmistakable murmur of voices. He blinked. Who was out and about, and talking, at this hour? He was sure there were cops and garbage men and cabbies and the like going about their business, and of course some portion of the city's homeless population might be awake, but they wouldn't be *talking* like that.

He heard a woman's happy laughter. Curious, he headed toward the sound, turning a corner without noticing which street it was.

There were tables on the sidewalk under a wide blue awning, and there were people seated at most of them, talking and drinking. He saw lit candles and empty bottles and glasses of melting ice, and a woman in a red dress wearing a white feather boa despite the warm weather, and a man with a goatee like a Spanish grandee of the 17th century. A waiter in a white shirt and black apron was balancing a tray of foam-topped beer mugs as he squeezed between the chairs.

He blinked. Who *were* these people?

The after-theater crowd should be gone by now, and these people didn't look the part in any case – their clothes were wildly varied, from sweat-stained T-shirts to starched ruffles. Only a very few were dressed appropriately for a night out clubbing, and he didn't know of any late-night clubs in this area, so that wasn't a good explanation, either.

He approached hesitantly, looking for the name of the café, but the awning was blank and no sign was obvious, and he could not see past the crowd to read whatever might have been lettered on the windows or over the door.

A young woman who sat alone at a table, leaning back comfortably with a cocktail glass in one hand and her other hand flung over the back of her chair, noticed him. She smiled, then sat up and beckoned.

Still hesitant, he approached.

She was wearing an old-fashioned black and white striped blouse, with a black beret atop long brown hair. She had high cheekbones, a narrow jaw, and a red-lipsticked mouth turned up in a wry smile. "Sit down," she said, looking up at him. "I won't bite. At least, not unless you want me to."

He took one of the unoccupied chairs at the table and settled down facing her. "Hello," he said.

"Hi there," she replied, leaning back again. "What brings you here at this time of night? You aren't one of the regulars."

"No, I..." He paused, unsure what he should say to this friendly stranger. "I couldn't sleep," he said.

"So you went out for a walk? Don't most people watch a late movie or check their email?"

He shrugged.

She sipped her drink. "What's your name?"she asked.

"Steve," he said. It was a common enough name that he didn't mind telling her the truth.

"I'm Yvonne," she said. She put down her glass and held out delicate hand. "Pleased to meet you."

He took her hand briefly, then released it – not so much a handshake as an acknowledgment that she had offered. "What brings *you* out so late?" he asked.

"Oh, *I'm* one of the regulars," she said, waving at the crowd. "That's how I know you aren't. I'm here most nights."

"But... who *are* all you people? Why is *anyone* out at this time of night?"

"We're just folks who keep odd hours," she said. "Night people."

"Can I get you something sir?"

He started; he had not seen the waiter approach. The young man seemed to simply appear beside the table, looking at him expectantly.

"He'll have a vermouth," Yvonne said, before he could recover. "Won't you, Steve?"

"I..." He could not seem to form words.

"He'll have a vermouth," Yvonne repeated, more definitely. She patted his hand. "It's a house specialty. You'll like it."

"I don't..." But the waiter was gone.

Trying to spot the waiter he looked past Yvonne, at the other tables, and he began to notice details he had not caught before. Two tables over was a man in pajamas, talking to two brassy blondes dressed like Vegas showgirls. At another table a woman in a long gown was talking to a boy in short pants. Three long-haired men in checked flannel shirts were hoisting beer steins. The woman in the feather boa looked much older than he had first thought, almost skeletal.

This was a very strange crowd, even for 3:00 a.m.

"Are you people here *every* night?" he asked.

"Oh, pretty much," she said.

"Even that man wearing pajamas?" He nodded in the direction of the oddly-attired threesome.

"Hm?" Yvonne turned to see where he was looking. "Oh, him. No, I don't know him. I think he came here looking for those girls." She smiled. "If he wakes up he's going to be very surprised."

Steve blinked. "If he wakes up?"

"Oh, yes. He's asleep, and dreaming. I can tell." She smiled. "If he can keep it going long enough he may be in for quite a night."

One of the showgirls laughed warmly, and took the hand of the pajama wearer. All three of them rose, and began threading their way out of the café.

"I wonder if he knows he's been sleepwalking," Yvonne remarked.

Steve looked up as the other man passed, and saw that his eyes were indeed closed. One of the showgirls looked Steve in the eye and winked.

And then they were past, walking up the sidewalk to the corner, and for a moment Steve thought he saw the pajama-clad man alone, the showgirls gone.

But then they were back, and all three vanished around the corner.

"That was weird," Steve said.

"Oh, it happens," Yvonne said. "We don't see a *lot* of sleepwalkers here, but there are some." She smiled at him. "We don't see many day people, either."

Nettled, he asked, "So how do you know I'm a day person? Just because I'm not a regular at this particular café?"

"Because you don't understand who we are," she replied. "Another night person would have figured it out right away, even if he'd never been here before."

"Well, then, who *are* you? You still haven't said."

She looked at him for a long moment, considering, then said, "I could tell you, couldn't I? It wouldn't matter, not really." Her expression turned suddenly somber. "Nothing I do matters."

"Why not?"

"Because I'm a night person," she said. "I'm not *real*."

"You look pretty real to *me*," he said, but even as he spoke he wasn't sure he was telling the truth. The beret, the blouse, her pointed chin and lush hair, seemed suddenly more like an image from a movie, or in an ad, than like a living woman.

"It's kind of you to say that," she answered, "but I'm not. I'm just a dream someone's having – or really, a great many someones."

He blinked. "I'm not dreaming," he said. "I'm awake."

Her smile reappeared. "Yes, you are," she agreed. "That's what's so unusual. You're real, and you're awake, but you found us anyway. That doesn't happen very often."

"If I'm awake, I can't be dreaming you."

"Oh, I wouldn't be too sure of that," she said. "There are daydreams, and hallucinations, and so on. But no, *you* aren't dreaming me; half a million strangers are."

"What are you *talking* about?"

Her smile widened. "You know there are seven or eight million people in this city, don't you? And right now most of them are asleep, and many of them are dreaming, and the entire city is just *filled* with that energy, with their imagination, with their secret thoughts and desires, with everything they've seen and heard during the day. When they're awake that energy drives them through their ordinary lives, but at night, when they're sleeping, their bodies can't use it. Do you think all that just vanishes into nowhere?"

He wanted to say yes, that was exactly what he thought, but the words caught in his throat.

"That energy pools and collects and interacts, and takes on human form – and here we are," she said. "The night people."

"That's crazy," he said. "You're just screwing with me, and I'm listening because I'm short on sleep and my tooth hurts and I'm not thinking straight."

Her smile dimmed. "You can tell yourself that, if you want."

"You really think you're a collectivized dream that thousands of people are having?"

"I *know* I am."

"If you *aren't* just messing with me, then you're crazy."

She shrugged. "Please yourself."

"No, really. I mean, what do you do during the day, when there *aren't* millions of people sleeping? Don't you have a home, a job, a family?"

She shook her head. "I don't exist during the day, Steve. I'm usually not here until well after midnight, when enough of the day people have gone home to bed."

"But... what, every night you just appear, here at this café?"

"Not *every* night. And not always here. Sometimes it takes me hours to find where we're gathering that night. Or sometimes the energy isn't right, and I don't appear at all, or I'm not quite myself. I've been a little girl, and an old woman, and a cat, and a dozen other things."

"That's crazy."

"There are many crazy things in the world, Steve."

The waiter was there at his elbow, setting a glass of dark vermouth in front of him. Steve looked up.

"Put it on my tab," Yvonne said. The waiter nodded and was gone.

"You run a tab?" Steve asked.

She smiled again. "He thinks I do."

"Is *he* real?"

Yvonne looked to either side, then leaned forward, and Steve noticed her blouse was cut lower than he had realized – or perhaps it was cut lower now than it had been before. "Do you know, I'm not sure? Usually I can tell instantly, but the staff here – I don't know *what* they are."

"Do you ever *pay* your tab?"

She laughed gaily. "Oh, Steve, of *course* not! What would I pay it with? I don't have any money. I can't hold a job. But I don't *need* to; I don't need to eat or drink, and sometimes I come into existence with a drink already in front of me. And no one ever asks me to pay."

"Doesn't it..." Steve started to say, but then he stopped. This was all completely insane, and there was no reason to ask how it worked.

"Don't let it trouble you," she said. "Remember, I'm not a real person; I'm just a manifestation of the collective unconscious. Nothing I do can matter. Nothing I do can change anything. I don't need to worry about food or shelter. I have no soul. I can't feel guilt. I have no family. I can't have children. My only friends are the people like you, who come along sometimes and talk to me; I can talk to other night people, but we can't *connect*, not really. And the day people I meet usually decide they're dreaming, that they weren't really here at all, or if they *do* come back to look for me they may not recognize me, because I may be completely changed. I never know whether I'll be here tomorrow night, or whether I'll be the same person if I am."

"Can you feel pain?"

She bit her lip. "Not *physical* pain," she said.

He was sorry he had asked.

He wondered for a moment whether perhaps he *was* dreaming, but the pain in his tooth convinced him he was awake.

"But enough about me," she said, sitting up straight, her smile reappearing. "Tell me about *you*."

He shook his head. "I'm no one interesting."

"Oh, I don't believe that! Tell me! Do you have a family? A girlfriend?"

He hesitated. "No girlfriend," he said. "Two sisters back in Rhode Island – one's married, the other lives with our mother."

"What are they like?"

And he found himself talking about his sisters, his nephew, his parents, his job, his dreams and ambitions, and before he knew it his vermouth was gone, though he barely remembered tasting it, and the sky in the east was starting to get a little brighter, and most of the tables were empty, and the waiter was stacking chairs against the wall.

He had not seen anyone leave, though.

He stopped talking and watched, and a couple in Victorian dress vanished from a nearby table. They did not get up and leave, nor did they flicker or fade; they simply weren't there anymore.

"The city's waking up," Yvonne remarked. "This place doesn't serve breakfast; when we're all gone they'll close until eleven, when they open for lunch."

Others were disappearing, as well.

"Your dentist will open in another couple of hours," she said. "I hope he can take care of that tooth for you."

The other tables were all empty now. He took Yvonne's hand. "You're still here," he said.

"I'm not usually here this late," she said. "You've kept me here. It's been a pleasure talking to you."

"You have to go?"

"I do. There are barely enough late risers to have kept me here *this* long."

"Are you sure? If I come back, will I see you again?"

"Oh, you know I can't tell you that! And you need your sleep; as it is, you won't be able to get anything done at work today."

"But I don't... I want to see you again."

"Maybe you will." She smiled, and patted his hand.

"Dream of me," she said.

And then she was gone.

Paul is Dead

Someone invited me to contribute to an anthology of alternate Beatles stories. Here's what I came up with.

"Excuse me," someone said. "Aren't you Paul McCartney?"

McCartney turned, expecting to see a leather-jacketed young Liverpudlian – after all, who else would know, or care, who he was? But then it registered that the question had been spoken with an American accent, and he found himself looking at an overweight middle-aged man in a garish and badly-cut overcoat, bundled up against the cold winter air.

"I might be, at that," McCartney said. "Who might *you* be?"

"My name's Fred Eberhart," the American said.

"My sympathies," McCartney replied. He started to turn away.

"Mr. McCartney, wait! Please. There's something I need to discuss with you."

"What would that be, then?" McCartney resumed his walk, allowing the American to hurry alongside.

"You were a member of a band called the Beatles, weren't you?"

McCartney grimaced. "Yeah," he said. "Me and some of my mates, we called ourselves that."

"What happened?"

McCartney threw the American a puzzled glance. "What do you mean, what happened?"

"To the band, Mr. McCartney. What happened to the band?"

"Three of us had a row and we decided to give it up. What's it to you?"

"What *happened*, though? You had a great future!"

McCartney snorted derisively. "Well, we didn't, did we? I mean, here we are, you and I, and I don't see John or Stu or Pete or George around."

"But you *could* have!"

"Stu didn't think so."

"But you and John, the two of you..."

McCartney stopped walking. "What do you know about me and John Lennon?" he asked suspiciously.

"I know that you and he were *great* together!"

"*I* don't know that. And it doesn't look like John thought so, either, or he wouldn't have let Stuart talk him into quitting the band."

"Stuart... is *that* what happened?"

"Yeah. Who did you say you were?"

"Eberhart. Fred Eberhart. But why didn't you get back together after Stuart Sutcliffe died? It's been four years."

McCartney stared him. "Are you a bloody lunatic? If Stu Sutcliffe died, then who's got that gallery show up in London today?"

"*Oh.*" The man's expression was almost comically astonished. He collected himself and continued, "I see. Well, that could have been worse, I suppose. And it's exactly what...well, I think I'm in a position to make you a simply *amazing* offer, Mr. McCartney."

"And what would that be?"

"What if I could take you somewhere the band didn't break up? Where you went on to become one of the biggest acts in the world? No, not 'one of' — *the* biggest act in the world."

"That would be a pretty good trick, Fred, since we *did* break up. I was there, I saw it with me own two eyes."

"I know, but...you wouldn't have heard of alternate reality, so...did you ever read any science fiction, Mr. McCartney?"

"Not to speak of, no, but how's that got anything to do with our band?"

"Have you ever read about time travel?"

McCartney realized he was talking to a total nutter. Without another word he turned and started walking again, shoulders hunched against the winter chill.

"Wait, Mr. McCartney, please! I know I must sound crazy, but this is real! I'm from the future, and I've come back to your era to fix something that went horribly wrong!" The American was practically running to keep up.

"How's that, then?" McCartney asked, still walking.

"The Beatles weren't supposed to break up! You were supposed to change the entire face of popular culture, reshape pop music completely! And you were *doing* it, you *did* it, but then something happened and it all changed and the band broke up in 1961, and that five years...well, now I know something changed when Stuart Sutcliffe left, something that made John quit with him, and it's *all gone wrong*!"

"I think Stuart might disagree with you about that. Just how was he supposed to die, anyway? A car crash?"

"No, a brain hemorrhage. *You* were the one who died in a car crash."

McCartney stopped dead and turned to face the American. "What the hell is *that* about, then? I'm right here! D'you mean to tell me I died and *didn't notice*?"

"No, no, no! You *didn't* die, here! And what I want to do is take you back to the way history was *supposed* to go, and you'll take the place of that other Paul McCartney, who died, and the Beatles will go on and...please, Mr. McCartney, I want to hear what you and John and George and Ringo will do with more time!"

"Ringo? You mean Ringo Starr, from Rory Storm's band? What's *he* got to do with it?"

"Oh, he replaced Pete Best as your drummer. Nothing against Mr. Best, but Ringo's a better musician and he was the final piece to really make the Beatles great!"

"Was he, then." McCartney stared at the American lunatic. He might be mad as a hatter, but he certainly seemed to know something about Liverpool's musicians, because Ringo Starr *was* a better drummer than Pete Best. He had filled in for a show or two in Hamburg, back in the day, and the Beatles really *might* have been something special with him on the throne as their regular drummer.

Not that they were bad in the first place. If Stu and John hadn't gone off to be artists the band might have got somewhere; they'd been doing all right for themselves in Hamburg. That was the peak of his musical career, back then – nothing had worked for him since. He decided to let the lunatic spin out his little fantasy.

"Suppose you tell me all about it, Mr. Everhard, and let me think it over."

"Oh, well, the way it should have happened, the way it originally *did* happen, was that Mr. Sutcliffe quit the band in June of 1961, and the rest of you went on without him, and in November 1961 you met

Brian Epstein, and he became your manager and got you a contract with EMI, and it all took off."

"Just like that."

"Pretty much, yes." Eberhart nodded vigorously.

McCartney considered this for a moment.

He had sometimes imagined what might have happened if he and John hadn't had that great row. They'd written some good songs together, and the band had been pretty good. He'd had some ideas of what they might have done if they'd stayed together – or daydreams, really, more than ideas.

"But that didn't happen," he said.

"Not in this version of reality, no," Eberhart agreed. "But I can take you to a reality where it *did* happen, but where you – the other you – died in a car wreck on the M1 just after New Year's."

"*This* New Year's?" He pointed at the sidewalk, as if the year 1967 was there at his feet.

The American nodded, but only a quick bob instead of the frenzied up-and-down of a moment before. "So far it's been hushed up, but if this is going to work I need to get you there to replace him as soon as I can, before word gets out."

"You said something about time travel?"

"Well, yes, I did..."

"Then there's no rush, is there? You and I can just travel to whenever we need to be."

Eberhart shook his head. "I wish it worked that way, Mr. McCartney, but it's far more complicated than that. You really need to decide *now*."

"You say I'll be rich and famous in this other world?"

Eberhart nodded so vigorously this time that McCartney thought it looked as if his head might come off.

McCartney stared at him for a moment, thinking.

His life wasn't going much of anywhere, as it was. He was out of work again, wasn't seeing anyone, wasn't on speaking terms with John or Stu; he really didn't have much to lose. The loony American was probably just spinning some mad story that wouldn't lead anywhere, but at the very least it wold give him something to tell the lads at the pub.

And if this rubbish somehow turned out to be true, he'd be rich and famous and writing songs with John again, and those five years after he got back from Hamburg, those five lousy struggling failure-filled years, would never have happened.

Rich and famous...

"Right, then I'd be a bloody fool to turn it down, wouldn't I?"

"I...I wouldn't know."

That gave McCartney pause, but then he shrugged. "Let's do it, then."

"Oh, thank you, Mr. McCartney! This way, please..."

* * *

"They told us you were dead," John said accusingly. "There was a car crash, they said."

"Well, about that," Paul replied. "There *was* a crash, but I think I'll let Fred explain."

Eberhart waved his hands wildly. "Oh, I'd really rather not," he said. "Can't we just take it as a miracle and let it go at that? Here's Mr. McCartney, very much alive, but with a bit of...well, there's been..."

"I can't remember bloody anything from the last five years," Paul interrupted. "It's all gone. You three will have to teach it all to me."

"*Five years*?" George exclaimed.

"Everything since Stu left."

"Oh, the record label's going to love this," Ringo muttered.

"We don't need to tell them, do we?" John said. "Let's just get on with the album. We can finish up with your good old Sergeant Pepper and get on with the rest of it."

"Let's, then," Paul agreed. "And I may not remember how we got here, but I might have a few ideas where we go next."

* * *

"Mr. McCartney!" Paul turned, startled, and found Fred Eberhart, unkempt as ever, standing in the doorway.

"Fred!" he said, smiling. "Fred the fool. It's been some time."

"I just heard the news. You quit? The band's breaking up?"

"That's right. I don't know whether the man back where I came from is any better, but *this* John Lennon is a right bastard, and George means well but he's...I don't know, we just aren't seeing things the same way. And I hardly ever knew Ringo, not to mention that man Klein!"

"But it's only been three years!"

McCartney said, "Well, that's three more than you had before, innit? And I think we did some good work in there, when we weren't all ready to murder each other."

"Of course you did, but only three years? I wanted thirty!"

Paul shrugged. "As our lad Mick says, you can't always get what you want."

Eberhart seemed to wilt, as if suddenly deflated. He let out a sigh. "I suppose you want me to take you back to your own timeline, then?"

McCartney blinked at him, astonished. "My own...what? Are you daft? I'm staying right here!"

Eberhart's jaw dropped. "But...but it's not your world!"

"That didn't seem to bother you back in 1967, that I recall. I like this world just fine, as long as I'm not in the Beatles. You think I want to give up Linda, or our kids? And really, how would you explain it if I disappeared?"

"Oh, well, I...um..." Eberhart blushed.

"Oh, my God," Paul said. "You were going to replace me again, weren't you? With someone who'd stick with the band?"

"It was just...I didn't mean any harm."

"Yes, you did. I know you can't take me away unless you get me back in your machine, and I'm not going. Listen, Fred, you're just going to have to accept it – the Beatles are over. The fact is, all of us have been drifting apart, it's not just me."

"But it's because...because you aren't *you*."

Paul shook his head. "No, it's not. It's because we've grown up. We're all ready to move on. And you haven't heard the last of us – all four of us will be doing solo work, you know. Besides, if you replace me again, the new fellow won't be me, either, will he?"

"If you hadn't planted all those clues about your death..."

"Oh, please. Most of those were John's, anyway, and some the fans just made up themselves."

"But...just three years!"

"Just three years. Go find something else to do, Fred; we're done here. I'm not leaving this universe, not for my old one or for any other." He turned and walked away, leaving Eberhart staring forlornly after him.

"No more Beatles," Eberhart whispered to himself. "After all I did, just three years, just a few albums." His shoulders sagged.

But then Eberhart perked up. "Something else to do," he murmured to himself. "He said I should find *something else* to do."

* * *

"Mr. Holly!"

Buddy Holly turned around to see a fat man in an ugly overcoat hurrying toward him through the blowing snow. "Who're *you*?" he asked.

"My name's Fred Eberhart," the man said, panting slightly, "and I'm asking you not to get on that plane..."

The House of the Spider

As a teenager I was a huge fan of sword & sorcery – Howard's Conan, Moorcock's Elric, Leiber's Fafhrd and the Gray Mouser. When I started writing fantasy, that's what I tried to write. I thought I was succeeding, but then I referred to my first novel, **The Lure of the Basilisk***, as sword and sorcery in front of Lester del Rey, the editor who had bought it. Lester got pissed and said, "I do not publish sword and sorcery!" So maybe it wasn't – but I tend to think Lester was wrong.*

That said, I gradually moved away from S&S, and didn't write any for decades – until I got an anthology invitation that specifically asked for sword and sorcery. I tried to get back into my youthful mindset, but discovered I couldn't quite do it straight anymore. Instead I wrote this.

There could be no question that this was the house he was looking for. A mile from any other structure, it was built of black stone, with towers at every corner, and two hulking black creatures resembling tiger-sized bulldogs were chained up on either side of the entry, watching him suspiciously. A forest of clearly unnatural, impossibly-dense thorn trees surrounded the rest of the structure, but the tops of the trees were half-hidden by strands of some sort of shiny gray material. Gordak had encountered wizards before, and most of them liked to make some intimidating display of their magic, but this was more blatant than usual.

He had agreed to rescue a young woman the wizard was holding prisoner, but he was not about to go charging in unprepared – though that might surprise his employer. It was entirely possible the man – not much more than a boy, really – expected him to charge in and get killed, and *wanted* that to happen for some reason Gordak didn't understand.

Well, Gordak did not intend to die if he could avoid it, which meant he would not be going in through the front door. Those guard dogs would almost certainly be a serious challenge, even if they didn't turn out to be made out of animate iron, or capable of instantly regrowing severed limbs, or otherwise more dangerous than they looked. The Ellemerians might call his people barbarians, but that didn't make him an idiot. Even if the dogs turned out to pop harmlessly like soap bubbles when stabbed, their defeat would almost certainly trigger warnings somewhere inside.

He could walk up, hat in hand, and ask to talk to the wizard, but that seemed very unlikely to lead anywhere useful. He imagined the scene – "Excuse me, but my employer says you're holding his fiancée prisoner. Could you please release her?"

"Oh, of course! I'm so sorry! She'll be right out; would you like a mug of ale while you wait?"

His mouth quirked in a wry smile. No, that wasn't going to happen.

Well, if he couldn't go in the front door, what other options did he have? He stepped off the path, testing the ground carefully with each step.

There didn't seem to be any traps. One never knew, with wizards. They tended to be over-cautious. Gordak didn't fault them for that; after all, wizards made enemies easily, particularly other wizards, and furthermore, they were always assumed to have treasure just lying around waiting for some enterprising thief to make off with it.

The locals Gordak had spoken to in the taverns had not spoken particularly ill of this one, Ammander Poritha. They all agreed he was dangerous, like any wizard, but he was not noted for an ill temper or excessive greed, and there was no evidence his sorcery had driven him mad – yet. He was not known for abducting people; in fact, except for Dolisar Kalen, the over-dressed, perfumed little fop who had bailed Gordak out of jail in exchange for running this little errand, no one knew anything about Poritha holding a woman prisoner, or doing anything else seriously objectionable. The wizard had no reason to go overboard with his defenses.

But Kalen said his fiancée Liniandra was in there. Assuming Kalen had told the truth, allowing wizards to hold women prisoner was bad policy, and Gordak wasn't going to stand for it. Kalen couldn't have known that the main reason he accepted the job was the same reason he was in Ellemeria in the first place, instead of back home – he had been sent into exile after killing the wizard who had abducted his sister. The clan whose crops depended on that wizard's magic had not taken it well. Addisa had been forgiven when everyone saw what the wizard had done to her, but Gordak had not. He had wandered to Ellemeria, where he was accused of theft and jailed.

Gordak suspected that Kalen had arranged for his arrest in the first place, in order to compel him to take the job of rescuing his fiancée, but Gordak didn't much care. He could attend to the little weasel later.

So here he was, and if this wizard was holding women prisoner, then that was worth Gordak's attention – especially if this Kalen would actually paid what he promised. The rich twit had probably thought that paying Gordak with his freedom as well was necessary to convince him to take the job, but honestly, the money and doing the right thing would have been enough.

And there was still time to back out, if it looked too dangerous or difficult.

Right now, though, as he walked carefully across the sunlit meadows around the house, it was hard to judge how difficult the rescue might be. One never knew what to expect with magic.

The tangle of strangely-draped thorn trees extended farther away from the house on one side; Gordak suspected there was a walled garden in there, though the thorns were too thick to give a clear view. Getting into the garden might be possible, but it was probably not a good idea; it was all too likely to contain exotic poisons that could kill with a touch, man-eating plants, or other hazards, possibly including the wizard himself – wizards were just as likely to enjoy puttering about in the garden as anyone else.

Gordak completed a circuit of the house without incident. There were no other roads or paths leading in, no other visible entries. There were plenty of windows, though, several of them visible above the thorn trees.

He had not seen any evidence of tunnel entrances anywhere, and those thorn trees undoubtedly had deep roots, so going under them did not appear to be an option. The dog-guarded entry was out. Cutting *through* the trees might or might not be possible – again, one never knew with magic – but would almost certainly be a very slow and difficult approach. Those thorny branches were very thick indeed.

That left *over* the trees, and in through a window.

Gordak considered his approach. Those thorns looked vicious, and might be poisonous; he would want to wear armor to climb over them, and not just the traveling clothes he had on. Those silvery strands might also be dangerous somehow; he doubted the wizard had installed them purely for decoration.

And of course, at any stage of his approach he might trigger some sort of magical alarm. When he did make his attempt the wizard might be watching his every move in a scrying glass. Some risks were unavoidable, though.

He took one final look at the mansion and its surrounding thorns, then turned and headed back into town. However he was going to try to get inside, he was not about to do it in broad daylight.

Twelve hours later, after buying an assortment of equipment and charging it all to Dolisar Kalen, he hauled a cart along the road, relying on starlight, memory, and touch to find his way. He could see lights in the mansion's windows; at least he wouldn't be in total darkness crossing the thorns.

He was wearing boiled leather armor, with a sword on his hip and three knives in his belt. A pretty blue stone hung on a cord around his neck; it was supposed to be a protective amulet, but Gordak had never found a way to test it. Wearing it might not do any good, but it should not do any harm, either. Over everything he wore a heavy cloak.

He had pulled the cart all the way from town by himself, rather than risk using a beast of burden that might make noise at an inconvenient time. Now he heaved it up off the road onto the surrounding meadow, and dragged it around to the side of the house farthest from where he believed the walled garden to be.

There he lifted out a ladder. It was the tallest he could find on short notice, but still only about twelve feet long, while the thorn trees topped out around fifteen feet. He hoped that the steel gauntlets and boots he wore would let him cover the last few feet safety.

He had also brought two broad planks and attached straps to them; now he slung these on his shoulder, set the ladder firmly against a tree, and began climbing. He moved slowly, to minimize the creaking of the ladder and his armor, and to keep the planks from bumping against anything, and had to keep his belly sucked in to avoid the points of thorns that protruded through the ladder, but he reached the top quickly.

He paused, looking at the black thorns and the gray filaments before him. He carefully touched one of the strands with a single finger.

It stuck to his steel gauntlet. A shake did not loosen it, and he could not pull hard without losing his balance.

He frowned, drew a knife with his other hand, and tried to cut the filament. It took several seconds of sawing and a surprising amount of pressure before he was able to cut it away. An inch or so remained adhered to his glove, but the severed ends fell away on either side. He picked at the remaining fragment with the point of his dagger, but could not detach it.

Whatever the stuff was, it was going to complicate matters, but he thought he could manage. He pulled one of the planks off his back, and placed it against the thorns, where it extended up onto the treetops. Carefully, he pushed himself along the plank, and as he had planned, it tilted under his weight until he was lying stretched out atop the trees, untouched by thorns or sticky strands.

The plank, however, was now firmly attached to the tree – he could tell that dozens of thumb-sized thorns had embedded themselves in the wood.

He had thought of using wide iron bars instead of wooden planks, but none were available on short notice, and the additional weight would have been exhausting. He would just need to pry the board up behind him.

He pulled the other board from his back, and lined it up ahead of him; then he slid himself forward from the first board onto the second. He felt it sink slightly under his weight as the thorns dug into it.

He did not try to stand up; even kneeling made the board wobble, as the tree branches beneath him were not as strong as he might have hoped. He turned, and tried to pull up the first board and set it ahead of him; that would be enough to get him perhaps halfway across the thorn trees. It took more strength than he had expected, and he came close to overbalancing, but at last he had it free – of the thorns. The gray filaments still clung to it, and he could not lift it more than a few inches.

Cursing, he drew a knife and began hacking at the threads, gradually lifting the board until it was free, though several gray strands still clung to its underside. Then he swung it around and placed it ahead of him.

He had thought crossing the tangle of thorn trees would take perhaps ten minutes, but the necessity of first prying up, and then cutting free, each board slowed him down considerably – especially since those severed gray strands remained on the underside of each of his two planks, so that there were more of them left dangling each time, and their adhesive, whatever it was, was gumming up his knife, making it less effective with each use.

The whole thing also made more noise than he liked, the boards rattling and creaking as he went. He also thought he heard some sort of rustling in the trees below him, and hoped it was his imagination.

At last, though, he reached the inner edge of the thorny forest, where a gap of six or seven feet separated him from the stone walls of the wizard's mansion. He had thought that at this point he would be able to drop down, or perhaps anchor a rope and climb across, but there was a complication he had not anticipated. The gray filaments did not end when the thorns did; instead, they stretched across the gap and were anchored to the walls beyond.

And here he could see a pattern to them that had not been visible among the tangled branches and their thorns. They were not random strands wandering through the trees, nor were they some sort of tenting such as caterpillars might leave; instead they formed an elegant web, about ten feet from the ground, that gleamed in the golden light that spilled from the windows.

A web very much like a spider's web, but with strands as thick as latch-strings.

Gordak chewed his lower lip as he considered this. *Had* a gigantic spider spun these webs? Or given their extent, had an entire *colony* of spiders made them? He did not *see* any such monsters, but the night was dark, and the thorn trees provided plenty of places to hide.

Well, spiders or not, he needed to get through that web if he was going to find a way into the mansion. Just trying to drop through it might leave him trapped; those filaments were tough and extremely sticky.

After a moment's thought, though, he devised a simple plan he hoped would be enough. He wrapped himself in his cloak, leaving nothing exposed, with his hands in front of his face, a dagger in each. Then he rolled forward and let himself fall from the end of his plank.

He was depending on the web to at least break his fall, so that he wouldn't be injured, and that seemed to work; he did not fall far, but found himself bouncing slightly. He was lying horizontally.

He pulled open the hood of his cloak and peered out.

He was indeed lying on the web. He had not plunged through it, as he had hoped, but he himself was not stuck; only his cloak was.

Maneuvering carefully, he twisted around and began cutting the strands of the web that held him. It was not easy; they were springy and sticky. At last, though, he had an opening he could fit through; he began lowering himself through it, leaving his cloak behind in the web.

Just as he was about to let himself drop, though, he felt the web moving. He froze. Then, very slowly and cautiously, he tried to turn to see what was happening.

An immense black spider was approaching, in no great hurry. Its central body mass was roughly the size of a large hog, but its legs covered the full width of the gap between the thorn trees and the wall of the house.

Gordak began struggling to slide out of his cloak as quickly as possible; seeing his movement, the spider picked up its own pace. It was only a yard away when he tumbled free and fell to the ground.

He landed hard on his right shoulder, then rolled over and got to his feet – just in time to see the spider drop down on a strand of webbing. Gordak snatched at his sword, but his shoulder had been injured enough in the fall that in his first attempt his fingers did not close on the hilt. He grabbed again, and this time was able to awkwardly draw the blade.

The spider landed on the ground perhaps two yards away, and for a moment the two stood, staring at one another.

Then the spider leapt at him, and Gordak swung the sword up. He could not strike a decisive blow, but he forced the spider aside before its jaws could reach him. Then he turned, and struck at the monster before it could attack again.

The sword bounced from its chitinous exoskeleton, leaving a mark, but not penetrating deeply enough to do real damage.

The spider, however, had clearly had enough; it turned and scuttled away, turning to climb up the wall and return to its web.

Gordak let out a sigh of relief. He was not really surprised, though; most beasts were not interested in fighting to the death, and would run from any sufficiently dangerous foe. He turned around, looking for the nearest way to get into the house, only to find three more of the gigantic spiders coming toward him from the opposite direction, one on the web above him, one on the wall of the house, and one among the thorn trees.

That rustling sound he had heard before was back, and was definitely *not* his imagination.

"Gods' blood!" he said. He looked up at his cloak, dangling from the web, and wondered whether they were somehow homing in on that, or whether they had sensed movement.

Whatever was attracting them, he did not want to be in their path. He ducked his head and charged forward, sword ready. A hairy leg reached out, and he slashed at it, removing the outermost joint.

Then he was past them. He glanced over his shoulder to see that one in the thorn trees, whose leg he had severed, was retreating into the black forest; the one on the web above seemed to have lost interest and was not moving.

The one on the wall of the house, however, was still coming after him; it had dropped down so that four of its legs were on the ground, the other four still on the wall. He turned, sword at ready, and met its charge.

This time he was able to strike it properly, and his sword sank into the creature's bulbous body. It staggered, its legs curling under it; he pulled the sword free only to find it was coated with dark ichor. He retreated, sword dripping, as the spider collapsed; as he passed a lighted window he could see that the ichor staining his blade was a deep blue.

He paused, asking himself whether he should go in through that window, or whether it would be wise to find an unlit one. He leaned over, peering in.

He saw what appeared to be a small, uninhabited sitting room, and decided he would risk it. After all, the house was allegedly only inhabited by a single wizard – the townsfolk had not even been aware of any servants – but at least half a dozen windows were lit.

Apparently he was careless about extinguishing unneeded lamps, or perhaps the light was produced by magic. Gordak could not see the light's source, but from the shadows he judged it to be on the wall to the left of the window.

He hoped the wizard was sleeping peacefully somewhere on the far side of the house, but he could not know.

That rustling noise was louder now, and was coming from several places in the thorn trees.

Whatever might be in that room, staying in this narrow, spider-infested alley between the thorn trees and the walls did not seem like a good idea. There might be dozens of spiders, or worse things than spiders, lurking around the next corner. He studied the window, and saw only a very ordinary latch. Switching his sword to his left hand, he drew his last clean knife and tried to wedge it between the casement and the frame.

His efforts were interrupted by the arrival of another spider, which he quickly dispatched. He was not happy to hear rustling around and above him growing louder; getting into the house was beginning to feel urgent. One spider at a time he could handle, assuming it wasn't significantly larger than the ones he had already encountered, but if half a dozen were to attack at once...

He was just beginning to wonder whether the latch might be enchanted, or if there might be some other magical protection on the window, when the bar finally popped out of its resting place and the casement came free.

The rustling was now being joined by a chittering noise, and he wondered whether the spiders could communicate and plan a joint attack. He quickly swung the casement open, and tried to climb through.

The opening was not as wide as he had thought. He dropped his knife and sword into the room, reaching as far down as he could to reduce clatter, but found he could not *quite* squeeze himself through, not even turning sideways. Hoping the spiders were not yet ready to attack, he stripped off most of his armor and dropped that, piece by piece, through the window. His sword belt and pouch followed next, and then he turned on his side and began heaving himself through.

Something touched his boot, and he forced himself through in one final rush, landing heavily on his armor and other equipment. He froze; if the wizard was anywhere nearby, he surely would have heard the thump and rattle of his landing.

But then, lying sprawled on the floor, he saw the tip of a black, segmented leg thrust in through the open window. That was a far more immediate danger than the wizard; he leapt to his feet, shoved the spider's leg back out, and yanked the casement shut.

Arachnid legs rattled against the glass as he snugged the latch back into place.

He was very glad that he had kept his gloves on; that leg was not something he wanted to touch bare-handed. Shuddering, he stared out at the darkness beyond the window, and saw a set of shiny black spider-eyes staring back at him. He stepped back, and picked up his breastplate.

He had just slid it down over his head onto his shoulders when a deep voice from behind him said, "Good evening."

His sword and knives were still on the floor. He had been caught woefully unprepared. Slowly, his open hands raised, he turned.

A tall man in a golden robe, almost as tall as Gordak himself but much thinner, was standing in the door of the room, holding a lamp in one hand and watching his uninvited guest intently. He was not holding a wand, staff, or other visible weapon, unless the lamp could be considered one, but Gordak knew better than to think that meant he was harmless. Unarmed as he was, he would need to talk his way out of this, not fight.

"Good evening, sir," Gordak replied, in his very best Ellemerian. "Ammander Poritha, I presume?"

"At your service," the tall man said, nodding slightly. "And you are...?"

Gordak was relieved that the wizard was speaking conversationally, and showed no signs of preparing a spell. "Gordak of the House of Balgar, of Darana."

"Ah. I'm afraid I've never heard of you."

"I'm a traveler passing through."

"May I ask what a simple traveler is doing, climbing in my window in the middle of the night? This is more the sort of thing I would expect of a thief."

"It is, I admit," Gordak agreed. "But I am not here to rob you, I swear by my gods. I came here seeking a woman named Liniandra, who I have been told is a prisoner here."

The wizard's eyes widened slightly. "*Prisoner?*" he said. "May I ask who told you this?"

"A man who says he is her betrothed. I do not want to name him yet."

The wizard's eyes widened further. "Her *betrothed?* Oh, this does bear investigation." He held out his empty hand. "Would you mind accompanying me? And please, leave your sword and other tools here."

Gordak was not in a position to object. Even if he were to catch the wizard by surprise and defeat him somehow, he did not see how he could get safely out of the house – the spiders and the giant watchdogs were still out there. He left his equipment where it was and followed as Ammander Poritha led him out of the room, along a corridor, and up a flight of stairs. They proceeded along another corridor, past several closed doors, until they reached one particular door, where the wizard knocked loudly.

A muffled voice on the other side of the door made a sleepy questioning noise.

"Liniandra? I'm sorry to disturb you, but I'm afraid I need to speak with you."

"*Now?*"

"Yes, now."

"It's the middle of the night!"

"Nonetheless. Open the door, please."

It had become very clear to Gordak that whoever this Liniandra was, she was not a prisoner. He had already been annoyed with Dolisar Kalen, but now he was becoming downright angry.

He heard footsteps, then the rattle of a latch, and the door opened. The head of a tall young woman with silver-blonde hair – a girl, really – appeared. She looked as if she was about to speak, but then she saw Gordak. "Who's *that?*" she exclaimed.

"This is Gordak, of the House of Balgar," the wizard said. "Gordak, allow me to present my daughter, Liniandra Poritha."

Gordak bowed deeply. "I am honored." he said. He did not for a moment doubt that she was indeed the wizard's daughter; the family resemblance was unmistakable. They shared the same sharp cheekbones and long nose, the same eyes.

"Gordak tells me," the wizard said, "that he is here on behalf of your fiancé."

"My what?" Liniandra said, startled.

"A man named Dolisar Kalen told me that his betrothed was being held prisoner here, and he hired me to rescue her," Gordak explained. "It seems he lied."

"Dolisar?" She frowned. "A small man with curly hair and fancy clothes? About my age?"

Gordak nodded. "That's the one."

"You know him?" the wizard asked.

"Well, I met him, anyway," she said. "At the Harvest Festival. We danced together, and he bought me some sweets and a trinket, and he did ask me to marry him, but I thought he was joking and just laughed."

"That's all?"

"That's all."

"He seems to have taken it more seriously than you did," the wizard said.

"I swear to you, Papa, it was nothing! He's a mad fool!"

"I'll agree he's a fool," Gordak said. "Apparently even more so than I thought."

"He hired you to kidnap my daughter?" the wizard asked.

"So it appears," Gordak agreed. "I apologize for breaking into your home, but Kalen had friends to confirm his story, and I had no reason to doubt him. Perhaps I am as big a fool as he."

"Oh, I don't know," the wizard said. "You've been civil enough."

"I fear I owe another apology, as well. I killed two or three of your spiders."

"Actually, thank you for that. They've been getting out of hand lately. In fact, I found you because when I heard the noise you made I thought one of them had gotten into the house."

"Papa, he *broke into our home*?" Liniandra exclaimed. "What if you hadn't caught him, and he'd kidnaped me?"

"I would have released you once I saw you were not being held against your will," Gordak said.

"*Would* you? You wouldn't have thought I was ensorcelled? For that matter, how do you know I'm *not* some poor ensorcelled captive?"

"Lini, please," her father said.

"I'm going back to bed, and he better be gone when I get up." She pulled her head back and slammed the door.

The two men stood silently for a moment in the corridor outside her door.

"Well," the wizard said at last, "I think that just leaves the question of what I should do with *you*."

"I am at your mercy. I hope you will be kind. I was deceived." Gordak did his best to sound sincere, but even as he spoke he was judging the distance to the stairs and wondering how fast the wizard could run if he made a break for it.

"If I let you go," Poritha said, "what will you do about this Dolisar Kalen?"

"I had not yet thought about it, but now that you ask, I do not think I will do anything. I will simply leave."

"That would leave him free to send some other dupe after my daughter, one less reasonable than yourself."

Gordak nodded. "Yes."

"You wouldn't feel it necessary to kill him?"

"No. Would you?"

"Tempting, but no. The thing about being a wizard is that if you once start killing people, no matter how much they may deserve it, you get labeled as evil and are considered fair game for adventurers, other wizards, and anyone else hoping to steal your possessions or build a reputation."

Gordak nodded. "If I kill him it would be seen as proof that I am a murderous barbarian, but whether I would be applauded, or hunted down and hanged, would depend on what his neighbors and family thought of him."

"Then perhaps we need some response short of killing him."

"Could your daughter simply tell him to leave her alone? That she is in her father's house by choice?"

"Did he strike you as the sort of person who would accept that? Besides, much as I care for her, I don't want it known I have a daughter, and Liniandra doesn't want it known that I'm her father. I took her in when her mother died three years ago, and I'm very happy to have her here, but our relationship is...complicated."

Gordak thought for a moment, then said, "I have a thought. You said you have more of those spiders than you need?"

"Considerably more. Why?"

Gordak smiled.

* * *

Dolisar Kalen was lying on a silken couch, staring glumly at his mother's collection of exotic flowers, when a footman entered the garden and cleared his throat.

"What is it?" Dolisar asked, without moving.

"Someone who gives his name as Gordak is here to see you, sir."

"Gordak?" Dolisar rolled over and glared at the footman. "I don't know anyone..."

Then he stopped. "The barbarian?"

"He does not appear to be Ellemerian," the footman confirmed. He hesitated, then added, "He is carrying a large sack."

"Let him in!" Dolisar screamed, scrambling to his feet. "I'll see him in the blue parlor."

A moment later he rushed into the parlor to find Gordak seated comfortably on a velvet sofa, while a very large canvas bag lay squirming on the floor at his feet. Dolisar stopped dead and stared.

Gordak gestured at the bag. "I found Liniandra," he said. "But the wizard had..." He hesitated. "She may not be what you expected."

"What are you talking about?"

"I will forego half my promised payment," Gordak said, holding out his left hand. His right was on the hilt of his sword.

"What? Oh." He turned to the footman. "Fetch my green purse." Then he turned to stare at the squirming sack. After a moment, he asked, "Aren't you going to let her out?"

"As soon as I have my money."

For a few awkward seconds the men glared at each other; then the footman returned and handed a fat green purse to Dolisar. He promptly tossed it to Gordak, who caught it easily.

Gordak bowed. "Thank you," he said. "Pull on that string, and the bag will open. I'm so sorry for what Ammander Poritha did." Then he turned and marched toward the door.

Dolisar rushed forward and pulled on the string; sure enough, the knots that held the drawstring easily came free, and the mouth of the bag widened.

A black, chitinous leg thrust its way out of the opening, and then another.

As he stepped out onto the street Gordak heard Dolisar's scream, and smiled. He had never said that Liniandra was in the bag, and if Kalen thought she had been turned into a spider – well, that might discourage him from bothering Ammander Poritha in the future.

The Jurors

The anthology premise was to choose three historical figures from different periods, throw them together, and tell a story about them. I immediately chose these three. Why them? I have no idea. I do know I had to repeatedly explain that yes, I meant Mary Wollstonecraft Godwin and not her daughter, Mary Shelley.

Three time travelers watched as the young man walked into the room and took the chair on the opposite side of the table. He set a small rectangular object on the table; colors flickered across its surface.

He cleared his throat. "Good morning," he said. "My name is Tobe Carlsen, and I am here to explain your situation."

The younger of the male time travelers folded his hands behind his head, leaned back, and said, "Please do. I understand we are in what we would consider the future?"

"That's right, Mr. Fitzgerald. You are roughly a century and a half from the time of your death."

Fitzgerald frowned. "Go on."

"First, I don't know whether you've introduced yourselves. Ms. Wollstonecraft..."

"Mrs. Godwin," she interrupted.

"I'm sorry," Carlsen said. "Mrs. Godwin, then. This is Mary Wollstonecraft Godwin, who died in 1797, at the age of thirty-eight, from complications of the birth of her second child."

As this exchange took place Fitzgerald sat up and unfolded his hands, giving the woman a curious look.

Carlsen turned to the older man. "General William Tecumseh Sherman, U.S. Army, retired. Died of pneumonia in 1891, aged seventy-one." Fitzgerald gave Sherman a startled glance, then returned his attention to Carlsen as the man said, "And Mr. F. Scott Fitzgerald, died of heart failure in 1940, aged forty-four."

"If we are dead, how is it we are here?" Sherman demanded. "Surely this isn't the afterlife."

"No, it isn't," Carlsen agreed. "This is the city of Seattle in the year 2096, and you were brought here by means of a machine that allows us to travel through time. We abducted each of you from as close as we could manage to the instant of your death, brought you to our own era, and cured you of the ailments that killed you, keeping you asleep while we did so. We also made lifeless copies of your bodies, dressed them in the clothes you were wearing when you died, and left them in your places, so that your absence would not be noticed."

"I assume you realize this is quite incredible," Sherman said.

"Oh, I know. It's still true. You may be wondering why we did this – why abduct anyone, and more specifically, why you three."

"Yes," Godwin said. Both men nodded.

"Recently a person named Rasheeda Cho led an insurrection against the governments of Europe and North America. Rasheeda was defeated and arrested, and was to be brought to trial, when we encountered a difficulty. Our law requires an impartial jury. Well, in Rasheeda's case, we couldn't *find* an impartial jury." He tapped his rectangular device. "We have methods of communication that had allowed everyone to watch the events of the insurrection, and everyone we approached already had a very strong opinion on Rasheeda's guilt or innocence.

"At the same time, the scientists – I'm sorry, Mrs. Godwin, that word is from beyond your time; the scholars – who had recently constructed a time-traveling machine were eager to find a way to put it to use, and suggested that we draw our jurors from the past, as a demonstration that their work could be of practical value. We agreed.

"We required jurors who read and speak fluent English, since the trial would be conducted in English. We needed people where we knew enough of the details of their deaths to be able to *find* them, and take them without being seen. We preferred people who had written extensively, so that we could analyze their attitudes and beliefs. From the candidates who met these standards, you three were chosen for your clarity of thought and your experience of revolutions and their effects."

"Experience of revolutions?" Fitzgerald asked, startled. "*I* was? I mean, Mrs. Godwin saw the French Revolution first-hand, and General Sherman fought in the War Between the States, but what did *I* do?"

"You closely observed the class conflicts of the Jazz Age and the Great Depression," Carlsen replied. "A social revolution, rather than a political one."

Fitzgerald grimaced. "I think you got the wrong man."

"Why only three of us?" Sherman demanded, before Carlsen could respond. "Or are there nine more in other rooms somewhere?"

Carlsen sighed. "I was coming to that. The operation was under way, and you three had been retrieved, when the entire project was shut down."

"Why?" Fitzgerald asked. "You decided it was too dangerous?"

"No. Because Rasheeda was assassinated while awaiting trial."

"Assassinated?" Sherman asked.

Carlsen nodded.

"So you don't have any use for us?" Fitzgerald said. "You went to all this trouble for nothing?"

"That's right." He shifted in his chair. "Well, not really for *nothing*. We proved our methods worked. You're here, and alive."

"All right," Fitzgerald said. "I suppose we should be grateful for that, but now what? Are we going to be returned to our deathbeds? Or rather, these two to their deathbeds, and I to the living room floor?"

"No. We are not going to save your lives only to kill you again. You will stay in this time, and you are free to go. We will assist you in adjusting to our era."

"You aren't taking us back to our own times?" Fitzgerald asked.

"No," Carlsen said unhappily. "We don't dare. We're afraid your presence would alter the course of history, so that our own time would not exist."

"I do not understand that," Godwin said.

"It is recorded history that you, Ms... Mrs. Godwin, died in 1797. If you were to be found alive in 1798, the world would change in ways we cannot predict – though in *your* case, we do know one change that would alter our world. If you had lived to raise your daughter Mary, she would almost certainly not have written the novel *Frankenstein*, with its theme of parental abandonment. The development of modern literature would be completely different."

Godwin's eyes widened. "What? What are you saying?"

"I hate to say it, Mrs. Godwin, but he has a point," Fitzgerald said. "*Frankenstein* was *unbelievably* influential, and not just in literature."

"My Mary became a writer? A novelist?" Godwin looked thunderstruck.

No one answered her. "That's fine for her," Sherman said, "but what about me? I was retired and no longer doing anything of importance, just giving speeches."

"We cannot say what effect your survival might have had, General. It's true there is nothing as obvious as *Frankenstein*, but you were still politically influential, whether you intended to be or not."

"I did not."

"Nevertheless."

"And I suppose you're afraid I might actually write that masterpiece I wanted to write," Fitzgerald said. "A book added, rather than lost."

"Yes, Mr. Fitzgerald. You understand. Though you will be interested to know that Edmund Wilson published your unfinished final novel, *The Last Tycoon*. Had you been able to complete it – but you weren't."

"He did...what? Well, damn!"

"If we can't go back, then what *are* we supposed to do?" Sherman demanded.

"Whatever you wish. I'm sure historians will be eager to interview you, and you might become speakers or lecturers – you are, of course, more knowledgeable about your own times and your own works than anyone born in our century can ever be, and many people are interested in hearing about your experiences. Your speeches will be in as much demand here as in your own time, General, though the crowds will be virtual, rather than filling lecture halls."

"What does *that* mean?"

"We'll explain that."

"I will want to read my dear child's novel – what was the title, again?"

"*Frankenstein*," Fitzgerald replied. "It's very good, but...perhaps not what you might expect."

Carlsen cleared his throat. "We will need to acquaint you with the basics of modern civilization. Simply putting you out on the street without guidance would be cruel. Mrs. Godwin, in your case we think we should also provide an interpreter; English has changed somewhat in the last three hundred years."

"I would appreciate that," she said.

"Good." Carlsen nodded, then rose. "We'll install one. I will be back in a moment." He turned, and left the room.

For a moment the three sat silently; then Fitzgerald said, "Install?"

"That is what he said," Sherman said. "What he meant I cannot say. This entire situation is extremely strange."

"You can say *that* again!" Fitzgerald agreed. "It's something I wouldn't expect to find in the most lurid pulp magazines, let alone experience first-hand!"

"Pulp magazines?" Godwin asked.

"Well, the General would know them as dime novels, I suppose, but I'm damned if I can think of an equivalent from your time. Newgate Calendars, perhaps?"

"Oh," Godwin said, looking only slightly less puzzled.

"I might not be entirely convinced this is real, even yet, if not for the incidental details such as these 'pulp magazines'," Sherman said. "I'd say this must be some last-minute delirium, save I don't believe I have the imagination to come up with it all, even in my death throes."

"And that from one of the more imaginative military men in our history," Fitzgerald remarked. "The idiots in command in Europe in 1914 hadn't half your intelligence or imagination."

"Was there a war in 1914? I wouldn't know," Sherman said, a bit stiffly.

"Of course not. But there was, and rest assured, the best of their generals were bumbling fools compared to you. I read your memoirs – you're a brave and talented man, General. The men running the World War were not. I volunteered in 1917 because I thought serving under them would be a more respectable way to die than outright suicide, but I didn't get sent to the front in time to pull that off."

Godwin listened to this with growing interest. "You wished to die?" she asked.

"Well, I thought so at the time. I got over it."

Sherman snorted. "I suppose a woman was involved?"

"Ah, you know romantic young men too well, General." He glanced at Godwin. "I seem to recall that your posthumous memoir mentioned suicide attempts. I concede you had more reason than I."

She blinked. "Posthumous memoir?"

"Your husband published it. I haven't read it, merely descriptions."

"It is very strange to hear that anything I wrote might be considered posthumous, since I am yet alive."

"Personally, I'm glad you are," Fitzgerald said. "I confess I haven't read any of your work, Miss Wollstonecraft, but I would like to."

"Hm," Sherman muttered.

Fitzgerald looked at him. "Her reputation as a writer and philosopher was much improved in my time over how she was viewed in yours, General, and that she was chosen as we were is intriguing."

"Not to me."

"I wonder how long they'll keep us waiting?" Fitzgerald asked.

"No telling," Sherman said. "At least here we don't have all those confounded moving images and colored lights and hums and clicks that were all over my hospital room."

Fitzgerald shrugged. "I made my living from moving images. Or at least, from words intended to accompany them, though most of what I wrote never made it onto the screen."

Sherman frowned at Fitzgerald. "And was this a respectable way to earn a living, where you came from?"

"Not really. It's what I was reduced to when my novels stopped selling."

"You were primarily a novelist?"

Fitzgerald sighed. "I like to think I still am, despite how I earned my bread for the last few years before they kidnaped me. Apparently I am sufficiently remembered as such that they considered me worth fetching here." He glanced at Sherman. "And I must say, General, that it is an honor to be treated as your peer."

"Hmpf."

"Excuse me, gentlemen," Godwin said, rising from her chair. She walked to the door they had entered through; it slid aside as she approached, and she stepped into the corridor beyond.

The door closed behind her.

"What's *that* about?"

"A call of nature, I suppose."

"I suppose." Sherman cast a look at the door, then turned back to Fitzgerald. "I would not be too sure it *is* an honor to be considered my peer, sir; the fact that they have put me in the company of a notorious and wanton madwoman like Mrs. Godwin does not speak well of my reputation here."

"Madwoman?" Fitzgerald threw a glance at the door, then smiled wryly. "Oh, she's no madwoman, whatever the people of your time may have thought. Believe me, I know a madwoman when I see one. I was *married* to one, and Mrs. Godwin is nothing like her, nor like any of the others I've met when visiting my wife in the asylum."

"You are doing nothing to dissuade me from my opinion."

Just then Carlsen reappeared, followed by three others, a man, a woman, and one whose gender was not immediately obvious; all of them wore blue pants and white tunics, similar in cut to the pale blue pants and tunics the time travelers had been issued. Each held two rectangular objects about the size of a children's book. "Where's Ms. Godwin?" Carlsen asked.

Fitzgerald gestured toward the door. "She didn't say."

"Ah. Well, I'll start with you two, then. General Sherman, this is Darine Ramirez." The clearly female person stepped forward. She handed Sherman one of the rectangular things.

"It's an honor to meet you, sir," she said. "This is your tablet; come with me and I'll explain how to use it."

"Perhaps we'll meet again, Mr. Fitzgerald," he said, as he allowed Darine Ramirez to lead him away.

The clearly male new arrival stepped forward. "Mr. Fitzgerald? I'm Caspar Tranh." He proffered a tablet. As Fitzgerald accepted it, the door opened and Godwin reappeared.

"Mrs. Godwin," the third individual said, stepping forward. "I am to be your tutor in your brave new world."

They reached out a tablet, and Godwin accepted it. "And your name?" she asked.

"Robin Walters. If you will follow me?"

She glanced at Fitzgerald.

"It has been a pleasure, Mrs. Godwin," he said.

"Farewell, Mr. Fitzgerald." Then she followed Walters.

Fitzgerald turned to Carlsen. "Will I ever see them again?"

"That's up to you," Carlsen said. "Now, if you would accompany Caspar..."

Fitzgerald did so.

* * *

One year later, Scott Fitzgerald sat in a café sipping some weird descendant of Coca-Cola – there were so many varieties that he did not try to keep them straight, but simply took whatever the machines first offered – when Mary Godwin walked in and looked around. He waved, and she crossed to his table.

"Mr. Fitzgerald," she said, as he rose and pulled out a chair for her.

"It's been over a year since I did that for a lady," he said, as they both sat.

"Many of the old niceties do seem to have been lost," she agreed.

A machine rolled up and set a glass of tea and a plate of tiny sandwiches on the table, then moved smoothly away.

"I do find some of the changes improvements, though," she said, sipping her drink.

"You ordered online?"

"Yes."

"I don't really have the hang of that yet. I always get some detail wrong."

"For my own part, I find these intelligent machines quite agreeable." She sipped tea again. "Will General Sherman be joining us?"

"I hope so. I did not get a straight answer."

She nodded. "And how have you been faring this past year?"

"Well enough. Carlsen was right that I would have an audience for whatever I might want to say, but I could wish for a *better* audience. I am very tired of answering stupid questions about *The Great Gatsby*."

"Your...third novel, was it?"

"Yes. And it seems to be the only one anyone remembers. I am further mortified that that fool Wilson published the fragments of *The Love of the Last Tycoon*, rather than doing the decent thing and leaving it alone."

"At least you are remembered for *your* work, even if not as you would have chosen. There *are* a handful of scholars familiar with my work, and I am credited by them as one of the early visionaries whose writings helped bring about the equality of the sexes now taken for granted, but to the vast majority of the population I seem to be known only as the mother of the author of *Frankenstein*. I am constantly being asked about a child who was barely ten days old when last I saw her, and about whom I know almost nothing."

"Did you read the novel?"

"I did. I found it tremendously sad. If I could only return to my own era and raise little Mary in a loving household!"

"Then it would not have been written."

"And would that be a tragedy? Perhaps she might write something joyous in its stead."

"Well, *I* would regret its loss – assuming I knew of it, which of course I wouldn't." He frowned thoughtfully.

"I also read my husband's *Memoirs of the Author of A Vindication of the Rights of Woman*. It is absolutely not what I would have published, had I lived."

"It did not serve your memory well," Fitzgerald agreed.

"Oh, here is the General!" Godwin exclaimed, waving.

A moment later Sherman joined them at the table, and accepted a glass of some amber-colored beverage from a serving machine.

"General," Fitzgerald said. "A pleasure to see you again."

"Is it?"

"Why, yes," Godwin said.

"You prefer a relic like me to the popinjays and perverts of this time?"

The others exchanged uncomfortable glances.

"A relic, sir?" Fitzgerald asked.

"What else would you call it? I have neither friends nor family, and serve no purpose in this place. I have accepted several speaking engagements, but they have all been done as talking images, rather than standing upon an actual stage, and the audiences are far less congenial than those of my own times. Interviews with historians have also proven less than enjoyable. I must thank you, though, Mr. Fitzgerald, for mentioning the generals of the First World War. I have been studying them, and I find it a far more appealing topic of research than this new world; I can *understand* them, and see where they went wrong. I wish I had been there to tell them what fools they were, and perhaps put them on a better path. Tens of thousands of lives could have been saved."

"It seems we would all prefer to return to our own times," Godwin said. "I to raise my daughter and see that my husband did not make a hash of my memoir, you to show the generals of Europe how to avoid needless slaughter, and Mr. Fitzgerald to finish his novel. Would that it was possible!"

Fitzgerald said, "You know, it's not actually *impossible*; it's simply forbidden."

"Oh?" Godwin said.

Fitzgerald nodded. "I've been studying it – time travel, I mean. They won't allow us to return to our lives because they're afraid we'll change history, but it's not that we *can't* go back. The machine that brought us here can take us back."

"You are sure of this?" Sherman asked.

Fitzgerald nodded. "Absolutely. And I have been studying the theory involved – not the actual physics, that's beyond me, but the theories regarding causality and what would happen if we *did* change the past."

"Go on, Mr. Fitzgerald," Godwin said.

"I'm afraid this is...well, it sounds insane, frankly, but the physicists..."

"The what?" Godwin interrupted.

"Physicists. People who study the science of physics."

"Go on," Sherman said. "What do these mad scientists say?"

"Well, the basic argument is that you cannot change what has already happened – which seems obvious enough, doesn't it? At any rate, if we were to return to our former lives, the universe in which we died would not be changed, because it can't be; it already existed, and if it didn't, we wouldn't be here discussing it. Instead we would create an entirely new version of reality existing alongside this one. They even have a word for this theoretical creation – a 'timeline.' Theory says that there can be multiple timelines, and that if we returned to our own times, we would create new timelines, entire new universes that would follow their own paths, while *this* universe, where we died on schedule, would continue to exist, blithely unaware of any changes. Our Mr. Carlsen and his friends are worrying about nothing in their determination to prevent us from going back; this reality will not be changed, and will be unaware a new one has been created. I read several articles saying as much. Apparently there is a consensus among physicists, but the politicians reject it."

"New universes?" Sherman said doubtfully.

"I was not aware the word 'universe' could have a plural," Godwin said.

"Say 'worlds,' then." Fitzgerald replied. "Or realms. Think of the worlds where we return to our old lives as realms like Faerie."

"And you say the time machine can take us to this Land Beneath the Hill, where we will have our friends and family around us again?" Godwin asked.

Fitzgerald nodded. "Of course," he said, "that would mean giving up everything we have here that was not invented yet in our own times. No medical miracles that brought us back to life and cured us of the diseases that killed us. No tablets that can answer every question. No foods brought from every corner of the world, regardless of the season."

"I'll take that," Sherman said. "No constant buzzing and humming from machinery everywhere, no flashing lights and moving pictures, no creatures who are neither men nor women."

"I quite like some of the machinery, though its ubiquity can be disconcerting," Godwin said. "I confess that I am not entirely comfortable with some of the changes in society, however, even though I argued for many of them; I am still a creature of my own upbringing, as are we all. But this is all nonsense; we have no choice. Perhaps the machine can take us back, but its keepers will not allow it."

All three were silent for a moment, though the café was anything but; there was a constant buzz of conversation, and unpleasant music playing.

Then Fitzgerald said, "I have a long history of doing things that weren't allowed. True, most were when I was either young and stupid or very drunk, but still. And since they repaired my heart and liver for me, I feel twenty years younger; I think I'm capable of being quite stupid again."

"I have never felt the need to let others dictate my actions," Sherman replied. "I think we can find a way."

"They did choose us for our familiarity with rebellion," Godwin mused.

"I have an idea of how we can get to the machine," Fitzgerald said. "We are celebrities, after all, and that gives us power. I don't know how to operate it, though."

"Perhaps I can help," Godwin said.

"Really?" Fitzgerald cocked his head.

"As I said, I have taken quite an interest in electronic devices, and I have made friends these past few months who are very knowledgeable," she said. "We may need some time, though."

"That can be arranged," Sherman said, "if you two are serious about this."

Fitzgerald smiled crookedly. "As serious as a heart attack," he said.

* * *

"I think this is a wonderful idea," Tobe Carlsen said. "I'm glad to see the three of you finally enjoying your celebrity. You know, I'd had some concerns about how you were adjusting, Mr. Fitzgerald."

"Scott," Fitzgerald said. "Please, call me Scott."

"Scott," Carlsen said, smiling.

"Are the cameras getting it all?" Fitzgerald asked, looking at the swarm of drones cruising around the laboratory.

"I'm sure they are." He glanced back as Mary Godwin and someone he did not recognize followed them into the big room.

"Mrs. Godwin wanted to bring a friend," Fitzgerald said. "I trust that's not a problem?"

"Oh, not at all! I'm pleased she's made friends!"

"That's good. I believe General Sherman may have brought a few, as well." He turned to the structure occupying the center of the laboratory. "So this is it, then?"

"That's it. Of course, it's shut down now."

"Of course." Godwin and her companion came up to stand beside Fitzgerald as he studied the time machine. It was smaller than he had expected.

Behind them General Sherman entered the room, accompanied by two very large men.

"Do you think you could turn on the power?" Fitzgerald asked. "Just so the lights come on, to make it look a little more exciting. You don't want our viewers to think the project has been completely abandoned. I mean, one point of today's exercise is to convince them that the money spent here wasn't wasted. "

"I think we can do that," Carlsen said. He ran a finger across the miniature tablet on his wrist, and a dozen screens and indicators on the time machine lit up.

"Thank you, Tobe – may I call you Tobe?"

"Of course!" Carlsen smiled, bathing in his own sense of self-importance.

Sherman had joined the party, his two men hanging back. Godwin was now close beside Fitzgerald, and her companion had stepped back a little as well, where she was doing something with a tablet.

"You're on in five," a voice said from somewhere overhead.

"Thank you," Carlsen said. He turned to face the largest of the drones, which had dropped down to eye level. A red light came on.

"Dear viewers," Carlsen said, "welcome to our special presentation on the International Physics Consortium's time travel program. I'm sure you've all heard about it, and perhaps even seen interviews with some of the people involved, but today we have the three people brought from the past, who have agreed to appear together for the first time..."

He rambled on for what seemed like hours, but Fitzgerald knew it was really just a few minutes. He noticed that Godwin looked nervous. Sherman looked alert, but calm.

Carlsen introduced each of them, and asked a few questions, which they answered. Then Fitzgerald saw Godwin's friend with the tablet nod.

"May we go inside?" he asked Carlsen. "Just the three of us? I don't think we can fit any more; it's not very big."

"Inside?"

Fitzgerald nodded. "I mean, we were unconscious when we were in it before, and I'd like to see what it looks like."

Carlsen looked uncertain.

"We don't mind if the drone comes in with us," Fitzgerald said. "I mean, we aren't going to break anything."

"Well, I suppose..."

"Won't your viewers want to see the inside, as well?"

"Yes, of course! Good idea. Ms. Godwin, General...?"

The three of them clambered through the hatch into the machine, Fitzgerald first, Sherman next, and Godwin last, a drone squeezing in between Sherman and Godwin.

And the instant Godwin was inside, the hatch slammed shut and the machine shifted from standby mode to powering up. Panels lit, and a loud hum sounded. The drone in the machine with them fell to the floor, inert.

"It seems your friend knows her stuff," Fitzgerald said.

"I trusted her, and I do not trust lightly," Godwin replied, tapping commands on her own tablet.

Something pounded on the hatch from the outside. Fitzgerald looked up.

"Don't worry," Sherman said. "My men know their job."

"You're sure you can trust them?"

"They were two of Rasheeda Cho's most devoted troops. They have no love for the government here, and will make sure no one prevents our departure."

"Mary?"

"There!" she said, with a final triumphant click. She looked at Fitzgerald. "I do hope you gave me the correct time and place."

"I hope so, too," he said, as the air around them began to shimmer.

* * *

They had not given much thought to the fact that there were dead bodies in their respective places, but the solution was obvious. Sherman and Fitzgerald heaved Fitzgerald's corpse into the machine just as Sheilah Graham entered the room.

"Scott, what the *hell*!" she exclaimed.

"Just a moment," Fitzgerald said. Then he stepped back as the hatch closed.

Harry Culver, the building's manager, was close behind Graham. He stared as the time machine flickered and vanished.

"What the *hell*," Graham repeated.

"What was that?" Culver asked.

"How about," Fitzgerald said, "we pretend none of this ever happened? Because I can't give you a reasonable explanation, but I can assure you it won't happen again."

"But...are you okay?" Graham asked. "I thought you were dead!"

"I'm fine," Fitzgerald replied. "I'm fine. And I'm not going anywhere."

* * *

Aboard the time machine, Sherman and Godwin both stared at Fitzgerald's corpse with distaste. There was no room to move more than a few inches away from it, but they did their best not to touch it.

"I'm afraid you'll have my body as well for the final leg," Sherman said.

"I will bear up," Godwin replied.

"I'm sure you will. While I may have entertained unkind thoughts about your beliefs and morals, Mrs. Godwin, since meeting you I have never once doubted your courage and resourcefulness." He hesitated, then asked, "What do you plan to do with this machine, once you reach your home?"

"I intend to send it into the distant past, where no one will have any notion what it is, or how to operate it, or how it came to have three cadavers in it."

Sherman nodded. "A good solution." He turned his attention from Fitzgerald's dead face to Godwin's very alive one. "How *did* you learn to operate it?"

"I did not think to study time travel, as our friend did," she said, gesturing toward the corpse, "but I found the devices of that place fascinating." She held up her tablet. "I learned as much about them as I could, with the help of Robin Walters and our friend Kris. There are those who teach themselves to use these machines illicitly; they call themselves hackers, and take pride in gaining access to forbidden information. Kris is one such. She was able to find out everything I needed to know to operate this machine; it is, after all, merely a larger device. All of their electronic devices operate on the same principles." Then she looked at her tablet, and said, "Shall we deliver you to your deathbed, General?"

* * *

Godwin's control of the machine had improved, and the two remaining travelers were prepared for the task of manhandling a body into the time machine, so they were able to manage the transition in Sherman's New York home more smoothly than the one in Fitzgerald's Hollywood residence. Godwin launched herself for home before anyone caught more than a faint glimpse of her transport.

At her final destination, though, she required her baffled husband's assistance in loading her doppelganger into the machine. After the machine's disappearance he demanded an explanation, and she told him, "You must consider it a miracle, dear William, and accept it as such. I cannot tell you more unless you would think me a madwoman. Know only that I am here, I am well, and I am eager to spend the remainder of my life with you and Fanny and Mary."

* * *

The Godwin family thrived, and no further mention was ever made of the strange apparition and miraculous cure. William inquired about the curious tablet his wife had acquired, and the manuscript she hastily copied from it – *Frankenstein, or the New Prometheus* – but received only evasion, and no real answer. The tablet went dark forever after a month or so; as for the manuscript, Mrs. Godwin refused to publish it, but presented it to young Mary on her twenty-first birthday. Whatever explanation she gave her daughter remained between the two of them.

The feminist movement led by Mrs. Godwin took root and grew, as well, though far more slowly than she liked.

"It is faster than it was previously, at least," she said to her husband, and once again she refused to provide an explanation.

* * *

After his miraculous recovery from pneumonia, General W.T. Sherman surprised everyone by taking ship for Europe, where he seemed determined to track down certain French and British officers and engage them in extended conversation about military history and practice. Upon Germany's surrender in 1916, several of the victorious generals credited their success to Sherman's tutelage.

* * *

F. Scott Fitzgerald's *The Love of the Last Tycoon* was published to critical acclaim in the spring of 1943; wartime paper shortages severely hampered sales, but in 1945 a second edition landed on the bestseller list. Fitzgerald's sixth novel, *A Time of Strangers*, took an unexpected turn into science fiction, but was nonetheless well received.

* * *

In October of 2097 Tobe Carlsen stared in horror at the empty space at the center of the laboratory floor. He waited for the world he knew to vanish around him, to be replaced by something alien – or by nothing at all.

Nothing changed.

He lost his job, of course, even though that final webcast became a popular success, with over three billion views. He checked feverishly to see whether he could find any difference in the world, but the histories of Mary Wollstonecraft Godwin, William Tecumseh Sherman, and F. Scott Fitzgerald were all just as he remembered them.

He tried very hard to ignore the possibility that his own memories had changed, along with all records.

Several people told him that this simply proved the diverging timeline hypothesis. Others suggested that the inexperienced people from the past had been unable to handle the machine properly and were lost in time, or had simply ceased to exist.

The two Rasheedists who had held security at bay during the hijacking were apprehended, tried, and convicted, but served only six months.

The time machine never reappeared.

* * *

In a fifth timeline, a mysterious metal box containing three corpses appeared out of nowhere on the island of Hokkaido during the later Neolithic era. The cult that grew up around this phenomenon became the foundation of the Ainu Empire that ruled much of Asia for some 1,100 years. Later archeologists studying the remains concluded that the box was a tomb of some sort, but no consensus on its origins was ever reached.

Distractions

In the late 1980s there was much online discussion of what the next trend in science fiction would be after cyberpunk had run its course. I jokingly suggested it would be New Age cyberpunk. (I also suggested vampire unicorns and a few other possibilities.) As an example, I wrote the opening paragraphs of a story called "Maidens in Mirrorshades." I was then challenged to complete the story, so I did. I sold it. In fact, I sold it three times over a period of more than twenty years, because the planned publications kept going broke before seeing print. It never did appear; this is its first publication. Warning: Includes sexual stuff and rude language.

Fingers jitter across the keyboard, the sensory inputs are hardwired but the run command's still gotta be typed, she doesn't use the mouse with the eyeset on. She hits enter and Amber's in the glade, angle of the light's wrong but a quick patch and that's fixed. The shadows are slow adjusting; someone must be eating bandwidth like M&Ms somewhere. She calls the file and the unicorn is there; the smile on her face is visible only in realtime, only where her mouth shows below the eyeset, in the glade she's calm and taking it all in.

She lets the 'corn see her, and the head comes up, the horn raised high as it looks her over; she thinks that if a man did that she'd call law, and her smile's wider than ever.

She's got a white lace dress keyed in, nothing like the realtime jeans, and she's enhanced a curve here and there, she knows she's a walking wet dream in here, and suddenly for a moment it all slips and she thinks jesus, why am I wasting this on a fucking computer program, and it's not even a man, it's a fancy horse...

And then the 'corn takes a step toward her, and the curves of its neck, the feathering on its hooves, the glow of its silvery hide are all perfect, all running smooth and clean and perfect as a Hollywood kiss. It's realer than real and she's back in her role. She lifts a hand, reaches out toward it, and the electrons surge, she knows she's breathing fast out there as it steps closer. Light's sparkling from the golden horn, virtual light that doesn't need a source. Golden eyes gaze at her, she can see into them like deep pools...

And a little too deep, the gold's gone and the image is breaking up, there's static, and then everything's gone and she's sitting at the console smelling nonexistent oranges, her vision kicked up into the purple for an instant as the eyeset flares out, as she drops back to realtime and the damn oranges are suddenly mixed with the smell of hair burning.

"Goddamn *shit!*" she says, snatching the plug from behind her ear and the eyeset from her face. "Goddamn fucking power surge!"

"Burned again, Amber?"

The voice comes from the door, and she looks up and it's Jess, with that thing on her shoulder like a severed hand except it's green as a frog and has those red, red eyes, like it's been out on a three-week binge.

"Damn right," she says. "You'd think they'd have VR debugged by now."

"They do," Jess tells her. "At least in theory. What they ain't got is the hardware and personnel to keep it all up and running, what with half the country out on VR."

"You're exaggerating," Amber says, turning back to the console. She thinks again and pulls away from the keyboard, but it's hard, it's like swimming in glue, like getting out of a warm bed on a cold morning when the heat's down, like letting go of a lover. The unicorn's in there waiting, or maybe it is, maybe the file's damaged and she'll have to go to backup, and the backup hasn't got that last level of detail, that final high-definition gloss, but if she checks she'll be in there for hours, if the power doesn't surge again, if the net doesn't go down, if some Trojan horse doesn't start eating data.

Jess is right, virtual reality is an addiction, it's eating people.

But by the Goddess, it's fun!

"I look on it as an interesting experiment in evolution," Jess says, leaning against the doorframe, speaking in a formal voice like a newscaster on CNN deep background, like a prof starting to lecture. The hand thing doesn't like the frame crowding close and scuttles down her red flannel shirt, onto the curve of her breast, two of its legs hooked into the shirt pocket.

Amber gives her the go ahead look, ready to rock and roll – when it's words she can give as good as she gets, she can dish with the best.

"If half the population veges out in VR," Jess says, "Western Civ's going down the toilet with the rest of the shit, and it's the vidiots who buy it. It'll be the rest of us, the ones who don't surf the net, don't watch the feed, who'll survive and rebuild."

"Oh, right, the people who don't know enough to run a box are gonna rebuild?"

"Hey, we can, but we don't. We know when to unplug." The hand thing looks up at Jess' face and waves a finger-foot idly.

Amber frowns. "Am I plugged in?"

"Is the system up?" Jess retorts.

Amber glances at the board and smiles. "Sure is," she says.

"So okay, you're not hooked that bad yet," Jess replies. "Maybe you'll pull through, along with those of us who prefer reality to a few gigabytes of dream." She reaches up and pets the hand thing, which is stroking two legs along the slope of her breast.

"Oh, you're never on the net?" Amber asks innocently. "You never call up a little happy talk when you're bored? Never do a little erotic software when you're horny?"

"Sure I do. But I don't skip meals. I don't blow off my job." She pulls the hand thing out of her pocket and puts it back on her shoulder as she steps into the room, away from the door.

"This *is* my job." Amber picks up the eyeset, doesn't put it on. "They pay me. Content provider."

"So why do you think I'm talking about you, then?" Jess smiles, she's scored her point and cut the game short. She approaches the console, moving with a slow sideways grace to see what's on the screen. The hand thing hangs on with three legs, uses its fourth to bat at the earring that dangles from Jess' earlobe, tangled in her black hair. The earring's in the shape of a spider clutching a tiny skull. "So what are you working on?"

"Unicorns," Amber tells her, punching a three-key sequence that calls up a 2D image, 3600 dpi resolution, on the display. The 'corn is there, the glade, but no woman, no virgin in white lace, and the 'corn's cycling through a simple loop animation, there's no life to it.

Jess lets her lip curl.

"I thought you were hot shit," she says, "girl genius of the web, twenty-six years old and you're still playing with My Little Pony? God and goddess, if all you want's a horse with a horn on it, I can graft you one, or gene it up and crash-grow. Take a couple of months, but it'll be real and solid, not just VR."

"Not a horse. Check the tail. Cloven hooves."

"Close enough. Minor gene rewrite. Get me a horse and I can grow you one looks just like that."

"Yeah, and it'll act like a horse, not a unicorn. Not to mention it'll eat and shit."

Jess blinks, thinking that over.

"I could maybe fix that," she says.

Amber stares at her.

"No shit?" she says.

Jess stares back, and a smile works its way across her face despite her, and she laughs.

"That's right," she says. "No shit."

"This I gotta see," Amber says.

* * *

The problem is harder than she thought, it's a stone bitch even with her head wired on flash and an illegal implant, and the flash wears off every three hours and she can't get a dermal drip, the market's gone bad, too many good old customers home with their heads plugged into the VR box, her connection says, the pipeline's running dry, get the flash while she can because it's all there is.

So Jess is flashing and working the genes, trying to clean up the loop, make the 'corn a closed system, no solid input or output.

She can get the end product down to not much, she can gene-rig it to about 90% efficiency, but that last ten percent, there's no way she can see. Maybe sweat it off, but not at horse size; run on sunlight, not unless it's green, and it won't exactly be running and dancing in the fucking moonlight at the energy level she can get from photosynth.

It's gotta be cyborg.

And Jess don't know shit about cyborg.

When she comes down off the flash again she stays down and does the tube of detox from her mother's bedside shelf, just to be sure, and she goes to check out what's on the market, what's on the web.

Right away she hits it, Russian nuclear waste in a sealed container, private corp that bought it on a gamble and can't use it, looking for someone who can. She reads the emissions catalog, figures the energy, and hits it: custom bacteria living off the heat, the 'corn lives off the bacteria, raw materials from air and water, waste material boiled off, lost in breath or sweat. Tricky, not impossible.

Tricky.

Because if you put that thing in a 'corn's gut, that'll be shielding enough to keep the NRC happy on the street, she can do that, but the mutation rate inside the 'corn, in that happy little bac colony, is going to make all her tinkering come apart like one of the old Soviet republics unless she can come up with a way to purify the strain on site.

Or keep the mutations in the right directions.

And on-site phages, the obvious fix, are gonna mutate, too.

Truly, an authentic killer. Back to the flash.

The models won't run. Jess stares at the screen, plugs in to get it right, sees the whole thing freeze up on her. Her system isn't S.O.T.A., hasn't got the raw ram to do a job this thick. Someone needs to tickle it down.

Or she can crack a Cray-Ola somewhere, get all the raw she needs, and get five to recon if she's caught.

She could buy time – if she had the juice, and hadn't spent it on flash and tissue samples and cold storage.

She unplugs and stares at the screen, and the hand thing crawls down her arm onto the keyboard. She snatches it off and sits there holding it, its finger-legs intertwined with her own fingers, its eyes looking up at her like the eyes of some Old Church pilgrim watching for God in the cathedral tracery.

She needs to have it tickled down. Or to get time somewhere, crack it or buy it.

She can't do those – but she knows who can.

And what the hell, it's Amber's damn 'corn in the first place.

* * *

In the back of her mind, or really somewhere in the right side of her cortex, Amber knows she shouldn't be here, she's been in VR too much lately, but the stud is just too much, the audience is applauding, and she can't remember if this is sim or inter, and it's all washing over her with an intensity realtime's never had for her, and she only half-remembers that that's because she spliced an illegal voltage boost into the sensory feed. He's got her on the bed and he's penetrating her in more ways than would be possible in realtime, he's more than human and so is she, and the audience is cheering and screaming and she wishes she could remember whether they're all just a bunch of electrons or whether she's let realtime people watch through the web...

And then there's a flash and everything goes white and she's coming all over and she feels herself slam against the back of her chair and realizes that that's realtime, she's coming out of the VR, somebody's done something, is it the cops, is the net going down?

And she remembers that that was inter, the stud was CGI but the audience was all inter, she was letting real people watch her fantasy, and the idea is horrible and wonderful at the same time, and she arches her back in another orgasm, and then she's sitting in the chair, the eyeset dark, and her back's bruised, her pants are soaked, the system's shut down, but she feels wonderful and sleepy and content and at the same time she wants to get back in, back on, do it all over again.

"Amber?"

It's Jess' voice.

Amber unplugs and places the jack on the desk by feel, the eyeset is still on, she's still blind. Then, reluctantly, very slowly, using both hands, she lifts the eyeset off and blinks at the screen of her monitor.

It's blank.

"You okay?" Jess asks. She's not on the monitor, she's standing six feet away.

"I'm fine," Amber snaps.

"You were moaning and twitching. And you practically broke the chair there at the end."

"I was coming, you asshole!"

"Sorry."

They stare at each other for a moment, until Amber sighs and asks, "What is it?"

"I got bugs. I need some hacking if you want this unicorn we talked about."

For a moment Amber stares up at Jess with no idea at all what she's talking about, Amber's still half in the fantasy, half on that frilly pink bed with her more-than-human lover and all those people watching, the net voyeurs – and then she remembers.

"You're really gonna do it?" she asks.

Jess snorts. "That was the idea."

"So what's the bug?"

Jess shows her a minidisk, and Amber plugs it in and then plugs herself in while Jess calls up the file. She sits there, intent and blind, while Jess waits.

"You need negative feedback," Amber tells her at last.

"I know that," Jess snaps.

Amber shakes her head, then waits for a second's dizziness to pass before saying, "No, I mean, you can hook the system up to a watchdog box. Like the cancer hunters the meds use."

That dizzy spell worries her. She has been in VR too much. When was the last time she ate? And she realizes her bladder is painfully full – with that realization comes relief that at least that's not what wet her pants, that'd be embarrassing, and the odor would give it away. Still jacked in, she checks the system time/date and almost chokes.

"Bad enough I need to use a nuke for power," Jess is saying, and Amber tries to listen, rather than dashing to the bathroom. "Now you want I should build in more gadgets? I just wanted you to help me model the gene variations, not come up with a whole new angle. Where would I get a watchdog?"

Amber smiles a lopsided smile and opens a desk drawer. Still smiling, she throws a catalog on the desk in front of Jess, a hardcopy catalog the size of an old Manhattan phone book, except that instead of columns of names and numbers the pages are covered with specifications for electronic hardware and software.

As Jess stares, wondering who the hell still prints catalogs on paper, Amber heads for the door, saying, "I'll be right back."

When she returns Jess is paging through the catalog.

"Some of this stuff..." she says, and her voice trails off. She knows now who still prints on paper. Paper can't be traced, hacked, shut down. There's stuff here that shouldn't be running loose.

"Amazing, isn't it?" Amber agrees. "Still think everybody's too busy on VR to produce anything?"

"Maybe not yet," Jess says. She points to an item. "Would this work?"

"Don't know," Amber says. "Check the specs on-line."

"You check – I don't know this stuff."

"What, you can't surf the web?" Amber stares in exaggerated astonishment.

"I can surf it," Jess says, angry, "but you're better at it. Can you hack genes?"

"Not like you," Amber admits. "Sorry, Jess. Hacking code is hacking code, but we've all got our own specialties." She takes the catalog and plugs in; keys rattle.

Jess watches, notices how thin Amber's gotten. She isn't nuked, and hasn't been eating.

Jess wonders if she could come up with something that would feed someone while she's in VR, something better than the standard IV or time-release granola bars, some kind of internal flora, maybe. Gotta be a big market for that; would mean she could drop the diddly-shit stuff she does to pay the bills, and live on royalties.

At least until the illegal clones wreck the market.

She reaches up and remembers that the hand-thing isn't on her shoulder, she left it back in her room. Suddenly nervous, she looks over Amber's shoulder at the monitor screen.

Specs flash up for a watchdog box, one centimeter by one by six, safe for implantation, runs off blood flow, maps genes, armed with electrochemical zap, tracks and kills whatever cells it's told to.

Range, ten centimeters.

"I need to cover a bigger area than that," Jess says, remembering the size of her power supply.

"So get a dozen."

"What's it cost?"

Amber points.

Jess chews her lip and thinks, she's got the juice but this wasn't what she'd planned for it.

But what the hell, she can hack it. Or Amber can.

"You buy me those, girl, I build your 'corn. Cyborg, nuke power – no food, no waste."

"No shit?" Amber stares at the screen. "How long will it take?"

"Maybe six weeks."

"You got it," Amber says. "You got it all."

* * *

The unicorn is beautiful, sleek and white, with its long golden horn and cloven gold hooves, and it's hanging motionless in the straps as Jess drains the tank. It's smaller than a horse, larger than a pony, alive and breathing shallowly.

Amber stares in awe. This is new. This is nothing she's seen in VR. The jungle smell of the nutrient fluid is thick and pungent, the horn shatters light into glitter. The white hide shines like a cat's just-licked fur.

Watching it grow has kept Amber offline half the time for weeks, more time in realspace than she's done in years. Now it's ready.

It's beautiful, and completely out of place in its jury-rigged surroundings.

Then it moves, and the eyes, when they open, are rich amber and strangely patterned, a complexity that Amber hasn't seen even in 3600 dpi fractals. The 'corn raises its head and looks at her. Its nostrils flare.

"I left out most of the stuff about virgins," Jess says. "Figured you'd want to be able to touch it. But I gave it the best sense of smell I could – dog genes. It's checking you out."

"It's still in the tank," Amber says.

"Tank's open at the top. It can smell us."

"And see us," Amber says.

"Of course."

"It's a female, you said?"

"Neuter," Jess says. "Two X chromosomes, but no genitalia at all."

"Damn," Amber says.

"It needs a little water, but no food. Burns off its wastes as sweat."

"Damn," Amber says again.

"So now that you've got it," Jess says, "What are you going to do with it?"

The unicorn turns its head, moving with a sudden sinuous flexing that no horse ever displayed, and studies its surroundings through the plexiglass tank walls.

"Ooooh," Amber says.

"Snake genes," Jess tells her. "For the musculature and some of the nervous system. It's got horse and goat and deer and other stuff, too." She glances at the 'corn, then back at Amber. "So what're you gonna do with it?"

"Um," Amber says, frowning. She had not thought about that. Virtual creations are easy – file 'em away on disk somewhere. Hardware's easy, too – just toss it in the corner or the closet.

But a unicorn?

The 'corn lowers its head, and at first Amber thinks it's studying its own forelegs, but then it's moving, sudden as a startled lizard, golden horn thrust forward. A sound like a paper punch the size of a semi, and plexiglass spalls, white instead of clear.

"Oh, shit," Jess says, running for cover.

The unicorn rears, and with a clatter of hooves leaps up and out of the tank, scrabbling at plexiglass.

This isn't any forest glade, it's a cluttered bio lab, and this isn't any fantasy 'corn, it's a real animal, with a half-meter of gold-plated spear on its head; Amber steps back, suddenly trembling.

She doesn't run, though, and the unicorn stops and sniffs, taking her scent. Then it ducks its head.

Amber tenses, certain it's about to jab that horn forward and impale her, not in any symbolic or sexual way but in a burst of pain and blood that would kill her dead dead dead. She gets ready to dive to the side, out of its path, the instant she sees it move.

Then the head comes up again, the horn is pointed at the ceiling instead of her chest, and the 'corn looks at her, and she reads disappointment in its eyes. It turns and moves, something midway between a trot and a slither, and then it rears and kicks and with a roar like white noise the corridor door shatters into a million half-centimeter safety-glass cubes and a dozen bent strips of aluminum alloy. Then the 'corn is out in the corridor, and then it's gone.

Amber lets her breath out.

"What the hell..." she says.

"I don't know," Jess says, climbing out from under a table. "What'd it do?"

"I thought it was going to kill me, and then it just looked at me like I'd hurt its feelings instead," Amber tells her. "What kind of behavior did you give it?"

Jess frowns. "I built in a bunch of stuff," she says. "I took a lot of pheromonal stuff from primates, gave it a killer vomeronasal organ that's its main behavioral input."

"So what does that mean? Was it gonna kill me or not?"

"No, no," Jess says. "No killer instinct at all. It's aggressive, yeah, but only socially, like a cat wants to be petted."

"No killer instinct? Look at this mess!" Amber waves a hand at the shattered door and the white-veined plexiglass tank.

"No one got hurt," Jess says defensively. "It was trying to be friends, I think."

Amber considers that, and sees that without the horn the 'corn's pose would have been submissive, a pet asking for attention. "Oh, shit," she says. Then she stops, and asks, "But why'd it leave, then? I didn't yell at it."

"Well, you did something," Jess says. "And so did I." She glances at Amber, then at the table she'd hidden under. "It didn't come near me."

Amber looks sideways at Jess. "Maybe it's what we didn't do," she says. "We didn't reach out for it."

"I was too scared!" Jess says. "I never made anything so big before. And that horn! And the smell..."

Amber had not consciously noticed the smell, but she knows instantly what Jess means; the 'corn has a strange, musky smell that hit something somewhere deep in the back of her brain, behind and below the human parts. "You didn't do that on purpose?"

Jess shakes her head. "Nope. Couldn't decide what it should smell like, so I just let that part happen."

"You were scared," Amber says. "So was I, when it pointed that horn at me."

"It can smell fear," Jess says, understanding. "That's why it left."

Awareness dawns; Amber looks at the door.

"Oh, shit," she says. "It left. It's out there somewhere."

"It won't hurt anyone," Jess says.

Amber wheels on her. "Who gives a flying fuck?" she shrieks. "Jess, we just turned an atomic-powered unicorn loose on the Shadyside Industrial Park! We've gotta go get it."

"Chill, Amber," Jess says. "It won't hurt anyone."

"Yeah, but what if *they* hurt *it*? Not to mention I don't know if it's legal turning a unicorn loose on the streets."

Jess frowns. She knows exactly how illegal the 'corn's insides are, and it's very. "Okay, we go get it," she says. "No huhu."

Together, they hurry through the diamond-sand of shattered glass into the corridor.

The 'corn is easy to track at first – two more shattered doors on either side of the lobby mark its passage. The plaza outside is blank, but the soggy patch of just-watered lawn beyond the plaza shows the distinctive mark of cloven hooves. Amber follows, past where she always turns for the parking garage, out to the street, and Jess follows Amber.

But then there's sidewalk, and no marks show. Amber stands on the walk, looking first one way and then the other, searching for some sign of the 'corn, as Jess trots up beside her.

"It must be moving fast," Jess remarks.

Amber doesn't reply at first; she's too busy noticing.

This is outside the industrial park. This is a main drag, offices and drug stores and travel agencies and delis, city-mandated urban greenspace breaking up the glass and stone. She had been looking at the street and signs and fixtures for a mark, a sign, some damage the 'corn had done, but then she saw the other damage.

It's late on a Thursday afternoon and the streets are empty except for a UPS truck at the curb three blocks down. The sidewalks are deserted, office windows dim, shop displays dusty. Dead leaves lie in the gutter, but no newspapers, no candy wrappers, no beer cans. A brass-reflective second story window across the street is cracked from top to bottom.

This street is a dead thing – not abandoned, not ruined, but lifeless and still.

"What happened here?" she asks.

"Where?" Jess asks, looking around. "Did it wreck something?"

"The street!" Amber says, waving her hands. "It's dead!"

"It's Thursday," Jess says, annoyed.

"It's not always like this?"

Jess hesitates, then admits, "Well, yeah, it is."

"No one comes here?"

"Do you?" Jess counters. She doesn't understand why Amber is asking this instead of following the 'corn. "You work at home, you shop the web, you get your kicks there – why go out?"

"I hadn't noticed it was like this," Amber says, staring at the UPS truck as the driver climbs back into the cab.

"You don't go out," Jess says. "When would you see?"

Amber doesn't answer. It's true – she doesn't go out.

She thinks maybe she should.

"Where's the 'corn?" Jess asks.

Amber shrugs. "I didn't see it."

Jess represses the urge to kick someone. "Come on," she says, "you look that way, I'll look here."

They separate, but are only a few meters apart when Jess sees movement in the vest-pocket park between wings of an office tower. "There!" she calls, as she begins to run.

A moment later the two slow and stop a dozen meters from the 'corn – and the man petting it.

He's sitting cross-legged on the grass, under a scraggly potted birch, stroking the unicorn's neck as it kneels before him and rests its head in his lap. The 'corn is staring up at him with those complex amber eyes, its expression unreadable from so far away, but its reaction to his appearance is obviously not the same as Amber's.

He's emaciated, a tangled, ragged beard pressing against his chest as he stretches out his hand, gray-streaked hair so dirty and disarrayed Amber can't be sure what color it originally was. His blue-glitter jumpsuit is still clean and bright as the unicorn's fresh white hide, his nails are short and his hands are healthy, but Amber is still repulsed.

And frightened. The golden horn is poised at the thin man's throat. The 'corn clearly means him no harm, but if it starts up suddenly the movement would drive that lethal point up into his neck.

He hears the women's footsteps, though, and looks up.

"Are you inter or sim?" He smiles, displaying discolored teeth. "I didn't even know I was still online until I saw the unicorn – I thought I'd lost my feed. Someone must've been messing with my head."

"We're real," Jess says.

"You aren't online," Amber adds.

He laughs. "Don't try to nass me," he says. "It's a unicorn, isn't it? There aren't any real unicorns."

"There are now," Jess says. "I made it. Engineered it, gene by gene."

He stares at them for a minute, then looks down at the unicorn.

"Naaah," he says.

"Listen," Amber says, "when you're online, how long is your beard? You got its growth programmed in?"

He strains to look down at his own beard and comes within centimeters of impaling himself on the glittering horn.

"It's real," Amber says. "Look at your hair. Look how thin you are. Smell the 'corn – do you have that much sensory data on your feed?"

He looks up and reaches for the VR headset over his eyes and it isn't there, his fingers touch eyebrow instead of plastic and he believes.

And he realizes the horn at his throat is real, and freezeframes.

"Is it safe?" he asks.

"It won't hurt you intentionally," Jess says. "It likes people. But it's inexperienced and that horn's sharp."

His jaw locks, Jess sees the tendons stand out, and he tips his head back while rolling his eyes to look down his own chin. The move would be funny as hell if it were Buster Keaton or Richard Pryor doing it onscreen instead of some half-starved wirehead in a grubby city parklet.

The unicorn looks up, like a cat wanting to know why the petting stopped, and the golden horn scratches the wirehead's chin ever so slightly and tears out a small tangle of beard.

The unicorn sees and smells his fear; disappointed, it gets smoothly to its feet and turns away.

He sits just where he is and lets it go.

"Grab it!" Amber calls. "Catch it!"

"You catch it!" he calls back.

Amber gropes for a reply, then sees Jess already trotting after the unicorn and follows.

"Jess," she calls.

Jess trots on without answering.

"Jess!" Amber shouts, trotting along.

"What?" Jess asks, running now to keep the 'corn's lead from widening.

"How are you going to catch it?" Amber calls.

Jess dead-stops, like a printer with a pulled power cord.

"We need a rope," she says.

"We need something," Amber agrees.

The unicorn has slowed and is sniffing the air; they watch as they start forward again, keeping it in sight as they talk.

"A lasso or something," Jess says.

"How strong is it?" Amber asks.

Jess dead-stops again. "Oh, damn," she says.

Amber stops, as well. "What? Why?"

"Because I put a fucking nuclear reactor in that thing, Amber – it's probably strong enough to drag us both along without even noticing. You saw what it did to the tank, right? And the lab door?"

"I saw," Amber agrees.

"You were the one who said we hadda go get it back," Jess accuses.

"Screw what I said," Amber says. "Let it go."

Jess looks at the 'corn again, then at Amber. "It's illegal as hell," she says. "And dangerous."

"And traceable?"

"Probably."

"But they'd have to catch it first?"

"Well, yeah," Jess admits. "But eventually they'll catch it."

"Maybe we can wipe the right records so a trace won't matter. Or forge the permits we need."

"It's dangerous," Jess repeats. "The 'corn, I mean, not the hacking."

"So we issue a warning."

The sound of a motor distracts them; the UPS truck is moving, and the 'corn is turning to follow it.

The truck accelerates, and so does the unicorn, and suddenly the idea of catching it on foot looks downright silly, as Amber estimates its speed at better than forty klicks.

"Warning it is," Amber says.

* * *

Sightings are easy. Sightings flash in by the hundreds. Once Amber's warnings go out, routed around the world through a dozen aliases but all directed back to this one city, a handful of people report seeing it.

Then others go looking for it. The arguments about whether it was a hoax, another netscam, fill immense amounts of bandwidth, until the sightings become too numerous to deny.

A unicorn is loose in the outside world. Not VR, not SFX, but a genuine cyborged animal is roaming the city, looking for people to play with.

It likes people. Amber explains this over and over when people ask why it isn't heading for the woods somewhere.

And people like the unicorn. More and more report not just seeing it from a distance but meeting it close up and personal.

But there are always doubters. "You aren't serious," a typical e-mail says. "A u-nuke-orn? In the so-called real world?"

And Amber, annoyed, writes back and says, "Get offline and see for yourself."

And more and more people do.

Amber issues warning after warning about the danger, but no one seems to care. A few people get scratched, some feet get stepped on, but hundreds more pet the unicorn, stroke it, play with it, and come away unhurt.

The 'corn likes to play fetch; it tolerates ring-toss with its horn as the target, but only briefly.

But try to grab it, even for a minute, and it runs.

And when it runs, nothing can stop it.

The cops try. It's a public menace, and they feel obligated to remove it from the streets. They do their best.

It isn't good enough. The 'corn punches through the side of a SWAT van. It shrugs off tranquilizer darts or gas.

"I figured a general immunity to toxins would be useful, since it might be drinking open water," Jess says with a shrug. "With no digestive tract, why not?"

The cops, after a few escapes, think it over, and consult the city council. Someone, with only a little e-mail urging from Amber, has the smarts to think of the possibilities.

People are getting offline to see the 'corn, and touch it, and play with it. EMT personal-neglect calls and hospital admissions for dehydration and malnutrition drop for the first time in three years.

The cops are told to leave it alone.

And Amber and Jess watch it all, on net and vid and sometimes out their windows. Amber isn't online as much as she used to be, and when she is it's more netsurfing and less VR.

And one day, as the hand-creature strokes Jess along the jaw, Jess says, "You know, sooner or later the novelty is going to wear off."

"I know," Amber says.

"People will get sucked back into VR."

"I know."

"Unless there's something new," Jess says.

Amber nods and leans back in her chair, pushing away the keyboard.

"I was thinking 'dragon,'" she says.

Harry's Toaster

When I wrote "Why I Left Harry's All-Night Hamburgers," I intended it to be a one-off story – no sequels or spin-offs were planned. But once it was done, the idea of a diner that got customers from a near-infinite number of alternate realities just had too many story possibilities to ignore. I've tried not to go overboard, but I've written a few.

"I shouldn't do this," Harry said, looking at the gadget and wishing it couldn't look back. "You sure you haven't got anything else?"

"I'm sorry," the little man in the shiny suit said. "I thought my money would be good here." His accent was like nothing Harry had ever heard before. Harry got a lot of strange customers in his diner, not all of whom spoke any language he recognized, but this guy – well, it was definitely English, and Harry could understand it, but what he did to it was downright unnatural.

Harry snorted. "It's not even good counterfeit. The United States of Columbia?"

"What's wrong with that?" the customer said, in a tone that conveyed such hurt Harry half expected him to start crying.

"This is *America*," Harry pointed out. "Columbia is in South America!"

The man blinked, clearly confused. "No, you mean Ameriga is in Southern Columbia...oh. Oh, I see. Is...is that really the way it is here?"

Harry nodded. "It really is." He had long since given up being surprised by the stuff his late-night customers said. He didn't know who these people were, or where they came from, but they kept him in business – even the ones who didn't have money usually came up with something he could hock, and in fact were often among his most profitable customers.

This guy was not looking promising, but the gadget, whatever it was, might be worth a few bucks at a pawnshop in Morgantown or Pittsburgh. Maybe.

The little man glanced at the pile of bills and coins on the counter. "And you can't take those?"

Harry sighed. "Listen, mister," he said, "I'd like to help, but around here that's just play money. I mean, the coins aren't even metal!"

"I know," the little man said, looking utterly woebegone.

"And you don't have anything else to offer me, besides this thing? Maybe some other gadget, or something with silver in it?"

The customer shook his head. "No," he said. "I'm sorry, but I just can't. They won't let me."

"Who won't...oh, never mind. But you can give me this?" He pointed at the shiny plastic thing that sat on the stool next to the little man, its face-like turret silently observing the conversation.

"Oh, yes," he said, nodding vigorously. "It won't mind at all, I'm sure. I don't have any use for it, but I'm sure you will!"

Harry looked at it dubiously. "What *is* it, anyway?"

The little man looked startled. "It's a toaster, of course!"

The bell above the door jingled, and Harry decided it wasn't worth arguing about. Whatever the thing was, it looked as if it was worth more than the meager meal the little weirdo had just eaten; he'd only had french fries and salad and a Coke, after all.

"Okay," Harry said. "Hand it over, and you can go – but if you ever come back, try to have something to pay me with, okay?"

The little man nodded, lifted the gadget up onto the counter, gathered up his worthless money, then scampered for the door.

Harry put the thing on the shelf under the counter, then went to wait on the new arrival. When he had gone the gadget whirred softly to itself and swivelled its double-lensed turret, looking over its surroundings.

Satisfied for the moment, it quieted. And it listened.

Something over an hour later, as the first faint glimmer of dawn showed in the east, there was a slow period, and Harry spared a few minutes to pull the gadget out and carry it back to the prep table in the kitchen. He set it on the metal surface and looked it over.

It looked back.

"A toaster?" he said. "How does *that* work? I don't see anywhere to put any bread."

The gadget unfolded a metal arm and held out a curved claw. Harry frowned. It had obviously heard him and wanted to cooperate. He turned and fetched a slice of bread, then tried to hand it to the gadget.

The gadget swivelled its turret to stare at the bread as Harry set it in the claw, but it did not close its grip. Instead it rotated the claw at the wrist and dropped the bread on the table. Harry grunted and started to reach for it, but before he could pick it up the gadget extended a rod, reached down with its claw, and wrapped the slice of bread around the rod, forming a tube. It then took the cylinder and pressed in one end against the table. That done, it lifted the result up, open end at the top, and looked expectantly at Harry.

"That's not toast," Harry said, looking back.

The thing looked at the cylinder of bread, then back at Harry.

Harry considered this. It seemed to have a very definite idea of what it was doing; its actions did not look random. It appeared to want Harry to do something – fill the bread with something, perhaps? Maybe it wasn't so much a toaster as a pastry-stuffer.

Before he could experiment further the bell on the diner door jingled, and Harry went to wait on the arriving customer, leaving the gadget where it was.

It watched Harry leave, its turret rotating to follow his movements; then it looked at the rolled-up slice of bread. It flung the bread away.

A moment later Harry came back into the kitchen on his way to the refrigerator and stepped on the bread.

"What?" he said, looking down. He turned to glare at the gadget, then peeled the bread from the bottom of his shoe and tossed it in the trash.

"What is the event?" the gadget replied, in a low but astonishingly deep and resonant voice. It spoke with the same peculiar accent as its previous owner.

"What?" Harry said again, startled.

"What is the event?" the gadget repeated.

"I'm waiting on a customer," Harry said. "Not that it's any of your business." Then he continued to the refrigerator to get a stack of sausage patties and cheese slices. He gave the gadget a wary glance on his way back to the grill, but didn't say anything more.

A moment later he was flipping a patty when a voice proclaimed loudly, "*I don't work here!*"

Startled, Harry almost dropped his spatula.

"I would be *proud* to work here, but I don't!"

It was the gadget.

Harry put down the spatula and came around the corner to glare at it. "Shut up!" he said.

"Is this the wrong time?" it asked, its voice low again.

"Yes," Harry said. "Please shut up."

It lowered its turret and retracted its arm.

Harry went back to the counter, where a bleary-eyed local whose name Harry thought might be Bob was sitting up straight, rather than in his customary slouch. "Who's back there?" he asked.

"Back where?" Harry asked.

"In the...back behind there. In the kitchen." He gestured.

Harry did not want to explain how he came to have that weird-looking gadget, with its disturbingly lifelike turret and fancy claw. "There's no one back here," he said. "Just me."

"Then who was shouting?"

"The radio," Harry said. "The volume's wonky sometimes. I've turned it back down."

"What was that about not working here?"

Harry shrugged. "Some stupid comedy program. I don't get some of this modern humor, you know?"

"Yeah, I can understand that. Hey, have you always had a radio back there? Because I've been in here a dozen times and I never heard it before."

"I don't play it much."

"Because of that volume thing?"

"No, I'm just not that interested." He turned back to the grill and checked on the customer's breakfast patty, then flipped it and slapped on a slice of cheese. "You want a refill on that coffee?" he asked.

"Sure."

"I would like a refill as well," said the gadget's voice from behind him. Harry almost dropped the coffeepot. He attended to his customer, then hurried behind the grill. He started to tell the gadget to shut up, but then he saw that it had once again extruded its arm and had picked a coffee cup from the stack near the table. It was holding the cup out to be filled.

"What do *you* want with coffee?" he asked quietly, hoping Bob would not hear.

"Is it not the correct beverage?"

Harry blinked.

Maybe, he thought, if he did what the thing asked, it would shut up until the customer left and Harry could deal with it in private. He poured coffee.

"Thank you," the gadget said. "What name does the celebrant prefer?"

"What?" Once again, Harry almost dropped the pot.

"What name does the celebrant prefer?"

Harry was not sure what the gadget was asking. "What seller brand?"

"The first."

Harry carefully set the coffeepot back on its pad. He tried to make sense of the question, but couldn't. Finally he simply made a random guess of what a "seller brand" might be. "Coca-Cola," he said.

The gadget lifted its cup so suddenly that Harry thought it was about to fling hot coffee on him; he stepped back involuntarily. Somehow, though, it managed to stop its motion without spilling a drop. "Ladies and gentlemen!" it said, its voice once again inhumanly loud. "I give you Coca-Cola!"

"No, that's coffee," Harry said. But then comprehension dawned. "You're a *toaster*!" he said. "You make *toasts*, not toast!"

"Heritage Products Mark VIII Deluxe Toaster," it confirmed.

"Wow," Harry said. "That's kind of..." He hesitated. "I was going to say that's kind of neat, but actually, that may be the most useless thing I ever heard of."

"Weddings a specialty," the gadget said. "When the best man is too drunk to serve, rely on your Heritage!"

"Harry, what the hell is going on back there?" Bob called.

"Radio's on the fritz again," he called. "I'll be right out." Then he turned back to the gadget. "I don't need any more toasts today; how do I shut you down?"

"Is the event over?"

“Yes, it is.”

“Shutdown is automatic. To reactivate, simply stand in front of your toaster and address it. When the arm extends, place the appropriate beverage in the gripper,” the device recited in a singsong tone, very different from the warm resonance of its previous speech. “Your toaster will record and interpret all conversation to improvise commentary, jokes, and appropriate remarks. Thank you for choosing Heritage Products.” Then it set the coffee cup down on the prep table, retracted its arm, lowered its turret, and went still.

“Harry?”

Harry turned and hurried back to the counter.

“I think my sandwich is getting a little over-cooked.”

“Damn!” Harry whirled and quickly scooped the sausage patty off the grill, leaving a ring of burning cheese. He plopped the patty onto the waiting bun, then looked at it uncertainly. He looked back at his customer. “Want me to re-do it?”

“Naah, I’m sure it’s fine.”

Harry assembled the sandwich and served it, then went to scrape the grill.

“You get that problem with your radio figured out?” Bob asked as he ate.

“Hmm? Oh, yeah.”

“What was it?”

Harry plunked the spatula into its tray. “Interference from my new toaster,” he said.

How I Found Harry's All-Night Hamburgers

This was the second Harry's All-Night Hamburgers story I plotted, but it took me about thirty years to finally get around to writing it. It's the darkest one I've come up with so far.

I was in my office, digging receipts out of drawers and trying to decide if I'd have to do my own taxes this year or if I could afford H & R Block, when this little guy knocked on the door and walked in.

"Be with you in a minute," I said, and I dumped the whole stack on top of the file cabinet, to be dealt with later. Then I motioned him to a chair, and while he pulled it over I sat down behind the desk and asked, "What can I do for you?"

He was a little nervous, which is normal enough for someone making his first visit to a private detective. He cleared his throat a couple of times, then told me, "My name's Bergin, Paul Bergin, and I want to hire you to find something out for me."

"That's what I do," I said, leaning back in my chair. "I find things out. You've come to the right place. What is it you want to know?"

He cleared his throat again, and reached into his jacket pocket and pulled out something about the size and shape of an egg.

"I want to know where this came from," he said, setting it on my desk.

I looked at it, and it didn't look like anything very special. It was a soft brown color, patterned, something like tortoiseshell, and shaped in a flattened ovoid, an inch or two thick, one side convex and the other concave. It looked a little like a bar of fancy soap.

"What is it?" I asked.

"I don't know," he said. "That's why I want to know where it's from, so I can find out."

"Where'd you get it, then?"

"There's this guy," he said. "He comes into my shop sometimes with stuff to sell."

"Your shop?"

"I run a pawn shop."

I nodded. "Okay. Go on."

"Right, so this guy comes in sometimes – maybe once every couple of months – and he's always got weird stuff to sell. Almost never any ordinary stuff like rings or laptops or musical instruments; instead he'll have coins from places that don't exist, and strange little gadgets – "

"Wait a minute," I said, holding up a hand. "What do you mean, coins from places that don't exist?"

"I mean he'll have coins that say they're from countries that aren't real, or that don't exist anymore, or that never had their own coins. Places like, say, the Republic of Texas, but dated from the last few years, not the 1840s. Or the Dominion of Darien, or New Sweden, or Deseret, or whatever."

"Like – play money? Or movie props?"

"Maybe. That's what I thought at first. But they look real, except for being from impossible places, and when I've had them assayed most of them are real gold or silver. I take those to a smelter, since they aren't worth anything as currency. The ones that turn out to not be real precious metals I give away as curiosities."

I sat up and cocked my head. "This guy has a *lot* of these coins?"

Bergin nodded. "He must have brought me a couple of hundred over the years."

"He won't say where he got them?"

"Customers, he says."

"Customers where?"

"He says he runs a business in West Virginia. He won't say what kind. I figure it's probably a second-hand shop or an antique store, from the kind of thing he brings in, and he's bringing me the stuff he can't sell back home."

"All right. Go on."

Bergin adjusted himself in the seat. "He brings other stuff, not just coins – jewelry sometimes, but not like any other jewelry I've seen, and gadgets like hand warmers and shavers and pocket flashlights, but they're almost always a little off, somehow, and they aren't any brand I recognize."

"So it's *all* weird?"

"Pretty much. I'm guessing that he takes the more ordinary stuff somewhere else, and only brings me the oddball items."

"Why? Why you?"

"Because I'll take it. I have a reputation for handling unusual goods – not just from this guy, but from other people, too. It's my niche, you know? I don't pay top dollar, to be honest I mostly pay pennies on the dollar, but I'll take almost anything that looks interesting. My customers know that, so if they want a conversation piece, or a unique gift for someone, they come to me. Which is why I took this." He pointed at the egg-shaped thing. "I thought it was just a paperweight, and I could get a buck or two from someone looking for a gift for a boss or a teacher, but then I handled it. He'd had it in a baggie, and I took it out."

"Oh?" I looked at the thing. "What does it do?"

He licked his lips and glanced to the side, let his gaze wander around my office, but I didn't rush him. I wasn't in any particular hurry.

"It feels good," he said at last.

I looked blank. I'm good at that; it's a useful skill in my line of work.

He sighed, reached out, and pushed the thing across the desk at me. "Try it," he said.

I picked it up.

It felt softer than I expected; it looked like hard plastic, but it was silky to the touch, and just a little cooler than I had thought it would be. I ran my thumb over it, and it felt *nice.* I don't know how to describe it any better than that. It reminded me of the back of an ex-girlfriend's neck, where there were very fine hairs, too pale and thin to see if you weren't looking for them, that made her skin feel impossibly soft and smooth and delicate.

It fit perfectly in my hand, resting on my palm where I could wrap my fingers around it and slide my thumb along the top curve. I found myself staring at it, drawing circles on it with my thumb, thinking about *nothing whatsoever.* Not about doing my taxes or what I would have for supper or Bergin sitting there watching me or how the afternoon sunlight was shining on the polished hardwood floor or *anything.* Not even about the object itself.

It's hard to describe just how wonderful that was, to think about nothing. No worries, no concerns, just calm.

And then Bergin reached out and took it out of my hand and dropped it back in his pocket.

"You don't want to do that for very long," he said. "It's kind of addictive."

"I'll bet," I said, staring at that jacket pocket. I suddenly wondered how long I had actually held the thing; the shadows on my office floor looked longer than they had been when Bergin came in.

"I want to know what it is," the little pawnbroker said. "And where it came from, and whether I can get more."

"I see," I said. I tapped a key to wake up my computer. "The guy who sold it to you – you know his name? Pawn shops usually require ID."

He reached into a different pocket and pulled out a folded sheet of paper. "Here," he said, handing it to me. "I did some searching myself, but I couldn't find out anything. No police record here in Pittsburgh – I have contacts on the force, in case someone tries to use me as a fence, so yes, I checked."

I opened the paper and saw a scan of a West Virginia driver's license in the name of John H. Praszky Jr., with a rural-route address in Sutton, West Virginia. The photo showed a middle-aged man who didn't look as if he'd ever been in good shape, and who certainly wasn't now, though I'd seen worse. Overweight, thinning hair, sagging clean-shaven jaw, tired eyes.

"John Praszky," I said, wondering whether I had the pronunciation right.

Bergin didn't correct me. "He never said his name, but he matches the picture on the license," he said.

"All right," I said. "I have somewhere to start, anyway. I'll need a retainer, and if I'm going to be traveling out of state I'll need to have a thousand up front. Are you sure it's worth that much to you?"

"You held it for almost fifteen minutes; what do *you* think?"

I nodded. I understood. And now I knew how long it had been, and it was longer than I'd thought, but not as long as I feared. I was surprised Bergin had let me hang onto it that long, but that brought me to another point.

"Can I take that thing with me, in case I need to show it around?"

Bergin bit his lip, staring at me, then shook his head. "I can't," he said. "But here." He reached into a pocket again and handed me a sheaf of photographs, showing the thing from a dozen different angles, several of them including a ruler – it was four inches long, a little over two across, an inch and a half thick.

"These should do," I admitted, but honestly, I wanted to hold the thing again. I wanted to take it with me. Hell, I wanted to *keep* it. "You wouldn't want to sell it, would you?" I asked.

He shook his head immediately, and not just a gentle back and forth. "I'll sell more if I get them, but I'm keeping this one," he said.

"I understand," I said, and that was absolutely true. I had a momentary thought of grabbing him and simply *taking* it from him, but I dismissed it quickly; not only do I try to be honest and do my business cleanly, and not only would he probably call the cops and I'd likely lose my P.I. license even if I stayed out of jail, but...okay, this is the weird part. I didn't think the gadget would like it. I didn't think it would feel as good if I took it without permission. I didn't want to upset it. Why I thought I *could* upset something that looked like a lump of plastic I don't know, but I did.

After that it was just details – exchanging contact information, getting his check and a cash deposit for expense money, and so on.

I didn't have anything else going except follow-up on a divorce case, so I finished out the afternoon with tax prep and paperwork, did some research, and the next morning I headed out.

I had an old Toyota – in my line of work it's a good idea to drive something that isn't distinctive, that will just blend in, and I had decided that it was about time to swap it for something newer because it was getting old enough to be noticed and wasn't as reliable as I would have liked, but I hadn't done it yet. It was still good enough to get me to Sutton – I-376 west to I-79, then a hundred miles south on the interstate.

The drive should have been pleasant – a sunny spring day, light traffic, a good road, and the Toyota behaved itself – but I found myself not enjoying it. I felt nervous. I am not a nervous guy, or I wouldn't survive as a detective, but that whole way I was uncomfortable, thinking about that thing I had held the day before. I hated the idea that I was driving away from it, and at the same time I was anticipating maybe finding one of my own, if I could find this John Praszky and learn where he'd gotten it.

I knew I was being irrational, that it was just a gadget, not anything important, but I couldn't help it. I was more focused on trying to remember how it had felt to hold it than I was on my driving, and I almost missed my exit. At the last instant I realized where I was and cut over, down the ramp onto the two-lane blacktop and into town – what there was of it.

Sutton's the Braxton County seat, but it's still not much of anything. Main Street runs along the Elk River, and there are a few blocks on either side, and that's about it. I had considered going to the county clerk's office and asking after John Praszky, but I thought it might be better to try an informal approach first, not put anything on the official record, since after all, I wasn't chasing a criminal, just trying to locate a shopkeeper.

I drove the length of Main Street and didn't see any secondhand shops, or anything with "Praszky" on the sign, so after I'd cruised all the way through town from west to east and then retraced most of it I stopped in at the Rite-Aid for a candy bar. The cashier rang me up, and while I was pretending to dig for change in my pocket I said, "Hey, do you know a guy named John Praszky?" Ordinarily asking a random minimum-wage employee would be a long shot, but in a town this size I thought it was worth a shot, especially if he owned a business. "I heard he lived in Sutton."

"Nope," she said.

"*Anyone* named Praszky?" I asked, as I counted out coins.

She hesitated, then called to the guy stocking the beer cooler, "Hey, isn't Harry's last name Praszky?" Her pronunciation was pretty close to my own, basically assuming the Z was silent.

"I dunno," he answered.

She swept up the coins and counted them into the cash drawer. "Who's Harry?" I asked.

"He owns Harry's Hamburgers, west of town," she said, as she closed the drawer.

Well, this Harry was a shopkeeper, anyway, and if he was John *H.* Praszky, *Junior*, maybe he went by his middle name so as to be distinct from his old man, or maybe John Praszky was a brother or a cousin. It seemed worth checking out, especially since it was getting on toward lunchtime. She handed me my receipt, and I asked for directions, which were pretty simple, Sutton being what it is. Finding a *home* might be a challenge, if it was somewhere back in the woods on an old logging road, but there were only so many places a business could reasonably be.

So back to the Toyota and west I went, and sure enough, there was this tacky little joint with a neon sign reading HARRY'S ALL-NIGHT HAMBURGERS and a parking lot big enough to hold a couple of semis but currently occupied only by two pick-ups and a rusty sedan.

Except for a little cabin out back, practically in the woods, it was all by itself, with nothing but trees around it. Seemed to me this Harry would do better in town, or down by the exit off I-79, but no one asked me. I pulled into the lot and parked between the pick-ups, looking around.

I didn't see anywhere that mysterious whatsit could have come from; there was no souvenir shop or secondhand store, just the restaurant and the cabin and a lot of trees. I collected myself, unbuckled the seatbelt, and got out.

It was quiet out there, the sort of quiet I didn't hear much back in Pittsburgh. I could hear the wind in the pines, a sound I hadn't heard in ages. When I walked across the asphalt I could hear grit scraping under my shoes.

Then I opened the door and stepped into Harry's burger joint, and the quiet was gone – the grill was sizzling, machinery humming, music playing over speakers in the ceiling, and someone I didn't see was laughing. It smelled pretty good. There was an old guy at the counter with a cup of coffee and a newspaper, but the half-dozen booths were empty. It was cleaner than I'd expected.

It didn't look like a place you could find anything like that gadget. It looked like an old-fashioned diner where you wouldn't find anything more exotic than key lime pie. My fingers twitched at the thought of the gadget.

Someone must have heard me come in, because a young man appeared behind the counter and waited while I crossed the floor and took a seat three stools down from the guy with the newspaper.

"What can I get you?" he said.

"A burger," I said, my finger tracing a circle on the laminate counter. Burgers were their specialty, after all. "Cheese and lettuce, no ketchup."

"Onions? And are chips okay? If you want fries you'll have to wait."

"Sure, onions, and chips are fine." I glanced down the counter, forced my finger to stop moving, and added, "And a coffee. Black."

The guy headed back toward the kitchen, and I looked around, hoping to see a picture of the proprietor somewhere. I didn't find one. There was a pecan pie under a glass dome that looked pretty good, and I realized I was genuinely hungry.

A moment later the guy who had taken my order reappeared, and I beckoned him over.

"This Harry who runs the place, is he around?"

"No, he mostly works the night shift. We're open twenty-four hours, he's not kidding about the 'All Night' in the name, and Harry usually does the graveyard shift himself. He's probably asleep right now."

"Does he live nearby?"

"That cabin out back."

"So you could go wake him up if you had to?"

"If I wanted to look for another job, sure."

"So is his last name Praszky?"

The guy looked startled. "How should I know?"

"He's your boss, isn't he?"

"Yeah, but he's just Harry. I don't know his last name."

I fished that scan of the driver's license out of my pocket and folded it so that only the photo showed. "Is this him?" I asked, holding it up.

He squinted at it. "Yeah, that looks like Harry. What's this about? Is he in trouble?"

"No, no. But there's someone in Pittsburgh who's looking for him, and hired me to find him."

"Why?" He looked worried.

"Harry did him a favor once, and he wants to see about maybe... well, I don't know exactly. Returning the favor, I guess. He doesn't mean Harry any harm, I can promise you. There might even be some money in it for him."

"Okay. He'll probably be in for the dinner rush."

"You get a dinner rush here?" I looked around. "I sure don't see a *lunchtime* rush."

"It's still early," the counterman said defensively. "It's not a *big* rush."

"Burger's up!" a female voice called from the back.

My guy turned and stepped back from the counter, and a moment later he set a plate in front of me.

It was a pretty good burger, I've got to admit. Nothing fancy, but fresh beef cooked just right, and the cheese was good sharp cheddar, which is my favorite. Somewhere around my third bite I paused and said, "My compliments to the chef."

He smiled. "I'll tell Ashley."

"Is it okay if I hang around? I want to talk to Harry."

He shrugged. "*I* don't care. It'll be awhile, though, and I'm off at four, so the evening guys may have something to say."

I nodded.

I took my time, but I wasn't going to let the food get cold. I got a refill on the coffee when the counterman cleared my plate away, and I took my cup over to a booth in the corner.

They did get some more customers eventually, and the old guy with the newspaper packed up and left. The young guy was prompt with the customers, but spent as much time as he could in the back, flirting with someone I assume was Ashley. Going by her laughter, she didn't mind a bit.

I tried people-watching – I do that a lot, in my line of work, and usually it keeps me entertained, but this time it wasn't really working. I kept finding myself curling my fingers around something that wasn't there, and sliding my thumb in little circles on my palm. I wanted that gadget in my hand, and not having it there began to *hurt.*

Besides, there weren't always people to watch; sometimes there weren't any customers and the counterman was in the back. I tried meditating, or thinking over old cases, or estimating figures for my taxes, but those weren't any better. The remembered feel of that gadget kept intruding. Its absence was the exact opposite of the calm, happy oblivion I had felt when I held it.

Around quarter to four, when I was the only customer in the place and had been rubbing my thumb across my hand so long that the joints in my thumb were aching and my palm was red and sore, a middle-aged guy came in and headed straight behind the counter. I looked up, but this wasn't the man in the license photo.

"Hey, Bill," the counterman said. Then he leaned forward and whispered something, and I saw Bill throw a quick glance in my direction.

Then a woman about my age or a little older came in, a thoroughly unnatural redhead wearing an apron; she settled at the counter and began chatting with Bill and Ashley's beau – I never had gotten his name, and Harry evidently didn't believe in name-tags.

A few minutes later Bill vanished into the back, and the redhead took over behind the counter. Ashley appeared – she was a cute brunette, well worth flirting with, but from the way the counterman put his arm around her waist and she leaned into him, there was obviously more there than a little workplace flirting. They left together.

"Need another coffee?" the redhead called, and I said I did. She brought the pot over and we talked a little, confirming that I wanted to talk to Harry as soon as possible.

"He'll probably be in for his breakfast soon," she said. "I'll let him know you're here."

I thanked her, she left, and I found my thumb making circles again. I forced myself to stop.

For a moment I wondered what I was really doing, spending the entire afternoon sitting in a greasy little diner in West Virginia, but then I remembered the feel of the gadget. I wanted one of those for *myself*, damn it, and this was where I needed to be to find one.

It was about five, and a couple of truckers were at the counter bantering with the redhead, when I heard a door slam somewhere in the back. I sat up.

And there he was, pushing past the redhead to get himself coffee and danish – Harry Praszky. He looked better than the picture on his license, but who doesn't? It was definitely him. He was maybe sixty, at a guess.

He brought his breakfast to the counter, then came around the end and settled on the last stool. I got up and carried my own coffee cup over, then sat down beside him.

"Hi," I said.

He didn't look at me or say anything, just sipped coffee.

"You're Harry, right? You own the place?"

"It's not for sale, and my bills are all paid, so don't try to tell me I owe someone money," he said.

"I wasn't asking that," I said.

He didn't reply, just took a bite of danish, so after a moment I went on. "You sold a friend of mine something, and he was hoping you might have more of them."

He stopped chewing and stared at the countertop for a moment. Then he finally turned to look at me. "Yeah?"

"We'd pay good money," I said, reaching into my pocket for the photos.

"I like money," he acknowledged, "but I probably can't help you."

I spread the pictures on the counter. He glanced at them. He frowned.

"That thing? He wants more?"

I nodded.

"Is this the guy from Specialty Pawn, in Pittsburgh?"

I nodded again. "His name's Bergin."

"I don't care what his name is," Harry said, in a tone of disgust. "I don't have any more. I don't even know what that thing is. I thought it was a paperweight, but I can't believe you'd come all this way for a paperweight."

"It's not a paperweight," I said. "It's... it's like a meditation stone. It feels good. And Mr. Bergin thinks he could get a good price for these."

"Well, good for him. I don't have any."

"You sold him this one."

"I sold him a lot of stuff."

"Well, where'd you get it?"

He sighed. "From a customer," he said.

"Could you be more specific? Mr. Praszky, I'm not trying to give you a hard time. We just *really* want more of these, and you're the only one we can ask. Even if you don't have any more, if you can put us in touch with this customer of yours, we can pay you a finder's fee."

Bergin had not actually authorized that, but *I* was willing to pay whatever it took to get myself one.

"I don't know her name," Harry said. "She was in here late one night, and tried to pay for her meal with a counterfeit bill, and when I spotted it she said she didn't have any other money, so we worked out a trade. She put a bunch of stuff in a plastic bag and gave it to me – some of it was jewelry, so I thought it would cover the costs. I drove it up to Pittsburgh and sold everything in the bag to Specialty Pawn." He pointed at the photos. "That was in the bag with the jewelry."

Bergin had told me he'd bought jewelry from Harry. He hadn't mentioned it was in the same plastic bag, or I'd have wanted a look at it.

"Is she a regular?"

He looked at me like I was wearing pink eyeshadow. "She tried to pass a counterfeit bill; what do you *think*? I never saw her before or since that one time."

"And you didn't get her name?"

"Nope."

I pulled out my pocket notebook. "What did she look like?"

For just an instant I thought I saw a sort of trapped, deer-in-the-headlights expression flicker across his face, but then he shrugged. "I don't remember the details; I mean, it's been at least a month. Kind of short, I guess. Hair a funny color, probably a bad dye job. Or maybe a wig. Beyond that I couldn't tell you."

"Fat? Thin? White, black, Asian?"

"She wasn't real fat or real dark. Seriously, I didn't notice."

"So she didn't make much of an impression, even with this whole mess with the bad bill and trading you a bunch of knicknacks?"

"I get a lot of weirdos at night, after anyone with a brain is home in bed, and I've taken barter before when customers didn't have money, so no, she didn't make a big impression. Sorry I can't help you, buddy; I'd have liked that finder's fee." He took another bite of danish.

I needed a moment to process that. He'd taken barter before? Often enough that it wasn't a big deal? And I remembered that he had brought Bergin all those fake coins and other odd stuff. I'd assumed he was running a secondhand shop, not a burger joint, until I got there, but once I got inside I hadn't seen any sign of anything but a diner. I had been too obsessed with the gadget to give that the attention it deserved; clearly, he accepted a *lot* of bartered items. What kind of a place was he running out here in the middle of nowhere?

I decided to try another angle. "So you thought it was a paperweight, and you never saw her again. Did you ever see another paperweight like that one?"

"Nope. People come here to eat, not to show off their stuff."

I looked down at the pictures and felt my hand trembling, desperate to hold the thing again. For the first time a thought struck me, one I should have come up with much sooner.

"Why'd you take that stuff to Pittsburgh, anyway? Isn't Charleston a lot closer?"

"I like Pittsburgh. I get better prices there."

"So you sell stuff there a lot?"

He shrugged, and sipped coffee.

"Is it *all* weird stuff you got in payment for meals? How often does that *happen*?"

He sighed. "Look, you got what I can tell you. How I run *my* business isn't any of *your* business." He turned away and finished his danish in another oversized bite

I didn't know what to say. He didn't owe me anything, and he probably really didn't know anything more about the customer that gave him the gadget, and if I hassled him too much he would have every right to throw me out, but I needed to know more. I *needed* to know how I could get one of those things for myself.

I could head back to Pittsburgh and tell Bergin it was a dead end, and go on with my life, but I wanted one of those gadgets. My fingers itched for one – they were twitching at the very thought, trying to close around a nonexistent one, as I sat there next to Harry.

I tried to think of what my next step should be, and Harry drank his coffee, and I beckoned the redhead over for a refill.

This whole business of Harry getting weird stuff in trade for his food – that didn't make any sense. I remembered what Bergin had said about coins from places that didn't exist; was Harry's joint somehow getting customers from those imaginary places?

That sounded ridiculous, but that gadget – something like that didn't exist anywhere in the world *I* knew. What was going on out here in the West Virginia hills? I had been there all afternoon, but I didn't want to leave yet. I was sure there was more to learn. I stayed where I was.

Harry finished his coffee, then went back behind the counter, around the corner where I couldn't see him.

The lunchtime counterman had been right; there really was a dinnertime rush. Oh, it wasn't huge, but it was enough to fill most of the booths and all the other stools at the counter at the peak, from maybe 6:30 to 7:00. But then it began to thin out again.

I got myself fried chicken and a piece of the pecan pie for my supper, and kept drinking coffee. The chicken was a bit greasy, but it tasted okay, and the pie was good.

Most of the post-dinner clientele seemed to be guys in hunting jackets.

Around 11:00 p.m. the truckers started to predominate, and the redhead, who I'd heard other people call Sherry, told me that was because the fast-food places out by the interstate had mostly closed for the night, so the more knowledgeable truckers pulled off the highway and came to Harry's.

Harry started working the counter alongside Sherry around 11:30, and not long after that she and Bill left, leaving Harry to manage by himself.

And business slowed down after midnight. Even most of the long-haul truckers were off the road by then, or at least weren't stopping at Harry's.

Around 12:30 Harry came over to me and asked, "You sure you don't want to head home, buddy?"

"I'm good," I said.

"Look, you've been here a long time; how long are you planning to stay?"

"Until I get another lead on where I can find more of those things."

"Buddy, give it up. I got *one* of them, *once.* It could be years before another one turns up, if it *ever* does."

"I'm staying a little longer, just in case."

Harry frowned. "Seriously, do you have anywhere else to go?"

"Sure. I have a nice apartment back in Pittsburgh."

"That's a three-hour drive. Shouldn't you get moving?"

I shook my head. "I'll head back tomorrow. Or Friday."

Harry sighed. "I don't want to give you a hard time, buddy – for one thing, you seem to be doing that to yourself, so I won't pile on."

He handed me a napkin from the dispenser; I looked at it, puzzled, then up at Harry, who pointed at the smear of blood on the counter. My hand was bleeding where I'd been rubbing it; I hadn't noticed. While I scrubbed at the blood Harry continued, "But I'll tell you right now, if you bother any of my customers, I'm throwing you out, and if you give me any argument I'm calling the sheriff, and I guarantee Sheriff Williams would not appreciate being woken up at this hour."

"I won't bother anyone."

Harry did not look as if he believed me, but he left me alone.

Half an hour after that I was beginning to fade. I'd had a long day, even if I'd spent most of it sitting at the counter drinking coffee. I didn't want to bother getting a room, but settling into the back seat of my Toyota for a couple of hours was definitely starting to appeal to me.

But then *she* came in.

I hadn't heard a car or motorcycle, but I assumed I'd just missed it, as groggy as I was. She was tall, probably six feet, with a shiny black helmet tucked under her arm, and dark blue hair halfway to her waist, wearing a black leather cat-suit, with a bright red logo I'd never seen before on the back. There were three red lines on one cheek, but I couldn't tell if they were make-up or scars or tattoos or war paint. She looked around warily.

I was the only customer in the place, so I tried to look harmless. I had no idea who she was, but it was pretty obvious to me that she didn't belong in a place like Sutton.

She marched up to the counter. Harry had emerged from the kitchen at the sound of the little bell on the door, and was waiting for her.

"You speak Angle?" she said.

"I speak English," Harry replied.

She nodded. "I have no local currency," she said. She held out a hand and dropped a few coins on the counter; they made an odd sound, not quite the normal jingle. "Will you credit these?"

Harry swept them up and studied them. "Gold?" he asked.

She nodded again.

"Yeah, I'll take these." He handed two of them back. "This should cover pretty much anything on the menu. And if you think you're going to *want* some local currency, I could give you a good deal on the others."

"I will think toward it," she said, as she took a seat. "What food do you offer?"

He handed her a menu.

This was apparently where some of those strange coins Bergin had talked about came from. I started to get up, but Harry saw it and hurried over. "Don't bother her," he whispered.

"I wasn't – "

"Seriously, buddy. Leave her alone."

"I was just – "

He put a finger to his lips, then turned back to her to await her order.

She pointed to something on the menu. Harry looked at it and nodded. "Club sandwich," he said. "Coming up. Want something to drink with that?"

She looked confused.

"I'll bring coffee," Harry said. He fetched her a cup and poured, then put the carafe back and headed for the kitchen.

When he was out of sight I moved to the stool beside her, the photos in my hand. I noticed a strange smell, a bit like licorice, but I ignored it.

"Excuse me," I said, "have you ever seen anything like this?" I spread the pictures on the counter.

She glanced at the pictures. "No," she said. Then she looked at my face. "You are a worldjumper?"

"I'm a detective," I said. "I'm trying to find more of these."

"I know them not." She sipped her coffee, and grimaced.

It wasn't bad coffee; I can only assume she wasn't a coffee drinker.

Disappointed, I gathered up the photos and returned to my own seat.

Unless she was a superb actor, she was not the source of Mr. Bergin's gadget. Harry had said the woman who traded it to him was short, which this blue-haired goddess definitely wasn't, but neither of them was exactly a normal diner's typical customer, and there were those gold coins...

Apparently Harry did get weirdos, plural, as late-night customers – but who were they? Where did they come from? Where did those coins come from, and the gadget?

Harry brought her sandwich, and she ate, and I beckoned Harry over.

"Could I see that coin she paid with?" I asked.

"Why?"

"Just curious."

He had it in the pocket of his apron; he fished it out and laid it on the counter. I leaned down for a good look.

It had a stylized picture of an owl, and letters around the edge that seemed normal enough but didn't say anything intelligible – it was all abbreviations, something like IMP AQ NOV ORD I SOL.

"Why'd you take it?" I asked.

"Because it's gold," he said. "I'm guessing it's at least twelve karat, and I estimate that melted down it'll be worth about sixty, seventy bucks. That'll cover her sandwich, and a decent share of the drive to Charleston or Pittsburgh."

I looked up at him. "You do this a lot?"

He put the coin back in his pocket. "Enough to know," he said.

I was going to say something else when the bell jingled again. I turned.

The three things that came in then *shimmered.* They were more or less human in size and shape, but I couldn't see their features, and they didn't really look solid. One wore blue, one solid green, and the third maroon, but I couldn't tell through the distortion whether those were jumpsuits or something else. I stared.

Harry didn't. He just held out a menu.

These three didn't seem to speak any English. They looked at the menu, conferred among themselves, and then the one in maroon tapped a picture on the menu three times.

Harry nodded, but then held out his hand and tapped his palm.

I couldn't see what they offered at first, but Harry waved it away. On the second try they apparently came up with something more to his liking, and he nodded and headed for the grill.

I stared for a moment, and realized my mouth was hanging open, but then I closed it and turned away; looking at them made my head hurt.

What was going *on* here? Who were these people, and where did they come from? What had Harry just agreed to accept in payment, and how did he know what it was?

I didn't know. I began to wonder whether I might be hallucinating.

I did know I wasn't going to sleep any time soon. I sat at the counter, watching and waiting.

The blue-haired woman did not speak to the ghostly trio; she ate her sandwich, drank her coffee, then left. Harry brought the threesome three cheeseburgers and three Cokes and accepted something I couldn't make out from them in exchange. They, too, ate and drank and left. They spoke among themselves in a variety of hooting sounds. I did not approach them; my tolerance for weirdness was not *that* high.

For a few minutes after they left the place was empty except for me and Harry, but then the bell rang again...

I never heard car engines, or trucks, or motorbikes. Sometimes there was a whine, or a thump, or a whoosh, but nothing that sounded like an ordinary vehicle. There were lights, but not like ordinary headlights. Some of the late-night people looked pretty normal; some did not.

Harry remained utterly unfazed by them all. He accepted normal currency when they had it, coins of gold or silver or platinum if they were offered, and assorted jewelry and other trinkets. A few times a sale took extended dickering, and Harry might wind up with a gadget, or a tool, or an article of clothing.

And sometimes they couldn't reach a deal. When that happened Harry would give the would-be customer a glass of water and a stale hamburger bun and maybe some onions and lettuce, out of pity.

I didn't see all that the first night, of course. I stayed. The weird ones stopped coming an hour or so before dawn. Once the sun came up and Harry went to bed, I went and slept in my car.

And whenever I could, whenever Harry wasn't looking and the customer spoke English, I would pull out my photos and ask about the device.

I was getting desperate, I admit it. My palm was raw from rubbing; I went down to the Rite-Aid and got myself some bandages, and I would wear through about two layers of gauze every night. Whenever

I wasn't actually talking to anyone, I would sit and remember how beautiful it had felt to hold that thing. Sometimes when I *was* talking, I would find myself staring wistfully at the pictures and rubbing at my bandage.

The sheriff came by a couple of times; he rousted me out of my car once, but I showed him my P.I. license and explained I was on a stake-out and he let me go. He had a long conversation with Harry that night, though, and afterward Harry told me that if I made any trouble at all, or bothered any customers, I'd have to go, and the sheriff had been warned.

I tried to be meek and say, "Yes, sir," at every opportunity.

Most of the customers I spoke to had no more idea what the thing in the photos was than I did, but on the third night a woman with a shaven head and a sort of holographic badge on her chest took one look and said, "Oh, that's a neural resonator!"

Relief flooded through me, like nothing I had ever felt before. I had a name for it. I hadn't hallucinated its entire existence. "It is?" I said.

"Sure!"

"What's a neural resonator?"

"*That* is! It's a mood enhancer. It uses touch and microstimulants to make you feel better when you hold it."

"Do you know where I can get one?"

She snorted. "Not around *here*, certainly."

"Where, then? How do I get there?"

"No, I mean not in this timeline."

I wasn't clear on what she meant by "timeline," but I ignored that. "How does it work? Could you help me make one?"

"Me? Not an inkling. That's not my lawn. I'm a test pilot, not a biotech."

That should have been interesting, that test pilot business, but I was focused on my target. "What do I need to do to get one?"

She sighed. "You're bottled, aren't you? Someone let you hold one unsupervised? One that had already formed for someone else?"

I had thought she spoke the same English I did, but I was beginning to wonder. "What do you mean?"

"I mean you held one that had already patterned itself for someone else, and now you're addicted."

"Patterned?"

"Sure. Everyone's chemobiology is different, so a new resonator attunes itself to the first person to handle it. After that, it can be dangerous for anyone else to hold it – or it might not work at all. It all trails."

That explained a lot, even if I wasn't completely certain what she meant by "trails." "Is there a treatment for this addiction?"

"Oh, sure! You just need your own fresh resonator. That'll repaint your neurons and put you on top of the branch – if it isn't too late."

"So I *really* need to find one."

She glanced at the bloody, torn bandage wrapped around my hand. "I don't know, playmate, you may be past the fence."

"But I have to *try*. Where can I go? What can I do?"

She looked me in the eye, and for the first time in three days I realized I probably looked like hell. I hadn't bathed or changed my clothes since I left Pittsburgh, or even combed my hair. I'd bought a toothbrush at the Rite-Aid, so my hygiene wasn't a *complete* disaster, but it was pretty bad. I'd eaten nothing but Harry's greasy cooking for three days, which probably hadn't done my health, or my breath, any favors – Harry was generous with the onions.

"Do you have any idea where I came from?" she asked. "Or any of the other people who come in here late at night?"

"No." I had noticed they were extremely strange and varied, but I had been too focused on finding the gadget, the neural resonator, to really give it much thought. It finally began to register that I *should* have thought about it. I would have, if I hadn't been rubbing my hand and dreaming about how it had felt to hold that thing.

"I'm from another universe," she said. "So are neural resonators. *Your* world doesn't have anything like that – not yet, anyway."

"What?" I must have looked like a complete imbecile. My mouth hung open, and I stared at her.

Just then Harry delivered her burger and fries. He glared at me. "Is this guy bothering you?"

"No, it's smooth," she said. She nibbled one of the fries, took a swig of her soda, and waited until Harry left before she starting talking to me again. But when Harry was out of sight, she gave me a crash course in parallel world theory.

I'd heard some of it before, of course. I wasn't a big sci-fi fan, but some ideas drift out into the mainstream. This was the first time, though, that I'd heard it discussed as a real thing, not just a fictional device, and she went into a lot more detail than I'd ever heard before, talking about the practical difficulties of navigating among infinite universes, and how the shape of what she called polyspace complicated it.

One of those complications was that there were just twelve spots on Earth where travel between worlds was easy – at least, using the method her vehicle used, though apparently other methods were possible. Most of the twelve were in the middle of one ocean or another. One was in Antarctica. One was in the Gobi Desert. One was in central Africa.

And one was just outside Harry's All-Night Hamburgers, or its otherworldly equivalent.

I had occasional problems with the way she used English. It was basically the same language, but some words and phrases had shifted meaning. Still, I could follow it well enough.

By the time she finished explaining her burger was gone, her soda was on its second refill, and her last few fries were cold. Four short guys in black robes had come in and taken a booth in the corner, where they were arguing intensely about whether their faith permitted them to eat fried chicken. A sort of flying drone thing had come in the front door at one point, but Harry had chased it back out with a broom.

"So," she concluded, "you can see why I can't bring you a neural resonator."

"No, I don't!" I exclaimed, loudly enough that one of the four in the corner looked up at me, startled, and I could hear Harry moving around in the kitchen.

"Because we *can't steer*," she said. "We've unraveled a few things about polyspace, but not enough to find any specific universe. I told you that. None of us can ever go home, except maybe by fluke – we can't find that one particular timeline. If I went traveling and found a bag of neural resonators and tried to bring it back for you, I wouldn't be able to find you. At the extreme best I might find someone *like* you, who's bottled the way you are, but the odds are a myriad to a minimum it won't be *you*."

"But what if I came *with* you?" I said. "Then when you found those resonators, I could use one."

She frowned. "There are at least three preventions," she said. "On top, it would be immoral to remove you from your own world without a possibility of restoring you. I wouldn't be able to find your world any more than I can find my own; I'd have to strand you in some other timeline. Next down the stack, my orders forbid it – my callers worried about spies or wreckers or disease vectors, and stuck it to my nose that I was *not* to fetch anyone along. That one isn't so significant anymore, since I'll probably never see any of them again, but then we get to the bottom, the one that really bakes the clay: I operate a one-person vehicle. There's no *room* for a companion."

I couldn't argue with that.

We talked a little more, but not about anything that mattered; then she settled up with Harry, using little strips of something silvery that Harry apparently recognized, and left. I went to the front window and pulled aside the curtain, and I couldn't see how *she* fit in that thing – it looked like a half-melted coffin. There certainly wasn't room for a passenger. It made a sound like a shotgun when it vanished.

I hadn't gotten the gadget I came for, but I knew a lot more about it now. I started approaching Harry's customers a little more boldly after that.

A couple of others recognized the neural resonator from the pictures, but nobody had one with him; most had no idea what it was.

It took five more days to convince someone to give me a lift. I think my appearance, particularly the damaged hand, frightened a lot of people off. Finally, though, I got a ride. He was an ordinary guy, and his vehicle looked like a boxy little van with black paint and golden tires; he said his name was DeVane. I was trembling with excitement when I climbed into his machine, and he cranked up the engine; it whined like nothing I had ever heard before I found Harry's.

We didn't seem to go anywhere except across the parking lot on that first little hop, but in this version of Sutton my Toyota was gone and Harry didn't recognize me. "I thought I'd start small," my driver said.

I asked half a dozen people. No resonators.

The next jump was longer, and we came out atop a glacier, with nothing anywhere in sight but ice and intensely blue sky. We obviously weren't going to find any resonators here, so I waited impatiently in the van while DeVane took pictures and made measurements.

After that came an ocean, where I discovered that the van was amphibious. The next stop was empty forest. Then we saw a radioactive wasteland, a sweltering jungle, another glacier, and then a diner, but the sign wasn't in any alphabet I had ever seen before and the woman running it had scars on her cheeks and spoke something that sounded Slavic.

At each stop DeVane read the instruments in his vehicle and took careful notes, and where it looked safe he got out and took photos and readings. I helped where I could. We talked a lot, but I don't think I was very good company – I was obsessed with neural resonators.

We managed to stay in human civilizations for awhile after that. DeVane had done some calibrating on his vehicle. He still couldn't really aim, but he could largely control the probabilistic distance we traveled.

I was with him for maybe a month, subjective time, and by then we were fed up with each other and I hitched a ride with a woman whose name kept changing according to a pattern I never really understood. She tried to treat my hand, but couldn't really do much. The closest to a resonator we found was a tracking device used in a fascist state – it injected some sort of opiate into the user's wrist.

Except it didn't work on me. I was too far gone in my addiction.

After her came Jottie and Kor, who wanted to adopt me, and then Big Stan, and by then my hand was gone, leaving just a stump, but that wasn't enough to stop me.

It's been about three years now, I think. For most of the last six months I've been back in universes where Harry's exists, even if the United States doesn't. One of them had the technology to make me this robot hand – you'd hardly know it's not real, would you? And it doesn't itch, and I can't rub it hard enough to damage it. The fact that I can rub with it at all means I still have my *other* hand.

So I'm back, I've found Harry's All-Night Hamburgers again, and someone here told me that *you* may have licked the navigation problem. Is it true?

You think you have? Oh, thank God! Oh, lady, you have no idea what this means to me. I'll do anything I can if you'll give me a lift.

What? No, I don't want to go home! Not yet, anyway.

But please, help me find a resonator.

The Prisoner of Shalott

I was invited to contribute to an anthology of Arthurian fantasy, and I had been listening to Loreena McKennitt's "The Lady of Shalott," putting Alfred Lord Tennyson's poem to music. I did a little reading on the legend of Elaine of Ascolat, also known as Elaine the White, that had been Tennyson's source material, and came up with my own version with a more positive ending.

Elaine stood defiantly before her father and looked him in the eye. "I have done nothing wrong," she said.

"You have brought shame upon our house," Sir Bernard replied, meeting her gaze.

"What have I done that would shame us?" she demanded.

"Must you ask? Throwing yourself at Sir Lancelot, begging him to bear your token into the lists..."

"I love him!"

"You are a child," her father replied. "You know nothing of love – and apparently, despite my best efforts and those of your late mother, you understand nothing of the laws of hospitality, and the duty a host owes his guest. Lancelot was here to compete in a tourney, not to court you, yet you would not leave him alone."

"I love him!" Elaine repeated. "And would he not be a suitable husband for me? Lancelot is a worthy knight – indeed, one of the greatest in the land, the king's favorite..."

"And the queen's favorite, as well, yet you insisted he show your favor, rather than hers. Do you not see how poorly this reflects upon my hospitality?"

"But I would marry him, which the queen cannot!"

Sir Bernard sighed. "Oh, my foolish daughter – have you seen any sign that *he* would marry *you*? He did not approach me to seek your hand; indeed, he gave no hint, either directly or through his servants, that he had any interest in you."

"He bore my token in the lists!"

"He is too gallant a knight to refuse a lady such a favor to her face – and when the tourney was over, and he fell wounded, did he keep your favor and display it? Did he kiss it, as he returned it to you? No, daughter, he did not. When I saw you look at him, I bade your brothers to speak with him, to see whether he had anything to say of your charms, your wit – and he did not. Not a word said he of you, not one word. Cannot you see that he is accustomed to women, both high-born and low, desiring his attention? Though you are of noble birth and fairy blood, he thought no more of you than he would of some milkmaid or tavern wench."

"You lie!"

Sir Bernard rose from his chair. "You *dare* address your father so?"

Elaine realized she had gone too far, and bowed her head. "I...I know you are wrong, Father. You do not lie, I know, but you are mistaken. My heart spoke before my senses could stop it, and for that I am sorry, but I know that Lancelot must surely love me as I love him. God could not be so cruel as to have it otherwise."

"I tell you he does not," her father said, still standing.

"And I say you must be mistaken. Let me go to Camelot and speak with him, and you will see..."

"Go to Camelot? Where you would force Sir Lancelot to deny you before the court, and shame us before the King himself? Nonsense! I forbid it; you shall not set foot beyond our lands until you have come to your senses."

Elaine stared at him, struggling to find the words that would make him understand, but before she could say a thing he turned. "I have said enough for tonight," he said. "I will retire, as will you, and perhaps in the morning our passions will have cooled, and we can discuss this more calmly."

She stood on the carpet before his seat and watched him go, certain that *her* passions would not cool until she had felt Lancelot's hands upon her. At last, though, she turned as well, and under the watchful gaze of her father's guards and her own maidens she made her way to her chamber.

Alone in her room, though, she did not undress; instead she crossed to the window and looked out at her father's lands, extending for miles in all directions.

Far to the west, she knew, lay the lands of Faerie, whence her long-lost mother had come, but to the northeast, little more than a day's ride away, lay Camelot, where dwelt her beloved. She stared in that direction, wishing that she had some magic that could transport her across that distance unseen.

She did possess some small share of her mother's magic, as did her brothers, but not enough to cross so many miles before sunrise, and none of her enchantments could withstand the light of day. Her father's mortal blood limited her; by day she was merely human, her gifts lost.

But perhaps, if she gathered all her skills, she could climb upon the moonlight to escape her tower room, and descend safely across the castle walls. Even without magic beyond that, she could be halfway to Camelot by dawn.

She opened the casement, then closed her eyes and gathered herself, drawing in the night's power, pressing aside her mortal weight and letting herself be as light as thistledown, as light as a dandelion seed upon the wind. She floated up upon the windowsill. Taking a deep breath, she stepped off into the night –

And the alarm went up upon an instant, men shouting, a bell ringing, startling her so that the spell broke, and she barely caught herself upon the sill, clambering awkwardly back into her room.

She had scarcely gotten back to her feet when the door burst open and two guards rushed in, followed by her uncle Kailen. Elaine stared at her mother's brother, astonished; her fairy uncle rarely involved himself with human affairs, preferring to spend his time alone, doing no one knew what.

"Child," he said, "that was rash. Did you think your father could be so easily deceived?"

"I..." Elaine hesitated, then admitted, "I did not think at all." She had never been able to lie to her uncle; she guessed that was an aspect of *his* magic, so much stronger than her own.

"I fear that will cost you dearly," Kailen said. "Though perhaps it will prove best for us all in the long run."

Then her father appeared in the door behind her uncle.

"Oh, Elaine," he said sorrowfully. "I had hoped that it would not come to this; I have no desire to lock my daughter up as if she were an unbroken horse, to be kept imprisoned until its spirit is tamed. You leave me no alternative, though."

"Then will you cast me into the dungeons?" Elaine asked, her voice wild. She was not entirely sure whether she feared or welcomed such a fate; it would certainly prove to her, if to no one else, that her father was in the wrong.

"No," Sir Bernard said, with a shake of his head. "You are still my daughter, and the daughter of a noble of Faerie, neither a traitor nor a common criminal. I will confine you in the tower on the island of Shalott, in the river seven miles hence, amid the gardens there, and I have asked my late wife's brother, your uncle Lord Kailen, to place enchantments upon you that will bind you, to keep you in that place."

"Is that why you are here, Uncle?" Elaine asked.

"I had been on my way to your chamber in hopes that I could sway you from your path in time to spare you this," Kailen replied. "Alas, that you were so quick to display your defiance!"

"I know the island of which you speak," she said. "And I will accept confinement there, until such time as you shall repent your cruelty – for shall I not be there seven miles closer to my beloved's home in Camelot?"

"Oh, daughter, you vex me sorely!"

"And you are blind to the truth of my love!"

At that, her father let out a wordless bellow of frustrated rage and turned away. "See to her confinement, as I have commanded!" he said, as he stormed away.

When he had gone, her fairy uncle said, "He does love you, you know, and seeks only what is best for you."

"But he will not *see* what is best for me – to be joined with my true love!"

Lord Kailen sighed. "In the morning I will see to your imprisonment, as your father has ordained." Then he, too, turned and left.

The guards, though, stayed.

* * *

In the morning a party was assembled, and Elaine the White was escorted to her new home.

The island lay in the center of the stream, between banks lined with willows, and beyond the trees fields of barley and rye stretched far and wide, covering the land in rippling gold from one horizon to the other.

On the island itself stood a single structure, an old watchtower that had not been manned since the bad old days before Arthur took the crown and brought the warlords to heel beneath his banner; there was no need for such a defense now that Camelot's peace reigned over England. Four gray stone walls, a turret at each corner, stood in baleful contrast to the bright lilies and graceful willows that surrounded the little fortress.

This was to be Elaine's home, and her prison, until such time as she and her father were reconciled. Although her maidens did not accompany her, and the servants were under strict instructions not to speak to her nor obey her orders, it was arranged that her meals and other necessities were to be provided.

To occupy her hand and mind, a loom was set up in her chamber, and to ensure that she did not slip away, her uncle placed a geas, a curse, upon her – she was to work upon this loom, weaving a tapestry, during all her waking hours, save only when her meals were brought to her. If she turned away, and left the shuttle unmoved for too long, then the full force of the curse would fall upon her.

"And what is this dire fate that will befall me?" she asked.

"I will not tell you that," her uncle replied, his voice little more than a whisper.

"Will I die, then?"

"So it would seem," Kailen answered, and then he fell silent and would say no more.

Her belongings were stowed, her bedding prepared, brightly-dyed threads for the loom set out for her, and then finally her father's party prepared to take its leave and return to the castle of Astolat. She said nothing to her father, and for his part he several times seemed about to speak, but never did.

When the others had gone, though, her uncle waited behind, and drew forth something from beneath his cloak.

"You will be lonely," he said. "Trapped at that loom, you will weary of the same four walls. I cannot give you your freedom; I have sworn to your father that I would not. I can give you this, though, to lighten your days." With that, he handed her a gleaming disk – a mirror of the finest glass, perfectly silvered, utterly without flaw. "This can show you whatever you might see from anywhere in this tower," he said. "Hang it above the loom, and so long as you obey the geas and continue to weave, you need not leave your labors to see the view from each window, or from any of the four turrets, or the parapets between. The mirror will show you whichever you please."

"Thank you, Uncle," she said, accepting the glass.

And then she was alone in her island bower. She placed the mirror above the loom as her uncle had suggested, and began her weaving.

In truth, she found it was not so very terrible; no one troubled her, and the tapestry gave her distraction when she wanted it, as she planned out her design and chose the colors, but it did not require her full attention when she preferred to think of other things. Knotting the threads, working the treadle, and sending the shuttle back and forth was familiar, comforting work that she could carry on while her attention was elsewhere – on dreams of escape, or on fantasies of what it might feel like to rest in Sir Lancelot's arms, her head pressed against his mighty chest.

She could also continue her work when she watched her marvelous glass, for the mirror performed as her uncle had promised; with a word, a gesture, or even a thought she could direct it to show her whatever view she chose. What's more, she found that in some regards it was even better than peering from the actual window, for she could instruct it to show only a portion of an image, whereupon that portion would expand to fill the entire glass, as if she stood much closer than the tower truly was.

She watched barges pass by her island, heavy-laden with grain and treasure bound for the king's court at Camelot. She watched the drooping branches of the willows on the banks brush against the stacked bundles as they passed through the narrows that surrounded Shalott. Branches that had dangled into the river drew dark lines of water upon canvas and wood, and then the barges emerged again into sunlight and moved on toward their destination, and the streaks dried swiftly.

There were small, light boats that passed as well, driven by vividly-painted sails that bore the arms of their owners, or for those that belonged to none of the great houses, fanciful creatures and intricate designs. These flashed brightly in the sun, then dimmed beneath the shade of the trees only to blossom forth anew when they had passed the island. Elaine realized these were carrying messages from town to town, and sometimes also held passengers who preferred the smooth water to the jostling of riding horseback.

She would have waved to these as they passed, but she dared not leave the loom, for fear of her uncle's curse.

Beyond the willows she saw the farmers in the fields, reaping the grain with sickles, or with scythe and cradle. She saw them loading their carts, and wiping the sweat from their brows, and through the open window behind her she could sometimes faintly hear them singing as they worked, songs that celebrated their labors and helped them keep a smooth rhythm as they swung their blades. On occasion, when she knew the songs of old or had heard enough to learn them anew, she sang along, and more than once she saw a reaper raise his head and turn to look toward the island tower, showing that her voice could be heard.

None ever dared approach, though; they would pause, listen, and then return to their work.

The singing helped to lighten her heart, though, and lift the weight of her captivity, so she continued to sing, whether the farmers sang or not.

A road ran beside the stream, and she could see those who passed along it – peasant children in brown homespun, friars in their dark robes, pages and couriers hurrying to bring their masters news of other places, women in colorful gowns fetching goods to market. Most, she knew, were traveling to or from Camelot, which lay but a dozen miles downstream.

Indeed, if she set the mirror in just the right way, she could see the distant towers of Arthur's castle – a reminder that her beloved was not so very far away, and that if she were free of this place, of her father's walls and her uncle's curse, she could go to him. She even saw the means by which that might be achieved – whether by accident or design she did not know, but she found that a small boat, without sail or tow-rope, lay abandoned upon the rocks at the northern end of her little island. If she dared to leave her tower she needed only drag that boat into the stream, and the current would deliver her to Camelot.

There were times when that knowledge cheered her, and she sang songs of love and happiness; there were other times when seeing the boat only reminded her of the walls and the curse that bound her, and all thought of music or gaiety left her.

At first she had thought that her stay on the island would be brief, that her father would reconsider, or that she would find a means of escape, or that Lancelot would seek her out and rescue her, but the days passed, and the weeks, and finally months. The golden fields were stripped bare by the harvesters, the rye and barley hauled away to barns or to market; the leaves of the willows yellowed and fell, the flowers withered and vanished. The travelers on the road were now wrapped in woolen cloaks, hoods pulled forward to shield their faces from the bitter wind. Her unseen servants kept fires going in the rooms below, so that winter's chill did not penetrate too deeply, and her fingers remained nimble enough to continue her weaving.

The tapestry upon which she worked had become a grand panoply of the king and his knights, woven from her memories of the tourney at her father's castle, but where most would have put Arthur at the center, she had instead placed Lancelot there, and had arranged everything else around him, like children around a hearth's fire. She wove his tabard of the purest white she could find, adorned with a cross of the brightest red her dyes could produce, and the face she gave him was worthy of the gods of old and seemed to shine of its own light. His armor gleamed like silver. The other knights were mere shadows by comparison; even Arthur himself was only a man among men, far less than his chief servant.

As the winter wore on, though, she sought more color to counter the drab grays and whites of the outside world, and the stands on either side of the lists were woven of red and gold, adorned with flowers in every color of the rainbow.

At last the days again grew longer, the sun brighter, and the snows melted away, revealing fresh black earth and sprouting green. The mirror showed her travelers' faces once again, and more of them; the farmers, too, returned, to plant the seeds of the new year's crops. The windows were opened, and although she could not easily turn to look out through the casements she could feel the fresh breeze finding its way to her chamber.

She had by now despaired of her father's love; it was clear that he would not relent, that if he had his way she would spend the rest of her life here unless she forswore her love – and that, she could not do.

At that, she sometimes doubted that her father even recalled her existence. Did he remember that he had a daughter, almost twenty years of age, locked away in this tower? Had he forgotten her and moved on with his life, as if she had died? What of her two brothers – had they, too, forgotten that they once had a sister, a childhood playmate? Neither of them had made any contact with her in all her long months of imprisonment.

Nor had her uncle, but that was less surprising; he was, after all, a lord of Faerie, with the cold and whimsical nature of his race, prone to forget how brief mortal lives might be.

And Lancelot had not come. Did he even know where she was? Might he be searching the kingdom for her, seeking her in every village and field, unaware that her own father had imprisoned her here, within sight of Camelot's spires? But surely someone would have told him; it was no secret in her father's castle, surely. Did he think she did not want him? Had her father lied to Lancelot, told him she was no longer interested? Or had her father forbidden Lancelot to come here, and he, noble knight that he was, respected that imperative, though it pained him?

Her moods varied from day to day; sometimes she worked at the loom gladly, singing as she wove, certain that in time her love would come for her. On other days she despaired of life, and passed the shuttle from side to side from simple habit, looking nowhere, ignoring both her tapestry's design and the world the mirror showed her.

On one such day she looked up at the glass and saw the farmers standing respectfully still as a column of knights rode by, their chargers churning the damp soil of the springtime road. Their banners whipped in the breeze – golden lions, and blue saltires, and green dragons, but nowhere a red cross on white. These were knights riding out from Camelot, but Lancelot was not among them, and none turned to look at her island prison as they passed.

Still, they were knights, Lancelot's companions, and she turned, as if to see what was reflected in the mirror, to see only the bare stone wall of her chamber.

"Shadows," she said, turning back to the mirror and the loom. "Only shadows. I am half-*sick* of shadows!" She grabbed the shuttle and flung it furiously across the warp threads.

The days passed, and her tapestry grew; she had completed the central scene of knights at tourney and was now extending it outward, to the lands beyond the castle walls, where magical beasts gamboled amidst bright flowers.

As the spring advanced more knights came and went; she guessed that the king had set the Round Table some new quest, and these men were traveling upon this business, whatsoever it might be. The fields grew green, the plants shooting up, stretching for the sun as the farmers tended to their crops. Flowers blossomed anew on the island outside the tower walls.

And then one day, when summer was almost upon her, she looked up from warp and weft and saw the image of a lone knight on horseback, riding down the road toward Camelot. He had already come alongside the island; the mirror had been directed elsewhere and had missed his approach. She could not see the front of his tabard, to see what sigil might be embroidered there, and he bore his shield on the far side of his mount, so she could not see his arms; his face was turned away, as well.

But she knew him. She had thought of him every day of her imprisonment, had dreamed of him every night. There could be no possibility of error. This was Sir Lancelot, greatest of the Knights of the Round Table.

And then he turned to look at the little tower, and there could be no mistake. It was he.

He wore no helm, as he was returning home, not facing any possibility of combat; his broad clear brow gleamed in the sun, and his black curls swept back from his face on either side, while his helmet rode upon the saddle behind him, a bright red plume waving from its crest as he rode. His greaves glittered like gold, and the steel that guarded his broad shoulders shone like silver. He rode upright, straight and strong. A cross as red as blood emblazoned his chest, vivid on a tunic as white as a summer cloud.

"He has come for me at last!" cried Elaine. She wanted to leap up, to run to the window call to him, but the shuttle in her hand reminded her of the curse; she could not leave the loom.

She would remain here until he had entered the stronghold, she told herself. He would find an entrance and come for her, and then she would fling the shuttle aside and throw her arms around him, and together they would find a way to escape the curse.

She tied off a thread, then unspooled another length and wound it on the shuttle; that done, she looked up at the mirror, to see whether Lancelot had yet found his way across the channel to the island.

He had not; instead he was still upon the road, and almost past the line of willows, close against the burgeoning green barley. He was no longer looking at her prison, but ahead, at the distant towers of Camelot, and she thought she could hear, ever so faintly through the open casement, his deep voice raised in happy song at the sight of home.

He had not stopped. He had not come for her. He would not be singing thus while he sought to breach the fortress that held her, so that was not what had brought him at all. He did not know she was here, she realized; he had not come searching for her, but merely chanced to be passing on some other business.

"No!" she cried, dropping the shuttle. "*No!*" She leapt to her feet and turned, trying to get her bearings – which way to a window where she might call to him? She had for so long seen the outside world only as reflections in her glass that she had lost all sense of how her prison was oriented.

She ran through a passage and found only an empty room, and windows that looked out upon barley fields and willows; there was no road, no passing knight, below her vantage point, but only water lilies upon the sun-dappled stream. She whirled and ran back the other way, flung open a pair of shutters, and again saw field and garden and river and tree.

But now, with two references, she knew where she needed to go. She turned once again and rushed up a short stair to yet a third window. Here she leaned out and saw the river between two rows of willows, and the road and green barley beyond. She let her gaze follow the road, and saw Lancelot riding away, the red cross upon his back as bright as the one upon his chest, the red plume of his helmet dancing upon his saddle as if to taunt her.

"No," she called again. "*No!*"

Wind rippled through the willows below, cool on her face. "Beloved!" she cried, "I am here! Come for me! Save me! *Lancelot!*"

But her voice did not carry over the wind, and over the growing distance between them. He could not hear her, shout as she might. Had it been night, when her mother's magic stirred within her, she might perhaps have reached him, have somehow gotten his attention, but in the warm afternoon sun she had only a mortal's throat to call his name, and it was not enough. He rode on, never looking back.

She watched him go, hoping that he might turn and see her, that he might casually glance back and catch sight of her, but no such miracle occurred; his horse carried him down the road away from her, his gaze fixed on the towers of Camelot.

And then she heard a noise behind her, a sound of strings snapping and wood straining. She turned.

Something twanged.

"Oh, no," she said. Then she leapt down from the casement and ran back to her chamber, to the room that had been her prison and her refuge for the past several months.

The loom had splintered, threads broken and tangled; her unfinished tapestry had unrolled and lay spread upon the wreckage. And above the stool where she had sat for so long hung the mirror that had shown her shadows of the world outside, but as she watched the glass shuddered and rippled, and the mirror cracked from side to side, the magical images vanishing so that the two pieces now reflected only the gray stone of the walls enclosing her.

"The curse," she wailed. "The curse is come upon me!"

And now, she knew, she was to die. That was what her father and uncle had agreed upon, should she abandon her labors, and she had left the loom too long as she sought to see her lover.

She was to die – but she did not know what form her death would take, nor how long she had before it befell her.

Even as these thoughts ran through her head, though, she felt a twinge in her belly, a tightening in her chest, and she knew her doom was upon her. She paused for a moment to snatch up a pot of dye and a scrap of cloth, so that she might perhaps leave a final message – she had neither paper nor ink, but the dye, she thought, would serve. It was the color of midnight, a deep, deep blue, and very beautiful.

She found the stairs and staggered down, the breath growing weak in her lungs. She wondered whether the servants were near, and whether they would speak to her in this final extremity, perhaps give a final message to her father, but she saw no sign of them.

She flung open the great oaken door at the base of the tower and stumbled out onto the graveled path, looking for that long-abandoned boat she knew lay on the island's shore.

She did not want to die on this island; if it took her death to set her free, then she would *be* free, no longer trapped in her stone walls, but out in the spring air and sunshine. And that boat – she could set herself adrift, let the boat carry her corpse past Camelot and out to sea, so that everyone would see what had become of her. Lancelot need not seek forever after his lost love; he would know she was gone, and could go on.

She swayed unsteadily as she walked, hoping she had time enough; it would be so...so *plain* to fall dead here, without leaving the island.

And though she could feel the strength leaving her limbs, she found the boat and righted it, setting it on the island's verge. Then she took her pot of dye and dipped the cloth in it, trying to think what message she might write, what her parting words might be, so that the world would understand the tragedy that was happening here.

"Here lies Elaine of Astolat," perhaps, "betrayed by those she loved."

But no, she was Elaine of Astolat no longer; she had been cast out of Astolat, her name taken from her. She took the stained rag and wrote upon the prow of the boat, as neatly as she could with her trembling hand, "The Lady of Shalott."

She had hoped to say more, but she could sense she had no time to spare, and her wits were fading, as well, so that she could not decide upon anything more. She tossed aside the dye and rag, and pushed the boat down into the river. As carefully as she could, she clambered aboard and felt her little craft drift free. As it found the current she lay down upon her back and folded her hands across her chest, waiting to die.

Clouds were gathering in the sky above, she saw – perhaps a spring shower was coming.

She would feel nothing of it, though. She closed her eyes.

She could no longer feel her legs or arms, but somehow her throat was still clear, and upon a whim she began to sing, composing her own dirge as she drifted down the river. How she found the strength, she did not know; why she still lived at all, she did not understand. Still, she sang, so that what little breath remained to her might not be wasted.

She sang as long as she could, but she had lost all sense of time, and did not know whether that was only a moment, or an hour. When at last she paused for a moment, she heard voices muttering.

Startled, she opened her eyes and found that her boat had already found its way as far downstream as the outermost houses of Camelot, where frightened people lined the riverbanks, watching her pass. There were merchants in rich velvet, peasants in drab wool, knights in gleaming armor, dames in shining silks, staring out at her. She saw townsfolk cross themselves in fear as she drifted by, and she wanted to call out to them, to let them there was no cause for concern, but now her voice was gone – she could not move at all, not even her eyes, any longer.

Her uncle's curse was stranger than she had anticipated. She knew, from the words she heard from the banks and bridges, that they thought her dead, a corpse laid out as though for burial, but she could still hear them, could still see them gesture, not just the making the sign of the cross but also the devil's horns, to ward off the evil eye.

Was this death, then? Surely not. This was some spell that her uncle had placed upon her, some enchantment.

"The Lady of Shalott," someone said. "What is Shalott?"

"An island up the river," another voice replied. "It's said a fairy lives in the tower there, and the farmers can sometimes hear her singing."

"We heard singing," a new voice joined in. "Perhaps this is she, then – the fairy who dwelt there."

"But what is she doing here? Why is she dead? There is no mark upon her of either blade or fever."

"Someone tell the king, or his wizard! Let him tell us what must be done."

"Tell the king!"

"A messenger has gone to the castle, since first the boat was seen."

Elaine could not move her eyes, so she could not see who spoke; she could see only the sky above, the undersides of bridges, and the faces of those who lined the nearer bank of the river.

But then she heard a voice that she did not need eyesight to identify. It was the deep, rich voice of Sir Lancelot, calling orders.

A moment later, at his direction, boat-hooks grappled with her little vessel, pulling it toward the shore. A moment after that Lancelot's face came into Elaine's field of vision, dark against the sky, his black curls framing his strong features as he looked down at her.

Elaine thrilled at the sight, and a thought filled her. Perhaps a kiss from this, her true love, would break the curse her uncle had laid upon her, as might happen in an old tale. Perhaps if Lancelot were to lean down and press his lips to hers she would be freed of this enchantment and would return to life, ready to live with him for the rest of her life.

She waited as he knelt down over her boat.

"The Lady of Shalott," he said. "She has a lovely face, a rare beauty; it is sad that we should only see it now, when she is dead. God in his mercy granted her this grace; I hope that it served her well while she yet lived, and brought pleasure to her and those around her."

Elaine waited for him to stoop down, to give her a farewell kiss, a kiss that would restore her to life, but he did not; indeed, he straightened and got back to his feet, still looking down at her.

"What a shame," he said, "that I did not meet her while she yet lived. Perhaps I might have found the means to save her from whatever fate has befallen her."

Then he turned, and signaled to the men with the boat-hooks to release the little craft.

Elaine was almost too shocked to notice when the boat drifted away from the dock.

"What a shame that I did not meet her while she yet lived," he had said. "*What a shame that I did not meet her.*"

He did not love her. He did not even *remember* her.

Her father had been right all along. She had been a silly girl, caught up in a romantic fantasy. Sir Lancelot had never really noticed her; she had just been one more foolish child drawn to his handsome face and manly form, and to the tales of his strength and goodness.

The boat drifted on, past the castle towers, the stone bridges, the soaring spires, the staring crowds, until Camelot was past and she was again in open country, beneath gathering clouds. She lay unmoving, trapped by her uncle's spell, unable to weep, unable to curse, wondering what was to become of her.

Then the clouds burst, and rain fell, and where the drops touched her she felt strength and sensation return. She could blink again, and flex her fingers; then she could turn her head and raise her hands to shield herself from the gentle storm. Her legs bent, and she was able to sit up and look around at the fields slipping past.

A willow dangled above the stream, and she reached up to grab its branches, pulling herself and her little boat to the shore. Still somewhat unsteady, she used the willow's limbs to pull herself upright, and to heave herself over the boat's side and onto the bank. There she let herself fall back, and sat upon the riverside, looking out at the intricate patterns formed by the willow's leaves and the expanding, interlocking ripples each fat raindrop made as it pierced the river's surface.

And then her uncle was there, standing on the shore a few yards away, watching her silently. She blinked and stared at him.

"I would not kill you," he said. "You and your brothers are all that I have left of the sister I loved. You should have known that, were you not so blinded by your infatuation."

"You *said* I would die."

"No," he replied. "I said it would *seem* that you died, and is that not what occurred?"

"Did you *know* that all this would happen as it has? Did you know Lancelot would not recognize me?"

"Not precisely," Kailen said. "I knew that he did not love you, and I knew you would not believe that until you saw it for yourself – not merely heard the good knight say it, for then you could say that he was denying the truth for some reason of your invention, but *saw* it, in a way you could not reject. I bent my spell to encourage the fates to arrange for such an encounter, but I did not know how that might be accomplished, nor how long it might take. The fates were kind, and found a way in less than a year. I am glad it took no longer; you mortals live such brief lives that it would be a shame to waste more of one than necessary."

Elaine stared at him, then said, "I know you have done me a great favor, Uncle, but I cannot yet bring myself to thank you. The pain is still too great."

"Of course. But *my* life is not brief, and I can wait." He glanced upstream. "And now, dear child, what will you do? Your death has been reported far and wide, but I am certain your family will gladly receive you back, should you return to Astolat."

Elaine shook her head before she had consciously made her decision. "No," she said. "I am a grown woman now, and I cannot yet forgive my father any more than I can thank you. I will find my own way in the world for a time; if I am careful I think I have enough magic and common sense to get by."

"I am sure you do," Kailen said with a nod. "Go, then, and find your path. In time it may bring you back to your father's halls, or perhaps to your mother's home in Faerie, or to the king's court in Camelot. If you ever feel you need help, always remember you have two brothers who love you, and a father who cares for you whether you believe it or not – and of course, you have an uncle you can call upon."

"I will remember," Elaine said. Then she turned and walked up the riverbank to the road, where she turned toward the sea, her back to many-towered Camelot. She glanced back, and as she had expected, her uncle was gone. He was a fairy lord, and did not need to go as mortal men did.

She managed a crooked smile, then walked on alone, eastward into the warm spring rain.

An Interrupted Betrothal

Here's another tale of the Bound Lands, again written for the "Lace and Blade" series. Where "Sorcery of the Heart" was set in the northwestern corner of the Walasian Empire, this one is set in the Cousins, the small nation-states east of the Empire.

Riassa watched from the shadows as the doors of the hall swung open, propelled by a pair of burly, wary-eyed guards. They scanned the room swiftly, taking in Lord Panris and his own half-dozen guards arrayed on the dais, but if they saw Riassa they gave no sign; apparently the first of the spells she had bought worked as promised.

Then the guards stepped to either side, standing with their backs against the doors, and a brightly-clad herald stepped in, trumpet in hand. He did not raise his instrument, however, but instead took a deep breath and announced, in a voice so loud it seemed to fill every inch of the room, "His Excellency Lord Arzam of Barva!"

Lord Panris stirred, straightening where he stood, as his guest marched in. He looked unimpressed – but then, he always looked unimpressed in public. That was deliberate, Riassa knew. Her uncle was too clever to reveal his feelings openly.

Lord Arzam did not look particularly impressed at the sight of Lord Panris, either, but then Riassa saw his gaze wander quickly around the lesser audience chamber, and she thought she saw a little more respect in his expression as he took in the gleaming marble and intricate gilding, the fine tapestries on the walls, and the glittering crystal pendants that adorned each lamp.

As for Riassa, she *was* impressed – Arzam was one of the tallest men she had ever seen, towering over his entourage, but he did not have the rough features or brutish mannerisms that many large men displayed. He stood straight, his shoulders back. His face was strong and handsome, his body perfectly proportioned, his movements graceful. He wore his black hair pulled back in a gold-banded braid that reached almost to the sword-belt at his waist.

Riassa noticed that the leather-bound hilt protruding from that belt was heavily worn; the weapon was clearly not just for show. That worried her slightly, but she did not let it distract her. The plan did not call for any violence, and she had her magical escape ready if she needed it.

She wondered whether her cousin Avinna might reconsider once she saw her suitor, because Riassa certainly found him appealing – but no, Avinna had sworn that she wanted nothing to do with *any* man, that her interests lay entirely with her own sex, and Arzam was perhaps the most purely masculine creature Riassa had ever seen.

She had no idea what his temperament might be like, though.

"I am here, Lord Panris, as we agreed," Arzam said. Riassa had expected a man of his size to speak in a rumbling bass, but instead his voice was a smooth baritone, and he spoke Kalithian with none of the barbaric accent his envoys had displayed.

"I thank you, Lord Arzam, for coming," Uncle Panris replied. "I know yours are a direct people; shall we dispense with the preliminaries and get directly to the presentation? I am sure you want to see your prospective bride."

Arzam smiled, an unexpectedly open expression Riassa found charming. "It would seem the Kalithian reputation for endless ceremony is undeserved," he said. "By all means, bring her out."

Panris raised a hand, and a waiting attendant drew back one of the curtains at the back of the dais. For a few awkward seconds nothing happened, but then Avinna suddenly emerged as if shoved, as indeed she probably had been. Her head was bowed as she stepped forward to her father's side. She wore a simple but beautiful gown of white silk trimmed with pale beads, and her hair was wound into elaborate curls that framed her delicate features.

She was trembling, Riassa noticed – probably nervous about her upcoming performance. After all, she was about to irretrievably ruin her own reputation.

For now, though, Avinna stood waiting and said nothing.

"Lady Avinna," Arzam said. "I see the reports of your beauty did not exaggerate."

Avinna did not move; her head remained down, and she neither looked at her suitor nor spoke.

"I would be pleased to hear your voice," Arzam added, his smile fading.

"I have nothing to say to you," Avinna murmured; Riassa could barely make out the words.

"Oh? Is there nothing you would ask, nothing you would tell me about yourself? Are you content to marry a complete stranger?"

Avinna's cheeks reddened. Finally she raised her eyes and looked at him.

"I don't want to marry *you*, stranger or not," she said. "If you would please me, Lord Arzam, then let me be and go home."

Riassa watched her cousin's face, trying to judge whether there might be some trace of interest once she saw Arzam's face and figure – but no, Riassa saw only nervous desperation, the same desperation that had driven the two of them to concoct their scheme.

For a moment after Avinna's words of defiance, no one spoke. Every man in the room seemed frozen in surprise; Riassa looked from one to the next, trying without success to judge what might happen. Then Arzam broke the silence, his tone surprisingly gentle. "You do not know me, girl. Am I so repulsive that you would refuse me without allowing me any chance to prove myself?"

"Yes!" Avinna exclaimed – but then she caught herself. She and Riassa both knew that men did not believe there was any woman alive whose passions could not in time be roused; they had discussed that often enough. For her part, Riassa found it hard to grasp just how thoroughly Avinna detested the idea of letting any man touch her, but she had at last been convinced that her cousin was completely sincere – she had no interest at all in boys or men, but only in women.

And both of them had overheard enough boastful male conversation to suspect that Lord Arzam would see Avinna's lack of interest as a challenge, rather than a disqualification.

"It is not *you*, my lord," Avinna hastily added. "But I already have a lover, and will have no other." And thus the scheme was launched; Riassa stood ready.

Arzam's eyes widened. He looked to Lord Panris, whose expression was one of shock. "I give you my word, Lord Arzam, I have heard nothing of this before this very moment!" he exclaimed.

"Did you think to *ask* her, my lord?"

Panris flushed. "I told her I had found her a fine and worthy husband, and she made no such objection at the time."

Avinna turned to her father. "I *told* you I did not want to marry!"

"But you said nothing of a lover!"

Avinna turned angrily away without answering.

Riassa was looking, not at the principals in this discussion, but at the various retainers. Her uncle's guards seemed to range from amusement to shock, while Lord Arzam's people appeared to be worried, or even frightened. Perhaps their master had a temper?

"It would seem, Lord Panris, that intentionally or not, you have misled me," Arzam said. His voice was calm; if he did have a temper, he was keeping it in check.

"That was not my intent, I swear!" Panris spread his hands. "I had no idea that her objection to the match was anything but adolescent foolishness."

"Perhaps you should have discussed the matter with her more closely before making an offer that would shape her entire life."

"What would you have me do? She is my daughter, and it is my *responsibility* to find her a suitable husband."

"She may have saved you the trouble." Arzam turned his attention to Avinna. "Tell me, girl, who is this lover? Where is he? Do you intend to wed him?"

"Yes, Avinna – who is he?" Panris demanded. "Please tell me you have not become besotted with some muscular peasant or handsome soldier."

Riassa tensed at that. She knew her uncle's jab was not random, but a reminder of how his own sister, Riassa's mother, had embarrassed the family. Not that Riassa considered her father an embarrassment; he was brave and strong and a loving parent, and she much preferred him to her noble uncle.

Avinna threw back her head and pointed – not quite at Riassa, but in the right general direction. "He's right there! He's a sorcerer!"

That word, "sorcerer," was the cue they had agreed upon; Riassa released her purchased magic, drew her borrowed sword, and stepped forward, suddenly visible – a reasonably tall figure in men's clothing, a hooded black robe worn loose to hide her face and disguise her shape.

"I am the one who has claimed this woman," she said, speaking in as deep a voice as she could manage.

Several of the men in the room started, and hands fell to sword-hilts as this new arrival seemed to appear out of nowhere, but then Arzam raised a hand. His men froze where they were, and her uncle's guards looked to Lord Panris, who also signaled for calm.

"Who are you, that dares intrude here uninvited?" Lord Panris said, his voice trembling – though with rage or fear, Riassa could not tell.

"I am Avinna's sorcerous lover. Surely you know a sorcerer's true name gives one power over him? Then you will forgive me if I do not tell you mine, nor insult you by lying to your face."

"Then you have no noble title, nor renowned family?"

"Indeed, I do not. My power, gained through study, is both greater and less worldly than any derived from birth." She and Avinna had discussed the possibility of claiming some highborn ancestry for their fictional magician lover, but had dismissed it; Lord Panris knew the pedigrees of every landed family in the region and would spot a lie.

"Yet you think yourself worthy of my daughter?"

"I do."

"And he's the one I love!" Avinna exclaimed, starting toward Riassa.

One of her father's men grabbed her arm and held her. That was *not* in the plan. At this point in their little act, Avinna was supposed to come to her side. Riassa wished she had anticipated this; a genuine sorcerer would probably have some little spell that could pry the guard's hand away, but Riassa had not included anything of that sort in her tiny magical arsenal.

But then, the trio of spells she *had* purchased had cost every copper she and Avinna could raise, and more – she still owed the Lornish magician a favor to cover the unpaid balance. She could not have afforded anything more.

"Release her!" Riassa demanded, her heart racing. She raised her sword. She was unsure what she could do if her demand was refused, but to say nothing would make her seem weak.

The guard looked to Lord Panris, but before he could speak, Lord Arzam said, "Wait."

Panris turned to his guest. "What would you have, my lord?"

"If I may, a few questions."

His tone was calm, which was not what Riassa had expected. She had assumed a barbarian lord would be enraged to have his betrothal disrupted this way. She let her blade down a little. "Of whom do you want your answers, sir?" she asked.

"Of our host, O nameless magician – at least, for now." Arzam turned back to Panris. "My lord, our negotiations were conducted through intermediaries, so perhaps I have misunderstood some points. I would like to clarify them."

"Lord Arzam, this is not the time or place..."

"It is *precisely* the time and place," Arzam roared, interrupting Panris. His right hand was closed on the hilt of his sword, and the sudden bellowing after his previous calm was shocking. "You appear to have brought me here under false pretenses, and I will have this matter clarified *now*. You may have issues to straighten out with your daughter and this young man, but you are not going to waste *my* time with them until our own situation has been clarified."

Riassa was impressed with both the volume of the Barvan's voice, and his command of Kalithian.

Panris frowned, but before he could reply Arzam continued, "My understanding was that you were offering me a beautiful virgin bride to seal the bond between our two lands. You were quite definite in your description, were you not?"

"Yes!" Panris said. He was about to say more, but again, Arzam interrupted.

"I can see that your daughter is beautiful," he said, "unless you have availed yourself of a glamour – perhaps this young man provided that, as part of some elaborate performance?"

"No!" Panris exclaimed, as Riassa burst out, "I have not..."

"But is she a virgin? The existence of this alleged lover casts doubt upon it."

Again, Panris and Riassa both spoke at once. Arzam held up a hand, then pointed at Riassa. "What do *you* say, sir? Has this young woman known a man's company?"

"I have shared her bed," Riassa replied. Which was true; the cousins had innocently spent many nights together as children. This was the very heart of their plan; Lord Arzam was now supposed to reject Avinna, dismiss her as unworthy of him.

For a moment Riassa thought it was working, as Arzam turned to Avinna, who blushed a suitable shade of crimson. "It's true," she said.

Her father looked shocked. "I didn't...how..."

Once again, Arzam's voice overrode everyone else.

"It would still be to the advantage of both our realms for an alliance to be made, and sealed in some way more binding than signatures on a piece of paper," he said. "Furthermore, I doubt it would enhance anyone's reputation save perhaps that of our magician friend were I to yield all claims and let these lovers run off together. So if certain concessions are made, I will ignore Avinna's misbehavior and her father's misinformation, and accept her anyway."

Riassa's mouth fell open, and she snapped it quickly shut, as Avinna wailed, "No! You can't!"

"My dear girl," Arzam said, "I most certainly can. I have three good men and my own blade, and your father has six men of his own; can your talented friend there defeat all of us? I doubt it. And if he can, any magic that might strike us down might kill your father, as well – are you so besotted as to want that?"

Avinna threw Riassa a helpless glance. She knew her cousin was not a real sorcerer. The plan had called for her to run to Riassa's side, and the two would then vanish in a cloud of smoke – but her father's guard was holding her back.

And they had not made any plans for what they would do if Arzam did not abandon his claim on her. The plan had been to keep Avinna out of sight until her Barvan suitor had gone home; then she was to reappear, saying that the magician had betrayed and deserted her. Avinna would stay on in her father's palace, disgraced and unfit for marriage – which was exactly what she wanted.

But it had all gone wrong.

"Now, Lord Panris," Arzam said, ignoring both his intended bride and her supposed suitor, "shall we renegotiate the terms of our agreement, in light of this new information?"

Desperate, barely remembering to keep her voice pitched low, Riassa called out, "No! Avinna is mine!" She stepped forward, sword ready.

Arzam's two guards drew their own blades and moved toward her, ready to defend their master, but Arzam waved them back. "So this boy wizard has the courage to fight for his beloved?"

Boy wizard? Perhaps her masquerade was not as convincingly manly as she had hoped. Her size was considered ungainly for a woman, but apparently she was still too slender to pass for a grown man.

But that was not important; her present need was to meet Arzam's challenge. "I do!" she said, desperately hoping that the barbarian lord would laugh, or turn away in disgust, and give up Avinna as not worth the trouble.

Arzam did neither. He casually pulled his own weapon from its sheath and advanced to meet her.

Riassa struggled to hide her trembling. She had been trained to use a sword, but never very seriously; after all, despite her size, she was only a woman. Her two remaining spells were a simple fireworks display intended to show she was truly a magician, and the transporting spell that would carry her and Avinna to safety, and neither of those would help her swordplay. Oh, the fireworks might dazzle her opponent briefly, and the other would let her escape, but she did not want to resort to that if she could possibly avoid it, since it would leave Avinna stranded here. She raised her blade into guard position and stood ready, hoping that Avinna or Uncle Panris would call out to stop the fight.

But neither did. Panris undoubtedly saw this as the simplest way out of an embarrassing situation; if Arzam killed his daughter's illicit lover and married her anyway, everything would be back on course. Avinna – well, Avinna was probably too frightened and confused to think of anything to say. Riassa loved her cousin, but Avinna had never been the most quick-witted member of the family; the plan had been mostly her own creation.

That escape talisman was becoming more tempting every second; her left hand slipped into the pouch holding it.

Then suddenly Arzam closed on her, moving with astonishing speed, far too fast for her to react effectively, but he did not thrust his blade through her heart or belly, nor slash at her; instead he somehow managed to lock blades with her so that the two of them were pressed together, swords crossed between them.

She stood, baffled, chest to chest with the barbarian, unsure what to do next, and very aware of his nearness. Now she could not escape at all; if she triggered the spell while they stood so close, she would take Arzam with her.

"Listen, sorcerer," Arzam whispered, "do you want to live?"

Riassa tilted her head but said nothing; she stepped back, as if forced.

"I couldn't refuse your challenge, nor negotiate openly with you," Arzam continued. "It would look weak, and I can't afford that. But I've no desire to kill you, or to keep you and Avinna apart. Now, we need to make this look good; shift your blade to the right. We'll swing around and lock again."

Riassa nodded, ever so slightly, and then pulled free; in a flurry of steel the blades swept around, clashed, and then they were once again chest to chest.

"I *need* this marriage," Arzam murmured, speaking swiftly but clearly. "My people – we *need* this Kalithian treaty. The Olzani are pushing us west, out of our grazing land, and we need wealthy allies and better weapons. My own idiot councilmen won't trust the Kalithians without something more than signatures on a piece of paper, though; they'll probably cut my throat while I sleep if I return without a hostage bride."

"Hostage?" Riassa replied, startled.

"You thought it was a love match?" He pressed forward, and she stepped back again. They were so close his scent filled her head, and his dark eyes filled her vision. "Don't be a fool. Now, yield to me, and we can make an arrangement to suit us all. Avinna and I will stage a wedding, but if she doesn't want me I won't touch her – the two of you can do as you please, if you're subtle about it. I can take you back as my new court magician. Fling your sword aside and raise your hands, and we're done."

For a moment Riassa seriously considered this offer, but an instant's thought told her it could never work. She was no magician, and did not want to be Avinna's lover.

But another thought struck her.

She felt Arzam tensing, and there was another staged flutter of their blades, this time without any spoken prompting. When they had again locked into position she whispered, "I can't do that. I'm sorry. But there's another possibility."

"What?" Arzam grunted, as he pressed her back another step.

"Avinna has a cousin, a year older than herself. Her name is Riassa, and she *is* a virgin, if not a beauty. I think she might be more cooperative. She's not a lord's daughter, but she's of noble blood."

Arzam blinked, smiled, and then stepped back, breaking away from his opponent. "What sorcery is this?" he shouted. "I cannot touch him!"

Riassa saw this as her best chance; she thrust her left hand deeper into the pouch and squeezed the transporting talisman. Smoke swirled up around her.

When the smoke cleared she was in her own bedchamber. Avinna was not with her, but that no longer mattered; she dropped her sword and quickly stripped off the bulky garments she had been wearing. Pulling on her nearest dress she hurried out into the corridor and down the stairs, only realizing halfway down that she was still wearing men's boots, and not her slippers. She straightened her skirts and ran on, hoping no one would notice.

The doors of the lesser audience chamber were still wide open; she ran in without pausing, rushing past too quickly for the guards to react.

Lord Arzam was standing before the dais, saying, "...saw what he did! Who's to say he could not transport himself into my bedchamber thus, and cut my throat before my guards could stop him?"

"Uncle!" Riassa called, as she came skidding to a stop at Arzam's side. "I saw a man *flying*!"

One of Arzam's guards grabbed her from behind; she did not resist.

"Riassa?" Lord Panris said.

"Uncle, truly, he was flying! I saw him soar off above the stables!" Her bedchamber's one window overlooked the stables.

Arzam turned to her. "Was he dressed in black, with a long sword?"

"Yes!" she said. "Did you see him, too?" Then she blinked, and attempted a curtsey that was severely impaired by the strong hold on her arms. "My apologies, sir; do I know you?"

"I am Arzam of Barva," he replied, with just a trace of a bow.

Lord Panris sighed. "Lord Arzam, may I present my niece, Riassa ter-Vallez?"

"I am honored," Arzam replied, bowing a little more deeply and meeting Riassa's eyes. He smiled. Then he turned back to Lord Panris.

"My lord," he said, "why did you not tell me that your home held *two* remarkable beauties?"

"What?" Panris said, clearly caught completely off-guard. Riassa suppressed a smile; she knew that her uncle had never considered the possibility that *anyone* might think her beautiful; she was too tall, her shoulders too broad, her features too pronounced. He preferred the petite delicacy of his wife and daughter. Riassa realized that Arzam's question was just flattery, but she still enjoyed hearing it.

"Her husband is a lucky man," Arzam continued.

"I am not yet married, my lord," Riassa said, casting her eyes demurely downward. She had suggested herself as an alternative entirely for tactical reasons, to save Avinna from a fate she dreaded, but now that it appeared about to be realized she felt her heart beating faster, not with fear, but with anticipation.

"Why, then..." Lord Arzam smiled again, that wide-open smile she had admired before. "Lord Panris, I believe I see a happy solution to *all* our problems! If you will simply substitute her name for Avinna's in every agreement, I think we will all be pleased." He turned to Riassa. "Assuming, of course, that she will have me."

Before either Panris or Riassa could respond, Arzam went down on one knee, snatching up Riassa's hand and freeing that arm from his guardsman's grip. "Riassa of Kalithia," he said, "will you marry me?"

"It's ter-Vallez," Riassa said. "And I will certainly consider it."

* * *

It was three days later, on the ride back to Barva after the negotiations were concluded, when the two of them were alone in the carriage, that Riassa was finally able to ask, "When did you know it was me?"

"The moment I looked in your eyes," Arzam replied. "It's fortunate no one else had seen the 'sorcerer' at close range." He hesitated, then asked, "Were you really Avinna's lover?"

Riassa blushed and shook her head. "Not beyond a few silly games when we were children, though I think she wished there were more."

"You prefer men?"

"Very much so."

"Then...I will not press you, and I am willing to accept whatever you decide, but will this be a marriage in more than name?"

"I certainly hope so." She smiled as she leaned toward him, ready for her first kiss. "And won't it make a fine story to tell our children, when they ask how we met?"

To See the New Jerusalem

I watched the movie "Things to Come," and got thinking about how utterly wrong it was in almost every respect in its predictions of the future. Then I tried to imagine how someone from the 1930s would react to the future we actually got, and this story is the result.

There are three further details I want to address. First, the title. I swear I thought "To see the new Jerusalem" was a quote from a famous poem of the early twentieth century, but I have been completely unable to identify a source; apparently I made it up without meaning to. Second, as a sort of in-joke, the characters' names are all those of prominent Princeton University alumni families. And third, the description of Times Square is based on a webcam view taken at the exact time in 2023 that the scene is set, which was exactly when I wrote it.

The three guests stared in awe at the humming apparatus. "It must have cost a fortune!" Frelinghuysen said.

"A large part of one, certainly," Powell agreed, as he placed the last hat on the coat-rack by the door. "Oh, I'm not in any danger of starving, but I don't think I'll be buying any yachts this year."

"What the devil *is* it?" Joline asked.

Powell turned to him, startled. "Why, it's a time machine," he said. "I explained that in my invitation."

"You mean you were *serious*?"

"Very much so."

"It *is* a bit much to accept, you know," Foulke remarked. "I know that German fellow, Einstein, seems to think that you can travel in time if you simply move fast enough, but the idea never really made sense to me."

"Oh, Einstein," Powell said. "Well, you know, I think he's already behind the times, but yes, his work was what got me started."

"Not Mr. Wells?" Frelinghuysen suggested.

Powell smiled. "Mr. Wells was indeed a part of my inspiration, but I could hardly draw on any theory he put forth, since he neglected to include any in his little fantasy."

"You really claim to have built a time machine?" Joline demanded. "One you can ride through time the way Wells described?"

"More or less," Powell said. "There are significant differences."

"Have you tested it?"

"No," Powell said. "I have *not* tested it, and I must say, Bob, I'm rather disappointed that you didn't read my invitation more carefully. I put considerable effort into writing it."

"*I* read it," Foulke said. "I wasn't sure what to make of it, but I read it. You want us to act as observers?"

"Observers and advisors," Powell said. "I have done the best I can in making my preparations, but I have done it all in the utmost secrecy, and I'm all too aware that I may have overlooked something of importance. I trusted the three of you when we roomed together, and I'm trusting you now to advise me, think of whatever I haven't – and not have me committed to the booby-hatch."

"I'm none too sure of that last," Joline replied.

"Oh, hush, Bob," Frelinghuysen said. "Powell may have got some idiotic bee in his bonnet and tossed away half the family funds, but he's hardly a raving madman. But Powell, I do want a promise from you before this goes any further."

"What sort of a promise?"

"I want your assurance that if this contraption of yours doesn't work, you'll give serious thought to the idea that perhaps there *is* something wrong with the old noggin, and not go rushing off into any other hare-brained schemes."

"I'll certainly consider it," Powell agreed cheerfully. "But I'll want to check for loose wires first."

"It seems to be running," Foulke remarked. "That would seem to militate against faulty wiring."

"It's warming up," Powell explained. "Building up potential. Doesn't mean everything's actually *working*."

"Well, assuming it works, just what will it do? Will we see it vanish?" Joline asked.

"Not the whole machine," Powell said. "Just me. See that platform there, between the field generators? I'll be standing there, and in theory, everything on that platform will vanish from this room, transported to some time in the future – I think the early twenty-first century, but you'll understand that there's been no way to calibrate it, so I can't be sure of the exact date. I will, I believe, experience a stay there of a few hours – I'm estimating between three and four – and then the temporal charge will dissipate, and I will pop back here to 1934. If I have the theory right, I'll only have been gone for a few minutes, from your point of view."

"How do you know you'll come back that far?" Frelinghuysen asked. "What if you wind up stranded in the middle of next year?"

"Then I'll present an interesting case for the missing persons department. I sincerely hope it won't happen that way."

"Why are you going to the future?" Foulke asked. "A trip to the past would be a better test – you'd know what to expect, and you could leave us proof somewhere that you'd been there."

"I can't," Powell admitted. "So far I've only figured out how to apply a *positive* temporal charge. And the interval to be traveled is also predetermined – time appears to be a quantum phenomenon, and my best estimate is that the quantum in question is around eighty or ninety years. Besides, I want to see the world of tomorrow!"

"This sounds horribly risky," Frelinghuysen muttered. "What if you land in the middle of...say, *where* will you land?"

"In theory, not far from where we are now," Powell said. "The Earth's gravitational field creates a sort of friction."

"And what if you come out inside a wall, or somewhere over the Atlantic?" Joline asked. "Assuming this thing works at all."

"Materializing in solid matter would require more displacement energy, so it won't happen; I'll be shunted a little to one side, either in time or space. Popping out in mid-air, or dropping into the Hudson – well, I can swim, and I'm hoping for the best."

"You're being a fool," Frelinghuysen said.

"Quite possibly. Nonetheless, I have built my machine and I intend to try it out. Now, I'm taking a canteen and an apple, and a few dollars in coins – the silver should be worth something even if the currency value is nil. I'll be wearing this suit, of course, which will undoubtedly be out of style but should not offend anyone's sensibilities, and carrying a camera, so I can record what I see. What else would you suggest?"

"A gun," Frelinghuysen said. "You said yourself you aren't sure just where you'll come out, and of course we don't know what the future holds – what if you land in the middle of a war?"

"If I land in the middle of a war, I don't think one little gun is going to help me."

"And if there isn't a war, it might get you arrested," Foulke said.

"Precisely."

"What do you *expect* to find?" Joline asked.

"Well, some people think we should all be living in a Socialist paradise by then, and I hope they're right. I expect to see Utopia."

"Judging by what's happening in Europe, I think a Fascist dictatorship is more likely," Frelinghuysen replied.

"You said eighty or ninety years?" Joline asked,

"I think so," Powell said. He did not sound very certain.

"Well, if your Mr. Wells is right, Fascism will have been wiped away in a general collapse of civilization before that, and we'll have your Socialist paradise once we've rebuilt."

"Where are you getting *that*?" Foulke demanded

"From his recent novel, *The Shape of Things to Come*. Which, to be honest, I think is largely nonsense, but then so is Powell's scheme."

"See? A paradise," Powell replied.

"It'll be a nightmare," Frelinghuysen said. "A regimented smoky industrial hell."

"Or it *could* be a paradise," Joline retorted. "I don't know about you, but even with the mess the world's in right now, I'd rather live now than eighty years ago. I *like* cars and airplanes, and streets that are paved with asphalt and not horseshit, and doctors who are more likely to help you than kill you. Eighty years from now – you'll probably be surrounded by miracles, Powell, old boy."

"Or burned-out ruins," Frelinghuysen said. "You don't really think the World War ended all wars, do you?"

"No, but people will always rebuild, and I like to think we learn a little from our mistakes each time," Joline said. "Progress does happen. Maybe eighty years from now we'll have learned better than to kill one another."

"We haven't yet, in thousands of years," Frelinghuysen replied.

"Excuse me, gentlemen," Powell said, "but I brought you here to advise and observe, not to argue. The only suggestions I have heard so far are to bring a gun, and be ready for anything, and I've decided not to take that first bit – for one thing, the machine's almost ready, and I don't have a gun in the house. So, anything else, or shall we get the show on the road?"

"Smoking ruins," Frelinghuysen said. "You'll see."

"Paradise," Joline snapped back. "Science and technology will make Earth a paradise."

Powell glanced at the dials on the front of the big machine, and said, "Well, I'm about to find out." He clapped his fedora on his head and stepped up on the platform. "Here we go, gentlemen. I hope to see you all again soon." Then he pulled down a lever, and the machine's hum rose in pitch and volume until it was like the scream of a falling shell; the three observers stared, caught off-guard by the speed of their friend's action.

And then, with a thump, Powell vanished, and a rush of wind blew into the space where he had stood, ruffling the observers' hair and sending their ties askew.

The machine's hum died away, and for a moment there was only a stunned silence; then Foulke said, "Well, I'll be damned. I didn't think it would work."

"We don't know that it *did*," Frelinghuysen said. "All we know is that Powell disappeared. He could be in the next room laughing at us – or his atoms could be spread between here and Mars."

"Or he could be in the distant future," Joline said.

"In your Socialist paradise?" Frelinghuysen asked.

"Maybe."

"Or he could be in next Tuesday," Foulke said. "He said he didn't *really* know how far into the future it would send him."

"That's true..." Joline began, but then a loud bang sent a new wind blowing out from the platform, disarranging hair and neckties anew, and Powell was standing on the platform, looking somewhat dazed. He had lost his hat.

"Powell!" Foulke exclaimed. "Are you all right?"

"I'm...I'm fine," Powell replied, a bit unsteadily.

"What happened?" Joline asked. "Where did you go?"

"Broadway," Powell replied. "Near Times Square."

"Yes, but *when*?" Frelinghuysen demanded.

"I think...I think it was 2023, from some of the adverts and displays."

"What was it like?" Joline asked.

"Like?" He took a deep breath, thought for a few seconds, then said, "It was amazing. There were billboard-sized movie screens everywhere, or something like them, but I didn't see any sign of projectors, and the colors were brighter than Technicolor. Most of them were advertising, but at least half the time I couldn't figure out what they were trying to sell. Everything was still in English, but there were words and phrases everywhere that made no sense. The cars were low and sleek, not like today's. Hardly anyone wore hats or ties, but some people had masks over their mouths and noses, like surgeons."

"So it wasn't ruins," Freylinghuysen said. "But what *was* it? Was it paradise, or was it hell?"

"Was it like the pictures on pulp magazine covers?" Joline asked.

"Was it a regimented nightmare?"

"Was it a war-torn wasteland?"

"Was it a technological paradise?"

Powell considered this for a moment, then shrugged and said, "It was New York."

When I See Rigel's Light Sleeting Through the Side of Heinlein Station

When I see Rigel's light sleeting through the side of Heinlein Station
Gleaming red from floating dust and bright on broken metal edges
Lighting the corridors a color the station's crew never saw
Through a hole where bodies drifted in final decompression
When I remember the centuries that this vessel drove through the void
Toward an unknown, an alien and hostile destination
When I feel the emptiness that fills it
That pulls my suit into a puffed and stiffened bubble
So that I am as awkward and strange in these chambers as Rigel's light
I wonder how the legends of Earth must lie, must hide the truth
I wonder why, what horrors our ancestors hid from us
With their tales of blue skies and green hills
And lies those tales must surely be
I know this when I see how they struggled to come here
If Earth were fair and beautiful, as they told us
Then how could they have left?

About the Author

Lawrence Watt-Evans has been a full-time writer for more than forty years, with more than fifty novels and well over a hundred short stories to his credit, as well as assorted essays, poems, comic books, and so on. His story "Why I Left Harry's All-Night Hamburgers won the 1988 Hugo for short story, as well as the Asimov Readers Award.

He lives in Bainbridge Island, Washington with his wife.

His website is at www.watt-evans.com.

www.ingramcontent.com/pod-product-compliance
Lightning Source LLC
LaVergne TN
LVHW020531100826
845148LV00010B/1414

* 9 7 8 1 6 1 9 9 1 0 6 0 7 *